PLATO'S CAVE

Larry Henry

Vietnam 1955 -1975:
A Novel, Part II

MCANALLY FLATS PRESS

McAnally Flats Press
4809 Riversedge Road
Louisville, TN 37777
www.McAnallyFlatsPress.com

LCCN: 2011901977
ISBN-10 0-9819209-1-8
ISBN-13 978-0-9819209-1-7
Copyright: TXu 1-704-863
v. 2.02

Cover Design: Ann Lowe
Images ©Larry Henry with the exception of the following: Painting on page one by
William Kidwell, from Dreamstime.com: Russian missels Vladimir Yanchenko., from
WikiMediaCommons: Israel flag MathKnight.
Typography: Minion Pro, Bordeaux Roman Bold

The songs, *Ball and Chain*, Janis Joplin, ©1967, Bro 'N Sis Music, Inc., Used by Permission.
MacArthur Park, Words and Music by Jimmy Webb, Copyright ©1968, Universal - Polygram
International Publishing, Inc.. Copyright Renewed. All Rights Reserved. Used by Permission,
Reprinted by permission of Hal Leonard Corporation..

Printed on acid free paper.

This Book Is Dedicated to
The Loving Memory of My Parents:

Mildred Geneva Butler Henry
Hugh Jackson (Jay) Henry lll

The Armed Forces of The United State of America

Sir Winston Leonard Spencer-Churchill

And God

Also by Larry Henry:
Garden of Eden
Noah's Ark
Against the Wind

Foreword

Larry Henry has captured the essence of the experience of millions of ordinary young men accomplishing extraordinary feats during hellish war. As the characters in his books, I shared similar honors as they did, theirs fighting on the ground; mine, as a Navy gunners' mate at nineteen in WWII, trying to kill other nineteen year olds who were trying to kill me. I served at Okinawa and Iwo Jima where 5,000 sailors died, mostly from Kamikaze attacks.

Henry writes with accuracy and passion. He has honorably served and lived during the period he describes in this remarkable painting of the life and times of so many of us.

This is the kind of book that rekindles the patriot's dream.

Gordon Sams
Knoxville, Tennessee

Chapter One

Johnson and Gunny

The Dandelion Field

First Platoon had been mauled in their bloody retreat through the jungle. A company of North Vietnamese Army regulars had been camped on their backdoor every yard of a two-mile trek through dense trees to an open field where the helicopters were waiting. They were exhausted, and down to their last rounds of ammunition. The fly boys had managed to save their butts with repeated bombing and rocket attacks against the enemy troops. The last helicopter lifted off under a hail of gunfire. Pasamenus and the others were lucky to still be alive.

John and Gunny lay dead in a pool of blood on the chopper floor. Gonzales was sprawled beside them, unconscious, with a spinal injury. The door gunner lay crumpled against his machine gun with multiple gunshot wounds. They were all wounded with the exception of Driggins, Henry, and Pasamenus. It had been a fateful decision by Gunny and Lieutenant Butler to remain in the valley for one final crack at Charlie. That had cost Gunny his life. John's too, plus five additional Marines. Now the lives of the wounded hung in the balance of a damaged Huey helicopter and the skills of its pilot.

The pilot, Captain Pataki, a Marine Corps veteran from the battles of La Drang and a dozen other places got them up to 1,300 feet, but there the machine began to smoke and vibrate. The coast was eleven miles due east. They had to make the beach for evacuation to the hospital ship, or some of the Marines would bleed to death. Red was gut-shot and bleeding all over the floor. Pasamenus was tending to his damaged friend, but the blood just kept coming. Gonzales had lapsed into a coma. His eyes rolled back in his head, and he trembled uncontrollably from shock and falling blood pressure.

The Lieutenant crawled over and gathered Gonzales in his arms to share his body heat. He stuffed a rag in the hole in Gonzales' back to stop the bleeding. Gonzales moaned, trembled some more, then lay still. Butler's fatigues were soaked with clotted blood from bullet wounds in his own legs.

Daniel Butler couldn't stop thinking that this lash-up was his fault. He and First Sergeant had agreed on a second ambush in the valley. At the time, it seemed like a good idea. The Air Force did their job chewing up that first company of NVA. The fly boys did an excellent job with their second ambush, but he and Gunny never figured on a third company of North Vietnamese Regulars. Tears ran down Butler's cheeks. He was ashamed and sad too about losing his men.

Gunny Abernathy was one of the best top sergeants in the Corps. The man was a legend, killed under his command. But more than that Lucian had become his friend, made him look good in front of the men when he was unsure about something, consulted him when Gunny already knew the answer. Lucian Abernathy had made him a better Marine.

The wounds in his legs ached like crazy.

Daniel rested his head back against John's silent chest, sticky with blood. Officer Candidate School at Quantico, Virginia had trained him to maintain a distance with enlisted men for the purpose of command. Sixteen days in the Ben Hai River, two successful ambushes, then getting their ass shot off had rendered that theory a moot point. These men had become his brothers. John was his favorite.

John's death hurt worse that those Marines killed under this command at Hue during the Tet Offensive.

"Dump your gear back there. We got boo koo battle damage."

The pilot was wrestling with the joy stick, goosing the fuel lever up and down, coaxing his engine, but the craft was losing altitude.

"Dump everything! Jock straps. Your mama's picture. All your shit!"

Bubba threw out red's M-60, his own M-14, then he disengaged the door gunner's M-60 machine guns and over they went. He crawled around the bloody floor throwing out all their weapons. When he came to Gunny's .45 caliber Thompson, he took off the heavy drum magazine and tossed it out. The Tommy gun he kept. It was all they had left of the man they had come to respect more than their own fathers.

"More! Dump everything! We ain't gonna clear them trees up ahead."

Bubba pulled off Gunny's boots and threw those out. Then he took off John's boots and out the door they went. He took all their boots, cartridge belts, bayonets, canteens, everything. All went hurtling down into the lush greenery sailing past beneath the struggling aircraft.

"That's good! That's good! We're almost lever. Gimme some more!"

Bubba pulled off Gunny's bloody clothing and threw that out. Then John's. Then Gonzales'. Then the wounded door gunner's. And finally Red's. The rest of them stripped and flung their bloody fatigues overboard.

The ridge was coming up fast.

"Hold on, men! Come on, Lu Lu Belle!"

The pilot was half standing, wrenching at the controls, banging his palm against the dials, pleading with his Lu Lu Belle for a few more feet. A few more precious inches. He flung his helmet out, his mike, his clipboard, everything in the cockpit. Then he unstrapped a pearl handle .45 given him by his father. Out it went.

The trees rushed at them, limbs slapping the skids underneath the helicopter, leaves flying around the open interior. It sounded like hailstones on a tin roof. A bushy limb slapped Driggins in the chest. They were down in the treetops, plowing through birds, monkeys, lizards, and tree limbs.

"Come on Lu Lu Belle! Sweetheart! Baby! One more time for Poppa!"

A big limb struck the right skid, ripping it loose. It dangled down, creating a drag in the trees. The craft lurched sideways, threatening to spin out of control. Captain Pataki banked hard left, kicking the foot petals, black smoke bellowing from his turbine engine. Henry was holding onto the side door with both hands, reciting the Lord's Prayer.

Dwayne Henry had been through four firefights with John and his fellow Marines. Survival was a better term for their experience at Firebase Hansel. What a cluster-fuck that had been. Dead men everywhere, mortar rounds and artillery shells pounding the hell out of them, gun fire pouring in from every direction. Then their 20mm self-propelled "duster" took a round and blew up. The supply helicopter was shot down. The first aid bunker took a direct hit from a 130mm shell.

God performed a miracle that January 31st through the person of a Marine Corps officer by the name of Abraham. Captain Abraham stayed on the radio coordinating air support when it looked like they were all going to die. Their miracle appeared out of the clouds in the form of a blue-bellied AC-130 gunship. When it fired, its 20mm Gatling guns made a grotesque buzzing sound at 2,000 rounds a minute. Dwayne later learned they called their four engine aircraft "The Thing."

This time it looked like they were going to buy the farm for sure. Dwayne was making their peace with God, thinking about his wife

Sophie, when another big limb ripped off their dangling skid, bouncing them up above the treetops. And they were free.

A beautiful green plain lay before them as they cleared the top of the ridge. Four miles out they could see the crystal blue water of the South China Sea. The salt air smelled delicious. Deliverance was at hand. A pair of F-105s appeared overhead. Two Cobra gunships came up alongside, accompanied by three more Huey helicopters.

"There's the beach up ahead. I'm gonna sit down and we'll transfer to those other choppers. Lu Lu Belle's done her best, but she's gonna conk out any minute. Hold on tight. I'm taking the old girl down."

They came down rattling and banging, round and round, smoke and red sparks billowing from their failing power plant. With one skid sheared away, the craft rolled over lazily on her side, ripping the blades off, which went flying through the air when they sliced into the earth. But they were down and still in one piece. The Huey's settled down beside them. It was a good landing. They were alive. Overhead, the F-105s and the two Cobras continued to circle in case any unwanted guests paid a surprise visit to the men on the ground.

The Huey's crews came running over, unloading the dead and wounded. Lu Lu Belle's fuel tanks caught fire. 60 seconds later she was an inferno.

"This one looks bad. Load him on Number Two. The rest of you, take their dead over to that chopper by the trees."

Gonzales was whisked into the Number Two helicopter and they flew away.

Then the Navy Corpsman turned his attention to Red.

"This guy's had it."

"You fix him!"

Two nearly naked Marines stood menacingly behind the young Navy medic. One with bullet holes in his thighs and blood running down. The other with the deranged look of a man who had seen too much death that day.

Bubba spoke again. "You fix him!"

Pasamenus adjusted his dark gaze on the Navy Corpsman from Maryland.

"Okay! Okay! Help me get him onboard."

Flying out to the hospital ship, lying beside Red and Lieutenant Butler, Bubba passed out from loss of blood, transcending into that far distant realm where dreams are made. He was with Suzie Brown at the Southern Circle Drive-In Restaurant in South Knoxville. Robert was home on leave, and they had themselves a picnic basket and a fancy bottle of French champagne.

Suzie suggested they go to the mountains and visit Gatlinburg, maybe buy themselves a Teddy Bear. Traffic on Chapman Highway was light so the drive up to Sevier County was peaceful. It was springtime and everything was green and in full bloom. Just above Sevierville, Suzie saw a snowy white field alongside the highway.

"Robert, look!" Suzie pointed to the picturesque setting.

"Sure is pretty, ain't it honey?"

"Let's have out picnic down there, by the river."

Bubba pulled off Highway 411 beneath a grove of hackberry trees, where they got out and unloaded their basket. Once down a red clay embankment with honeysuckle and kudzu vines, they found themselves on a broad, level field lush with thousands of white dandelions.

"Oh, Bubba, it's like magic."

"Suzie, honey, you're somethin' else."

"I love this place. It's perfect."

They made their way across the white field to the riverbank beside a long line of cedar trees and leafy sugar maples. The river, which ran through the center of Gatlinburg, wasn't broad but it was deep in places with an assortment of trout, shiners, and smallmouth bass.

Suzie spread their blanket and arranged the food on the hand-made quilt while Bubba wrestled with getting the cork out. Then he poured their champagne into two Dixie cups, handing one to Suzie.

"To you, Suzie Brown. The best thing that ever happened to me."

Suzie bowed her head and began to cry.

"Honey, what did I say wrong?"

"Nothing, Robert, I just … I care about you so much."

"I know I'm not good with words, Honey. I don't say it often enough. But I love you, Suzie. I love you with all my heart."

Then the waterworks really started. Suzie flung her arms around Bubba's neck, spilling their champagne, crying into his chest until his shirt was wet.

"I love you, Robert. I always have."

He moved their picnic over onto the soft green grass, lay her down gently on the quilt then Robert slid her pink panties down off her ankles. He pulled his trousers down, positioned Suzie in a more comfortable position, and began their rhythmic labor of love with the woman he adored, amid the merriment of the birds singing and the beauty of the dandelion field.

"Wake up! Can you hear me, son?" Wake up!"

Bubba opened his bloodshot eyes to the spectacle of four Navy orderlies sliding him off his bloodstained stretcher onto a metal gurney covered by a white linen sheet. Dreams of Suzie Brown faded away. A physician was taking his pulse.

"My buddy Red? Is Red all right?"

Chapter Two

Coming Home

May 20, 1968: The South Korean cargo ship Kobukson docked in Los Angeles at 1600 hours. Onboard were twenty-nine veterans from Platoon Forty Three, First Battalion, Third Marine Division. Their sea voyage had lasted twenty-seven days. Bathroom facilities onboard the aging vessel were spartan so their uniforms were somewhat soiled and they smelled a bit less than high society, but it was swell to be back in The World again after Viet-by-God-Nam. Their thirteen-month tour of duty was over. Time now for cocktails and dinner before finding a place to sleep for the night.

Three of their rank had been killed during the Tet Offensive. Four others were blown away by explosive devices on search-and-destroy patrols along the DMZ. Two more had been sent home to the Bethesda Naval Hospital. Those less seriously wounded had recovered from their battle injuries in Da Nang hospitals, and were among the smiling veterans waiting to disembark. Their's was a feeling of hope and great joy to be back stateside again. The rigors of war and their no-win situation in Vietnam had left its mark. Many of the men felt betrayed, but they were thankful the whole affair was behind them now.

"Look at them cutie pies down below."

"I like that tall blonde with the big boobs."

"Fellows, you better read their signs. I don't think this is a welcoming committee."

"I can't make that out, Sarge. What's it say?"

" 'Make Love Not War.' That big one up front reads, 'Baby Killers.' "

"Baby Killers? I don't get this."

"Those are some of the war protesters you been hearing about. They don't like us, Catfish. They're all hippies."

"Shazam! I never bargained on this crap."

"They're lowering the gangplank. Grab your gear. Let's vacate this tub."

The Marines made their way down a narrow steel stairwell to the wharf below where they were confronted by a noisy group of protesters waiting with eggs, placards, and angry attitudes. An egg hit the gunny sergeant on his sleeve as he was stepping off the gangplank. In the background he spotted a dozen Port Authority rent-a-cops just waiting for the Marines to react to the situation.

"Keep your cool, men. We got blue-bellies in the outfield."

A shower of eggs and assorted vegetables came raining down, striking all but a few of the Marines.

"Baby killers! … Boooo! … Go back to Vietnam! … Boooo! … I hope you die! … Marines are cowards! … Go to hell! … Boooo! … Killer pigs! … Your mother's a dirty whore! … Baby killers! … Boooo! … Marines are murderers! … Boooo!"

"We oughta teach them pukes a lesson."

"Take names and kick some puke asses!"

"Do not respond. That's an order! They're just waiting to throw us in jail. Maintain your cool, men!"

A muscular body builder, dressed in gay attire and sporting a stylish red beret, came sashaying up and spat in the sergeant's face. The crowd cheered. The rent-a-cops were now standing behind the protesters, laughing and jeering the Marines. Master Sergeant Henry Thoreau Duval wiped the spittle off with his hand, husbanding his anger while leading his Marines away from the crowd across the Queens Way Bridge toward the neon lights of the city.

"Los Angeles! Corn Hole Capital of the World! Remind me never to come here on vacation."

Catfish's caustic remark made the sergeant laugh.

Jerry Glenn chimed in. "That queer fucker looked like my old Aunt Sally."

Jerry had survived two AK-47 rounds through the stomach.

"That tall blonde with them hooters? Man! How can a woman look so good and be so damn dumb all at the same time? She probably blows old Aunt Sally."

Dwayne Temples was a connoisseur of bodacious ta-tas, winner of the Silver Star, and walked with a limp from a North Vietnamese mortar round.

Catfish continued with his monologue. "A pure waste of female plumbing. I got just what that lady needs to get her back on the straight and narrow. A boo koo application of Catfish Cassidy's Down Home Wild Root Tonic!"

"Right on!" Dudley Eckford Calhoun had dropped out of Columbia University to join the Corps. "A serious grudge fuck would do that bitch some good!"

In spite of their unofficial greeting home, the men had regained their sense of humor. After what they'd been through in South East Asia a few eggs seemed almost funny, if not pathetically ignorant and tragically un-American. They found a Trailways bus station and used the restroom to clean up as best they could with soap and paper towels.

Biddle Hutchins pulled a Vietcong dagger from his duffle bag which they used to scrape off their eggs *au naturel*. Half an hour later they came across an Italian restaurant on a side street beside a dilapidated five-story hotel building. A blue neon sign out front read "Luigi's." Sergeant Duval went in alone to ask the manager if they would be welcome for dinner.

When the owner spotted the sergeant, his face broke into a broad grin. The place was empty except for a young couple eating up front by the window.

"You a Marine! My son a Marine too. My name a Luigi. You come a eat now. I fix you plenty good a food."

"Mister Luigi, sir. There's twenty-nine of us."

"Luigi my first a name. You call a me Luigi. No 'mister,' please. You bring in a da boys. We got a plenty a room. Mama in a da kitchen. Mama plenty good cook."

Duval signaled for his men. They filled up the empty tables. The young couple eating beside the window hurriedly paid their bill, and left in disgust.

"I don't think this town likes us much."

"Luigi likes us. That's good enough for me.

"Right on, man. That dude's Number One."

Luigi brought his wife out from the kitchen to meet their dinner guests. "This a Giovanna. We a married a thirty-one a years last a June. She a good a wife and a good a cook."

All twenty-eight Marines followed their sergeant's lead, rising to their feet to show their respect for the middle-aged beauty with the jet black hair and the dancing black eyes. Luigi beamed with pride. Giovanna blushed, nodding her head in appreciation to the circle of smiling men. Then she went about the task of bringing out bottles of Chianti from her kitchen for each table.

Giovanna paused by the master sergeant's table. "My son's in Vietnam. He's a sergeant now. I worry about him, but Luigi tells me we must believe God will bring him back to us. My husband's from the old country. I grew up here in LA. We're very proud of our Celio."

"Your husband's a good man, Giovanna. You're a lucky woman."

"Yes, I know, but I pray for our little Celio. We have just the one child. He's in a place called Hoi An with the I Corps Marines."

"That's up north where we were." Then Duval lied. "It's quiet up there, nothing much going on. I'm sure Celio will be all right."

Giovanna smiled, touching his cheek. "Thank you, sergeant. I know you aren't telling me the truth, but thank you so very much."

The food was delicious, and the wine just kept on coming. An hour later everyone was stuffed and somewhat inebriated. Gunny Sergeant Duval asked Luigi about lodging for the night. Luigi nodded his balding head up and down, enthusiastically informing Duval that he owned the hotel building next door and they could stay there for nothing.

The gunny sergeant pressed three one hundred dollar bills into Luigi's hand, while the stocky Italian danced a jig in protest. Then he hugged Mama Giovanna goodnight, and led his Marines next door to the red brick building. He inserted Giovanna's brass key, then stepped forward into an ambient elegance none of them had ever seen before.

Chapter Three

Catfish

Lawrence Fitzgerald Cassidy was born in 1944 in a town called Greers Ferry, Arkansas, near Greers Ferry Lake and the Little Red River in a rural community of farmers, country stores, and avid sportsmen. World War Two had just concluded and job opportunities grew on trees, following a twenty-four percent unemployment rate during the Great Depression. Larry's uncle had been killed at the Battle of the Bulge. His father had served in the Pacific with the Marine Corps. Lieutenant Colonel Jonathan Fitzgerald Cassidy returned home with two Purple Hearts, a Bronze Star, and tales of military adventures which enthralled his young son.

Larry's mother was a lady of refinement and Southern upbringing, a finalists in the 1943 Miss America Pageant at Atlantic City. Colonel Cassidy met her while completing a work assignment for the War Department. They took to one another like two lovebirds in a blackberry patch, married in a whirlwind romance, then off he went again for two more years in the Pacific.

On a fishing trip with his father when he was seven years old, Larry hooked a catfish so big it dragged him down the riverbank and into Greers Ferry Lake. Colonel Cassidy waded in after his son, grabbed young Larry and the fishing pole, then pulled them both ashore. There he handed his son the pole while holding onto Larry, allowing the excited youngster the thrill of landing the big catfish. Turned out the catfish was a fifty-four pound shovel-bill which was about what young Cassidy weighed at the time. Thus was born the nickname "Catfish," which the boy wore with glowing pride.

Lawrence evolved as a lady's man. His masculine good looks plus daddy's money afforded him a bevy of hot and willing femme fatales in high school. Following graduation he moved to Atlanta to attend the university at I-75 and 10th Street, where he majored in Beer and Women. Halfway through his sophomore year at Georgia Tech, Lawrence fell in love. Believing he had found his future wife, Larry hung up his rock -and-roll size twelves.

One week before Christmas, he discovered his roommate in a compromising position with his sweetheart, Miss Head and Heels. He called her Miss Head and Heels because that's about all that touched the bed when they were making love. A fistfight ensued. He knocked out his roommate, dragging him into the hallway by the hair. Then he flung Ken's shoes and clothing out into the corridor. Larry allowed Darlene time to get dressed. He felt he owed her that small consideration.

Darlene wept and begged for Larry's forgiveness, citing too much Christmas cheer as her excuse for pulling her panties down. But Larry was devastated, in tears himself. The woman he loved and planned to marry had betrayed him in the very bed they had shared on so many joyous occasions. He threw her pocketbook out in the hallway, yelling at Darlene, "Get out!"

His love shack had been struck between the eyes and set on fire. Brokenhearted, Larry cried until he caught the hiccups. All the love and affection he felt for Darlene, his dream of their life together, was going up in smoke. He felt adrift on a stormswept sea, a lovesick fool caught up in a blizzard of hurt and emotional despair.

When the cobwebs started to clear in Darlene's head, she realized she had made a dreadful mistake. This went beyond getting pregnant at age fifteen by an aide she met at a political rally in Washington, DC. Her privileged lifestyle supported by her father's law practice could not bail her out this time. All those years of pampered behavior as one of Boston's prized debutantes had just blown up in her face.

Darlene called again, begging Larry to forgive her and take her back. But spoiled little Darlene was up against the age-old traditions of family and honor taught him by his Marine Corps father. No amount of promises or being sideways drunk made any difference to Larry. He listened to her sobs and excuses for two minutes, then hung up.

The mind sometimes pulls back the curtain of truth at the most inopportune times. He recalled a horrific event described to him by his father, which the older man had witnessed in the South Pacific during a sea battle with the Imperial Japanese Fleet. Because of her betrayal and his own hand in the drama, Larry Cassidy saw for the first time what he had become. Darlene was a manifestation of that sad vision.

A stark realization was dawning on Larry, with knife-edge clarity, that he was a wastrel, a long-haired bullshit artist. A foppish young man who chased around after women most of his overly indulged life with little regard for his future. He had become the laughing, carefree boulevardier pimp rolling down the el burro of life, humming his tune, with a hot demimonde on his arm. The ferocious bulge in his jeans stood out as a proud reminder to all the brothers and sisters that Cool L C had his astral cord hooked into the Bodacious Church of Elvis … via an occasional toot up the snoot with Peruvian Marching Powder.

Then it happened. Barreling out of the sun came the kamikaze, straight down toward the vulnerable deck of his Freudian flattop. Parked libidos, armed and ready for takeoff. He filled the air with shot and shell, hammering salvo after salvo. On it came, on and on and down. A hit! Another and another! Please, God, why me? With smoke and flame trailing a sinister black plume it struck the main hangar deck, detonating in a psychoneurotic orange fireball which set off the aviation fuel in his stranded fighters. Then the bombs and rockets began exploding. USS Cool L C was doomed.

Next morning, through a cold fluorescent haze, he could see the great carrier wallowing down by the stern and slowly sinking. The inferno still billowing inside her tortured bowels, his dying collage of vanities and superficial dreams. How soon and swift it all came to pass for Little Boy Blue.

Just then the telephone rang.

It was the great man himself, Darlene's cousin, leader of the Clan Fitzpatrick, and a powerful political figure on Capitol Hill. He held half of Washington in his political pocket. The other half were careful not to make an enemy of the senator.

"How are yew, Larry, my boy? My, it's been a long time. How's the family?"

"Well, sir, and yourself?"

"Never bettah. Listen, I called about Dahlene. I understand you two lovebirds had a little quarrel."

"Yes, sir, we did."

"Women are emotional creatures, Larry Boy. They do foolish things. Dahlene is sorry for her mistake. She misses you. I want you to forgive that girl."

"I can't do that, sir."

"Listen to me carefully, boy. Be a man about this thing. I can make it worth your while. Dahlene is my favorite relation. I want her to be happy. You too, my boy. I'll set up an account in yoah name, plenty of money in thah. Lots more where that comes from."

"Thank you, sir, but I just couldn't do that."

"Larry, you're not being realistic. I want you in the family. My family. Marry that girl. Have babies. I'll set you up in business, engineering, law. Whatevah you desiah! Make you a politician, like me.

"Now thah's a thought. Politics, Larry! You'll become a membah of The Club. Have evahthing you evah wanted. Taxpayahs pay for it all. Yachts, women, money, fancy cahs. The world will be your oyster, Larry Boy. Rub elbows with the rich and famous. Live high on the hawg."

"But, sir …"

"Gosh darn it, look at the time. I have a speaking engagement in half an houh. Call Dahlene. I'll take care of evahthing, bank accounts, new Mercedes. Goodbye for now. Give my best to your family, Larry Boy. Goodbye."

The line went dead.

"Larry Boy!" I'm his fucking Larry Boy!"

For the second time in as many days Larry's feelings had been hurt, his sense of pride trampled beneath the feet of the very people who professed to care about him. The gasbag from Congress was trying to buy him off. Pieces of life's puzzle began falling into place. Darlene was amoral. A Bean Town tart. Perhaps the political system was amoral too.

He wanted nothing more to do with Darlene Fitzpatrick, an engineering degree, finding a job and settling down, Washington politics, or being the long-haired buffoon. The party was over!

He called Darlene and apologized for his behavior, explaining to her that their relationship had been a mistake. Larry said he was sorry for hurting her feelings. He wished her good luck, a Merry Christmas, and told her goodbye.

The next day he joined the United States Marine Corps. Twelve days later he was having his hair sheared off at the induction center at Parris Island, South Carolina.

Chapter Four

Mistress of the Universe

The interior of the hotel was the exact opposite of its exterior. Giovanna and Luigi had gone to great lengths and considerable expense to restore the interior to its original sixteenth-century architectural beauty. Frescos adorned the stucco walls and the thirty-foot ceiling in the ballroom. Arched windows contained brightly hued leaded glass. There were grand wooden columns, with bridging corners, supporting a Baroque balcony overlooking the ballroom. Intricate mahogany furniture sat among bronze sculptures of Plato and Aristotle, hanging tapestries, and in the center of the great hall against the eastern wall, a magnificent marble and stone fireplace.

Above the cypress mantel hung a painting of St. Peter's Cathedral in Rome. On the south wall stood a beautifully columned shrine with a majestic marble Madonna inside. It was as if they had entered a holy place, for indeed they had. It made them humble, and brought tears to the eyes of some who had lost comrades in battle.

Temples was awestruck, as was everyone else in the room. "Sarge, this is the most amazing thing I have ever seen. It reminds me of that big church in Saigon, but this is far more elegant."

"This is unbelievable. Peachtree Christian Church in Atlanta looks a little bit like this."

Catfish was blown away by the beauty of the ancient Italian Renaissance.

"Men, this is one of those once in a lifetime experiences. I'll buy the wine if some of you will go get it. There's a liquor store a block west from the restaurant. Let's celebrate our good fortune before we head home tomorrow."

Catfish volunteered, plus Temples, Calhoun, and the quiet one they called Swede. Sergeant Duval gave them $100 and off they went. They purchased two cases of red, one white, plus a case of brut champagne, and were on their way back toting their goods when the blonde with the bodacious ta-tas, the gay bodybuilder, and four rent-a-cops rounded a corner and bumped into them.

"Well, I see you Marine trash are still here." She spoke with accustomed authority.

One of the rent-a-cops poked Swede in the belly with his nightstick. "Baby killer!"

Swede set down his case of wine, as did the other three Marines. Pretty Paul sashayed up, preparing to spit again, when Calhoun lashed out, breaking the man's jaw. Pretty Paul's stylish red beret went flying through the air. He hit the deck cold as a cucumber.

Rent-a-cop raised his nightstick to strike a blow for the Bathhouse Boys, but Temples kicked his feet out from under him in one direction, slamming his body with his forearm in the opposite direction. The man crashed to the concrete, stunned and bleeding.

Swede grabbed another rent-a-flatfoot, swinging him around headfirst into a brick storefront. Down he went, unconscious. Catfish judo-chopped the third cop in the throat and he collapsed, clawing the sidewalk with broken fingernails, gasping for breath.

The fourth cop stood frozen with fear, a long urine stain spreading down his pants leg.

Then he ran into the night.

Hooters Galore, Mistress of the Universe, squealed for help, but she was fresh out of rental folk. Temples slapped her across the mouth to calm her down. Her mind went blank, stunned and disoriented. She reached out for the storefront to keep from falling. Nothing of that nature had ever happened before.

She had been head majorette, the senior high school prom queen. She was a straight A student at Berkeley University. Didn't they understand who she was? She was Mistress of the Universe!

Karl Marx spoke to her from his haven beyond the marble orchard. Vladimir Lenin, Leon Trotsky, Che Guevara, all her socialist heroes inside her head were addressing her from their pages in the history books. Urging her to do something significant to impose their political ideologies, subjugate the bourgeoisie, dominate the evil United States Marine Corps.

Saul Alinsky came forth, Fidel Castro, Joseph Stalin, all telling her to indoctrinate those USMC outlaws with more government, re-distribution of the wealth, and sexual freedom. Which was superior, indeed, to Wall Street, capitalistic greed, and that antiquated Jew, Jesus Christ.

Mistress Galore, also known as Belinda Boxer, had no real un-derstanding of her American heritage, the American Armed Forces, or her United States Constitution. 1776 was just a number to her. So was the War of 1812, World War One, World War Two, and Korea. Vietnam was of no concern to her or any of her associates. What mat-tered in her world were good intentions, socialism, making the dean's list, and looking pretty. People fighting and killing each other was for criminals, drug dealers, and Marine Corps murderers. Those swine standing before her weren't fit even to look at her. She feared them absolutely, but she also loathed and despised them.

Mistress Galore regaled them with her concerns for the down-trodden proletariat, her belief that capitalism was an inherent evil, why everyone should be given the same opportunities as everyone else, why war was not the answer, and why Corporate America and Wall Street should be regulated by government for redistribution of their accumulated wealth. She warned them that her parents had political connections downtown. It would go badly for them if they harmed her.

The four Marines did stare at her, but not in a way she imagined. Swede felt sorry for her. She was such a pretty girl to be so blissfully ignorant about so many things in life. They had just returned from the fighting, some of them died there, defending her freedoms and the freedoms of the Vietnamese people. Belinda Boxer understood noth-ing about the political ideologies at play in Vietnam, or for that matter around the world. How sad, Swede thought. What would become of her out in the real world once she graduated from school?

Calhoun felt contempt for Belinda, her and her self-righteous world view. It was all about her, Belinda, the center of attention. Isn't she just the prettiest one? He felt utter disgust for the hippie icon of the American antiwar movement. His best friend was dead, murdered by the Cong. Thousands more like him killed and injured in the war. She knew nothing about hunger, disease, poverty, or death. It consumed Vietnam. It consumed half the planet. At Berkeley it was just another school project, a book assignment to be studied and debated in the air-conditioned comforts of a lousy classroom.

Temples gazed at her ripe, luscious body, wondering what it would be like having sex with a gorgeous female like that? Certainly a lot more enjoyable than the three-dollar Boom-Boom Girl he paid for in Vietnam. What a trip that had been, stoned to the max on begonia weed and watermelon wine. But could he stand listening to her afterwards? GOOD GOD! He would probably blow beets or jump off the nearest bridge!

Catfish looked, thinking great tits, nice ass, no brains. Arm candy. Good for a few laughs. Larry Cassidy was a man who saw most things for what they actually were. Darlene had made him a part-time cynic, but Larry had changed into an intellectually honest individual. Mistress Galore was a stone-cold disappointment to the four men standing before her on their shared concrete walkway of contempt and sadness.

"Gentlemen, what we have here is a perfect example of Mother Nature's marvelous achievement … the complete hippie nincompoop."

After the laughter died down and Temples gave her a farewell salute, the Marines picked up their four boxes of wine and walked away. Belinda stood there in shock and humiliation, tears leaking down her pretty cheeks, frustrated, her jugs hanging out in the evening breeze with nary a man in sight to service her account.

All five of her male escorts had fled into the night.

Chapter Five

Chronicle of the 20th Century

"It was, above all, a decade of dissent. The civil rights and antiwar movements drew millions of people into their ranks, where public protests raged. Bloody riots erupted, and cities and flags burned. But new rights were also won and the troops, Kennedy's 'watchmen on the walls of freedom,' were beginning to come home from Vietnam.

"It was a decade of dynamic change for the nation's youth, the new generation to whom JFK said 'the torch is passed.' Long hair, mod dress, drugs, sexual freedom, and antiestablishment ideas were hard to find ten years ago; now they were everywhere, as affluent kids embraced a counterculture fueled by rock music and a sincere yearning for brotherhood and peace.

"It was a decade of tragic death, not only for the soldiers in Southeast Asia but also for John Kennedy, Martin Luther King, and Robert Kennedy. Who can forget when Martin was killed and Bobby tried to console a crowd in Indianapolis by explaining that his brother was killed by a white man too.

" 'What we need in the United States,' he said, 'is love and wisdom and compassion toward one another, and a feeling of justice toward those who still suffer within our own country, whether they be white or they be black.' " Two months later, Bobby was dead.

The sun was setting on 200 years of American tradition and religious custom. People with the antiwar movement were advocating everything from free love to the violent overthrow of the Federal Government. This included academia and the major news media. Millions were caught up in the intoxication of all the drugs and sex. It was a time of merriment, adventure, and change. Few thought about the ramifications of where this would lead someday. The majority of those young Americans lived for the moment.

Che Guevara was held up as a political icon. None knew that Castro had betrayed him to the Bolivian authorities who murdered him. The Black Panthers came into vogue. Timothy Leary advocated the use of LSD. The Supreme Court overturned state laws banning abortion. Marijuana evolved as the drug of choice. And welfare became a way of life. For many, the sense of entitlement was born. LBJ's Great Society had vastly expanded the size and role of government. The march to Socialism had begun.

Chapter Six

Hot Patootie

The next morning, after a special Italian breakfast with Luigi and Giovanna, the Marines said their goodbyes. It was an emotional time for them. They had just spent the very best and the abysmal worst thirteen months of their lives in a tropical paradise where little brown-skinned men, often as not, tried to kill them. Some wept. Others just smiled and hugged their buddies. Words were not necessary.

Combat does strange things to men. Sometimes they curse and fight, play nasty tricks on one another, ridicule their comrades, but deep down inside they're blood brothers. They're bonded for life, more so than any wife or any sweetheart ever can be. To fight in battle with fear clawing at their guts and death howling all around, to slaughter enemy soldiers, to see one's friends blown to pieces or shot between the eyes, that changes men into something different. In some ways they become ruthless and cunning like savage animals. Other times they cry at the sight of a dead child or an old person. But always, they stand together as brothers. Marines are special people. They love and defend God and America.

"What is that?"

"Looks like Hare Krishna."

"What does Hairy Christian mean?"

"No, you goofball. It's a religious order."

"Men singing and dancing in dresses?"

"It's their thing, man."

"Looks like the whole damn place has gone to hell since we been gone."

"That about sums it up out here in La La Land."

"They look like hairy sumbitches to me."

"You're just mad 'cause you expected hot tamales."

"We could use some sexy dancing girls, that's for sure."

"Let's bug out before they come over here with them collection bowls."

"Yeah. We need our dough for babes and beer."

Calhoun and Cassidy elected to remain in the city an extra day. The others had exchanged names and phone numbers, then gone their separate ways, heading for home on leave. The two Marines checked their gear at the train station, then went back out wearing their civilian clothes, hoping to find themselves a couple of hot dates. They hadn't gone very far when they spotted Butch's Backdoor Tavern. The marquee read, "Talent Contest Tonight."

The entrance was around back so they moseyed on in for a cold one.

The lady on the door was gorgeous. Tall with broad shoulders, long blonde tresses, wearing a low-cut pink gingham dress that made both jarheads perform a double take. Her physical features were curvy and alluring, long beautiful legs, high cheek bones, and demure brown eyes. She smiled and rose to greet them.

"Well, hello there, good-looking. You're just in time. Our show starts in fifteen minutes."

"What kinda show is it?" Catfish was in love!

"Pretty ladies, singing and dancing. It's fun. You'll enjoy it. Cover is five dollars."

They paid the five bucks. Then the hot babe offered them a doobie. "How much?"

"No charge. That's for welcoming newcomers. It's really good shit."

"Wow! Thanks!"

Catfish was impressed, and on the verge of drooling. "Are you busy after the show?"

She smiled and shook her head, no she wasn't. Then informed them she had a pretty girlfriend.

Calhoun warmed to the invitation, caught fire actually. Neither Marine could believe their good fortune.

"Her name is Marsha. I'll give Marci a call. We'll meet you out here right after the show."

Catfish and Calhoun were grinning ear to ear like two foxes staring at a tasty blonde cottontail.

"See ya after the show, pretty lady. Say, what's your name?"

"My name is Phoebe. Phoebe Buckingham."

They went on in and found themselves a table in the center of a big room down near the stage overlooking the dance floor. The place was almost full with men and women laughing, smoking and drinking, and having a big time. A burned-out looking waitress with excessive orange rouge and frizzy red hair brought their beers. Then Catfish fired up their marijuana joint. It was, to say the least, some good shit.

Three tokes later, the atmosphere changed abruptly. Light coming through the rear door reminded them of smoke grenades or angel hair or some damn thing … it streamed in, drifting in currents, ghostlike. It was like no sunlight they had ever seen before. Elton John was blasting away from the speakers up on the stage … the sunlight took on the appearance of opaque liquid. Blurred, shimmering … a room full of Jell-O pudding … what kind of pot was this? … purple shadows drifting back and forth. The pot was too good. They could barely sit up straight. The stuff was megaweed!

"God-A-Mighty!"

When the waitress returned, she resembled a zombie. She had on black eye shadow, reminding them of dead men they had seen in the jungle. Calhoun winced, looking away, staring down at the tabletop. Catfish got to his feet, reaching out a hand to steady himself … instead, he got hold of a pretty blonde. She was made up like Marilyn Monroe.

"Shit!" She groped his ya-ya!

"You look good enough to fuck, honey."

"Holy cow! I'm not really …"

"Sure you are!"

Miss Monroe grabbed Cassidy's shoulders, giving him a wet kiss right on the mouth. Then she squeezed his butt with both hands.

"Oh, wow!"

Catfish sat back down, kaplop. The joint was jumping. Wall to wall fandango. *MacArthur Park* came on over the loudspeakers. It seemed like everyone was on the dance floor at once. A jamboree of Jezebels and Nimrods, some willing, some not, a few souls lost in space. The rest were there just to escape the lunatic world outside.

> *"I don't think that I can take it*
> *'Cause it took so long to bake it*
> *And I'll never have that recipe again*
> *Oh Noooo …"*

The music was blowing them away. They closed their eyes. Rainbow colors. They opened them again. Party time!

"Far out!"

It felt good, grand, delicious. Too fucking much! The dancers reminded the stoned Marines of savages cavorting around a bonfire someplace out in the boondocks … their courtship ritual … prelude to bodacious sex.

Calhoun stumbled away from the table, angling for the Men's Room. He watched the shadows dancing on the walls beyond the imaginary flames. Gone with the wind? Not fucking likely. The South shall rise again!

He jumped … someone had felt his bottom.

A well-dressed "alternative lifestyle" stood there smiling back at him. He had the bluest eyes Calhoun had ever seen. Mister Fashion Plate looked a bit like Elvis.

"What's your sign?" the dilettante asked.

"My sign?"

"You're very good-looking," replied Elvis. "Going my way, sailor man?" He lisped exaggerated Mae West semaphores, hand on hip, cigarette drooping down from his pouty painted lips.

"Well … uh … no … I ain't gay."

"Don't knock it unless you tried it, honey."

Elvis was wearing purple eye shadow, similar to the waitress. He was giving Calhoun those "up from down under whammies" with his store-bought eyelashes.

"No … I don't believe …"

"Your eyes are all red, sugar. I've got some Vietnamese shit out in the pimp mobile. Come on outside, honey pie. I'll give you something no woman can. Make you change your mind about us fellas."

Calhoun was getting the hang of what it felt like to be a female. This bird wanted to do him!

"I'll make you feel like a woman, and cum like a truck driver!"

"I ain't believin' this!" The megaweed was driving Calhoun down a strange highway. He thought for a second about busting the guy in the chops … but then … he shifted gears. This Elvis person was flat-out corny. He had used those same dumb lines on dudes in other bars. The Marijuana Shuffle made it abundantly clear.

Calhoun deadpanned.

"You say that to all us hunks, I bet."

The cocksure stranger, accustomed to his own backdoor buckaroos ala Butch's Backdoor Tavern, flared at Calhoun's jest. "I certainly do not!" Actually it was his time of the month – PMS with balls.

"Sure ya do. You'll just screw me, then never call or nothin'."

"Well, if you're going to play hard to get …"

"Hard, hell! You'll break my damn heart. Probably get me pregnant!"

Calhoun was enjoying himself. Elvis didn't know whether to powder his nose or break wind.

"You ain't takin' me to no pimp place to read my Tarot cards, Mister Blue Eyes. I expect a relationship!"

"Well, of all the nerve. You're just awful!"

"You ain't getting none, period. I wouldn't let you fuck me with Paul Newman's dick!"

With that, Elvis whirled in umbrage, pirouetted as it were, lifting his narcissistic honker up toward the dusty plumbing overhead, then sashayed off in a bodacious huff … to the blaring lyrics of "Duke of Earl" by Gene Chandler.

Catfish was back at the table, a beer in one hand and a Lucky Strike in the other, becoming one with the music. Eyes closed, feeling the musical notes as they peppered over his body. He flashed back to Miss Head and Heels at Georgia Tech in Atlanta.

God, what a head trip that had been! Self-pity was the most unattractive quality, on stage or off. A prolonged exercise in kamikaze physics. He wondered, philosophically, if he still had a glass-jaw heart.

> *" … S-sitting down by my window now,*
> *All around I felt it,*

All I could see was the rain.
Something grabbed a hold of me, honey,
Felt to me, honey, like, lord, a ball and chain ..."

Janis Joplin was up on stage, beneath the spotlights, pantomiming her heart out to *Ball & Chain* with Big Brother & The Holding Company... at least he was dressed up like Janis. Complete with prison garb, a black leather biker's cap, and dragging a fake ball and chain around behind him. Ninety-eight heads turned in unison to address this new phenomenon unfolding before them, center stage. All eyes were glued to the moment, whether in hard-dick fascination or mouth-agape wonder.

Mistress Janis was right in the groove, doing her number ... she was BIG ... enormous ... the audience was going over the falls ... ones, twos ... a whole table ... then all, en masse ... they adored their Janis Joplin ... a star was born!

"... Honey, just because I got to need, need, need your love
I said I don't understand, honey, but I wanna a chance to
   try
Try, try, try, try, try, try, try
Honey, when everybody in the world will need the same
   lonely thing
When I wanna work for your love, daddy ..."

Lady Joplin was decked out in a black-and-white striped inmate's jacket he had managed to wrangle from Folsom Prison, a white feather boa, silver heart-shaped granny glasses, black mesh hose for his bare legs, and a pair of black leather fuck-me pumps. He was sultry, devastating, their condemned prisoner of love.

Perhaps she was their evil twin, their doomed personal Id, forever wandering the corridors of hell ... their depraved mad Ego, with a bloody chainsaw back in the trunk and a box of Gummy Bears up front in the glove compartment … their secret desire for a Singapore ass whupin! Whatever it was, Mistress Janis had struck an unbridled nerve. A sadomasochistic mind fuck.

The crowd began following him around the front of the stage. Janis Joplin, their love goddess, their legend in the making … "Let me touch her!" … stuffing dollar bills in his glittering rhinestone garter belt. He was exceptionally good at pantomime, a divine inspiration, a well-known Hollywood actor, their Paradise Lost.

The journey ended … cheering … emotional crescendos … palpitations of the heart … had there been any sacrificial virgins handy, they would have landed, ass-end over tea kettle, on stage before his nine and a half size tootsies.

Calhoun returned from his journey to the head, just in time to be seen by none other than Miss Belinda, Mistress of the Universe, who was seated at a front table with Pretty Paul whose teeth were wired together to accommodate his broken jawbone. Pretty Paul's spitting days were over for a spell.

"It's them! It's them!" she wailed.

Everyone began looking around to see what all the fuss was about.

"It's them!" she hooted again, getting up on her chair and pointing toward the two Marines.

Cassidy and Calhoun got up nonchalantly. Then began a quick stroll toward the rear door.

"They're the ones that attacked us!"

Calhoun and Catfish had just made the exit foyer, when the two transsexuals they originally thought to be hot patooties jumped up to greet them.

"Darling!" cooed Phoebe. Throwing his arms around Cassidy's neck.

Marsha was just as enthusiastic, latching on to Calhoun's arm. "You are a cutie pie!"

"Uhhhh … sorry, ma'am … we got a train to catch."

With that, they shucked off the two gender benders, kicked the exit door half off its hinges, then ran like a couple of scalded canines. The ruckus flooding out the door right behind them sounded like, could have been, a runaway locomotive. Screams and howls from the gay menagerie, unrequited love, backdoor thespians of the nocturne, revenge on the half shell, and two pissed off transsexuals left standing at the starting gate in drag.

Catfish yelled over to Calhoun as they were fleeing down an alleyway. "From now on you're gonna be the Duke Of Earl!"

Calhoun cackled with laughter as they rounded a corner with the station in sight. "Right on, and you're our Little Miss Buckingham!"

In spite of everything, all the hurt and disappointment, it had been a memorable weekend for the two young Marines. The chain still lay broken at Lady Liberty's feet.

Chapter Seven

Samantha

Official Business

Samantha Fox Jackson was busy at her work desk the day two Marines pulled up in the Alcoa Aluminum Company parking lot. Orders for sheet aluminum and aluminum ingots were pouring in on a monthly basis from Lockheed Corporation and the Furukawa Electric Company, for their wartime production of aluminum parts for helicopters and fixed-wing aircraft. Aluminum went into the production of just about everything from soft drink cans to American automobiles, refrigerators, and Uncle Sam's war machines. Samantha's secondary task was public relations and dealing with visiting dignitaries. But the majority of her time was spent filling orders for the huge smelting plant out back. The Vietnam War was good for business.

A rectangular gravel parking lot served as visitor parking for the two-story office building on Washington Street. The small brick structure had been constructed in 1910, becoming the aluminum company's regional headquarters in Alcoa, Tennessee. The home office was Pittsburgh, Pennsylvania.

John's last letter, dated three weeks earlier, was tucked away inside Sam's Austin Reed jacket hanging on a coat tree beside the office door. It was his best letter yet, professing his love for her and how much he missed her and thought about her on a daily basis, while relating his affection for his buddies. He called them his "Brothers," telling Sam they relied on one another in performing their military duties. He never mentioned the fact that those duties included the killing of enemy soldiers, and their constant struggle to stay alive while on search-and-destroy missions out in the jungle. Instead, he wrote about the parrots and monkeys and all the beautiful sights they observed on patrol. It was reassuring for Samantha, halfway believing that John and the others were never actually treading in harm's way.

Sam was extremely proud of her husband, the way he had matured after he joined the Marine Corps, and his devotion to her following their short-lived honeymoon in Atlanta. John was good for Sam. She loved and respected him with all her heart. They were going to have babies, watch them grow into fine individuals, and be together always as soul mates once he returned home from the war. But always, right at the edge of her conscious thought lurked the specter of fear.

When her office door opened and Samantha looked up and saw the two Marines standing there in full-dress uniforms, all the sunshine disappeared from her world. Without a word being spoken, she knew John was dead. A great chasm opened up around her, pulling Samantha down, down, down into an underworld of utter chaos and pain. Her agony was complete. It hurt so bad the tears refused to come. She gasped for breath, feeling as though her lungs were being torn from her body. Then she did cry, great retching sobs from the very depths of her soul. John was gone. The specter was real. The dream was shattered into a million insignificant pieces.

Suzie was working at the beauty parlor when the call came in. The Marine sergeant on the other end of the line explained the situation, telling Suzie that Samantha had asked for her while they were driving Sam to the hospital. Samantha had collapsed in her office and had to be carried by the Marines to their automobile. One of the aluminum company officials led the way to Blount Memorial Hospital in Maryville where he ordered a private room for Samantha. She was placed in bed and given a sedative to make her sleep.

Forty minutes later Suzie Brown walked into Sam's hospital room. "Tell me what happened."

"Ma'am, the details we have are pretty sketchy. We know they set up an ambush against a superior enemy force up near the Demilitarized Zone. That one went well. A second ambush they were involved in went badly for them."

"Were any more Marines killed?"

"Yes, ma'am. Three that we know about."

Suzie swallowed hard. She felt the vice of fear tightening around her ribcage. "Do you have their names?" she asked, her voice trembling. Suzie was on the verge of crying.

"I have two names, ma'am. The other one we don't know yet. One was their gunnery sergeant, Patrick Abernathy, the other is ..."

"Is Robert Smith dead?" she blurted out. Suzie felt woozy, about to faint.

The Marine corporal grabbed her arm, steering her to a chair beside Samantha's bed. "No, ma'am. He was wounded, but PFC Smith was not badly injured."

Suzie grabbed his hand and held it, tears streaming down both cheeks. "Thank God!" she whispered. "Thank you, sergeant. Thank you for my Robert."

A nurse brought in water and orange juice for the three men and Miss Brown.

After her orange juice, feeling somewhat relieved, Suzie remembered Red. "Is Billy Kidwell still alive?" she asked. "I don't have that name, ma'am. The other Marine we know about was PFC Albert Green."

In the days that followed Samantha was comforted by her mother, Suzie Brown, Bubba's parents, John's mother and father, and Billy Kidwell's mom and dad. The pastor with Blount Memorial Hospital stayed up with Sam her first night, praying with her and comforting Sam whenever she awakened, lost and afraid, crying over John. John's mom and dad were devastated but they held tough for Samantha, sharing themselves with their young daughter-in-law whom they loved. It was a terrible ordeal for everyone.

June 6, 1968: Samantha had been back at work two and a half months the day Robert Kennedy was shot in Los Angeles, California. The next day he died, twenty-four years to the day after the Normandy Invasion of Occupied France.

John Fitzgerald Kennedy had been assassinated four and a half years earlier, November 22, 1963, in Dallas, Texas. Followed by Martin Luther King, Jr. in Memphis, Tennessee, April 4, 1968. The Old World was dying, being swept into the dustbin of history. New tin pots and tyrants were taking center stage. The New World would breed additional corruption, propaganda, and disappointment for millions around the globe.

Three American statesmen lay dead, felled by bullets from hate-filled assassins. Thousands of miles away in Southeast Asia, thousands more Americans were being felled by political lies and political stupidity, coated with a thick, greasy layer of political arrogance. John and Gunny were among the dead. Work was not going well for Samantha. She retired to the powder room often, where she sat and cried. Her therapy with Alice Finkel helped, but the empty place in her heart was always there. That night Samantha experienced a strange dream.

She found herself alone on an alien shore, barefoot, on a long stretch of sandy black beach beside a majestic burgundy ocean. She was wearing her white wedding dress, and a pink Easter bonnet given her by John. The countryside was surreal, jade green bushes and jade green trees. Flowers all the colors of the spectrum bled down the beach into a nuclear colored sky.

She felt herself to be a single grain of sand. Tiny. No significance at all. Thousands more were gathered there, just like her. All young women in wedding attire. The nuclear sky was fantastic, magnificent, but somehow foreboding and frightening to look at. Far out on the horizon John's mother appeared above the waves holding a jeweled chalice in her left hand. In her right hand she held a silver box. Sam strained to see more but couldn't for all the fluttering sea birds.

Patrick Abernathy came walking down the beach wearing a tuxedo, with top hat and cane. High above him, her mother's face, Red's mother's, and the faces of other mothers filled the heavens among the wistful clouds. Kevin, a dead Marine from Firebase Hansel, rose up from the surf with seaweed trailing behind his ghostlike apparition. Then Captain America came forth from the sea, dripping red sea water, and chalk white in death. More silhouettes appeared, many more, populating the alien landscape behind Gunny with their capsized ranks from beyond the pale. Samantha fell to her knees in the black sand and prayed for the lost boys.

Her dream changed from the black beach to the Iwo Jima Memorial in Washington, DC, that day in August before John returned home from Parris Island. Samantha had driven up to Arlington National Cemetery during her vacation to see just what being a Marine was all about. Pamphlets and a talk given by a young Marine attendant described the 1954 dedication of the bronze memorial, Marine Corps' battles since 1775, the six boys on the flagpole, and the story about the thirteen hands.

Behind the seventy-eight foot statue stood thousands of white crosses, row after row of her nation's heroes. Men and women who had given their lives defending the United States of America.

Samantha was told that the first Marine setting the pole in the volcanic soil atop the rocky surface of Mt. Suribachi was Harlon Brock. Brock was later killed in the fighting on Iwo Jima. Next on the flagpole was Rene Gagnon from Manchester, New Hampshire. Gagnon survived the Pacific war.

Third was Mike Strank, their twenty-four-year-old leader. Strank was killed several days later by a Japanese mortar round. The last Marine at the rear of the monument with his arms raised high to help support the metal pipe was Ira Hayes, a Pima Indian. Around the far side of the statue was Franklin Sousley from Hilltop, Kentucky. He, too, was killed in the fighting before the island was secured. Last, on the backside, almost out of sight, was John Bradley, a Navy Corpsman from Antigo, Wisconsin.

Six thousand eight hundred and twenty one Americans were killed securing Iwo Jima, soldiers from the Army, Navy, and the Marine Corps. There were 19,217 wounded, the majority being United States Marines. Japanese dead were estimated at 20,000, with 1,083 Japanese soldiers taken prisoner.

Samantha questioned a Marine guard about the thirteenth hand, saying she couldn't find it on the flagpole. He told her that was an old fable, the thirteenth hand being the hand of God. Samantha silently vowed that day that she would become the thirteenth hand on the Marine Corps standard, holding the banner high for John, Red, and Bubba. And all the brave men and women with the Armed Forces of her beloved country. God was needed in other quarters of the world. Samantha would relieve Him, bear His burden proudly until He chose to return and reclaim His rightful place of honor.

Samantha needed God now to come take His place and relieve her. She awoke at dawn with the Marine Corps monument still vivid in her memory, experiencing a dull pain in her stomach.

Chapter Eight

The Visitor

Landing onboard the hospital ship, Bubba was taken straight into surgery where they shot him full of penicillin. There the attending physicians dug out two AK-47 rounds from his upper thighs. A third round had passed through, leaving a hole in his lower buttocks the size of a dime. Hence his hospital nickname, Double Barrel.

Red was dying. One Naval physician described his condition as "broke dick dog." He had bled out over half of his O Negative onboard the rescue helicopters. His doctors were cautiously optimistic. Even if they saved Red he might come out of surgery a mental defective due to lack of circulation to the brain. Three hours and nine minutes he lay on the operating table while they stitched him back together. They lost Red once, but managed to bring him back with their defibrillator paddles. Finally the operation was over. He was placed in ICU under sedation beneath an oxygen tent. They stuck a catheter up his penis, and an IV in his arm.

Pasamenus was a different story. He was suffering from battle fatigue accompanied by the infamous 1,000-yard stare. There were fancy words for what he had, but it boiled down to severe shock. He and Red had killed so many of the enemy, fighting their rearguard action while fleeing through the jungle, that his mind had closed a door to shut out all the horror and screaming. Watching all those North Vietnamese soldiers burn to death with napalm was a macabre experience. Twice he woke up screaming before the doctors gave him a shot to knock him out for twenty-four hours.

When Major Abraham learned that Gunny was dead, he became angry. Gunny was his best friend, his Marine Corps brother. They had served together in Korea. Patrick Lucian Abernathy had taken a Chinese bullet meant for him at the Battle of Inchon. The Marines had gone ashore that day in 1950 to reinforce the South Korean Army, throwing a monkey wrench in the victorious advance by the North Korean People's Army. General MacArthur had called that one right. The communist offensive collapsed when their supply lines were severed. The Reds were driven back all the way to the Yalu River.

Next day Major Abraham was onboard the hospital ship berating the wounded Lieutenant Butler, demanding to know what the hell went wrong. Lieutenant Butler quietly accepted the Major's wrath. He already blamed himself for Gunny's death. Daniel Butler felt responsible for all the dead and wounded under his command.

But after Major Abraham calmed down, he realized that Gunny was instrumental in their decision to remain in the valley for one final crack at Charlie. That was just like his brave and crafty Marine Corps Master Sergeant. With tears in his eyes he apologized to the young lieutenant, shaking his hand and thanking him for his service to the Corps. Then he went in search of the others from Gunny's platoon.

Pasamenus was still asleep. They had Carlos rigged up in a traction device, and he was beginning to get feeling back in his feet and ankles. The major spent twenty minutes talking with Carlos. Double

Barrel was up and rolling around in his wheelchair. They chatted a spell. When the Major came to Red's bedside his eyes again filled with tears. Red hair and all, there lay a younger version of his dead friend whom he had served with for twenty-two years. Major Abraham knelt down beside the boy's bed, took his pale hand in his, and prayed.

"Dear Heavenly Father,

"Sir, You got two of my best Marines up there, Patrick Lucian Abernathy and John Henry Jackson. There's good people, Lord. Two of the finest. This boy they call Red reminds me of Lucian. Acts like him too from all the stories I've been told about him and the others while Lucian was still alive.

"Please smile down on this Marine, Lord. He's just a squirt, but if You allow him some more time, he'll do You proud just like he does our Marine Corps proud. I know I'm not much of a Christian, Sir. And I don't pray very often. But please, God, let me keep this one.

"Blessed Father in Heaven. Amen"

Major Abraham rose to his feet, ramrod straight, saluted, leaned down and kissed Red's hand, then executed an about face and walked out of the hospital ward. Three nurses standing in the hallway outside were busy wiping away their tears. Two days later Red regained consciousness.

The first salvo landed 400 yards astern, hurling a column of water three hundred feet into the air. A second shell burst 200 yards directly behind the ship. Sailors on the fantail felt the concussion.

"Hard aport!" came the cry from the captain's quarters, where he was scrambling into his uniform jacket to hasten up to the bridge

A third round landed 100 feet forward, showering the vessel with falling water from the blast.

An American escort cruiser, 1,000 yards to starboard and tracking the incoming shells on radar, opened fire with her six- and eight-inch guns. The rapid reports spread across the South China Sea like rolling thunder. She continued firing for another three minutes, with one final enemy salvo landing between the cruiser and the hospital ship. Whoever it was had picked the wrong day and the wrong target. Heavy detonations back in the hills signaled an end for the enemy gun crew's brief reign of glory.

The roar from the guns jarred Pasamenus awake. He sat up in alarm, frightened and confused, fighting his bed sheets, believing he was back in the jungle again. Nurse Hanley rushed to assist him, alighting on the side of the bed, taking his hands in hers while speaking to Pasamenus in a calm and reassuring voice.

He relaxed then, looked her in the eyes and frowned. "You look tired today," he said. "We've been expecting you."

Nurse Hanley shook him, firmly but professionally. Then held his face between her hands.

"You've been away. To a bad place. But you're safe now. Your friends are here. They're waiting to see you."

"Captain America was killed up on the mountain. Kevin died up there too. Sixty-four men died that day. Gunny got his down in that field where the grass was yellow and green. John is out there waiting for me. They're all out there waiting. I have to go back."

Gayle lay him back against his pillow, leaned down beside him, slid her arm beneath his neck, and held Pasamenus as one would hold a child. She had seen it performed many times before on the hospital ship. Physical contact and talking to them helped the young soldiers find their way back from their personal hells. She stroked his brow, her head beside his on the pillow, her long brown hair flowing all around.

"You're safe now. You're onboard a hospital ship in the South China Sea. You were hurt, but you're going to be just fine. My name is Gayle Hanley. I'm your nurse."

"My men need me. I have go back and relieve Gunny."

"Those Marines are with God now. You're alive. You belong here with us. Your buddies need you. I need you too, sergeant. Please come back. We need you here on this ship."

Pasamenus had not cried since he was a little boy. He cried then, quiet and gentle sobbing. Gayle held the sergeant and rocked him, tears leaking between her long brown lashes. Finally he began his painful journey back to the hospital ship.

Red was awake. His eyes were open but he couldn't speak. Then he would lapse back into a post-traumatic slumber, a fretful sleep, much like a dog when it dreams about chasing rabbits. Red would twitch and moan, then wake up again. But he never said a word.

They hooked him up to various laboratory equipment to determine his brain wave activity and heartbeat; lungs, stomach, urine tests, and blood analysis proved inconclusive. He appeared to be normal, but no words came out of his mouth. Nor did he recognize where he was, the ship's personnel, or any of his Marine buddies. Red simply lay in bed and stared up at the overhead. His doctors were beginning to wonder if lack of blood to the brain had caused permanent damage.

"Wake up, you son of a bitch! Goddamn you! Wake up, Red!"

Bubba had hobbled in and was yelling at Red, hoping Red could hear him wherever he was inside his damaged inner sanctum . He slapped him, hard. Then again. But Red just lay there staring up at the white ceiling.

Bubba knelt down and hugged his cousin. "Please, Red. Please come back. I can't lose you and John both. Please, Red. It all sucks with you guys gone."

The enormity of losing his best friend, plus Gunny, with Red on the verge of becoming a head case was taking a heavy toll on Robert Smith. Terrible nightmares pursued him in his sleep. He felt alone and afraid. Again and again he dreamt of their flight through the jungle with the NVA hot on their heels. Him and Lieutenant Butler getting shot, a Marine he didn't know being blown to pieces in front of him, and the Air Force overhead.

He dreamed in Technicolor. The napalm smelled like kerosene. John was loading their dead master sergeant onboard the helicopter, then standing in the doorway firing Red's machine gun. Red lay on the floor, wounded, firing another M-60. The door gunner was blazing away with his machine gun when pieces flew off the wall of the Huey, and John fell across the master sergeant. John looked over at Bubba, whispered Samantha's name, and died.

That night when everyone was asleep, save for the night crew, a blue glow appeared in Red's private chamber.

He opened his eyes and spoke. "Have you come for me?"

A shadow moved from the end of the bed and stood beside his nightstand.

"Am I going with you tonight?"

The shadow leaned over the bed, bent down, and kissed Red's forehead. "Gunny will come when it's your time."

"Then why are you here? I don't get it."

"Gunny and the others thought it best I come pay you a visit."

"Why? I'm sick of this damned place. I want to go with you."

"Suck it up, Marine. You still have a job to do."

"Why? So I can get my ass shot off like you and Gunny? I've done my time in hell. Pasamenus blew a fuse. And you want me to go out there again?"

"It's your job. You're a Marine."

"Fuck it! I quit!"

"Marines never quit! And neither will you!"

"Shit on it! I ain't goin'. Semper Fi can kiss my ass!"

"Pasamenus is going back. So is Bubba, Driggins, Johnson, all the others. They need you Red, especially The Brain. He relies on you more than you know. I don't think you ever realized this before, but the men looked to you and me when Gunny and The Brain were off someplace doing their shit. You're a leader, Red. You owe it to the men. They rely on you. You and that cheap-ass radio of yours."

"You sure know how to make a guy feel like a jerk. An' stop insultin' my radio!" Red laughed then. "Yeah, I reckon you're right. I wouldn't quit if they paid me. I love those dumb bastards. Every damn one of them. I love you too, John. I wish you could stay here with us. Me and Bubba miss you. I bet Samantha is having a bitch of a time."

"Yes, she is, but that will end soon. Sam will join me before long."

Red reached out to touch his friend, but it was like holding smoke. The glow grew brighter and Red could see his friend a little better. He reached again, and it was almost real.

"What's it like where you are?"

"That's hard to explain. It's peaceful and wonderful, but I think I'll wait and let you see for yourself. Crossing over was the hard part, but that doesn't take very long."

"Will many more of us be coming your way?"

"Some, but we have other things to talk about tonight. You're going on a mission, something special and important. There will be problems. The men will look to you and Lieutenant Butler to lead them. That's why you're going back. To help Pasamenus, and to help protect the men.

"We were good together, weren't we?"

"Gunny said you an' Bubba an' me were three of the best he ever served with. That's something coming from that old salt."

"Yeah, I'm proud to have served with Gunny. I'll go see Madame when I get outta here. Take her some flowers. Make her feel better, maybe."

"Good idea. If you recall, Madame likes chocolate covered cherries."

"Is there anything special I need to know?"

"Just this. When it looks like you ain't gonna make it, use the railroad."

"Use the railroad?"

John was fading. "I have to go now. Remember to stay low and keep moving."

"I will. I'll take good care of the men too. So long, John. Thanks for coming to see me."

"Goodbye, my friend. Remember the railroad."

The light dimmed. And John was gone.

Next morning Nurse Mayo found Red sitting on the side of his bed, asking what they had for breakfast. Nurse Mayo was overjoyed. His doctors couldn't explain it, but Bubba sensed correctly that something strange had taken place. He never asked why Red had become so serene and peaceful. He was just happy to have his cousin back.

Pasamenus was once more himself, reflective, intellectual, friendly, and smiling, but his life had taken a turn for something extraordinary. Nurse Hanley had taken an interest in him. She found him different from any man she had ever known before.

It was the first time in his life The Brain had experienced serious thoughts about a female. At first he was confused, but after a few days he accepted Gayle because of her inquisitive intellect, not to mention all the rest of her female accoutrements.

Gayle had a BSN from Loyola University in Chicago and was an ardent student of science fiction, which was The Brain's favorite reading material. They discussed Clarke, Bradbury, Asimov, *Metropolis, The War of the Worlds*, Roswell, on and on for hours when she was off duty. Gayle had studied literature as her minor, so she was well-versed in the classics. One evening she surprised Pasamenus with a book from the ship's library. *All Quiet on the Western Front* was a tale about German soldiers on the Western Front during World War One, and the hardships they endured.

Pasamenus had never read a war novel before and devoured the pages, identifying with Paul Baumer, Erich Remarque's main character. Gayle then brought him another book, *Comrades of War* by Sven Hassel. Gayle's grandmother had lived in Paris during World War One, marrying a "doughboy" from Black Jack Pershing's General Staff.

The Marine and his nurse soon found themselves deeply in love. A few nights later she came to Pasamenus' bedside, bent down, and whispered, "Follow me." She led him to the Dead Room where they prepared the bodies before storing them in the ship's morgue. Gayle stripped, revealing her ample front armor plating and beautifully rounded buttocks.

Pasamenus shucked off his navy PJs. The Brain got up on the preparation table and lay down with his noggin on the headrest for dead people. Gayle climbed on top of him, straddling his waist with her thighs, taking him inside her eager, supple body. It was magic, better than either one of them imagined. It lasted only a minute. Then they made love a second time, a long and delicious union.

"You're such a man," she whispered, out of breath. "I could get used to this."

"You're marvelous, Gayle Hanley. I've fallen in love with you, really hard."

"I noticed the hard part."

They both chuckled.

"I feel the same way about you, Eshkhan. You're so different, but it frightens me. I'm afraid I might lose you. "

"The things we do as Marines aren't that bad."

"You're lying to me, Eshkhan. I know what you do out there."

"Well, sometimes it does get complicated."

"That's what scares me."

"To be honest, our retreat through the jungle scared me too. That's when we lost John and Gunny."

"I remember when they brought you in. You looked like *The Thing From Another World*."

"I apologize if I frightened you."

"It's my job, sweetheart, saving jarheads like you."

"I rather like being saved by you."

"Yes, dearest, you're a keeper. My sweet and adorable Armenian Marine."

"I have a proposal for you, Gayle Hanley."

"A proposal for little ole me?"

"Yes, dear."

"What is this secret proposal of yours, Eshkhan?"

"Will you marry me?"

"Oh, honey! Oh, you darling man! God, yes, I'll marry you. And give you all the children you can stand. I love you, Eshkhan. I knew it when I brought you those damned books."

"From now on I promise to be extra careful. I want to come back to you, Gayle. We can live anywhere you choose back in The World. I'll work diligently and be your faithful, loving husband."

"Yes, my darling. We'll be very happy together. And live to be old folks tottering around the house, goosing each other's behinds."

"Speaking of which, would you care to make love again, my dear?"

"Oh, my God! I've died and gone to heaven!"

Nurse Hanley and Sergeant Pasamenus were married by the ship's captain, with Dwayne Henry giving away the blushing bride. All the nurses and Marines onboard attended the ceremony. It was a beautiful marriage in a war-torn part of the world where horror and violent death were everyday events.

A week later First Squad was transferred to a regular hospital in Da Nang. Hanoi had launched a second offensive and all the hospital beds onboard the ship were needed for the soldiers coming in from the carnage taking place in the hamlets and villages up and down the Vietnamese countryside. Pasamenus kissed Gayle goodbye, then returned to his battle-scarred arena of bombs, bullets, and bandages.

Chapter Nine

Garden of Eden

The Legionnaire carried Madame upstairs, undressed her, then tucked her into bed. Next morning he called Major Abraham to ascertain the funeral arrangements. Madame had drunk herself into oblivion, sitting with her confidante, Gargoyle, outside in the courtyard following the Major's telephone call the evening before.

Mimi Le Beau would forever remember that night, a June moon, the stars overhead, the butchered face of her friend the Legionnaire, the smell of orchids in the damp night air, and the two little laughing thrush nesting in her ornamental sanh tree. She would forever remember the face of Lucian Abernathy as well.

Patrick Lucian Abernathy was to be buried in Arlington National Cemetery in Washington, DC. John Henry Jackson was going home to Knoxville, Tennessee, where he would be interred in Woodlawn Cemetery. Madame chose not to attend the graveside services in Washington, but to view Lucian's body one last time at the Da Nang airfield. The following day Major Abraham sent a limousine to pick her up. He was waiting at the terminal when she arrived.

"I wish I could take his place, Mimi. Patrick was the best we have."

"He was indeed. And I loved him for it. I feared it would end this way. Our world is not the same without Monsieur Abernathy."

"No, ma'am, it sure isn't." He took her arm. "He's over here in the service hangar."

They entered an airplane hangar with a B-26 Marauder bomber sitting inside. The oiled .50 caliber nose guns glistened in the early morning light. Bullet holes in the wings had been patched over with sheet metal, secured by stainless steel rivets. Eleven metal caskets sat in a row inside a large freezer locker which housed sides of beef, coffee, and numerous containers of ice cream.

"This is the one, Mimi."

The Major unfastened it, then raised the lid. Madame caught her breath, her hand quickly covering her mouth. The man she loved and planned to marry lay before her, cold, white, and still.

"Give us a minute, Saul."

Major Abraham turned and walked outside, taking a chair beneath the 20mm tail cannon of the B-26 bomber.

"Oh, Lucian … my darling … my love … I miss you, *mon Cheri*. I lost you once before, then God gave us the second chance … Now you've slipped away again. *Mon amour, toi et mon–Ca ne changera pas. Je vous aime* … Paris was ours for the taking. You would have loved it there. We could have shared such memories, loving one another, making the new friends, strolling the Champs-Elysees, growing old together. Why did you have to die, Lucian? *Je ne comprends pas*."

She wept then, her bereaved heart shedding its tears of finality and loss as the Major came back inside, gently closing the lid. Then he led her away from the room of the dead, with the coffee and ice cream and its silent warriors.

Major Abraham drove Mimi to a combination tearoom-boarding-house on the outskirts of Da Nang. It was a place used often by members the Central Intelligence Agency and the Israeli Mossad. Money and official documents changed hands there. Only Major Abraham and the CIA in Washington knew the history of the woman who owned and operated the two-story establishment.

Fraulein Decker had served as an American spy with the OSS during World War Two in Nazi Germany. The food was good, and the rooms were clean and comfortable. Some of the men and women who came and went there were of the clandestine nobility.

"Well, Saul, I see you've acquired yourself a pretty lady friend. It's about time. We were beginning to think you swung the other way."

"That'll be the day! Gabriele, this is my special friend, Mademoiselle Mimi Le Beau. Her fiancé was killed recently in a firefight. Mimi, Fraulein Gabriele Decker."

"*Mein Gott, ich habe schmutzige Gedanken!* Please forgive me, Mademoiselle."

"It's quite all right. I'm pleased to make your acquaintance, Gabriele."

"You poor thing. May I bring you some of my herb tea?"

"Yes, please. *Merci, Fraulein.*"

"Call me Dixie. Suits my personality. The usual, Major?"

"Yes, ma'am."

Fraulein Decker retired to her kitchen to prepare their refreshments. Then Major Abraham revealed the reason he had brought Mimi to the inn.

"You have a unique organization for acquiring information," he said. "Men talk when they're with women. Some brag, others become careless, some just talk because they feel the need to unburden their souls. Men need women. It's not just a sex thing. It's the desire for companionship, a need to share their dreams and aspirations. That's a fatal flaw in espionage."

"You have a surprising understanding of the opposite sex, Major. And the cynical view of your fellow man."

"War makes people cynical. And the things I do. I could use your help, Mimi."

"Lucian spoke of that. He told me you are the patriot."

Six foot two, two hundred and eighteen pounds, the red man from the Karankawa Tribe of Corpus Christi, Texas, frowned, placing his muscular forearms on the tabletop.

"I never told anyone this before, but I always looked up to Gunny. I admired him for his wisdom and his heart. He inspired others, which is a trait only a few men possess. He was a brave Marine and a happy warrior. I loved Patrick Abernathy like my own brother."

Tears came to Madame's eyes.

"I'm sorry. I didn't mean to upset you."

She nodded. "Seeing him lying there was a shock. Lucian was always the happy one. So full of life. He made others happy just being with him."

Fraulein Decker returned with Mimi's tea and the Major's cup of mulligatawny broth. Dixie joined them at the table with a mug of peppermint schnapps.

"*Prost!*" she said, holding her cup at eye level. "To you, Mimi. To you, Saul."

There where no customers at that hour, so the Major spoke freely. "I've asked Mimi to come onboard. Dixie is a confidante. We've worked together since what, 1962? Any questions you have, she can answer for you."

"My man is dead. And you ask me to become the spy for you?"

Dixie took Madame's hand in hers. "Your man was one of us. There are Northern agents all over South Vietnam. Whenever Lucian suspected one, he informed the Major. Lucian Abernathy accounted for over twenty enemy spies. Major Abraham makes them disappear."

Mimi Le Beau was dumfounded. For a full minute she sat gathering her thoughts. The American Indian and the German OSS agent said nothing, awaiting her response.

"Lucian did all of that?"

"Yes, ma'am. For his country and his Marine Corps."

"I never knew that about him," she said. "Not his secret life. I suppose ..." She paused. "I suppose he never mentioned it to protect me."

Mimi drew herself up straight in her chair and lit a cigarette. She was recalling the last time she saw Gunny, waving goodbye to him on the sidewalk outside her Garden of Eden as they drove away. First Squad was with him. That had been a joyous weekend for her and Lucian. A time for love. Her dream had come to pass. Lucian had proposed to her the night before, and Mimi had accepted.

"This is the difficult thing for me to do." She closed her eyes, composing her thoughts. "I swear before God ... I shall maintain the crusade ... this secret business ... for Vietnam and America ... and for my brave and courageous Lucian Abernathy."

Dixie and the Major both left their wicker chairs, hugging Mimi at the same time.

"*Moege Gott mit dir sein. Gott beschuetze uns alle.*"

She cried then, tears streaking what was left of her mascara. Mimi dried her eyes with her little silk handkerchief, stood up, squared her shoulders, then held her cup out before her.

"To Patrick Lucian Abernathy!" Mimi took a sip of herb tea ... then dashed her cup against the tile floor.

"To Patrick Lucian Abernathy!" Dixie and the Major repeated the words, drinking and smashing their cups in like fashion against the tile floor.

A hundred miles away First Squad was slogging through the jungle on a secret mission which would have sent the White House into a vitriolic rage. Meanwhile, back in Hanoi, a third offensive was being planned to compensate for the failed Tet Offensive last January, and their failed minioffensive again in May. Once again, General Giap had been overruled by the Politburo of North Vietnam.

Chapter Ten

Miss Sooty Belle

Return to 'Nam

"What was it like … your relationship? With your lady friend? How long did it take you to get over her?"

"Too damn long," he answered. Then he laughed.

"Do you think it will take much longer, for me?" she asked. Giving him that look that women do when they need a righteous fuck.

"Not so long as you might think." He returned the righteous gaze.

She lowered her eyes … smiling. "I hope it won't hurt … much longer." She raised her head, gazing into his pale baby blues. A mirrored reflection of her own sad journey.

"It won't. You're farther along than I was."

He reached over then, touching the golden down on the woman's tanned shoulder.

She looked relieved, smiled again for the gray man, tracing her fingertips along the heavy veins on the back of his hand. She was built for the night. A sensual body like men dream about, reminding him of his lost romance with Trudy Peters. Anita reached in her handbag, handing him her business card. He felt in control again, for the first time since coming home.

"Would you like to have a drink?" he asked.

… the car's headlights picked it up in its yellow beam on the side of the road in front of the mailbox. Familiar black mound … silent … still … tears welled up in his eyes before he could stop the automobile. The gray man rushed over to his fallen companion.

"Sooty Belle … my little Sooty Belle."

He gathered up the mangled cat, guts and all, clutching it to his chest with both hands. The furry black body had already become stiff, sticky with clotted blood which soiled the driver's coat and tie.

Tears streamed down his cheeks. Eyes clamped shut, he sat down in the grass by the side of the pavement and wept, great racking sobs, the little comrade cradled pitifully in his blood-stained arms. He cried for Miss Sooty Belle, and all the misery he had known since he came home from Vietnam. He cried a long time.

After a while the man lay back in the dew-speckled grass, resting himself against a damp, wheeling earth. His tear-stained face turned outward toward infinity. "Star light, star bright, first star I see tonight." Man's age-old question, the eternal cosmic God. Their favorite program, watching the planets and the shooting stars on a mysterious night stage far, far away.

The dead cat lay sleeping on her master's tummy. Where she had sat in times past, telling him of her day or making bread or simply dozing … before the boys in the pickup truck ran her down and killed her.

He felt broken, gutted. His world had become, finally, that night, an empty fucking shell.

A personal black hole of receding phantoms and guilt … dead

men he had known and fought beside in Vietnam … guilt that he was still alive.

The last thing he loved on earth was gone now. He had been fighting emotional quicksand for eleven weeks. Every night it came to his bedside like a bad habit, a discontentment of the soul which ate and clawed and consumed his spirit. He didn't understand why. Why after returning home from the war, why did he feel like he was losing his mind?

It felt as though he had fallen down the rabbit hole into Alice's Wonderland. His mind rebelled at the pagan behavior of the long-haired hippies, student sit-ins, peace marches, the antiwar movement. A Mad Hatter on every street corner. The whole thing flew in the face of his Christian upbringing, and his patriotic feelings about America. He missed his parents. His mother's teachings about the Bible when he was a boy, and his father's beliefs in kindness and one's personal honor. Finding his Marine buddy hanged in the jungle by the Vietcong had turned him into a killer, volunteering for six sniper missions. When he left Vietnam he had accounted for fifteen enemy soldiers.

Sooty Belle was the last straw. The man closed his eyes and spoke softly to his sleeping companion as one gives solace to a friend or loved one. The same way he cradled a mortally wounded corporal in a bloody rice paddy on the Plain of Jars. Then he prayed to his higher power, for Miss Sooty Belle, for himself, for his deceased parents, for the whole fucked-up planet to a god unknown.

There are star fields, billions of them, as numerous as there are human beings, hidden away inside the endless constellations of the human mind. Where man's feelings, every emotion, all thought, every vice, every good and evil exists in that particular vortex of time and energy. Silent, serene, waiting for the right chord, that appropriate kick in the shins, a turn of the screw, to engage, release, activate, that particular electrical spark … love, hate, erotica, madness, suicide … all are there. Small lifeboats on a galactic tide, awaiting their summons, their final countdown. Most will lay dormant, unseen, and eventually perish with their particular host. Yet there are others, like Dudley Calhoun grieving Miss Sooty Belle, who exhibit the raw emotions people carry around inside their heads. They wear the thorn crown. Their numbers are few.

Being back in The World was not what he expected. After the closeness and camaraderie of his Marine Corps brothers in mortal combat, the fear and heat of the jungle, their riotous drunks on two-day passes, three-dollar whores and cheap whiskey, civilian life appeared phony and inappropriate. Calhoun felt lost, sometimes afraid.

That particular morning, downtown at the City-County Building, he had walked into every woman's secret nightmare. A pregnant Mexican illegal had gone into labor, and was having her baby right there on the concrete floor in front of God and the Information Desk. A crowd had gathered, the usual rubbernecking menagerie. One young voyeur was leaning over sideways, up on tippy toes, "so's he could see," mouth wide open, staring up the woman's naked thighs.

The Mexican lady was being assisted in her breathing efforts by two older women who worked inside the City-County complex. Her gasps of pain came in short labored bursts, accompanied by brief intervals of crying out to "Sweet Lord Jesus!" and "Bring it on home, goddamn it!" This went on for some fifteen minutes before she gave vent to one final howl of agony, and the baby was there.

Calhoun couldn't believe this shit was happening. What a damn fool! Getting herself and her wetback kid caught up in such a precarious predicament. Damn! Were they all that weird? The whole collection of the human condition? He walked up the stairs to the second floor to retrieve a legal document for his cousin, the scene with the baby forever seared in his memory … rewinding his mental tapes … tapes he wished would go away.

That pregnant mama san in that village up in the Highlands with a Vietcong hand grenade. She, with her unborn child, trying to frag his Jeep, and PFC Simpson blowing the woman away, and half the block, with a .50 caliber machine gun mounted in back.

Later that afternoon he was buying gasoline from a raghead service station in a poor section of town when a muffled "bang" rang out from an old warehouse across the street. He paused a minute, thinking, then pulled his 9mm Smith & Wesson from the glove compartment and walked across the intersection to investigate. Someone might be in trouble.

A black man sat facing the rear parking lot, propped up against the corrugated side of the building, mumbling spit and nonsense.

At first he thought the Negro was just drunk, pissed off at his empty jug. But there was red drool running down from his lips, down off his chin onto the front of his shirt. He looked like he was having a fit. Then the gray man with the 9mm pistol saw the back of the Negro's head. Five inches above a red stained collar, a jagged round hole. The young man had placed a revolver in his mouth and blown out the back of his skull.

He was a nice-looking fellow, twenty-five or thirty years old. A dozen color photographs lay scattered across his lap and down on the ground beside his motionless hands. Bits and pieces of his miserable existence.

They never taught him in school how to cope or make a living in the white man's world. Or how to appreciate the joys of being a free individual in the land of milk and honey. It was mostly liberal invective regarding the merits of the NAACP and Equal Rights and the Black Panthers and Students For a Democratic Society and Federal subsidies, and on and on. Only Uncle Toms did Mas'suh Charlie's work.

An empty pint of Old Number 7 sat upright against his faded denim crotch, beside a blue steel .38 Police Special. Finally he slumped forward and became silent. Except for the soft dripping of the blood, where it fell down in a spreading pool of deep crimson between his knees.

Calhoun sat down in the weeds and shadows beside the dying Negro. Just sat there watching him. Slackjawed, high cheek bones, brown eyes glazing over, plaid cotton shirt, ragged-ass coveralls. And down at the heels brown brogans with not a trace of shoe polish anywhere.

The shoes more than anything else summed up the poor wretch's life. He didn't have enough money to make his shoes look nice. That upset the gray man more than the blood or the bullet hole in his head. He looked down at his own $30.00 wingtips and felt anger … rage. This pitiful son of a bitch had worked all his life, and all he had to show for it, bottom line, was a free trip to the morgue.

No decent clothes, no automobile, Goldberg's roach emporium for a pillow, whores and cokeheads for neighbors, street punks, brain-dead cops. The usual lifers down at City Hall. Not even shoe polish! Just an empty bottle of Jack Daniels whiskey and those Brownie color photographs of his life as a nigger.

The white man reached over to touch the still hand of the black man. It was still warm, limp as wet newspaper. They sat there together, blood brothers, comrades of an unjust world, the dying man's callused fingers held gently in the strong white ones, as his newfound friend passed over silently into eternity.

"Fuck it," he muttered. "Fuck them all!" he shouted pounding the ground with his other fist until his knuckles were raw and bleeding. Tears welled up. Rage against the war protesters, the media, the politicians.

Finally he, too, slumped forward, staring off across the asphalt into his own tattered existence. Their lost innocence, side by side, in a weed-infested parking lot. The black man had US ARMY tattooed on his right wrist. They resembled a pair of salt and pepper bookends. A Cracker and a Darkie, traveling that last mile together, waiting for a call from the governor, hoping for some kind of reprieve. A pair of flea market specials.

He cried as he had for Miss Sooty Belle. There was no bottom to it, just a terrible empty place where his heart should have been. He was lost. Down in the Pit. His life was as devoid of meaning and happiness as that empty glass bottle between the black man's legs. He was still blubbering when the police rolled up and hauled him away downtown.

The dark was settling in, marshaling its tidal forces, girding him with a mantel of corruption and decay. Draining his ability to resist. The terror was coming through the walls. It hurt so damned bad, his fall down through a black void into the lake of fire.

He thought about death. How welcome it might be. But fear too. He didn't want to die, not yet, anyway. Maybe there was still time. Surely there was more to life than this, this creeping depression which sucked the beauty out of everything since Vietnam.

"God damn!" he blurted out. "Fuck you!"

If God was responsible for all this shit and nonsense, he hated God. He wasn't a forgiving God. A decent and all-knowing Heavenly Father. All this poverty and disease and bullshit.

"Fuck you, asshole … and fuck your apple tree!"

God was a divine cock sucker. He began weeping again, waving his arms about, trying to find his way, flailing blindly … then suddenly … maybe … Yes! That was it! Finally, sure … that had to be it. The gray man stumbled on through an emotional fog for two more days before he established a clear mental portrait.

When Jesus Christ was nailed to the cross for the sins of man, man was supposed to get his act together. Straighten up and fly right. Cut out all the crap and bullshit. But did man do that? Hell, no! Every power since Rome right down the line to Uncle Adolf had done their level best to bend society over and fuck her in the ass.

So God finally threw in the towel. "I'm outta here!" said the Lord.

While Hippiedom was getting high, pulling her panties down, and throwing the bird to Jesus, the whole cosmic cracker went straight in the dishwater. LBJ and drugs and anarchy and me, me, me! Set the murderers free, Mixmaster the unborn in the womb, hoist the Jolly Roger, and sue on sight! Polecat politicians sucking up to every clown with a bogus complaint. Madness, suicide, a nation of victims. The US Government was on the ropes, and nobody had a fucking clue. Just charge it to the next generation. Or rewrite the Constitution. Or haul out the Smoke & Mirrors … ONE MORE TIME!

God had joined the Union.

Calhoun was on the telephone to Catfish in Greers Ferry, Arkansas, one hundred and fifty miles south.

"Right on, bro. I've had a belly full of peaceniks, John Lennon, Timothy Leary, sleazy politicians, and all the usual Bozos telling us shit I know ain't true."

"I know, Dudley. But there isn't much we can do about it now, is there?"

"We could leave."

"And go where, for Christ's sake?"

"We could go back to the boonies."

"You mean 'Nam?"

"Yes!"

"Holy shit! You are crazy!"

"At least back there we know who our friends are."

It was a troubling conversation for Larry Cassidy, which lasted another twenty minutes. Going back to Vietnam had crossed his mind too, but he knew the odds of getting hurt were just as bad, maybe even worse than before. Finding a job wasn't hard, but dealing with the general public had become an issue for him just as it had for Dudley

Calhoun. So many of them had become loud and obnoxious, disrespectful of the accepted ways of doing things. Welfare was coming out of the woodwork, the antiwar movement resembled a three-ring circus, even the cops were smoking ganja. And every day the paperboy brought more.

That night Larry talked with his father until two-thirty in the morning. Next day he called Calhoun's number in Ozark, Missouri.

"I thought it over … I'll go with you."

"Far out, Larry. Major cool. Could we meet at your place this weekend?"

"Sure. Come on down. I've told my parents a lot about you."

Nineteen days later they landed in Saigon. It was foggy and raining. There were metal caskets sitting on wooden gurneys on the puddled runway where they offloaded from their military transport out of San Francisco. Major Abraham was there in the fog and rain waiting to greet them.

"That is one big fucker!"

"The copilot said the Major requested us. Wonder why?"

"You're Mister Boom Boom. I'm Mister Pest Exterminator."

"Sounds reasonable. Come on, Duke. Let's meet our new boss."

The Major returned their salutes, then stood patiently by while they retrieved their duffle bags from the cargo hold.

"I guess you're wondering why I asked for you two jarheads."

"Yes, sir."

"I picked you out from a list of experts. There's a squad of Marines in Da Nang short a couple men. I'm going to place you with them because of your experience. This squad was specially trained by a friend of mine. I'm going to ask you from time to time to perform certain tasks. It's strictly volunteer stuff, outside military channels. Do you have a problem with that?"

"No, sir. We came back because of what's happening back home. The place is being overrun by political ass-wipes and traitors."

"Calhoun, did you actually shoot that gook colonel from a half-mile away?"

"Three-quarters of a mile, sir, in the left temple."

"Cassidy, your report says you blew a tunnel full of Vietcong."

"They told me over a hundred, sir. I got another one two months before that with about twenty inside."

"Welcome home, Marines. You're just what the doctor ordered."

Chapter Eleven

Big Girl Panties

Suzie was helping Samantha finish dressing when her doctor returned to the examination room. The pain in Samantha's stomach had not gone away. If anything, it had gotten worse. Suzie was concerned. Samantha was losing weight and not sleeping well since the news about John arrived, when Sam broke down and was taken to Blount Memorial Hospital. Sam was experiencing panic attacks, which frightened Suzie almost as much as they did Samantha.

Doctor Samuels was a young Jewish internist, not accustomed to dealing with two gorgeous WASPS who turned heads up and down the hospital corridors. Doctor Samuels had grown fond of both women who first appeared in her office three weeks earlier. The news she was about to deliver gave her pause to gather her medical courage. Physicians weren't properly schooled for such unpleasant tasks, but it had to be done. Melissa chose the direct approach rather than beating about the social shrubbery.

"Samantha, you have pancreatic cancer."

Samantha blanched white, then sat down on a hospital chair. Suzie's hands flew to her face, covering her mouth.

"I'm sorry, Samantha. It's advanced and inoperable. Some has spread to your lymph nodes. We can give you radiation therapy, which will slow the process and may send it into remission, but as the disease progresses you will require pain medication."

Samantha swallowed hard. "How long do I have, Melissa?"

"Six months. Maybe a year. I wish I could say something more positive, Sam. I'm terribly sorry to burden you with this shitty diagnosis."

Suzie burst into tears, hugging Samantha's face into her breasts. Samantha rose from her chair, hugging Suzie with the vacant stare of someone lost.

"It's okay, baby. It's okay."

"Oh, Sam. First John. Now this."

"It's okay, Suzie. Take me to Pero's for a drink."

The drive from The University of Tennessee Hospital to Pero's Restaurant on Kingston Pike was a dismal chore for Suzie Brown. Her best friend had terminal cancer. Suzie was devastated, but she was struggling to try and appear strong for Samantha. No sooner had they pulled into Pero's parking lot than Suzie burst into tears again, flinging her arms around Samantha's neck.

"Oh, God, Sam. I love you so much. What can I do to help?"

"It's okay, baby. Just be your crazy old self, and stop getting my dress wet."

Suzie laughed then, clutching Sam's hands in her own. "Well, the least I can do is buy you some lunch."

Samantha kissed Suzie's cheek, wiping her tears away with a Kleenex. Suzie was trembling emotionally, so Sam placed her arm around Suzie's waist, walking her across the parking lot to help steady the young woman. Once inside, the waiters recognized them, ushering the two ladies to a booth in the bar area away from the rest of the lunch crowd.

Samantha ordered a Bombay Sapphire gin martini with crushed mint leaves. Suzie asked for one too. Two martinis later they were both a little high.

"I remember the first time I met John. It was Bill's Barn a year and a half ago. He was the best-looking thing I ever laid eyes on. John was with Robert that night. We hit it off, dated, broke up, got back together. Then he asked me to marry him. He took me to Atlanta on our honeymoon. Lord, honey, that man could never get enough, but I loved every minute. He was tender and sweet, and he made me feel like a woman. I don't think a lot of men understand that about women, making us feel special and loved. John was good to me. I miss him such an awful lot."

"Yes, sweetie. Bubba told me in his letters how John talked about you all the time. John was a good husband. I remember he laughed a lot. I miss that about him."

"He did laugh a lot, didn't he? He was a happy person. Spoiled rotten, but that changed after we got married. The Marines did that for him. Then they took him away from me ..."

Samantha withdrew into herself, feeling the loss, the dull ache in her stomach, the empty place in her heart, dabbing at her eyes with her Kleenex. Then she remembered their going-away party at the Deane Hill Country Club.

"Remember when Bubba proposed to you? That was such a wonderful evening. And when we all went to Freddie Morton's Down Under, and Bill Paul met Susan Preston. Oh, Suzie, we did have fun, didn't we? While it lasted ... before the war."

Samantha's thoughts drifted away again. A tear ran down Suzie's cheek. They were each on their third martini. Suzie was stymied, at a loss for words. Then the waiter came by to check on them.

"May I bring you some water? Do you ladies need a menu?"

Samantha looked up from her mental fog. "What? No. I have everything I need right here. My friend Suzie Brown and this drink."

The waiter looked puzzled. Then went away.

With tears running down her cheeks, Suzie reached across the table and held Samantha's hand. "Sam, what can I do to make it better? I can't stand seeing you like this."

Sam's answer shocked Suzie. "I'll be dead soon so it really doesn't matter."

Suzie burst into tears. Samantha got up from her side of the booth and slid in beside Suzie, placing an arm around Suzie's shoulders.

"John used to say everything happens for a reason. If it's meant to be, it happens. If not, well it doesn't. I've been thinking just now, about life, about John, about me dying. Maybe my cancer is part of a plan, an invitation from God. John has gone to a place where I can't be with him. Do you think maybe in six months or a year we'll be together again?"

With tears streaking her mascara, Suzie nodded yes.

"So maybe I … no, we, shouldn't be so sad. Because where I'm going is a better place than here, and … and John will be there waiting for me. Do you believe that, Suzie?

Suzie lay her head on Samantha's shoulder, placing her arms around her friend, nodding yes, her tears wetting the shoulder pad in Sam's dress.

"I love you, Suzie. You're such a good girl. Soon I'll be going away to be with John. You'll stay here with your Robert. You'll have kids, worry yourself sick over them, grow old together. Then someday we'll all be together again. I truly believe that. I believe in heaven we'll be young and happy and always in love."

Suzie held on tight as her tears flowed down into Samantha's garment. "I love you, Sam. I'm going to miss you so much. You're the best friend there is. You always were. Thank you for accepting me as your friend."

"We still have time to do things together. We'll take Miss Martha out, have dinner, maybe go to the beach. I would love seeing the ocean again."

"Then let's do it. Next week, maybe. Or the first of the month. Talk to Martha and we'll go. I'll take a leave of absence from the beauty shop. I've never been on a vacation before."

Samantha was regaining her footing for the first time in weeks. And Suzie was beginning to see the glass as half full again. Both women had come to that fork in the road where hard decisions are made which would affect their lives the rest of their days on earth. They finished their martinis, poured themselves into Suzie's red Mustang convertible, and drove out Chapman Highway to consult with Miss Martha in Colonial Village.

There's an old saying down South among country people regarding young women who face hard decisions which are sometimes painful, but always challenging. "Big Girl Panties." Suzie and Samantha had just slipped into their big girl panties. It would change them in the days and weeks ahead in ways that neither one of them could have imagined possible before they met and fell in love with Robert "Bubba" Smith and John Henry Jackson.

Chapter Twelve

Reunion

Red had recovered from his stomach wounds and was back on his feet again in his usual rambunctious manner, pissing and moaning over "some serious by-God payback for them commie rat bastards." Bubba had saved Gunny's .45 caliber Thompson submachine gun while they were flying Red's shot-up behind out to the hospital ship when it looked like Red was bound for Glory. Pasamenus presented the weapon to Red their first night back in the barracks, after First Squad had finished checking in with I Corps Headquarters.

John and Gunny were dead. Gonzales had been shipped stateside for back surgery at Walter Reed Hospital. Lieutenant Butler was home on leave recovering from leg wounds and visiting his dying mother. Red accepted the weapon from Pasamenus, holding it reverently in his arms.

"This was Gunny's chopper. I'm going to name her Vera Lynn after that British babe that sang 'We'll Meet Again' during the Battle of Britain. "

Pasamenus had taught them many things, including the history of the Second World War. Giants trod the earth during the first half of the twentieth century, Hitler, Churchill, Stalin, Franklin Delano Roosevelt. Winston Churchill had kept Great Britain in the fight with his dogged determination and fiery rhetoric. England fought on alone for nineteen months against the incredible odds of the Nazi juggernaut. Hitler then made his prophetic blunder, following Pearl Harbor, by declaring war against the United States, December 11, 1941. Prime Minister Churchill went to bed that night knowing England was saved.

Bubba nodded his head with approval. "Right on, my man."

Corporal Johnson pulled out the switchblade knife given him by Pasamenus from the barroom brawl in San Diego.

"The Indians had a ceremony for becoming blood brothers. They made cuts on their hands, then mixed their blood by holding their hands together. Will you fellas join me as my blood brothers?"

"Go for it, man."

Johnson flicked the razor sharp blade across the base of his thumb. The others gathered round. He gave each Marine a small cut similar to his own. Driggins lit a candle, set it on the floor, then switched off the lights.

Red, Pasamenus, Bubba, Henry, Driggins, and Johnson all joined hands, sitting in a circle on the hardwood floor with the candle in the center of the circle between them. The cuts were shallow, but droplets of blood fell down on their spit-shined boots.

Johnson spoke. "I declare this circle of Marines to be blood brothers, like the Cheyenne Dog Soldiers of the Western Plains. Marines serve God and country. Our pledge of loyalty is Semper Fidelis. We will avenge our absent brothers, so help us Almighty God."

Red lathered his blood onto the stock of the submachine gun, rubbing it vigorously into the wood. The weapon was passed around the circle, each man rubbing his blood into the wooden stock. It produced a dull crimson sheen, which before had been the dull gray color of linseed oil.

"I christen you Vera Lynn, in honor of First Sergeant Lucian Abernathy and John Henry Jackson."

Dwayne Henry said a prayer.

"Dear God, bless these Marines. Grant us safe harbor through the valley of the shadow of death. Grant us brave hearts, Heavenly Father. Give us wisdom and guide us to do thy good works. Help us in our fight to free the people of Vietnam from communism. Watch over our brothers and sisters who tread in harm's way. And please, Lord, protect our loved ones back in The World. In Your Holy Name we pray. Amen."

A silence fell over the room. The six Marines gathered there in a circle on the squad bay floor with one another's blood on their hands and a flickering candle between them knew something unusual had just taken place. They were brave soldiers before, but this was different. A special bond of honor and loyalty had been forged. They didn't know it then but they were about to become an elite fighting force, feared and hated by the North Vietnamese with a bounty on each one of their heads.

August 19, 1968: Major Abraham called a meeting at 0800 hours in the barracks with Sergeant Pasamenus and his five Marines. When he walked in he had two more Marines with him, Larry Cassidy and Dudley Calhoun. Major Abraham returned the Armenian's smart salute, then asked the group to make themselves comfortable. He introduced First Squad to Cassidy and Calhoun.

"These men are your replacements to bring First Squad up to strength. I picked them myself. They're good Marines, volunteers, with a year in the Highlands under their belts. Calhoun is an expert rifleman. His longest kill with one of your M-14s was 1,300 yards.

"Cassidy can do things with explosives powder monkeys only

dream about. He booby trapped an enemy supply tunnel with C4, then waited two days until the place was full. Estimates of enemy dead ran over one hundred casualties. He has an amusing nickname. They call him "Catfish" because a big one pulled him into the river when he was just a little feller."

First Squad gathered round, shaking hands with the newcomers. Then Abraham resumed his briefing.

"Patrick Lucian Abernathy was my friend. We served in Korea together. He probably saved my life at Inchon. I carried him back to the aid station after he jumped in front of me, taking a bullet from a Chinese rifleman. He was a gentleman and a great Marine. Gunny Abernathy will be missed.

"I know a little about your John Henry Jackson. Nineteen years old from Knoxville, Tennessee. Lucian spoke to me about John several times. He told me about all you Marines with First Squad. I think John was his favorite. Pasamenus was always the brains of the outfit. I admire that, Pasamenus. We need more leaders like you. Henry was a favorite, too. Lucian believed in God. We talked at length about religion in Korea. Driggins and Johnson I can't say enough about. Lucian respected both of you men. Then there's Red. Something of a rebel like Gunny. You remind me of Lucian when he was a young buck private. How's that stomach of yours, son?"

"Sir, it would be a lot better if they could rustle up some Southern-style vittles in the mess hall. The chow up here ain't nearly as good as what we had on that hospital ship. Southern fried chicken an' mashed potatoes with chicken gravy and sourdough biscuits would taste mighty fine."

"I'll see what I can do about that, Red."

"Sir, will Gunny be buried in Arlington Cemetery?"

"Yes, Robert, that's been taken care of. I asked John's wife if she wanted John buried there, but she preferred Woodlawn Cemetery in Knoxville where she can visit him."

Pasamenus spoke up. "Major, sir, the last time you and Gunny got us together, we tracked down a psycho in the A Shau Valley. Is today another one of those special operations you have in mind for us?"

"Sergeant, that's why Gunny relied on you. He always said you were one step ahead of the game. Yes, I'm here with a mission request. This is strictly volunteer stuff so feel free to tell me to butt out any time. This one is behind enemy lines, and is not sanctioned by our Pentagon or the White House. If one of you is captured or your body and dog tags recovered by the enemy, we could all be in trouble. Don't leave anything behind that could identify us. If one of you is killed and the others can't get him out, bury the body. We'll come back later for the remains. I've assembled a special team of individuals for you to work with. These men are professionals."

"Sir, what kind of trouble are you talking about?"

"We decided a year ago that the White House is losing the war. Some of us are trying to turn that around. If exposed, we could all be drummed out of the service and sent to Leavenworth."

"How far behind enemy lines, sir?"

"Ten, maybe fifteen miles from the Laotian border. We'll chopper you in when it's raining. We have bases there. That way there will be less chance of the helicopters being spotted when they touch down. You'll be operating in an area along the Ho Chi Minh Trail. The North Vietnamese are suspected of having an underground bunker in there. Intelligence believes the Chinese are down there assembling missile components. I don't believe it's missiles. They'd need special trucks or a railroad for something that big. Probably not Chinese either, but we need to find out what's going on. We've tried, but we can't find it from the air."

"Sir, what happens if we do find it?"

"We have the area broken down into grids. You radio the location, our B-52s will do the rest."

"Sounds simple enough, if we don't get the ole bean shot off."

"That's true enough, gentlemen. The place is lousy with enemy soldiers."

"Hell, if it was easy it wouldn't be any fun."

"I suggest you men sleep on it tonight. You can give me your answer tomorrow."

"Sir, I heard you were with the CIA."

"I can't discuss that, Dudley. I can tell you this. I've been on seven of these missions myself, but that was in the early days of the war. I'd like to go on this one, but I have too many responsibilities to risk getting killed."

Next morning, First Squad walked into the chow hall where they were met at the door by the mess sergeant.

"Follow me, boys."

He escorted them to a back room where Major Abraham sat waiting for them, drinking coffee.

The mess sergeant signaled his team waiting in the hallway. Out came the goodies Red had requested the morning before. Southern fried chicken, mashed potatoes, sliced tomatoes, onions, fried okra, collard greens, cornbread, chicken gravy, scrambled eggs, sausage, hominy grits, baked ham, assorted fruit, buttered biscuits, and quart after quart of sweet milk.

"Men, you don't owe me a thing. This is in appreciation for your excellent job in the A Shau Valley. You're a special group of individuals. Certain brass know about you people. I'll leave now and let you enjoy your breakfast."

Pasamenus rose to his feet. "Sir, stay with us and have breakfast. We talked it over last night. The vote was unanimous. We'll do the mission."

Major Abraham went from man to man, shaking hands and thanking them for their patriotism and Marine Corps loyalty. Then the man with the classified secrets in his head and the war's burdens on his shoulders sat down at the table and led First Squad in the Lord's Prayer.

Something about the setting reminded Dwayne Henry of something he had seen before, but he couldn't put his finger on it. The food, the table … *déjà vu*. He thought and thought. He recalled Father McCreary and the Catholic Church in Manhattan where Dwayne had found peace of mind away from his father, the pimp, and his mother, Poppa's high-priced prostitute. Dwayne searched his memory of the Bible for a clue. Then he counted the people in the room. Eight Marines, the Major, and four mess boys. Thirteen. What was it? What could it be?

Slowly it dawned on Henry. Leonardo da Vinci's famous portrait of The Last Supper he had seen at the Metropolitan Art Museum. A chill ran down his spine. He wondered if God would protect them during their return into the gathering storm?

Chapter Thirteen

Laos

The CIA base camp, Delta X Ray, was located eighty-four kilometers southeast of the Mu Gai Pass beside the Se Bang Fui River in Laos. It was situated on a rocky plateau overlooking the waterway with a fifteen hundred foot runway. Air America flew in and out of the camp, sometimes five and six times a day. Secret military missions, spies, saboteurs, sniper units, and the usual fare ferried back and forth from the CIA stronghold. The machine gun bunkers, airfield and tents, supplies and munitions, were all part of Special Operations which was headquartered with I Corps back at Da Nang.

Delta X Ray was a special camp. They didn't go by the book, and they didn't fight by the rules. Major Abraham saw to that. They fought to win, to turn the tide of war against the no-win policy of the White House. The politicians and the Pentagon never found out. They were kept in the dark, being told Delta X Ray was used primarily for assisting the locals against the Vietminh and the Vietcong, monitoring the Ho Chi Minh Trail, and resuppling for the ARVN and American troops in the field.

Major Abraham and his aircrews were true patriots. They saw Washington as the problem, not the solution. There were other clandestine camps scattered throughout Laos and Thailand, with a few in Cambodia, but Delta X Ray was the Big Kahuna for the Central Intelligence Agency's top secret agenda in Indochina. Two four-star generals at the Pentagon plus a brigadier general in Saigon sanctioned the field operations through Major Abraham and his men at Delta X Ray. A major general took care of bomber command in Thailand. Three bird colonels were in the loop with I Corps at Da Nang. William Colby in Saigon was thought to be the mastermind behind the whole operation, but that was never confirmed.

Hmong tribesmen living in the region were recruited heavily by the Marines, the CIA, and US Special Forces operating inside Laos. They were called "Mongs" by the Americans and their military allies. Hmongs became a credible militia force protecting the American camps against the communists, while assisting in the war effort against Hanoi and the Ho Chi Minh Trail. Airplanes flown by Air America were mostly World War Two vintage, C-47 transports, PT-6s, A1 Skyraiders, B-26 bombers, plus an assortment of cargo planes, and smaller fixed-wing aircraft and helicopters.

Because the Hmong lived mainly in the highland areas of Southeast Asia and China, the French colonists had dubbed them the Montagnards (mountain people). But this should not be confused with the Degar people of Vietnam, who were also referred to as Montagnards. Both the Hmong and the Degar were fiercely independent of the lowland dwellers, especially the Vietnamese communists and their Laotian allies, the Pathet Lao. The Pathet Lao in Laos were the equivalent of the Vietminh above the DMZ, and the Vietcong below the DMZ in Vietnam. The Hmongs and the Degar fought against the communists throughout the Vietnam War.

The war in Laos, the so-called Secret War, was an independent conflict, but also intimately related to the war in neighboring Vietnam. It was a multisided conflict involving nationalist, pro-Western forces, neutralist, and communist troops. North Vietnam was directly involved in Laos, while the United States played a covert role using its CIA in support of the anticommunist Hmong. Communist China and the Soviet Union supplied the Pathet Lao in Laos and the communist forces in North Vietnam.

The "Secret War" in Laos began in 1965 when the low-level operations were replaced by major military maneuvers. Battles were fought during the dry season, the monsoon rains slowing military operations to a crawl between June and September. By 1968 there was major fighting in Southern Laos where the Ho Chi Minh Trail crossed over from North Vietnam into Laotian territory near the 17th Parallel. The Trail ran the length of Southern Laos, all the way down through Cambodia to the Mekong Delta. All along the perilous route munitions and supplies were ferried across the Laotian border into South Vietnam to reinforce the North Vietnamese Army and their Vietcong guerrillas.

A break in the fog and rain found Red sitting on a crate of 20mm ammunition admiring the scenery overlooking the river from Delta X Ray. Pasamenus and the rest of his fire team were lounging around Red drinking homemade Hmong wine. Major Abraham had delivered them that morning from Da Nang aboard his C-47 cargo plane. The major was busy in the Operations Tent, making certain they had as much information as possible before deploying for the mission.

Red was musing with Pasamenus, as they often did, about life, the war, and their role on the cosmic stage as soldiers. Young boys a year before, carefree and gay, they were no longer young, and no longer boys. Pasamenus was twenty years old. Red was going on nineteen.

Mentally, each man had evolved far beyond their particular orbits around the sun.

"Killing people is a strange way to make a living. I never dreamed I'd be doing this shit back in high school. All I ever thought about was getting loaded and getting a piece of tail. Look at us now. Abraham's Assholes, getting ready to knock off some Chink rocket factory. It don't get no weirder than this."

"Abraham's Artful Assholes. It has a certain charm about it." Catfish chuckled, engaging another swig of homemade wine.

"No, this one's better. Abraham's Assassins Against Asian Assholes." Driggins cackled merrily, hefting his jug for a healthy pull of forty proof.

Pasamenus was feeling no pain himself. He then breached a more serious subject. "Our cause is just. Soldiers like us fight and die for a reason. It's the politicians and the generals that are unjust. They covet another star or winning their next election, while men like John and Gunny give their lives fighting to free those unfortunate souls enslaved by dictators like Stalin and Mao, Hitler and Mussolini.

"Major Abraham understands. Gunny understood too. Remember when he said that war is like a big chess game to the politicians and lawyers in Washington? Chess games are won by deception and attack. President Johnson has failed because he refused to play his options, bombing the North, cutting the Trail, mining the Harbor. Congress and the Pentagon are failures too, because they refuse to challenge his failed tactics. They're political pawns, weaklings, afraid of losing their jobs. Gunny Abernathy understood those shortcomings."

"Then why the hell are we here?" Bubba was angry and about three sheets to the wind. "John and Gunny are wasted and what fucking purpose did that serve? We didn't free jack shit. Now we're fixin' to get our asses shot off again. And for what purpose? Some political puke in Smoke & Mirrors Land? Or General Gutless Wonder down at the Pentagon? Fuck them lousy bastards!"

"I can answer that." Red turned around to face his cousin. "We're here because we volunteered, and we could make a difference. Major Abraham believes in kicking ass, and maybe turning this war around. He says half the clowns in Washington don't have the balls for it, and the other half don't have the brains. We had the commie rat bastards on the run following Tet. Maybe we can yank a knot in their tails again with this missile business. It's worth a try."

"It sounds like a crock of shit to me. We could all get killed fucking with Charlie and his gook rocket factory. I got Suzie to think about. What if we get captured?"

"Marines don't get captured. You're talking like a pussy, cousin."

"Fuck you, Red! I ain't no pussy!"

Pasamenus walked over and sat down beside Bubba. "I know you miss John. We all miss him, and I've upset you. I apologize for bringing up the generals and those sorry-ass politicians. I'm sorry I said it."

Bubba looked at Pasamenus with tears in his eyes. "I do miss him. I miss John every day." Bubba broke down in tears.

Red settled himself on the other side of Bubba. "I apologize for calling you a pussy. You're a brave Marine. I had no call to say that."

Calhoun knelt down in front of Bubba. "I had a best friend my last tour of duty. The VC caught him and hanged him. We found Billy with his hands tied behind his back with his boot laces, and his feet about three inches off the deck. His guts were hanging down in the leaves where they cut him open. That's why I came back."

Bubba drained the last of his wine, stood up, and flung his empty jug down the side of the mountain. "I reckon it's my turn to step up to the plate. I don't mean to sound like no pussy. But I do think about John an awful lot. That same day we damn near lost Red. I don't know what I'd do if Red bought the farm too. Does caring about your buddies make a man weak?"

Dwayne Henry spoke up with a quote from his biblical background. " 'Greater love hath no man than this, that a man lay down his life for his friends.' Semper Fidelis is our bond and our Marine Corps heritage. John and Gunny were faithful to the end. No Bubba, your feelings don't make you weak. They make you stronger and bless you with the love of Jesus Christ."

"Now that's a mouthful." Catfish wasn't being sarcastic. "I never met nobody like you people before. I'm glad I came back with Dudley. This may sound plumb queer, but I feel safe around you turkeys."

Johnson rose up with his switchblade glinting in the noonday sun. "I think it's time we inducted these two jokers into the brotherhood. Red, bring Vera Lynn over here."

The cuts were made and Johnson spoke again about the Cheyenne Dog Soldiers. Then their blood was mingled together, and lathered into the wooden stock of the submachine gun. Dudley Calhoun and Larry Cassidy were welcomed officially into First Squad as blood brothers of the United States Marine Corps.

Chapter Fourteen

Tony

Tony (Dungchien)

"This is Tony. We call him Tony because his real name is difficult to pronounce. Tony is a Tiger Scout. Tiger Scouts are former VC who came over to our side to fight the commie rat bastards, as Red calls 'em. Trust his judgment. He saved my life two years ago in Cambodia. Tony knows the signs the VC and NVA leave behind to warn their people about booby traps. If he says 'Stop,' you stop. If he says 'Run,' haul ass. I've trusted Tony with my life on three occasions. This man is one righteous individual."

Major Abraham stepped aside to allow Tony to address First Squad. Tony was small, about five feet five inches tall, one hundred and twenty-five pounds soaking wet, almost frail-looking had it not been for the sinews which stood out in his neck and arms. There were scars all down his left arm and on the left side of his face, but his eyes were what caught First Squad's attention. Tony's eyes were opaque black, the eyes of a hunter. When he spoke, there was laughter in his voice.

"I talk okey-dokey American. I show you safe way in boondocks. Major Abraham my friend. Number One. Not kill when he find me hurt. Someday I go to America. We all go to America someday, big happy family."

Major Abraham motioned for his Marines to come to the front of the tent. Then he escorted Tony from man to man, shaking hands as they went. When they came to Red, something akin to electricity passed between the two men. Staring into each other's eyes, the two smallest members of the squad somehow knew their destinies were intertwined.

Red smiled. "Welcome aboard, Tony."

"You Red. Major Abraham tell me you good Marine."

"That's me. A whup-ass special."

"We whup-ass together. Kill boo koo VC."

Johnson opined. "Another candidate for the brotherhood."

Everyone laughed, including Major Abraham.

"Take good care of Tony. He's my personal bodyguard and my friend. Weather report indicates rain tonight and all day tomorrow. If the rain holds, you'll be leaving at 0500. Two choppers since there's nine of you. All your gear will be onboard. I'm sending you up to the north quadrant to work your way south. Keep your eyes open for anything unusual. I'll have planes in the air trying to draw fire. If that happens it could be what we're looking for. So be careful. No smoking. No grab-ass. No radio. This is VC country. Tony will be dressed as VC. Bury everything—cans, toilet paper, everything. Stay off the trails. Pasamenus has the maps. Synchronize your watches in the morning. Don't forget your foot powder and bug juice. If you get in trouble, get on the horn and I'll have the Skyraiders there in twenty minutes."

"Sir, if we find this Chink place, how soon will the B-52s show up?"

"Forty-five minutes to an hour. They have to get airborne over Thailand. Takes a few minutes for 'em to warm up. One thing to remember. Get at least a mile away. Concussion can kill a man if he's too close. They're loaded and ready to roll. Also, if there's a strong jet stream those bombs sometimes land all over the place."

"What kinda bombs, sir?"

They'll be five bombers. Two will be carrying 1,000- and 2,000-pound blockbusters. The other three will have the standard 500- and 750-pound bombs."

"Sir, if we do get in a jam and you can't find us, what action should we take?"

"Head east. I'll be in the air and we'll find you. You have my word on that. We lost a Mong team in there six weeks ago when they walked into an ambush.

Tony was VC for three years. He knows his stuff. Tony won't allow that to happen with you Marines. Now get over to chow and get yourselves a good meal. I'll see you off in the morning."

The meeting adjourned and the men headed for chow. Tony went with them, proud to be a member of the team. As they entered the mess tent, Bubba was thinking about Gunny and John. Red was too. The eight Marines and Tony were about to embark on a perilous journey that would land them in the annals of military history that nobody besides Delta X Ray, Major Abraham, some brass in the CIA, three colonels, and a handful of generals would ever know about.

Operation Ruc de Madeleine was underway.

Chapter Fifteen

Rue de Madeleine

Robert McNamara left the office of Secretary of Defense in February, one month after the Tet Offensive exploded across the headlines of the world, over his differences with President Johnson and the Joint Chiefs of Staff regarding Vietnam. A public relations nightmare was unfolding for the Johnson Administration. President Johnson declared he would not seek the Democratic nomination for a second term that March, due to the chaotic turmoil taking place across the country, and distrust of him by his own party. His failing health also played a contributing factor. Martin Luther King, Jr. was shot and killed April 4th, 1968, followed by Robert Francis Kennedy two months later. America was tearing herself apart over partisan politics, the Great Society, and the Vietnam War

On the other side of the world a special fire team led by Sergeant Pasamenus, and sanctioned by Major Abraham and his CIA confederates in Washington, had embarked on a secret mission to try and salvage some political capital, and to punch another hole in the seriously damaged communist war machine

The monsoon rain was coming down so hard the helicopter pilots had trouble seeing where they were flying. Red was sitting in the left doorway staring down at the green canopy as it swept past underneath the HU-1 Huey helicopter. Tony was in the opposite doorway watching for signs of anything suspicious. It was 0527 hours, and Operation Rue de Madeleine had been underway since 0505 that morning when they departed the Delta X Ray airfield.

The second helicopter with Pasamenus and the second half of First Squad followed a hundred yards aft behind Red, Tony, Bubba, Johnson, and Henry, and the two pilots and their door gunners. Red smiled to himself, remembering the last time he rode in a Huey helicopter when he cheated the Grim Reaper, twice, by escaping from a herd of pissed off NVA, and being gut shot all in the same day. Red glanced over at Tony, thankful they had a Tiger Scout with them who could identify the markings left behind by the Vietcong.

"Man, it's raining cats and dogs."

"Yes, indeed, cats and dogs." Pasamenus smiled. "Do you know where that phrase originated?"

"No. I never thought about it."

"I believe it was England or maybe Scotland. Farmers had thatch roofs where their dogs and cats would make themselves beds in the thatch for safety and to keep warm. When it rained they sometimes lost their footing and came tumbling down off the farmer's roof."

"Sergeant, is there anything you don't know?"

"Well, I was wondering if we'll ever see the Garden of Eden again."

Catfish was curious. "What's that, this Garden of Eden?"

"It's a place outside Da Nang. A very special place. I'll take you there when this mission is over. You'll meet Gunny's fiancée, and some very special ladies."

"Special ladies, like a whorehouse?"

"Something like that. Only this one is different."

"How can a bunch of whores be different from any other bunch of whores?"

Pasamenus rose to his feet, glaring at Larry Cassidy. Nobody had ever seen the sergeant angry before. The veins in his neck stood out, and his eyes glistened with a strange intensity that made Driggins wonder if the pressure of command was affecting The Brain.

"That was uncalled for, Cassidy."

"I didn't mean nothin' by it, Sarge. I'm sorry."

Pasamenus sat back down beside Dudley Calhoun, withdrawing into himself, remembering his friends, Lucian Abernathy, John Jackson, Madame Le Beau, and the pretty girl from Thailand. His thoughts turned then to his bride onboard the hospital ship. He wondered if somehow he had violated Gayle's trust by defending Madame and the Thai woman. At any rate, he would not tolerate disrespect for Madame Le Beau or her ladies of the evening where he and First Squad had spent such a memorable weekend before John and Gunny were killed.

He thought again about his first sergeant being shot while waiting for the remainder of their platoon to climb onboard the last helicopter in the A shau, John standing in the doorway, and the enemy machine gun that nearly got them all. His nightmares persisted, seeing John on the floor, and Gunny beside him covered with blood. Captain Pataki wrestling with the controls of their shot-up aircraft. The doctor had given him sleeping pills but the dreams persisted, refusing to go away.

'Don't pay him no mind, Sarge. Little Miss Buckingham had a bad experience back at Georgia Tech."

"Little Miss Buckingham?"

"There's a clearing … over there. Let's set these crates down and vamoose."

The two pilots landed in the northeast quadrant laid out by Major Abraham and his intelligence team. Somewhere in a jungle rectangle, seventeen kilometers wide by forty-five kilometers long, was thought to be an underground compound with Chinese technicians. If nothing was located within ten days, the choppers would rendezvous by radio and pick them up again. Besides all their usual equipment and ammunition, they carried two radios in case one failed. Cassidy had a pack filled with TNT. The other seven Marines carried five additional bricks of TNT, plus two claymore mines apiece. Tony carried no explosives. His job was looking after the fuses and detonators.

Seven seconds on the ground and the helicopters were up and gone. The rain was coming down in sheets, so the men hightailed it into the jungle where they located a small patch of dry ground beneath a triple canopy of hardwoods and evergreens. Pasamenus got out the map, allowing each man to study it just as Sergeant Abernathy had taught First Squad months before on previous missions. If Pasamenus was killed, they would know their position for contacting Delta X Ray.

"Lock and Load!"

They shouldered their weapons beneath their ponchos, and set out marching south. The rain made excellent cover for moving undetected. An hour later they found themselves on the banks of a raging torrent which two days before had been a peaceful tributary. Pasamenus dug the map out again, locating a narrow ravine half a mile upstream.

Major Abraham's weather forecast had turned into a tropical deluge. Lightning danced and spiderwebbed across a gray shrouded horizon. Thunder cracked and rolled in the heavens. The wind was gusting at twenty knots. Rain cascaded down from a towering thunderhead two miles above the column. Hearing was nearly impossible with the drumming of the raindrops amid the explosive bursts of thunder. A gathering of pale mist lay about in the ground depressions. The fog reminded Driggins of previous missions in the A Shau Valley. The Montagnard tribesmen living there called the place the Valley of the Shadow of Death.

Progress away from the flood plain into the jungle was slow because of all the creepers and broken branches, everything being slippery and wet. Johnson slipped, sprawling down in the wet leaves and mud. Lightning continued to flash, illuminating a sullen dawn sky. The crashing thunder reminded the men of artillery fire.

"Shit, Miss Agnes!"

Red stepped into a hole full of water up to his kneecap. Then fell over a moss-covered log, backwards, cursing a blue streak. Lightning struck a dead tree up ahead and that was all she wrote.

"Let's find a place outta this shit for a while."

Farther on they located an outcrop of limestone jutting out from the side of a vine-covered hill. There they took refuge out of the storm.

"You think these M-14s might attract lighting, Sarge?"

"Cassidy, were you ever addressed as Little Miss Buckingham?"

"Calhoun told, didn't he?"

"I'm afraid so, Corporal. I didn't mean to fly off the handle back there. The Garden of Eden is a special place where our top sergeant took us when he was still alive. Madame Le Beau operates the establishment. She and Gunny had planned to be married. She's a fine lady. If we don't get killed chasing moonbeams, I'll see to it you get liberty there."

"Sarge, I'll make it my special jarhead duty to see we don't get waxed. I like the sound of this Garden of yours."

"Fair enough, Miss Buckingham."

"Duke of Earl! I'll get you for this!"

Two hours later the storm had blown itself out, save for a light drizzle still coming down. Pasamenus led them away from their limestone shelter into a steep wooded ravine where they found several trees down across the flooded tributary. It was swift and deep, so they tied themselves together before crossing over one of the fallen logs. Driggins slipped and would have fallen in had it not been for the tether line.

"We'll engage a zigzag pattern. We're more likely to find it that way, if it's here. Red, you take point. Tony, you follow Red. Use your compass. We'll head southwest about five clicks, then break until nightfall. We can use the stars to navigate our way southeast. If it's overcast, we'll wait until first light. Sling arms. Let's move out."

Two kilometers into the march they saw something none of them had ever witnessed before. Two Bengal tigers, a female and a big male, about twenty meters off to their right eating a fresh kill. They were beautiful animals with sleek wet coats, and massive heads. The female let go a roar, warning them to stay away.

"Damn, I never seen one a them things before."

"Big sumbitches, ain't they?

"I'd hate to bump into one at night."

"Damn straight! Our bumpin' days would be over, bro!"

"Wonder what they weigh?"

"That big one might go six hundred. The other one about five."

"Man, I'm glad it's still daylight."

They journeyed on another two miles, where they came upon an abandoned campsite with creepers and small bushes starting to sprout back up. A flooded creek swirled and eddied at the bottom of the hill. Two wooden boxes with Chinese lettering indicating they once contained ammunition, lay abandoned beside a recent fire pit. An empty rice tin sat on top of one of the boxes. The Vietcong had been there.

"I gotta take me a dump. Be back in five minutes."

"Tony, go with him. Keep an eye out for Charlie"

Tony picked up his German 7.92mm bolt-action sniper rifle, and set off through the trees behind Red.

Fifteen minutes passed. No Red. No Tony. Pasamenus sensed trouble.

"Spread out. Five yards apart. No talking."

The sergeant led his six Marines into the trees to determine what had become of the missing men. Each Marine carried a fifteen round, fully automatic M-14 assault rifle, mounted with telescopic sights. The seven men moved among the trees, silently, intent on locating their missing companions.

Up ahead they heard talking, shouting. The men froze, waiting, listening. Pasamenus moved forward, one step, another step. Thirty yards ahead he caught a glimpse of something that made him wonder if they could get close enough in time.

Tony and Red had propped the Tommy gun and the Mauser rifle up against a tree to relieve themselves. Five Vietcong had appeared out of the jungle, and were standing between them and their weapons. The pair had their hands in the air, with their pants down around their ankles. Tony was explaining in Vietnamese that the American was a deserter and wanted to join up with the guerrillas.

"You lie! You traitor! They more of you?"

The Vietcong leader drew a long machete from a scabbard, advancing toward Tony with a malicious scowl on his face. Red began pleading for Tony's life, shaking his head back and forth, gesturing with his hands in the praying position.

One of the Vietcong smashed Red in the face with the butt of his rifle.

"No! No! We're all there is."

Red spat blood.

"We want to join you guys. Kill boo koo Americans. Hey! Don't fuck with him!"

The advancing Marines were within twenty paces, undetected. Enemy concentration was in the wrong arena. Death was coming through the trees. The man with the machete poked Tony in the chest. Blood stained the front of his Vietcong jacket.

"They more of you? You tell! How many?"

He jabbed Tony in the face, slicing his cheekbone open.

"You tell. How many?"

Fifteen meters and closing. Urgency now in their stealthy approach. But the trees were blocking their fields of fire. Tony was speaking in French, hands in the air, telling the guerrillas again that Red was a deserter. The young Vietcong struck Red a second time, splattering blood from his nose and mouth. Red staggered to the ground, spitting out a tooth.

"How many? You tell now." He raised the long blade to strike a blow.

"You fucking assholes!" Red was coming up off the deck.

The roar of the M-14s shattered the quiet of the jungle as the Vietcong's head exploded in a red cloud of teeth, brains, skull, and eyeballs. His machete went somersaulting into the bushes. The other four VC never had the opportunity of engaging their weapons. All four were dead before they crashed to the forest floor.

"What took you fuckers so long?" Red was grinning in spite of his busted mouth.

"Me happy you come now. Number One! Number One!"

"Come over here, Tony. Let me take a look at that cut of yours."

Henry cleaned the wound, then applied sutures while Driggins held the medical kit. Tony just smiled, thankful to be among men who cared about him. Red had pleaded for his life. That made Tony proud. The wound in his chest wasn't bad, just a nasty scratch.

Johnson slapped Red on the back. "Dang, you look like Alfalfa.. You can whistle at the girls now with that front tooth out."

"Guys, thanks for coming when you did. Another minute or two and me and Tony were fucked. How you feeling, man?"

"I hunky-dory. We have chow now?"

In the days to follow, they would discover that Tony was a chow-hound. But that was cool. After their brush with death, Tony turned his full attention to the signs left in the jungle by the Vietcong and their North Vietnamese allies.

Chapter Sixteen

The Winding Trail

Catfish rigged a tripwire across their trail after they made their exit across the swollen creek from the battle scene where five Vietcong had just met up with Lord Buddha. M-14 gunfire was quite unique from that of the AK-47. Either way, the sound carried for miles. Soon they would have visitors to see what the hell was going on in that neck of the jungle.

An hour later and well clear of the bivouac area, they heard a loud "Boom!" behind them.

"Damn, Catfish, you did it! That'll slow their asses down."

"Sure as hell will. I used rocks first time around up in the Highlands. Makes a terrible mess. Place a little pile on your charge, none bigger than a golf ball. Blows holes big as your fist."

"Wonder how many they are back there?"

"Probably pals of the ones we killed. But they's less of 'em now."

"I'd hate to have a damn rock blown in my ass."

"Yeah, might hurt just a skosh."

The monsoon rain was pissing down their backs as they proceeded in a southeasterly direction through tall timber. Suddenly, Tony threw up his hand. Each man stopped, motionless. Tony lay down his pack, disappearing into the giant fronds and jungle gardenias directly in front them. Moments later he was back.

"We in bad place. Smell rice cooking."

"Which way, Tony?"

"Uphill. Get away this place."

Quietly, they slogged up the side of the hill in the falling rain. Near the crest of their climb, well above the tops of the greenery down below, they could see an open field with thirty to forty enemy soldiers eating their supper under a tentlike structure with open flaps on the sides. Two trucks were parked back in the tree line.

"Looks like a regular NVA platoon. Probably taking a break from driving Uncle Ho's Trail. They'll be down around Saigon by the time we're done in here."

"Tony sure spotted those jokers. I'd a walked right in and stepped in their danged rice pot."

"The Major was right. Tony knows his stuff."

"Maybe we could take him with us to that Garden of Eden. Red said the babes there are real lookers."

"That's an idea. We could chip in and pay his way. I think he just saved our lives."

"Right on, man. He sure as hell did."

They slogged on another kilometer through the fog and rain until the moon disappeared behind a cumulus formation blanketing the horizon. Pasamenus called for a break. After some searching, they located a dry place beneath a stand of tualang trees. Tualangs were giants, known as "bee trees," reaching up over two hundred feet, with all manner of parasitic vegetation attached to their trunks and branches. Monkeys, lizards, and parrots lived there, among the honeycombs of the bees.

Tony reappeared from his reconnoiter around the camp. He'd been out half an hour making sure the coast was clear. Red and Pasamenus stood up when he walked into the bivouac area.

"Okey-dokey. No VC. We hunky-dory."

"I saved ya some beanie weenies, man. Come over here by the fire."

Red handed his small comrade a metal spoon. The heat tablets gave off a pale blue flame as Tony seated himself beside the tiny circle of stones. Pasamenus watched approvingly. So did the rest of First Squad.

"Thank you!"

"You done good today, Tony. We appreciate that."

"Major Abraham my friend. He tell me be safe for Marines."

Calhoun walked over and knelt down beside the fire. "Americans and Vietnamese don't get along very well, I guess because of our different brass. Don't sweat that stuff, man. You're one of us now."

Tony looked up at Calhoun, smiling, touching his damaged cheek. "Number One." Tony said. "Marines Number One."

By eleven hundred hours they had reached their destination toward the South China Sea. There they swung back southwest in a diagonal in the direction of the Ho Chi Minh Trail. The rain had stopped and they were making good progress. Four kilometers later, deep inside the skeletal remains of a forest defoliated with Agent Orange, they came across a heavily traveled pathway. There were boot prints and sandal impressions, hundreds of them, all leading east. The Vietcong and North Vietnamese Army were using the trail to reinforce their troops at Dak To and Quang Ngai. Right on down the Vietnam peninsula to Kantum, Plaiku, Qai Nhen, and the whole of South Vietnam.

"Sarge, should we leave 'em a calling card?"

"Yes, Cassidy. Rig something special this time."

"Guys, I need me four holes, eight inches deep, twenty feet apart, right here on the side of the trail. Scratch me a trench four inches deep, hole to hole, for the det cord. The rest of you, see if you can scare up some small rocks."

Red, Pasamenus, and Bubba went off into the dead trees searching for stones. The others set about digging holes and scratching trenches. Twenty minutes later the trap was armed. Cassidy had rigged the eastward charge with a tripwire running across the path inside a stand of dead grass. When it blew, the detonation cord would ignite the other TNT charges simultaneously, strategically covered with rocks and leaves. Excess dirt was scattered back in the jungle. The site was then dusted with a dead bush just like Gunny had taught them in the A Shau Valley. Everything looked as natural as when they first arrived.

"Saddle up, men. Tony, you take point."

They had gone another mile and were taking a five-minute break when a tremendous explosion rolled through the trees behind them.

"You're batting a thousand, Catfish."

"Somethin' tells me we better lam outta here. That was close. They're sure to pick up our trail."

Tony spoke. "Sarge, make trail easy. Booby trap again."

"That's an excellent suggestion. Men, break a few weeds for the next fifty yards.

Catfish picked a spot where several limbs stuck out from a fallen tree. They made it appear they had taken another break, snapping a twig on a small sapling and leaving behind a pack of Lucky Strikes. Cassidy ran his tripwire to a grenade at crotch level, directly in front of the cigarettes.

Forty-five minutes later they heard the telltale "Bang!" of an Mk 2 fragmentation grenade.

"I doubt if they'll be following us anymore today. We've hit them three times in a row. They have dead and wounded to look after. Good job, Cassidy!"

A plane flew over low. It was one of Major Abraham's pilots searching for the hidden installation. He couldn't see them for the trees, but it was comforting to know they had a friend up there in the clouds.

Day Three

They emerged from the trees on a plateau overlooking a wide expanse of green valley. Jungle covered most of the valley floor with a small river meandering snakelike out in the middle. On the far side they observed a dirt roadway, part of the Ho Chi Minh Trail. Traffic was heavy, all moving south, bicycles, soldiers, trucks, laborers. A river of men and women which represented a small portion of the communist war effort. Sixty percent would be killed or destroyed by the time those still alive reached the end of their journey.

Suddenly the men ran, ducking for cover.

"Incoming! Hit the deck!"

Hundreds of fiery explosions.

Trees, bodies, bicycles, trucks were blown high in the air. One truck landed fifty yards out on the valley floor. Bodies rained from the sky like hailstones. Whole trees somersaulting end over end. It was terrifying. Concussion after concussion rolled across the valley floor like something sinister and alive.

It was a B-52 bombing raid. The planes flew so high nobody knew they were there. Then came the cries of the injured and dying, as though the bowels of hell had split open and the souls trapped inside were screaming to get out.

"This is the worst fucking thing I ever saw."

"Me too, man. This sucks!"

"Mother of Christ! Let's get outta here."

Pasamenus addressed them as their superior. "You jokers listen up! Those assholes over there are the enemy. So fuck them!" No one had ever heard The Brain curse before. It shocked them, reminding the men of Sergeant Abernathy.

"My job first and foremost is to keep you fuckers alive. Second is this mission. So don't you be going soft on me. Lieutenant Butler and Major Abraham have faith in you people. Don't you let them down!"

Red and Bubba looked at one another, bewildered. Then Red spoke up.

"Brain, we didn't mean nothin'. We're just spooked, that's all. We ain't never gonna let you or Lieutenant Butler down. I speak for every man here. Right, Tony?"

"Okey-dokey. Me too, boss."

Henry joined the conversation. "Sergeant, we've been through hell and high water together. Most of us would have been killed back there at Firebase Hansel, but Gunny pulled us through and we're still together. We'll stick with you wherever that takes us."

The powerful Johnson walked up before his sergeant.

"Semper Fi, my brother."

Pasamenus lamented his feelings. "When John and Gunny died, I guess a part of us died that day too. But this is how I see it. They live on in us, in the Corps, in Madame, in Major Abraham. We soldier on after John and Gunny have gone home to be with God. It's something I feel inside that's almost sacred. Maybe it is sacred. We're Marines. Maybe that's sacred too."

"I wish I had your way with words, Sergeant. What you said is how we all feel."

Johnson pulled out his switchblade. "Tony, I got something here for you. We want you to join our brotherhood."

Tony glanced at the switchblade, remembering the Vietcong who cut him with the machete. He swallowed hard, then backed up a step. "You no hurt Tony?"

They all laughed.

They adjourned back into the trees to escape the stench of tritonal and the accompanying stink of death. The ceremony began amid the chirping of birds, the chattering of tree monkeys, and hundreds of dead people strewn across the landscape on the opposite side of the river. It concluded with Tony rubbing his blood into the wooden stock of Vera Lynn.

"Major Abraham my friend long time. Now I got boo koo friends. I happy you my friends. All go home someday to America. Okey-dokey?"

They followed the rim of the canyon another two hours, making camp for the night atop a high hill overlooking the valley. The fog was heavy, making the valley floor appear to be on fire. It lay like a white blanket, only the tops of the trees were visible.

The fog reminded Bubba of his and John's plane ride from Knoxville to San Diego when they passed over an ocean of clouds in Oklahoma. Bubba mused about John and his friendship as boys in South Knoxville, all the fun they had together, the Southern Circle, and Suzie and Samantha. And the day John died and Red getting shot. Red had changed since their Southern Circle days, become a dedicated, hard-nosed Marine Corps leader. He trusted Red's judgment the same as he trusted Pasamenus'.

Bubba fell asleep, dreaming about Suzie Brown the night he asked her to marry him at the Deane Hill Country Club. He missed his carefree days with John and the old gang at the Southern Circle Drive-In. He missed Suzie and Orbit, the frat rat. Then Gunny appeared in his dream with Captain America, the little South Vietnamese trooper killed at Firebase Hansel. His mother and father were in the dream, and drill instructor Kohn, the Cherokee Indian from Parris Island.

They were back at Firebase Hansel the morning of the Tet Offensive. Mortar fire was coming in, heavy mortar fire. And high explosive rounds from the 130mm field gun. The ammunition was all used up, and the Vietcong were coming up the hill. He couldn't find his rifle The mortar rounds were landing closer. They were going to die.

Bubba opened his eyes to find Driggins shaking him.

"You were dreaming, man, making too much noise. Go back to sleep."

Day Four

They were having breakfast, C rations and lizard tail with Texas Pete hot sauce, when Red stood up pointing toward the mountains. Then Tony stood beside him, pointing in the same direction.

"There's something out there … it's gone now … but it flashed for a second. Like sunlight on metal, base of that second mountain. "

"Me see too. Maybe people we hunt?"

"Finish your chow, men, then clean your rifles. We'll go about halfway, then wait for some weather. If this is it, they'll have sentries posted. Rain will cover our tracks and any noise we make."

Two hours later they were halfway to the mountain range. Calhoun found a small cave in the side of a limestone formation where they holed up, waiting for the rain. The men slept while Pasamenus stood watch. At 1600 hours the rains commenced.

"Tony, you take point. Red, you stick with Tony. The rest of you stay alert. We don't know what we're dealing with out there. Lock and load."

Tony disappeared into the green fronds and cypress branches wearing a poncho over his pack and rifle. Red followed right behind him. The men disappeared one by one, until only Pasamenus remained. The sergeant tried to think of anything he might have overlooked.

Gunny's face shimmered before his eyes. "Got your shit together, Marine?"

"Aye, aye, sir!"

Then The Brain followed his men into the jungle.

An hour later, slogging through wet leaves and bushes, they spotted a lone sentry. He was North Vietnamese Army, not Chinese or Vietcong as they had expected. The man was armed with a rifle. They watched as he walked his post, back and forth, in and out among the trees. Once in a while he paused and listened, then resumed his walking routine.

"Man bored. See way drag feet?"

"Think you can get close enough?"

"Give me gun make no noise."

"Driggins, give him your .38."

With the rain coming down it wasn't difficult for Tony to crawl within five meters of the sentry. He lay silent in a stand of bushes until the NVA walked directly in front of him. They barely heard the silencer when Tony squeezed the trigger. Johnson and Calhoun stashed the body back in the greenery.

Half an hour later they arrived on the banks of a narrow river. On the opposite shore, west of them some twenty-five yards, two NVA soldiers were sitting under a lean-to of saplings and tree branches. They had a fire going, enjoying a fish dinner. The current was swift, and the water six feet deep from the monsoon rains.

"Henry, you and Driggins go upstream and find a place to get across. Work your way down behind those jokers. Once you're in place, signal with your flashlight. We'll create a diversion. Use that Police Special. No rifles unless you get into trouble."

Red and Tony worked their way downstream on their side of the tributary, opposite the lean-to, until they were several yards below the enemy position. The rest remained where they were. If the situation went south, the North Vietnamese would be caught in a crossfire.

It took Henry and Driggins twenty minutes to ford the waterway and crawl up behind the lean-to without making any noise. It was almost dark. A three-quarter moon shown down through the rain clouds and drizzle. One of the Vietnamese came outside for more firewood. Driggins sighted carefully down the barrel of his revolver, and squeezed the trigger. The silencer went "Pomp!" The man fell to the ground with a bullet in his brain. Sensing something was wrong, his comrade came out of the shelter with a rifle in his hands. He called to his friend. No answer. Then he walked around the side of the lean-to and found him sprawled in the leaves, dead. Driggins was kneeling beside the rear of the makeshift structure. The man swung his rifle around.

Driggins pumped his five remaining shots into the NVA. The man stumbled, dropping his weapon, fell to the ground, got up, then toppled facedown into the waterway, floating away with the current.

"Get him! There may be others downstream."

Johnson splashed into the water up to his chin, dragging the body out on the far bank where they hid the dead men back in the boondocks. There was enough fish and sticky rice for everyone, so they huddled around the fire and ate supper.

All of them had wet clothing so they hung their fatigues up above the fire, taking turns out behind the lean-to in their skivvies to watch for enemy soldiers. By 0200 hours. everyone was dry. They doused the fire and moved out toward their objective.

At the base of the mountain they located another cave in the side of a high marble bluff and bedded down for the night, sharing quarters with a curious family of friendly raccoons. Tony and Red fed the raccoons with crackers they carried in their food packets. The raccoons made little twittering sounds and came right up to Tony and Red. Pretty soon all of First Squad were sharing their crackers with the masked bandits.

Day Five

Early next morning Calhoun was joshing Red with wild tales about Miss Head and Heels and the sloe-eyed beauties at Georgia Tech. Red's curiosity was aroused with visions of sunny-dimpled charmers, 38D front armor plating, and sex-starved Southern Belles standing on every street corner in Atlanta, Georgia. Catfish had just concluded two hours of standing watch outside in the rain, with the noisy monkeys and heavy fog. The Duke of Earl busied himself preparing breakfast to keep from laughing.

"Buggerville! You wanna know about Buggerville? Tighten your shoulder straps, Brother Kidwell. Strap on your Venusian antigravity belt. Then hit FULL TILT BOOGIE! Understanding the female spe-cies, Georgia women in particular, is like trying to catch moonbeams in a damn Mason jar.

"Best way to know one is to chug down a pint of loudmouth, stick your thumbs up your ass, then ride your elbows to Menstrual Cycle County. Son, it's a parallel universe, mentally, physically, and by-God spiritually. You'll become fallopian tube conscious once you've achieved orbit. This has to do with the earth's gravitational fields, the mag-netic declination of the moon, female ovulation, and satanic by-God rituals.

"Once there, you'll free fall into the Mind Fuck Kingdom. You'll be steppin' and fetchin' for a shot at that man in the boat between the little girlie's legs. Meaning you're fucked too, you just don't know it yet once you've performed the ole boom-bobba-boom-bobba-boom. Mister Happy leads us all astray, Brother Kidwell. Straight to Buggerville. A fate some consider worse than an Alabama ass whupin. But, man, what a ride!"

Red's mouth had fallen open, as had several others. Then he burst out laughing. "You two work as a team, don't you?"

"Something like that."

The Duke of Earl and Little Miss Buckingham were grinning ear to ear, like two possums eating coon shit.

"Well, tell me then. Do we ever graduate from this Mind Fuck place?"

"About as likely as pigs flying. Understanding a woman is like drinking loudmouth. You feel like hell the next morning, but by sun-down you're at it again."

The men were clapping their hands when Henry walked in from outside.

"We got company."

The rain had stopped and the fog was beginning to dissipate. A pale sun was shining down through the overcast. Everything was wet and lush green. They were on a shallow earthen rise at the base of a four-thousand-foot mountain.

"Holy shit! Look down there."

Seventy yards away, a column of enemy soldiers was winding its way through the trees, traveling east through the jungle. Some carried weapons. Others were carrying wooden boxes.

"Five'll get you ten, if we follow those jokers they'll lead us straight to it."

"Get your things together. We'll move out as soon as the column passes us by."

Agent Provocateur

Madame was watching a Bob Hope special on TV when a mental door opened, releasing a volatile mix of emotions mankind keeps locked away inside a dark room called the subconscious mind. Madness, suicide, love, murder, hate, they're all there. Watching, patiently waiting, always seeking a way out, an exit to the conscious world outside. Logic came to a grinding halt. Nothing made sense anymore. The bedroom furniture and the television set looked alien to her. Even her hands appeared to be those of a stranger. She felt as though her mind was slipping away in the pale reflection of the television screen. Terrified at what was happening to her, Mimi fled downstairs in her house robe and outside into the rain.

The Legionnaire overheard the strange commotion. He slipped out into the courtyard holding his 9mm in his hand. Madame was standing beside her little sanh tree, soaking wet, trembling with fear. Gargoyle took her hand, speaking gently to her, leading her back inside, away from the terrible loneliness.

"You had an attack, *mon cher*. I've seen it before with the soldiers in Algiers, and the prison camp. It is caused by the fear, stress, anger. All those things you feel about losing your man."

"It was terrifying, Henri. It felt as though I were losing my mind. Nothing made sense anymore. I was alone, drifting away, horribly alone in a dark room."

"You must get out of those wet things. Then hot tea for Madame."

"Yes, Henri. Hot tea would be wonderful."

She changed while Gargoyle looked the other way. He adored Madame, but would never reveal the true nature of his feelings. He understood and respected her love for the deceased master sergeant. Gunny had been his friend too. Henri was her bouncer, Madame's protector, her confidante, a loyal and trusted servant.

Next morning, Major Abraham paid them a prearranged visit. The girls were sent upstairs. Gargoyle sat listening while Madame and the Major conceived their plans.

"Your ladies, are they trustworthy? Can they keep a secret?"

"My girls are trustworthy, and surely they trust me. But secrets? They gossip like young ladies at a Parisian fashion show."

"Any ideas, Gargoyle?"

"Pensri, the Thai woman. Her fiancé was a communist. He was killed in the la Drang Valley. She is the conservative. Pensri saves her money. She has mentioned to me several times she wishes to go to America."

"Of course! I'm not thinking this morning. She's intelligent, and quite the beauty."

"Perhaps if we approach her with some promise of reward?"

Henri continued. "I know she hates the war, and she dreams of becoming the American. There may be danger in what you ask of her. If you would help Pensri become the US citizen, and promise her enough money to start the new life, I believe she would serve you well as your agent provocateur."

"I can arrange those things. In the meantime, find out how keen she might be about all this. I have a mission to attend to. I'll meet you people back here this weekend."

"Come to Sunday brunch, Major, ten o'clock. You can meet my girls then. If Pensri is up to the task, I will introduce you after the meal."

Chapter Eighteen

Hootenanny

Harvard University, located in Cambridge, Massachusetts, was founded in 1636 by the colonial Massachusetts legislature, sixteen years after the Pilgrims landed at Plymouth. Harvard was the first corporation chartered in the United States, and is the oldest institution of higher learning in the country.

Puritan philosophy was the central theme of the founding fathers. The college was never affiliated with any particular denomination, but many of its early graduates went on to become clergymen in the Congregational and Unitarian churches throughout New England. That began to change in 1708 when John Leverett became the first president who was not a clergyman, which marked a turning away from Puritanism and into the waiting arms of intellectual independence.

Harvard is consistently ranked Number One among national and international academia.

Harvard and its affiliates, like many American universities, are considered to be politically liberal (left of center). Conservative author

William F Buckley, Jr. quipped he would rather be governed by the first 2000 names in the Boston phone book than by the Harvard faculty. Richard Nixon famously referred to Harvard as the "Kremlin on the Charles" around 1970.

The Charles River stretches from Echo Lake in Hopkinton, flowing eighty miles northeast to Boston Harbor where it empties into the Atlantic Ocean. Much of the student body is politically left of center, the same as their liberal professors. ROTC is not allowed and Harvard does not offer athletic scholarships. The Harvard Crimson is the oldest continuously published college newspaper in America. The Harvard Library System is the largest academic library in the country, second in size only to the Library of Congress. Harvard University, like Columbia and Yale, is a bastion of liberal endeavor and social education.

"Ja hear about the Hootenanny?"

"Where?"

"Harvard Stadium, two o'clock tomorrow."

"You shitting me?"

"No, man. Big antiwar rally. Singing. Dancing. Speeches. It'll be cool, man."

"You think the Black Panthers will be there?"

"Not likely. Those cats are too heavy, man. I'm bringing Marty. See if you can round up Mickey, and that weird dude from Denver."

"You mean Alfie. He's into Timothy Leary, tune in, turn on, drop out. But I'll see if I can get him out of the house. Mickey will for sure, especially if Marty is there."

"She is one hot mama. Best looking babe on campus."

"What I wouldn't give to get in her pants."

"Righteous, man. I'd walk a mile for one of her Camels."

"Does she sleep with anybody you know about?"

"I don't believe so. She's into her Zen Buddhism, meditating all the time, searching for her Buddha-self. She told me once that to find your Buddha-self, you have to locate your nature first."

"I'd give my nature to the Salvation Army if she'd pull down those bun wrappers for me."

"Fat chance, Soul Man. You gotta find your nature all by your lonesome."

"Bring some grass, man. Maybe we'll find our nature with a head fulla Panama Red."

Next day, at the rally, nearly six thousand people had gathered in attendance, students, professors, Bostonians, flower children, and the local news media. Soul Man and Hasty Pudding didn't recognize the instructor who was addressing the crowd when they walked down the stadium steps with Marty, Mickey, and Alfie.

" … my friends, we are gathered here today to witness an historic event in the evolution of this great nation. Westmoreland has been shipped home, and deservedly so. Johnson has thrown in the towel. We've taken LBJ down, him and his malicious crowd of murdering thugs. The Vietnam War is on the ropes. Tet marked the beginning of the end. American soldiers and airmen were defeated by the People's Republic of North Vietnam. A great victory has been achieved. Walter Cronkite said so. England and France are with us. Members of Congress are on our side. *The New York Times* and *The Washington Post*. We are winning in spite of the odds stacked against us by the military industrial complex.

"There will be setbacks, more loss of life for Vietnamese civilians, more of us going to jail, but we must persevere. Never give up. Right is on our side. Together, we can overcome the odds …"

Marty spoke. "Isn't this amazing? All these people? I'm so glad you asked me to come. It gets me out of myself and into nature. And these people! I just love this."

"Marty, sweetie, I'd take you to the moon if you wanted to go. Here, have a toke. Good stuff, babe."

"Ummmm. It makes me high."

"It does do that. Let's find a place to sit down."

"Over there, behind that lady with the red hat."

"Oh, wow. This is some great weed, Hasty."

Alfie was flying solo, eight miles high on Purple Haze. Sitting down behind the lady wearing the red hat, he reached out a hand and touched her pale green dress. She turned and smiled.

"Do I know you?"

"Uh … no ma'am. I just … I'm admiring your colors. They … they're really cool."

"Is he stoned?"

"Yes, ma'am, but he's harmless."

"All right then, you may admire my dress."

Alfie carefully slid his hand across her shoulders. The colors danced off the material and floated up in the air above her head. "Oh, wow!" Her light blonde hair glowed with the pristine radiance of spun gold. Alfie's slender wrist resembled the feathery neck of a pink flamingo. People sitting around them pulsated with the earthbound serenity of life, surreal and opaque, all the pretty colors in art class.

"I love your hair, ma'am. It reminds me of autumn leaves … when I was little."

"Where are you from?"

"Colorado."

"I've never been to Colorado. Is it nice there?"

"Well, yes. It's… ah … it's nice."

Alfie lost his train of thought. Marty spoke to the lady wearing the red hat to fill the void. The woman was attractive and well dressed, a few years older than Marty's menagerie.

"Lots of mountains and snow. Colorado people are very friendly. It's pretty there."

"Tell me about your friend here. He seems interesting."

Hasty Pudding answered. "Alfie lost his older brother three weeks ago in Vietnam. They were very close. Tripping is his way of dealing with it. Alfie is working on his PhD in Political Science. He's a good person."

"I understand, introspection is the inner pathway to revealing one's nature."

Oh, my God! You're searching for your Buddha-self too."

Mickey was awestruck with Marty's psychic intelligence and sensual beauty. And stoned to the gills.

"You're so smart. And soooo good-looking."

Another speaker was pounding the podium, yelling at a Harvard graduate standing in the audience directly in front of the stage.

"How dare you question my patriotism. It's patriotic of me to question any unjust situation. The Vietnam War is a stain on the fabric of American society. Vietnam was scheduled for free elections, but we blocked them. Ho Chi Minh would have won if it hadn't been for President Diem and our crooked Central Intelligence Agency. Our government leaders are the criminals here, not Hanoi."

"The only criminals I see around here are you and your communist pals up there on stage. None of you people served in the Armed Forces. You're up there shooting your mouths off because you think it makes you look good. What the hell do you know about politics in Southeast Asia?"

"Shut him up! He isn't one of us. Fuck the military!"

The crowd was becoming angry. They didn't appreciate the Army Ranger questioning their moral authority against the Vietnam War. Sensing a potential conflict, the band director struck up Ten Thousand Men of Harvard. Students and alumni began to sing. A flower child stepped out onto the grass and started to dance. In minutes, hundreds of people were dancing and singing around the football field.

"I'm Marty. What's your name?"

"Dora McGhee. I work in Admissions."

"Have you practiced Zen long?"

"About four years, ever since I found my best friend in bed with my husband."

"Awww, man. I hate that."

"So did I. What about you, Marty?"

"Two and a half years now. I'm in Psychology. I just changed majors. English wasn't my bag. I need more of a mental challenge to do my thing."

Alfred Octavius Jones was tall and slender, a handsome young man with long brown hair and a full mustache. He was a tenderhearted individual, intelligent, loyal to his friends, and the only surviving son of a middle class mother and father living in Denver, Colorado. He was wearing blue jeans and a white Vietnamese sport jacket sent home by Chris, his older brother. Christopher had protected Alfred from the bullies in school when Alfie was a little boy.

"Your hair is beautiful."

"Why thank you, Alfie. Would you like to touch it?"

"Yes, ma'am. I sure would."

Dora removed her hat, leaned back, taking out her barrettes, allowing her long blonde hair to cascade down in Alfie's lap. He held her tresses in both hands, tears glistening in his sad brown eyes, gazing down into the golden fields of that far away world where he and his brother played together as children in the pastures of Colorado.

Sensing something was wrong, Dora turned around. Seeing Alfie in emotional distress, her heart went out to the damaged young man with his scholarship in Political Science, and misery and self-loathing running out the tops of his shoes like rainwater in a summer storm. Old memories came flooding back. Dora turned inward to her Buddha-self, sanctuary, her escape from the cruelty of the physical world. Realizing she had abandoned a fellow traveler outside, alone in the storm, she returned, taking his hand in hers, smiling for Alfie.

Hesitating momentarily, then pushing caution aside, Dora whispered to Alfred, "Honey, would you like me to cook dinner for you tonight?"

"Yes, Dora … I would very much."

Marty overheard and was delighted. Blonde and attractive Dora had taken Alfie under her wing. Her first date in four years. Marty thought it would be just the right medicine to bring Alfred back from that place he dwelt in the nether reaches of his acid sojourns, grieving the loss of his hero brother.

"Ladies and gentlemen, our time has come. We must seize the reigns of power. Get involved in politics, join your hometown civic organizations, school boards, newspapers, city planning. Work your way up the political ladder. Patience and hard work, that's what it takes. And a sincere desire for government expansion. Through government we can control every aspect of the American way of life, our economy, education, banking, Wall Street. There will be no more opposition from the military industrial complex. Those people will be working for us!"

A standing ovation was heard a mile away for the Harvard professor.

The band began to play "Kum Bay Yah." Soon the whole stadium was singing.

"Kum Bay Yah, my Lord, Kum Bay Yah."

Flower children took to the playing field whirling and singing in stoned delight. Many in the audience were high on marijuana and cocaine.

"Mickey, you okay, man?"

"Oh, wow, man. I am fucked up."

"Lay off that shit a while, okay?"

"I got'cha covered, bro."

Hasty Pudding and Soul Man were sideways looped themselves, but still able to communicate without speaking in tongues. Marty was in her element, laughing, singing, pursuing her inner nature. Alfred was blown away on Purple Haze. Dora was the only sober member of the group.

"I like you, Dora. You're a cool lady."

"My real name is Darlene. I'll fix you a good dinner tonight, Alfie."

"I like Darlene best. May I call you Darlene?"

"Of course, honey, and I'll call you Alfred."

"Where you from?"

"Franklin, Tennessee."

"What's it like there?"

"Well, it's small and country and flat. Nothing like Colorado. Tennesseans are some of the friendliest people anywhere. Lots of farmland. And we have the Grand Ole Opry in Nashville. Do you like country music, Alfred?"

A man in a wheelchair was being lifted up on stage. The podium was pushed over to one side to make room for the wheelchair. The crippled man was handed a microphone.

"Friends, I just got back from Vietnam. We're getting our butts kicked over there. Look what happened to me. We're losing people every day because of the Pentagon and Johnson's phony war. I'm going to tell you about ..."

"Phony, my ass! You're the phony. I saw you get in that wheelchair outside in the parking lot. There's nothing wrong with your legs, you lying sack of shit!"

The Army Ranger leapt on-stage, yanking the man to his feet. The crowd roared in protest. The Ranger slapped him hard across the mouth, drawing blood. The "crippled" man ran down the steps, disappearing into the crowd with people swearing and throwing things at him.

"You want to know what's happening in Vietnam? I'll tell you what's happening. We're winning every battle, but Washington refuses to let us win the war. And it's the media, and the antiwar protesters like you people who are responsible."

The crowd went ballistic. Bottles and debris rained down on the podium area. All the programmed dignitaries ran for cover.

"Booo. Get off the stage! Booooo."

An empty pint bottle struck the Ranger in the brow. He stood his ground facing them, blood spilling down onto his uniform. A hush fell over the crowd.

"I fought in Vietnam for the Vietnamese people. Some of my buddies died over there. I went there with the belief that I was protecting your Constitutional rights as Americans. You have this misguided notion that siding with our enemies is the right thing to do. All of you should be ashamed of yourselves. You have betrayed your country. And you have betrayed yourselves as Americans."

The Army Ranger threw the crowd a military salute, turned and walked away. His passage through the audience resembled Moses parting the Red Sea.

"Holy shit! Did you see that?"

"I saw it, man, but I don't believe it."

"Do you think he was telling the truth? About Washington not letting us win and all? I never heard that before."

Dora spoke to the group. "What he said was true. I have a cousin at the Pentagon who tells me what goes on in Washington. It's pretty awful the things politicians do. I'm not in favor of this war, but the way it's being conducted is criminal."

Alfred slid an arm around her waist, laying his head down on Darlene's shoulder.

"I'm sorry, baby. I didn't mean to upset you."

"Can we go home now?"

"Yes, Alfred. I hope you like dogs. I have a little dachshund."

"Christopher and I had a dog when we were boys. Mitzi was a Heinz 57 and my best friend. I was playing in the yard when a man came up to the house to apologize. Mitzi had run in front of his car down on the highway. I guess I lost interest in dogs after that."

"You'll like my doggie. I call him Barky Dog because he barks at me when I leave for work in the morning. Then when I come home I sit down on the couch, and he hops up beside me to have his tummy scratched. I love little Barky Dog."

The drug was starting to wear off. Alfred was coming down from his Technicolor voyage to the outer planets, his refuge away from the harsh realities of war and physical death, the end of childhood, and the collapse of make-believe. He found himself astonished at his good fortune that afternoon in the football stadium. Darlene was not what he expected at the antiwar rally. She was charming and witty, a true Tiffany personality that gentlemen often dream about, but seldom experience. His spirits took flight, seeking the sunlight for the first time since the terrible news from Vietnam.

"I'm grateful I sat down behind you, Darlene."

"So am I, Alfred. I've waited a long time for you to come along. Come on, honey. We're going home."

Chapter Nineteen

Stalin's Legacy

The Mountain

They were following behind the enemy column when the Vietnamese soldiers veered off to the right. Tony pointed up into the trees. Several had their tops pulled together with heavy ropes, hiding any activity on the ground from passing aircraft.

Camouflage netting was stretched between the trees above the new trail. They saw more and more sheets of the material as they followed the NVA deeper into the jungle. The column was advancing toward the second elevation, which was the same mountain Tony and Red had pointed out the day before. Up ahead they heard the faint whine of machinery.

"Leave trail now."

"Men, follow Tony. Single file. Johnson, you cover our rear. No talking. Move out."

"Boss, over there."

Through the trees sat a dual-mount rocket launcher inside a sandbagged parapet. Two Russian antiaircraft missiles gleamed in their steel cradles in the early morning light. Each weapon resembled a telephone pole with metal fins. Camouflage netting concealed the missiles from observation from above. One lone sentry occupied a wooden chair beside the control panel covered with plastic.

"Red, you take this one."

Without a word Red slipped into the foliage. It was easy because of the music playing from a battery-powered radio. Red slid his trench knife out of its sheath on his web belt. At the last moment the young Vietnamese realized he was en route to join his ancestors. Johnson pulled the body back in the trees.

"Can you booby trap this thing?"

"Well, it works on electrical power. All ya gotta do is hook up a detonator to the cables with a stick of boom boom. Charlie turns on the switch. *Adios, amigos.*"

Another hundred yards and they encountered a second antiaircraft battery with two sentries guarding the weapon. One was walking patrol while the other man was cooking bamboo shoots and rice for breakfast. Red crawled beneath the bushes and fronds.

When the sentry walked past Red, Red stood up and shot the man in the back of the head. The second Vietnamese heard the silencer's "Pomp," but Red had already closed the distance between them. It was just a boy, maybe fourteen. Red beckoned with his revolver. Not a word was spoken. He was going to spare the young man's life. The boy ran, and Red shot him twice in the back.

Cassidy rigged a pound of TNT underneath the left rocket cradle.

"Move out."

They soldiered on another two hundred and fifty yards when Dwayne Henry sang out. "Over there! Look!"

"Hell's bells! There's enough stuff in there to blow the ego off A. M. Rosenthal!"

"Who's that, sir?"

"Editor, *New York Times*."

A natural cave had been dynamited and hollowed out using heavy equipment to warehouse arms and ammunition. Artillery pieces, vehicles, mortars, machine guns, everything needed for another offensive. Camouflage netting, tons of the material, was strung everywhere. Wooden platforms had been constructed to disguise the entrance to the subterranean chamber as part of the mountain.

A shot rang out, holing Henry's canteen with a 7.62 round. Charlie had found one of the dead sentries. More shots, clipping tree bark and leaves around them.

"Hold 'em a minute while I set this thing up."

Calhoun and Bubba fanned out right and left, setting their M-14s on full automatic, catching the NVA in a crossfire.

"Fall back! Fall back!"

Cassidy reeled out the wire from the claymores and waited. The enemy was reckless, running through the trees without any thought of caution. Catfish detonated two M18A1s, blasting out hundreds of steel pellets into the onrushing troops. The charge collapsed. Men hit the ground dead. Others screamed in agony, one with his legs blown off.

"Move out! Move out! Call in our position!"

"Rue de Madeleine. Rue de Madeleine. This is Red Dog Two. Red Dog Two. Grid Seventeen. Mountain A 7. West Side of the Range."

"We read you loud and clear, Red Dog Two. What is your situation?"

"About five hundred assholes! Get the lead out!"

"Grid Seventeen. Mountain A 7. West Side of the Range. Confirmed. They're scrambling, Red Dog. We're sending the Skyraiders. ETA twenty minutes. Make smoke when you hear them."

"Affirmative. Hurry the fuck up!"

"They're warming up now. Good luck, Red Dog Two."

Enemy fire was coming from behind and to their left. AK-47s, Enfields, M-1s, then a heavy machine gun opened up. Leaves fell, wood chips flew, covering the Marines with the confetti of war like a Madison Avenue parade.

Tony came scurrying out of the foliage on his hands and knees from reconnoitering the trees up ahead. "We go now. Hurry, please."

"Follow Tony. Move out!"

Mortar shells came crashing down, bracketing their position. Tracers were streaking through the trees around them.

"Move it, Marines!"

They hauled ass, and for a few seconds they were clear of the gunfire. "Remember what the Major said about those bombers? We're too close. Make tracks for that cave we stayed in last night."

"Shit! I'm hit!"

Johnson had caught one through the fleshy part of his arm. Blood poured down. Henry tied a rag around his bicep. A mortar shell exploded directly behind them, knocking Driggins to the deck, showering the men with glowing sparks.

"Awww, God! It hurts!"

"Take Driggins and go! I'll rig another charge."

"I stay with you." Tony opened the flap to his pack of detonators.

Cassidy placed four bricks of TNT against the backside of four young trees, running tripwires between each tree. Tony ran the detonator cord tree to tree, covering the cord with twigs and leaves. Then they ran!

Loud Explosion …cursing, yelling.

"What's that all about?"

"Splinters. Those jokers are full of tree splinters."

"Remind me never to piss you off. How's it hangin', Johnson?"

"Like bein' stung by a damn scorpion. I'm good."

"Driggins?"

"Hurts like hell. I need a shot, bad."

Henry gave Driggins another injection of morphine. "Hang in there, ole buddy. Move out, Marines!"

Driggins was experiencing difficulty walking. Another mortar shell burst in the trees above their heads. The situation was going to hell in a handbasket. They could hear the communist troops talking in the forest behind them. Then they heard the familiar drone of the Skyraiders.

"Pop that smoke grenade. No, pop two uh those sumbitches!"

"This is Red Dog Two. We're making smoke and traveling east. Making smoke and traveling east. Charlie is forty meters west and closing."

"We see your smoke. Continue east. We understand Charlie is forty meters west of purple smoke. One hotfoot coming up."

A squadron of five Skyraiders peeled off, one by one, concentrating on the jungle aft of the purple smoke. The first aircraft jettisoned a pair of six-foot canisters which ruptured in the tree limbs, showering down on the soldiers below. First Squad heard the familiar "woooosh" of the deadly mixture, then the heat, followed by the cries of the men in the fire.

The planes maintained their attacks, first with jellied gasoline, then with 250-pound fragmentation bombs. First Squad maintained their trek toward their small cave. Driggins stumbled, going down on one knee, dizzy from his multiple wounds. The back of his fatigues was soaked with blood.

"Time check."

"They'll be here in ten or twelve minutes."

"Bubba, carry him."

"Take my rifle."

Bubba knelt down while Tony and Red positioned Driggins on his shoulders in a fireman's carry.

"Move out!"

Mortar rounds and rifle fire were banging and popping behind them, but the Skyraiders had slowed Charlie's pursuit. The Skyraiders were firing rockets into the jungle on both flanks and behind First Squad. Nevertheless, the North Vietnamese were gaining ground.

"There it is up ahead, fifty yards. You okay, Bubba?"

"Yeah, but this sucker's got lead in his pockets."

Truck horns began blaring inside the warehouse cave. Then a loudspeaker came on.

"What is it, Tony?"

"'Planes come. Man battle stations.'"

One of the antiaircraft batteries exploded in an orange fireball. Then the other battery blew up. Cassidy's booby traps had worked.

"That'll give 'em something to aim for."

The Skyraiders flew away to make room for the bombers.

"Smith, get a move on!"

Bubba slipped and went down in the wet leaves.

"I got'cha, bro."

Marcus Johnson hefted Driggins up into his arms and took off running. Bubba grabbed Johnson's M-14 and lit out behind him.

Two kilometers behind them they heard the shriek of the first bombs. Loud explosions. Rolling thunder was coming through the trees. Pasamenus glanced over his shoulder. Limbs and debris were flying into the air.

"Run! Run!"

A third antiaircraft battery salvoed its missiles. Then a fourth pair went streaking skyward toward the American bombers. The B-52 crews were dumping flares. All four missiles missed the target, chasing after the burning magnesium.

Iron bombs were gaining on them, rapidly closing the gap. The earth began convulsing. Johnson fell. Calhoun and Henry grabbed Driggins by the arms, dragging him through the open mouth of the cave with Johnson scrambling on hands and knees right behind them. A dozen explosions swept past their entrance then stopped. That load of ordnance had run its course. More explosions a mile back. Bombs blasting rocks and trees from the side of the mountain. Heavy detonations, big bombs were impacting.

Suddenly the floor was yanked out from under them. A terrific detonation rocked the countryside. Flying debris, weapons, men, and materiels burst from the mouth of the warehouse cave, followed by a violent megablast ripping the atmosphere as tons of shells and munitions went up in sympathetic detonation. The men were bounced around inside Mother Nature's marble womb like dice in a leather cup.

Their side of the mountain had erupted with volcanic fury, blasting boulders the size of houses high into the atmosphere. Down they came, crushing giant trees into kindling wood, destroying the North Vietnamese on the ground. It reminded Pasamenus of the biblical Armageddon. Henry was busy tending Driggins' back. Johnson sat on the floor holding his bloody arm while Calhoun wrapped tape around the bandage to help stem the flow of blood.

Tony stared out the entranceway, shielding his eyes in disbelief. "Look like end of world."

Devastation swept the valley floor. The jungle was in flames. Hundreds of trees had been blasted to pieces, uprooted, broken in half. Above it all, a fireball the size of the USS Constellation was boiling into the heavens.

"Red Dog Two. This is Lone Ranger. You guys still with us?"

"We got wounded down here. Send some help."

"Choppers are on the way. Where are you?"

"Base of the mountain. There's a clearing down to our left. We'll make smoke down there."

"ETA in six minutes. Make tracks, Red Dog Two."

They were getting Driggins on his feet when he mumbled a joke. "What has eight eyes and sixteen teeth?"

"I give up, what is it?"

"The night shift at the Krystal."

Chapter Twenty

Thailand

Thailand was a tropical Asian paradise comprising 514,000 square kilometers, seventy-five provinces, beautiful mountain ranges, jungles, rivers and deltas, exotic animals, and ancient temples, with a surrounding border of 5,022 lineal miles. Laos lay to the north and to the east. Cambodia was southeast. Bangkok and the Gulf of Thailand lay directly south. Burma was west, connecting with Laos in the north. In 1965 the country boasted a population of 30,000,000 souls.

Formerly known as Siam, Siam's absolute monarchy had become constitutional following a bloodless coup in 1932. In 1939 the kingdom officially adopted the name Thailand (Land of the Free). Education was highly prized, so the literacy rate among the population was considerably higher than the surrounding nations of Indochina.

Thailand managed to stay out of the First Vietnam War. The Thais disliked the French as much as they disliked the Communist Vietnamese. But Thailand was friends with the United States, so when the Second Vietnam War got under way the Kingdom sanctioned the use of Thai airbases for the Americans. Officially those bases were under the jurisdiction of the Thai government, but that was for political show only. During the Vietnam War, eighty percent of all USAF sorties over North Vietnam were flown from bases in Thailand.

Bangkok University, known previously as the Thai Polytechnic Institute Library, was founded in 1962. Pensri enrolled there as a freshman in the fall of 1963. She was the only child of a merchant couple who lived in Nong Khai, the northeastern most province of Thailand which bordered the Mekong River.

Her subjects in school included English, Mathematics, Thai Dance, and Asian History. But soon she discovered her true calling was International Diplomacy. This she taught herself from the law books she read at the Polytechnic Library.

While enjoying a picnic one Sunday afternoon her sophomore year at Benjakiti Park, a young man approached Pensri exclaiming how beautiful she was. Pensri ignored him, telling her would-be suitor to go away. But he persisted and made her laugh. He was very handsome and fashionably dressed. Soon she relented, inviting him to share her picnic. Following their first encounter, they never parted.

The young man came from a well-to-do import-export family in Rangoon. Bo was a communist, serenading her daily with the virtues of Karl Marx, the neo-Hegelian version of history, and the struggles of the proletariat classes against the bourgeoisie. Pensri didn't object to his high-minded pontificating, believing that some day he would mature from such political nonsense, and they would be married. She loved him dearly and planned on having his children. But it was not to be. With the war escalating in Laos and Vietnam, young Bo dropped out of college their junior year and journeyed north to join the communist forces. Three months later Pensri's mother and father were killed in a communist terror attack at the Nong Khai marketplace where their seafood stall was located. Pensri arranged for the cremations according to Buddhist tradition, sold their belongings to the neighbors, then returned to the Institute, a sad and angry young lady. Sad that the communists had murdered her mother and father. Angry that the man she loved was himself a communist who had abandoned her to leave and fight the Americans.

Chapter Twenty-One

The Battle of la Drang

The two-part battle took place November 14 through 18, 1965, in the Central Highlands of South Vietnam. American forces consisted of the 1st Battalion, 7th Calvary, the 2nd Battalion, 7th Calvary, and the 2nd Battalion, 5th Calvary of the United States Army.

The Vietnamese forces included the 33rd, 66th, and 320th Regiments of the People's Army of Vietnam (PAVN). And the National Liberation Front (NLF) of the H15 Battalion.

General Westmoreland and his staff wanted to test their newly developed airmobile cavalry, helicopters being the new military mode for transportation. A search-and-destroy mission was planned to track down an enemy force that had attempted, unsuccessfully, to overrun a Special Forces camp at Plei Me, about twenty-five miles south of 3rd Brigade's home base at Pleiku. The area chosen was the la Drang Valley, a longtime communist sanctuary.

It was soon discovered there were 1,600 communist troops on the Chu Pong Mountain, northwest of Plei Me. The Americans were told not to attempt scaling the mountain, bombers would do the job. What they didn't know at the time, there were additional communist forces in the valley superior in numbers to the Air Cavalry forces.

Just before 1300 hours on the first day, the Vietnamese attacked in force. At first, all went well. Casualties were inflicted on the enemy. But soon the situation grew critical. Massive attacks, repeated frontal assaults, flanking maneuvers. The enemy was relentless, attacking again and again. The Americans held on, calling down artillery and air strikes against the communist forces besieging them from every direction.

Valor became a common virtue those first forty-eight hours. The United States Army stood their ground against a relentless enemy that seemed impervious to death. Hundreds were slaughtered, perhaps a thousand injured. An accurate count of enemy casualties was never recorded. Seventy-nine Americans were killed and one hundred and twenty-one wounded. The battle was won. A great victory had been achieved. Colonel Brown then requested permission to withdraw from the battlefield. His troops were exhausted, having not slept for two days, and more PAVN soldiers were reported in the valley.

General Westmoreland refused Brown's request, stating he wanted to avoid the appearance of a retreat. B-52 Stratofortresses were on the way from Guam to bomb the Chu Pong Mountain, so the Americans began their march to a safe zone away from the target area.

They walked straight into the 8th Battalion, 66th Regiment, 1st Battalion, 33rd Regiment, and headquarters of the 3rd Battalion, 33rd Regiment of the PAVN.

A nightmare ensued. Vicious hand-to-hand fighting. Air strikes were called down which resulted in American casualties by friendly fire. The tide of battle ebbed and flowed. In the end, an additional one hundred and fifty-five Americas lay dead and another one hundred and twenty-one were wounded. General William Westmoreland had just made his first tactical blunder of the Vietnam War.

Chapter Twenty-Two

Bitter News

Pensri was in dance class the day she received word that Bo was killed at the Battle of Ia Drang. Her mother and father were murdered the year before by the communists. Now the man she loved and planned to marry, the man who believed in Friedrich Engels and Karl Marx, was gone. Her plans for a life together as husband and wife collapsed into broken shards of yesteryear. Tears fell like the monsoon rain. The last vestiges of her belief in Buddha turned to dust.

A month later she wandered away from school and into the back alleys of Bangkok. A lost soul in search of happy endings. She went to bed with the first man who asked her. Then the next. And the next. Months later she came to the attention of Madame le Beau who was in search of a new girl for her stable of beautiful prostitutes. Madame was particular. Pensri didn't care if the sun came up. Madame recognized something of herself in the young beauty from Nong Khai. A bargain was struck.

Pensri hated the communists. She hated the Vietnam War. But she had come to believe in Lady Liberty and Uncle Sam. Someday, she believed, she would go to America and start a new life there, a life free from war and heartache. In the meantime, selling her body had become her occupation. She enjoyed sex, so the men she entertained were of little consequence to Pensri.

When her friend Gargoyle, with his battered and mutilated facial features, approached her with a proposition for spying on certain clients, she was flattered but also intrigued. Men often told her things they would never tell their wives or even their priests. The die was cast. Pensri was scheduled to meet with Major Abraham the following Sunday.

"You understand what I expect from you?"

"I understand, yes."

"On occasion there will be men I want information from."

"I understand."

"Are you sure?"

"You want me to use my body to gain information."

"That is correct. This is serious business."

"I have one request, Mister Abraham. I want to go to America."

"You have my word, young lady."

"You will protect me if there is danger?"

"That is something you need not worry about."

"Henri said you were a man of honor."

"I will protect you, Pensri, and see to it you have everything you need when the time comes for your trip to the United States."

"Then I will do whatever you ask of me."

"Good. And remember. None of the others must know, for your sake as well as my own."

"No one will know. Only you and Madame."

"You may confide in Henri."

"The four of us, then?"

"Yes, the four of us."

Three weeks later the first situation arose. A Da Nang government official suspected of selling military information to the communists paid a visit to the Garden of Eden. Madame le Beau steered him to Pensri. She flattered his male ego, got him intoxicated, then entertained her Vietnamese client from the city. In the process, he spilled a few beans about his connection with a certain general in Hanoi. Four days later his body was discovered floating in the Han River. Pensri realized the kind of man she was dealing with in Major Abraham. Her fears vanished. She had found her passport to America. Pensri placed her life and her future in the hands of the handsome American Indian from Texas with the hard eyes and the black raven hair.

NVA Guard

The Chess Game

Deep in the jungles of the Thanh Hoa lowlands, south of the Red River Delta and well north of the Demilitarized Zone, two men sat at a table inside the gaming room of a French plantation, playing a game of chess and sipping jasmine tea. The structure was surrounded by a platoon of elite North Vietnamese Army personnel. Five twin-mount, radar controlled 37mm antiaircraft batteries sat strategically located among the trees, hidden from passing aircraft by camouflage netting. The two chess players wore rubber sandals and loose-fitting shorts, with white short-sleeve shirts to accommodate the high humidity and summer heat. They were on holiday.

The older man was tall and slender with sparse gray hair, a long angular face, and a gray mustache and goatee. The younger man was of average height, stocky build, with dark hair, a receding hairline, and bushy eyebrows. Twenty-two years separated the chessmen, the older man having been born in 1890. The weight of war lined their faces. The man with the goatee was in failing health, which showed in his emaciated features. The younger man revered his older companion. Between the two of them, they were responsible for the deaths of over a million of their fellow countrymen killed in battle.

Since the 1940s when they fought against Imperial Japan, they had orchestrated two political revolutions which culminated in two regional conflicts. The First Vietnam War, fought against France, was decided in a bloody fifty-six day battle near the tiny village of Dien Bien Phu. Lady Victory smiled upon them that May 7, 1954. The Second Vietnam War, against a more formidable United States, was not going so well.

The two men were Vietnamese Nationals. Both were intellectuals who had mastered the communist philosophy of Mao Zedong and Karl Marx. They were discussing the American war and how to deal with a recent turn of events.

"The American victory came as no surprise. I warned them, but Le Duan and his followers refused to listen."

"You were wise to take medical leave in Hungary. The Politburo might have scapegoated you."

"Our guerrilla fighters were slaughtered. Many wounded, scattered throughout the jungle. A stupid, useless waste!"

"Hard heart, comrade, hard heart. The American media favors us now."

"As do the war protesters. But our losses, Uncle Ho. Terrible!"

"Keep your eye on the prize, my friend. Never look back. Your move, General."

"Well, let me see … knight to queen's bishop three."

"Do you still believe Johnson holds back over China?"

"As Commander in Chief, Johnson is our greatest ally. They know nothing of history, our 2,000 years of war and revolution against China. Arrogance and fear strangle their military ambitions. They should bomb our cities and blockade the Trail. The South would run out of supplies and ammunition in three weeks. Instead, they bluster and talk and make speeches. Then ask to negotiate."

"They are a strange race. I almost feel pity for them."

"The Imperialists must be driven from our homeland. Otherwise, we will become a colony of servants for Uncle Sam, just as we were for the French."

"Remember how the men labored, some died, dragging those artillery pieces through the mountains to the Arena of the Gods? Then you pounded the French until they broke. We suffered greatly, but we won. The Americans, too, have a breaking point. Their love of life and luxury is their Achilles heel. One of them for every ten of us. They have no comprehension of the Asian mind."

"I apologize for my fears, Uncle Ho. Being with you has restored my spirits. I wish it were me with your heart ailment. Our people love you. You give them hope. You are the Napoleon of Vietnam."

"Me? The Napoleon? Nonsense. You are the real Napoleon. And our brave Wellington, to boot. You will lead us to victory. I may not be here to see it, but you will carry the day, my brave general."

"It's your move, uncle."

"So it is. Let's see now. What can I do to place you in a pickle?"

"A pickle?"

"You don't understand? Maybe I shouldn't reveal this secret new weapon. But I will, for my great general. It's a saying I heard when I worked in New York City. It means to place someone at a disadvantage, in a losing position."

Ho Chi Minh made his move, which did place General Giap in a position of grave danger on the chessboard. General Giap studied his dilemma, then did something Ho Chi Minh had not foreseen.

Uncle Ho captured the "poison pawn."

Eight moves later, after Giap sacrificed a rook, Ho's king was in "check."

"My faith in you has never wavered a single day. That pawn move was brilliant. There is no escape for my poor king. I concede the game, General."

"Thank you, Uncle Ho. You are our shining beacon of hope and unwavering faith on a future horizon for all Vietnam to see and cherish. For our brave soldiers, for me, for our great destiny as a nation. In the words of Winston Churchill, 'We shall fight on the beaches, we shall fight on the landing grounds, we shall fight in the fields and in the streets, we shall fight in the hills. We shall never surrender.' "

A tiger roared in the jungle. Followed by the sounds of elephants trumpeting the beast away from the little ones in the herd.

"I love the sounds of the jungle. They always remind me of my childhood. My carefree years as a boy. If only we can return to those happier times, when there will be no more killing and bloodshed. No more heartbreak. Where our children can grow old in a world of their own. That is my dream, General. My prayer to Buddha."

"And so it shall be, my dear Uncle. I swear this on my honor as a soldier before you and our blessed Lord Buddha. The philosophy of Marx shall prevail. The capitalists will be driven from our beloved homeland. This, I swear to you."

"Have you found out anything more about that camp in Laos?"

"Not as much as I would like. We have our spies in Hue and Da Nang. We know their commander's name is Abraham. He's an American Indian. The others are Marines, and pilots with Air America. They have several Hmong tribesmen living with them."

"It appears they have killed scores of our troops. How is that possible?"

"Abraham is a renegade. Washington talks and negotiates. Abraham acts on his own. We should be thankful there are no more like him. His men are just as dedicated as he is. I sincerely wish they were on our side."

"What can you do to stop this band of assassins?"

"We have a bounty on their heads. That's standard. We also know they have a Tiger Scout with them. If we could find some way to turn him back with us."

"What about his mother and father? Brothers? Sisters? Is he married?"

"We've been looking into that. I believe his relatives are all dead. No record of a wife has been found. It would be easier if we had them in custody. I remember the fear I felt when I learned the French had arrested my wife, and my dear father and sister. Later I was told they hung my beautiful Nguyen by her thumbs, and whipped her to death. They murdered my father and sister, and my sister-in-law. That was the last time I shed tears of sadness."

"The French are a sorry race. They brutalize captives and lose wars."

"I was a humble man during my lotus blossom days with Nguyen. The French changed all that. I'm married now to the Army. My lover is the warm breech of a Chinese cannon. Our words of love the engaging sounds of Soviet ammunition entering her breechblock. Her cries of ecstasy the report of shells and missiles bursting among our enemies. Our children of steel will transform themselves into mountain gods and river demons. We will drive the invaders into the sea."

"Spoken like Sun Tzu. You are the dragon god, Vo Nguyen Giap. That camp in Laos? Can it be silenced?"

"There is a woman in Hanoi. A very beautiful woman who speaks English. She may be of use to us."

"That sounds like something the British or the Germans used during the war."

General Giap smiled. "Where do you think I got the idea, uncle?"

"Yes, that might work."

"We'll see. In the meantime our spies are turning over every stone."

What about Hue? I heard the Americans destroyed the Citadel."

"Some of our troops who made it back told me parts of the city were bombed into rubble. Thousands of civilians killed. We lost something like forty-five hundred men there. Battles raged on both sides of the Perfume River. Much of the Citadel was destroyed."

"That is most unfortunate. I visited there several times as a younger man. It was a beautiful city."

"We didn't think the Americans would bomb inside the city. But we were wrong. The same way General Thanh was wrong about the Tet Offensive."

"What's done is done. The American media called Tet a defeat for Westmoreland and their Thieu-Ky Regime. Militarily, we suffered a terrible blow. Politically, we scored a great victory. That is not what we expected, but it bodes ill for the Americans."

"Total losses may run as high as fifty thousand. The Vietcong were virtually wiped out. Tons of weapons and munitions lost. It will take years to rebuild their ranks. Our NVA must take up the fighting now. We are hurt worse than the Yankees realize."

"Johnson has ordered another bombing halt. That is a sign of political weakness. Martial your forces as best you can. Take care of the wounded. Issue new weapons to those who lost theirs. Encourage the men. Give them hope. I will come speak before the Army if you need me. I'm going to bed now. It's late and I'm tired."

"Good night, Uncle Ho."

"Good night, my friend."

General Giap sat alone at the table sipping his jasmine tea and pondering Vietnam's fate. Supplies were pouring in daily across the border from China. Haiphong remained intact. Cargo ships from Russia and the Communist Bloc were busy unloading night and day. The transportation system was in relatively good condition. And the Ho Chi Minh Trail did not appear to be under any threat of blockade by the Americans.

His thoughts drifted back to 1939 when he married his pretty Nguyen. Vo had not thought about her in several days, not until his discussion with Ho over the Tiger Scout and the American Indian.

He wondered sadly how long she suffered before she closed her dark eyes beneath the cruel lash of her tormentors? He missed his family. The French were arrogant bastards, but they suffered, too. He paid them back a thousandfold in the valley of tears, and every step of their two-hundred-and-fifty-mile march to the prisoner of war camps. And again during their humiliating armistice. Now he had the powerful Americans to deal with. They were a strange race of people, but a far deadlier class of warriors than the arrogant French.

Vo walked outside for a breath of air and to admire the beauty of the summer night. He loved the smell of the jungle, the sweet scent of orchids and chrysanthemums, and the chaotic serenade of the night creatures. The tiger roared again. So many tigers were in Asian folklore. He thought again of the Tiger Scout, wondering if the woman in Hanoi might get close enough to attempt luring him back to their side.

The faces of the soldiers returning from Tet kept appearing in his mind's eye. Hollow-eyed men, beaten silhouettes, some still in shock. The Politburo following their Chinese doctrine of direct confrontation had almost cost Hanoi the war. His brave Vietcong were no longer a cohesive fighting force.

Khe Sanh had gone just as badly. His personal miscalculation over the dreaded B-52 bombers resulted in the loss of a whole division. Ever since Ho became ill and stepped aside, he was forced to deal with foolish politicians. Some of them had never worn a uniform before.

His guards kept a respectful distance of eight paces. They were a superstitious lot, eight being a lucky number. General Giap stopped for a moment focusing on something Ho Chi Minh had said, "Their love of life and luxury." Could that be one of the keys to victory? It might, if he could increase the American death toll. If he could prolong the fighting. If more politicians and American celebrities spoke out against the war.

Many of the world news agencies were on the side of the North Vietnamese. France and England, China, Russia, the American universities and war protesters. Hollywood and several key politicians. President Johnson was stepping down. What would Nixon be like if he won the election?

General Giap resumed walking. His thoughts drifted back to the Battle of Ia Drang. The last two days of fighting were close-in hand-to-hand combat, making it impossible for the Americans to effectively deploy their superior airpower and field artillery. The PAVN had paid a heavy price. But so had the brash Americans. If he could get his NVA inside the American perimeters, there would be no American bombs and artillery raining down on their heads. If not that, he could utilize Mao's guerrilla tactics. Hit and run, then hide in the jungle.

"Ten of us for one of them."

He let the words roll off his tongue. Uncle Ho was such a gentle man, yet exceptionally wise as a military tactician. He had lived among the Imperialists and studied their ways. He read their Constitution as well as their Bible. Too bad President Roosevelt died when he did. Vietnam might have gained her independence without all the years of fighting and dying. But that was water under the bridge now. Close-in fighting and guerrilla tactics. That far outweighed the frontal assaults employed by the Politburo and their failed Tet Offensive.

General Giap stopped in mid-stride when he noticed the eyes staring at him in the dark. His guards rushed to his side, rifles raised, preparing to fire. Giap's hand rose in the air.

"Don't shoot!"

The great beast stood watching him, slowly swishing her tail back and forth. She stood there a full two minutes before she strolled off into the undergrowth. The guards began to chatter and point their fingers. Giap held up his hand for silence.

He believed the tiger to be an omen. Vietnam's destiny, perhaps. Did she bring defeat or had the gods of Valhalla favored him with a mountain demon?

He envisioned the brave tiger as Uncle Ho's goddess warrior. His men looked on with awe as he went to the place where she had disappeared into the forest. He saw her there, some ten paces away, watching him as though she were waiting for something. There was a strange serenity about the fearsome jungle creature with her orange and black stripes, and her long elegant tail.

In Hanoi, two hundred miles to the north, Su Ling sat reading *The Observer* in her lavish penthouse condominium overlooking the Ho Tay Lake. An invitation, received the week before, lay on the coffee table, requesting her presence at a special dinner party. The note was signed with his customary, "Giap."

Su Ling glanced down at her invitation and smiled. Last time she worked with General Giap, he paid her $15,000. A Saigon general she lured into their hands had revealed important military secrets before he died. This time the fee was $50,000, a princely sum of money. She could live like a Trung princess, go on holiday around the world, buy herself a new Mercedes. Again she smiled, contemplating a luxurious lifestyle with the successful completion of her new assignment.

Chapter Twenty-Four

Red, Calhoun, and Bubba

Delta X-Ray

"You men have accomplished the extraordinary. You made a difference out there. A big damn difference. What Intelligence thought was a small missile compound turned out to be a staging area for another enemy offensive. We have no way of knowing how many NVA were killed, but my people estimate, judging from the devastation, that your cave contained enough weapons and ammunition to arm twenty to twenty-five thousand enemy troops.

"Tony has been beside himself ever since we got you people back. He talked for an hour, nonstop, about how you saved his life, Red and his bloody Tommy gun, something called Buggerville, blood brothers, booby traps, and how our B-52s blew the mountain all to hell. He thinks you people are something else. And gentlemen, you are something else. Each one of you is a credit to our United States Marine Corps.

"Sawbones got the shrapnel out of Driggins' back. He's going to be okay. No serious damage done. The doctor tells me he'll be up and around in two or three days. Johnson will be out of the hospital by the end of the week. They had to sew a muscle back together in his arm. I've arranged a liberty for you jarheads. Madame has a surprise for you back at the Garden. Tony asked if he could go. I told him it was up to you people. How do you feel about that?"

Red stood up. "Sir, Tony is welcome to go with us any time, any place. Being Vietnamese don't mean shit to me or none of the others here. He saved our lives more than once out there. I don't understand why some of our brass don't like the Vietnamese people. Tony is as good as any man in this room."

"That's what I wanted to hear."

The Major walked to the flap of the tent where an armed Hmong tribesman stood guard. "Go fetch Tony."

Five minutes later Tony walked in with a big smile on his face, dressed in fresh dungarees and a Marine Corps dungaree cap. The Marines rose to their feet. They were honoring a Tiger Scout, a small-ish man they had come to trust and respect.

"Gentlemen, thank you. This young man is like my own flesh and blood."

"Sir, he can go out with my sister any time he wants!"

Everybody hee-hawed with Catfish.

"Come to think of it, I ain't got no sister"

"Get the hook. Don't let him get started."

Pasamenus took the floor. "Major, sir, is it possible to recommend Tony for some type of military award?"

"Sergeant, you can ask some of the damnest questions. I don't know, but we'll award him one just the same. What did you have in mind?"

"I'm recommending Tony for the Bronze Star for saving our butts out there when we almost walked into a camp full of NVA, and for bravery above and beyond the call of duty in the face of heavy and relentless enemy attacks. He led us through some rough terrain, sir."

"Done!"

Major Abraham reached under the podium and pulled out a half-gallon of Jack Daniels bourbon whiskey. Then he opened the lid of an ice chest filled with Cokes and 7-Up.

"I understand some of you men shared a taste with Gunny now and then. I'd consider it an honor if you'd have a drink with me and my young friend here."

Tony had tears in his eyes. Before the Major found him half dead from an artillery bombardment, then drove him to an American aid station, he had been thrust into military service and mistreated by the Vietcong. This was special, beyond any boyhood aspirations, beyond even his imagination as a young man. Each Marine came forward, spoke with him briefly, then shook Tony's hand. Red handed him a glass of Jack Daniels and Coca-Cola.

"Semper Fi. You done good out there, little brother."

Chapter Twenty-Five

Madame's Surprise

Su Su was ecstatic to see Johnson again. It had been nearly three months since First Squad's last visit to the Garden of Eden. She ran up and grabbed him around the neck, kissing him tenderly.

"Ouch! My arm!"

"I sorry. I happy see you again."

Red recalled a promise he made, but couldn't remember to whom he had made his promise. Just the same, he walked through the front door with a big bouquet of red roses, a box of chocolate covered cherries, and a battered leather briefcase. Madame hugged Red, kissing him on the cheek.

"I'm sorry we lost him, Mimi. Seven of us didn't make it that day."

"The Major took me to see his body, but I am happy for you. *Merci* for my pretty flowers. Your visit today is my pleasure. My gift to you and these brave men who served with my Lucian."

Gargoyle stood in the arched doorway to the dining room, smiling. The Major had called the night before asking him to pick someone special for Tony. Henri had just the lady in mind, the Cambodian girl from Phnom Penh. Veata was like the wind, fresh, sweet, a sensuous beauty with long black hair and sparkling black eyes. She spoke perfect English with not a hint of a Cambodian accent. Tony took one look and fell like a ton of bricks.

"So, you're the hero they told us about?"

"I no hero. I just Tony."

"You're my hero, Tony. May I fix you a cocktail?"

"You like Tony?"

"Yes, Tony. I like you very much."

"Yes, please. I like you much too."

Veata took him by the hand, leading him over to the sofa in front of the fire. She prepared two chilled glasses of Schnapps with lemon slices, one for her hero and one for herself.

"Drink this, Tony. I want you to feel at home with Veata."

"Okey-dokey." Fifteen minutes later Tony was all grins and jabbering like a douc monkey.

Bubba took a seat at the dining room table with Henri and Madame. Pensri joined them. She traced a crooked scar along Bubba's temple with her fingertip. A bright crimson scar which ran back into the hairline.

"You make bad men afraid. Did you know that?"

"We're Marines. They're supposed to be afraid."

"But it's true. I hear them talking in the marketplace. Some say Marines drink human blood."

"You don't believe that, do you?"

"No, but they say it just the same."

"Let them. If it puts fear in commie rat bastards so much the better. Last time I tasted blood it was mine. This biker dude busted me in the chops in a bar in San Diego. Knocked me flat of my ass. Pasamenus kicked his butt, big time."

Pensri and Gargoyle laughed.

Madame posed a question. "Tell us about his wife. Is she pretty?"

"She's very pretty. They're like two teenagers in love. It's really funny watching them. They can't stop looking at each other. She's a nurse on this big hospital ship. The Brain has changed since he married Gayle. He watches over us now like an old mother hen."

Gargoyle spoke. "Wasn't Gunny like that?"

"Gunny was every rifleman's friend. We trusted him with our lives. The Brain is getting more like him every day. He even curses now. Brain never did that before."

Madame squeezed Bubba's hand. Her eyes were misty, but she was smiling.

Red connected with the same gorgeous redhead and the same shapely brunette as before. Up the stairs they went. Calhoun and Cassidy were in hog heaven, drinking and laughing, trying to decide who they wanted to match up with. The decision was made for them when a pair of pretty German girls sat down between them.

Su Su and Johnson were seated together at the mahogany bar. Johnson's arm was still in a sling. Su Su kissed the hand of his damaged arm, smiling up at him with a twinkle in her eyes.

"I miss you long time. How much they hurt you?"

"Not too bad. I was slippin' when I shoulda been slidin'. Or peepin' when I shoulda been hidin'. I ain't sure which one."

"You funny man. I like you much."

"You're a keeper, little mama."

"I keeper for you, Meester Johnson."

"I thought about this a lot, Su Su. If I get nailed, I'm going to leave $2,000 of my insurance money to you. Mama gets the rest. Pasamenus said he would take care of it for me."

"*Ban that tot*. I much care for you. Mama good woman have nice son like you."

"What happened when Madame got word about Gunny?"

"Ohhh, bad. Much bad. She better now, but Madame sad."

"Is there anything we can do for her?"

"Just be friend. No get killed."

"Losing Gunny was hard on ever' body. And John Jackson. John came from East Tennessee. They have mountains there and rivers just like here. But no humidity like you guys, and it don't rain half the time neither."

"No got monsoon?"

"No, but it snows sometimes. Do you ever get snow here?"

"No got snow."

"It's pretty and white, and it covers everything like a big white blanket."

"I want love you, Meester Johnson."

Su Su had done something that women in her profession are warned not to do. She had fallen for a client. Often that leads to trouble and heartbreak. But Marcus Johnson was not the typical soldier on leave looking to get laid. He, too, had developed an affection for Su Su. It troubled him that he cared for a prostitute. He wondered what his Baptist mother would say. He wondered too if he would ever see his mother again.

She led him up the stairs to her bedroom where she carefully removed the cloth sling from around his neck. Then she undressed Marcus and bathed him in the tradition of her mountain people. They made love, a passionate, intense, almost desperate union. The two of them using the other's body to escape the horrors of war, and the uncertainty which lay before them. Su Su seldom experienced a climax, but with Marcus it happened twice. They slept then. And Marcus Johnson dreamed.

Marcus dreamed he was home on leave in Magnolia Springs. The wisteria were in full bloom, hanging down from the tree branches in great purple clusters resembling grapes. And the pretty dogwood trees with their pink-and-white blossoms, symbolizing the crucifixion of

Christ. Mama had prepared a cherry pie, his favorite. She wore her handsewn kitchen apron with the double knit shoulder straps over an old print dress she purchased at the church bazaar. Hair pulled back in a bun, Margrete had been a handsome woman in her day. Now her hair was graying and she had that faded look that women acquire who live their lives in poverty. Marcus held her hand and bowed his head while Mama said the blessing.

A train whistle blew. Old Number 9 was rumbling along the tracks behind the house, traveling south with boxcars of weapons and munitions, and flatcars stacked with treated lumber and military trucks bound for Vietnam. The engineer always blew his whistle for Mama. They had attended high school together during the Second World War.

The scent of magnolia blossoms hung ambrosialike in the early morning dawn. Outside a golden sun shown down on the mockingbirds and robins pulling up worms in Mama's backyard. There was peace and serenity in Mama's world. Marcus was enjoying his pie, thinking about a chipmunk he'd tried to catch when he was a boy.

He had chased that chipmunk into a hollow tree. He built a small fire with dry leaves at the base of the tree to smoke out the tiny creature. But he allowed the leaves to flare up, causing the poor creature to come scampering out through the heat, singeing its fur. Whereupon Mister Chipmunk bit down on Marcus's thumb and held on, causing Marcus to dance a jig around the tree, yelling bloody murder, with the chipmunk firmly attached. Finally it let go and ran away. Marcus felt bad about hurting the chipmunk, but it had its revenge. He still had the scar to prove it.

Marcus dreamed about the time a neighbor came to the house telling about the Klan and what they had done to a black man down on the beach. They had staked him down at low tide, leaving him to die a terrifying death when the tide came back in. Days later the police found the body. By then the birds and the crabs had made a meal of the black man. For years after that young Marcus had nightmares about the crabs.

Su Su's face appeared. Somehow Marcus was above the scene looking down. She was sitting beside a sailor on the living room couch in front of the fireplace, sharing cocktails. Soon they were ascending the stairs together, going up to her bedroom. She undressed the sailor, bathing him in the same manner she had bathed Marcus. He kissed her. She kissed him back. Su Su began taking off her clothes.

"Stop that! Don't do that!"

But she didn't pay him any mind. Off came her clothing. She lay down on the bed, reaching for the seaman, spreading her legs for him, smiling up at Marcus.

"Su Su! No! Stop It!"

Then he heard the voices of John and Gunny. They were angry, raising a ruckus, asking why Marcus wasn't there when they got in trouble? He was trying to tell them he was onboard another helicopter with a wounded Marine he had carried through the jungle, but they couldn't hear him. John was furious and cursing Marcus. Gunny called Marcus a coward.

Captain America appeared in the dream, the little ARVN soldier. He said Marcus didn't care about him, all he cared about was saving his own skin. The little Vietnamese began to cry with his one good eye, the other was a bloody hole made by an AK-47 round. Marcus was yelling, trying to get their attention, but it was no use. They couldn't hear him.

"Guys, please!" he hollered. "I was on another chopper. I didn't know you were in trouble. I swear to God I didn't know."

But they went on cursing him, in a rage at Marcus. Captain America was inconsolable, blaming Marcus for his being dead.

Kevin rose up from his foxhole at Firebase Hansel with the top of his head shot away. He pointed at Marcus. "There he is. He did it. No good pogey-bait bastard. Yellow belly coward!"

John and Gunny picked up their weapons and started toward

Marcus. In the background he could hear the thunder of the jets, and the cannonade of the artillery fire, exploding napalm and the cries of men being burned to death. Captain America pulled the pin on a hand grenade. They were going to kill him.

"Guys, I didn't know. Please believe me. I didn't chicken out. I swear I didn't know."

Gunny opened fire with his Thompson submachine gun. John was blazing away with his M-14 assault rifle. Marcus could feel the bullets, but he didn't die. Then Captain America threw the hand grenade. He was running away, the bullets striking him all over, stinging him like bees. The grenade exploded, hurling him through the air.

"Stop it! Stop it!"

"You wake up, Meester Johnson."

"You crazy assholes!"

"Bad dream. You wake up now."

Marcus opened his eyes. Su Su was standing beside the bed naked. Her mouth was bleeding. The nightstand lamp lay on the wooden floor, broken.

Gargoyle was pounding on the door. "Su Su! Open this door!"

Su Su slipped into her housecoat and unlocked the bedroom door. Gargoyle was standing there with a club in his hand.

"No stick. He got bad dream."

Henri entered the room, still holding the club. "What's wrong with you? Do you require a physician?"

"No! No doctor. I was … I was … John and Gunny were trying to kill me. They thought I ran out on them. I didn't. I was on another chopper. I didn't know." Johnson began to cry. "I didn't know they were in trouble. I swear I didn't know."

Gargoyle laid aside his weapon. "Come downstairs, son. I'll fix tea and we'll talk. I, too, have the bad dreams. You will feel better after tea."

Downstairs, Johnson was upset with himself over hurting Su Su. She made a fist at him, then laughed and patted him on his damaged arm. Madame had joined them at the dining room table, wearing her kimono houserobe. Henri entered from the kitchen carrying a large tray with an ornamental teapot and cups for everyone.

"It's natural to have the guilt when you live and your comrades die. I still have the bad dreams about the battle, and the little valley where so many of my Legionnaires were killed. In time it becomes easier, but it never goes away. Not completely."

"Last time out they nearly got us. It was almost as bad as the A Shau Valley. It feels like … it feels like I ain't goin' home again. I think something is wrong with me. I have nightmares. I keep dreaming about dead people. I'm all right when I'm awake, but in my dreams … I'm afraid in my dreams."

"I, too, am the fearful one in my dreams, but don't think badly of yourself. You have the traumatic stress that so many soldiers acquire. I, too, have it. You'll go home. It's all the matter of being the soldier. You witness things in war that civilians can't imagine. They would react much the same way. War is a filthy occupation."

Bubba wandered in from his downstairs bedroom and sat down at the table. "You people were making such a racket I figured I'd come join you. What's going on out here?"

"I had a nightmare and banged Su Su in the head."

"You hit 'im back, Su Su?"

"Hit hard. Knock Meester Johnson on butt."

Madame chuckled. It was the first time she had laughed since Gunny had been killed. Gargoyle poured Bubba a cup of tea.

"Serves him right, big goldbrick. You know, The Brain's been having them dreams too. Buckin' an' snortin' in his sleep."

Madame spoke. "You must all be extremely the careful ones. I do not wish to mourn the loss for any more of you. Lucian's men, all of you, have become my family now."

Henri held up his cup of tea. "*Salud*, Madame."

They all saluted Madame with their cups of tea.

Red came down the stairs from his bedroom on the second floor. He was wearing his navy blue pajamas given him onboard the hospital ship. "Mind if I join the party?"

Madame smiled. "Please do."

"I heard what you said. That's a Number One compliment coming from you, ma'am. Now I'd like to make a toast."

Gargoyle poured a cup of tea and handed it to Red.

"To you, Mimi Le Beau. The finest lady I've ever known, besides my own mama of course. And the best friend a jarhead could ever hope for. During our last mission together, Gunny asked me to deliver this in case he couldn't be here." Red handed Madame Gunny's Marine Corps insurance policy made out to her.

"This was with it." Red placed a blue suede jewelry box on the table with a diamond ring inside.

"And this." Red set a worn leather briefcase on the table in front of Madame.

Mimi was so overcome with emotion she couldn't speak. Gargoyle opened the case for her, turning it toward the light so everyone could see. Inside were all of Gunny's military decorations, faded photographs of him as a schoolboy, his graduation picture from Parris Island, and photos of his deceased mother and father. There was a signed photograph of Gunny and Major Abraham when they served together in Korea.

At the bottom of the case was a folded Japanese battle flag, a German Luger with Nazi insignia stamped in the frame, and packets of hundred dollar bills. Resting on top of the money was a note with Sun Li's address in Hue, Gunny's former girlfriend, instructing Madame to send her $40 a month in the event of his death. Mimi read the note through her tears, smiling, nodding her head with approval.

"I shall attend to this. It was so like my Lucian to see to everything in case something went wrong. *Mon Dieu*, I miss my *cheri*. My brave and wonderful Lucian."

Nurse Hanley

Major Abraham sent a helicopter so Sergeant Pasamenus could visit his bride onboard the hospital ship. Meanwhile the rest of First Squad were getting their ashes hauled back at the Garden of Eden, Bubba being the exception to the rule with Madame Mimi's hay-market brigade. Miss Suzie in Knoxville was his slap-and-tickle princess. But he went along to be with his buddies, and to partake of the good food and the excellent spirits.

When Pasamenus saw Gayle he dropped his satchel on the deck, swept her up in his arms, and held her with his face buried in her perfumed hair. The roughness of his masculine physique stole her breath away. It felt like magic. This intellectual young man they called "The Brain." This Marine Corps hunter of men. This magnificent individual she loved and adored, her lawfully wedded husband.

"Follow me," she whispered.

She led him to a private room below decks which had been prepared in their honor. Gayle closed the door and locked it, then turned and kissed him passionately. She ran her hands through his hair, over his shoulders, his buttocks, savoring their urgent kisses, breathing in his scent, losing herself in the moment, feeling his hardness against her pelvis.

"Eshkhan, I love you."

She unbuttoned her blouse, slipping off her bra, revealing her magnificent breasts. Off came her skirt and panties, while Eshkhan peeled away his uniform and Marine Corps skivvies. She curled a hand around his manhood, guiding him down gently onto the bed.

Pure magic!

He rode her like a golden Palomino until she was flushed and panting, her knees up beside his shoulders. A perfect union, the battle-hardened Marine and his lovely Navy nurse. On they voyaged beneath a star-spangled night, intertwined as one through the rolling swells of the South China Sea to their ultimate climactic rendezvous.

"Oh, Eshkhan, I'm so happy. I love you, my darling husband."

"I love you, Gayle Hanley. You're everything I ever dreamed about. You and I were fated for one another in this crazy, insane world. Our destinies are now sealed as one, throughout all eternity."

"I want your child, Eshkhan. I want your seed inside me tonight."

"A wonderful thought, my darling. But goodness gracious, let the little fellow rest a few minutes."

"I think I'll call him Mister Happy. Your cock is a perky sort, always cheerful and happy to oblige."

"Mister Happy it is. And what shall we call yours, Nurse Hanley?"

"You have to choose my name. I chose yours."

"Well now, let me see. Muffin? … No. China Beach? … No. Miss DMZ? … makes you sound like a manic depressive. Hmmmmm … what about … Miss Saigon?"

Gayle laughed. "I like it! Mister Happy and Miss Saigon. A perfect combination for a Marine and his horny nurse."

"Let's do have a child." Pasamenus was intrigued by Gayle's invitation. "I can't think of a more fitting gift between the two of us."

"Make love to me, my husband. Get me pregnant."

They seldom left their quarters during his three-day pass. Neither one could get enough of the other. They made love like a couple of love-struck teenagers. And, indeed, they weren't much older than teenagers. Their second evening onboard ship, they were invited to dine with the captain. But other than that, they ventured out only for food.

"I love you too much, sweetheart."

"Not true. I love you too much."

"Then we both love each other too much."

"What then shall we do about this?"

She straddled his hips, taking him inside her, placing her arms around his neck, giving him little butterfly kisses. Gayle was a passionate, sensuous lady. She taught Pasamenus the joys of love that only women appreciate and understand.

Their naked bodies blended perfectly with their love and desire for one another. They celebrated the kissing, the happy emotions, wrestling in the throes of ecstasy, discussing their future together, laughing, holding each other while they slept, then waking and doing it all over again.

Their last evening together she held him and cried. Eshkhan made love to her, slow and gentle. It lasted a long time. Eventually he delivered his seed. Afterward, she lay shaky and spent, blissfully happy but afraid.

"Please, please be careful. I could not stand losing you."

Her thoughts flashed back to the wounded soldiers she had nursed back to physical health, but their emotional scars were another matter. Some of the worst were the men who were paralyzed. Others had lost limbs, genitalia, their eyesight. She cringed remembering the young soldier from Wisconsin with no face. He killed himself with a steak knife. They found him with his wrists cut, and the note he scribbled, without benefit of sight, thanked her for her kindness and words of encouragement. She cried for half an hour over Paul.

"Yes, Gayle. I promise."

"I wish you didn't have to go back."

"I'm beginning to appreciate that line of reasoning. There's more to this war than people understand. For one thing we aren't fighting to win."

"Then why all the fighting and killing?"

"Washington politics. World communism. A biased news media. Generals at the Pentagon more interested in another star than military victory."

"Then why not desert? I'll go with you, Eshkhan."

"No, Gayle, don't even tease about that. I have to go back. The men depend on me. I have to be there in case … well, you know."

"I love you so much."

"I love you too, sweetheart. But this thing with the Marines, it's sacred to me. I don't know if you can understand, but I'm bound to the men just as surely as you are bound to saving lives as a nurse."

"I understand, Eshkhan. I was being silly when I mentioned desertion. You're not that kind of man nor I that kind of woman. I just pray to God that you come back to me." Gayle began to cry again.

"Don't cry, sweetheart. I'll come back. I promise."

"You better! I'll pray on my knees every night to Jesus Christ to bring you home safe and sound. You're too good and too honorable to be used up like old field bologna."

"Field bologna? Where did you hear that?"

"A photographer named Mike came through a month ago from Chicago. He called the men out in the boondocks 'Field Bologna.' I never thought about it at the time, but it is rather descriptive."

"It sure is. I'm going to run that one by Major Abraham."

"It's nearly one and you have to get up at six o'clock. You need your sleep. I'll sit by the bed if I'm a distraction. I want you to be fresh and rested for your trip."

"May I hold you while I sleep?"

Gayle snuggled down beside Eshkhan and closed her eyes. They slept like two babies. It had been a marvelous three-day liberty. The nurse and the Marine had bonded together as soul mates. Gayle didn't know it then, but she was carrying their daughter, Christine.

Chapter Twenty-Seven

Knoxville

When John Jackson's mother and father were informed by Suzie Brown that Samantha had pancreatic cancer and her days on earth were drawing to a close, Frank and Mildred telephoned Miss Martha in Colonial Village that same day. John's death had broken their hearts. Now they were losing their beloved daughter-in-law to cancer. They extended Martha Fox a dinner invitation for the following evening.

Five o'clock arrived with Miss Martha knocking on the front door of the Jackson home on Larry Drive. When Mildred opened the door, Martha was standing there with a photo album in her hands. The pictures of her twenty-year-old daughter were Miss Martha's most prized possession.

"Please, come in. Frank is waiting for us in the playroom."

The Jackson home was huge compared to Martha Fox's frugal residence in Colonial Village. She marveled at the marble fireplace as they proceeded through an air-conditioned living room with polished wooden floors. And the kitchen had a dishwasher and a double sink, something Martha wished she could afford. When they entered the playroom Frank handed them both a highball. Frank had a cozy fire going in the stone fireplace.

"Martha, is there anything we can do to help? Anything at all?"

With tears in her eyes, Martha began the story of how Samantha came to be her little girl. She was hurting and needed to talk. She opened the photo album and began to show them her pictures. Frank and Mildred understood. They watched and listened in silence.

Martha Fox related how the young man she had planned to marry was killed in a naval engagement in the South Pacific with the Japanese Fleet. After Fletcher died, she lost all interest in dating. Martha went about her daily routine working as a secretary for *The Atlanta Constitution* with little concern for the future.

One spring morning in 1948, she heard a baby crying. Going outside to investigate, she found a basket sitting on her front stoop with a pink blanket inside and a little note attached. The note was scrawled in lead pencil.

> *Please take care of my baby. My family would kill*
> *me if they found out. God forgive me.*
> *S.*

Martha took the baby girl inside, called in sick for work, and never looked back. Next day she picked up a baby book with names and scoured the S section. She saw the name Samantha, and that's how she named the little girl. Never one to leave loose ends lying about, she conspired with a girlfriend at the Atlanta Courthouse, who stole a birth certificate from Piedmont Hospital, which they forged and registered. Samantha Gail Fox had become a legal citizen.

"But why did you leave Atlanta? What brought you here?"

"I was afraid the baby's mother might come back. Knoxville was a sleepy little town after the war so I felt safe here. Plus, I wanted a nice

Christian atmosphere for my child. South Knoxville was the perfect place."

"I'm thankful they had each other for a little while. We love Sam like our own daughter, but what can we do to make things easier for Samantha?"

Frank spoke up. "Is there anything she always wanted to do? Something she dreamed about as a little girl? A trip to Paris, maybe?"

Miss Martha thought for a minute, then she remembered Suzie inviting her to go with them to visit the ocean.

"Well, they talked about the beach. And Suzie asked me to go with them. I can't think of anything else."

"Honey, you've been to London and Paris. Can you think of anything?"

"I don't think that's the answer. Sam's illness will make her weak. She won't be able to get around to see the sights. We need something that requires a minimum of walking."

"A nice motel on the beach in Miami or Charleston? What about Los Angeles or San Francisco?"

"California is out. That requires a lot of flying, changing planes, then they'd have to deal with the tourists and all the traffic."

"A sea voyage, maybe?"

"Martha, that's perfect! I'll arrange it. You go with them. We'll stay here. Our presence would just remind her of John."

"John was lucky to have parents like you."

"We're lucky to have you and Sam as part of our family. Bubba talked about you two before he left. He said some really nice things about you and Samantha."

"Thank you so much. You don't know what this means to me. I'll find out where they'd like to go. The girls will be thrilled."

Mildred and Miss Martha hugged one another. Frank sat back in his easy chair smiling with pride at the two women.

"Now that our travel plans are settled, may I fix you another drink?

Chapter Twenty-Eight

Dog in the Manger

"I called you people together today because Madame and Gargoyle are in trouble."

Major Abraham had asked First Squad to rendezvous at the tearoom-boardinghouse where he had introduced Mimi Le Beau and Frau Decker. As soon as the Major had spoken, First Squad were on their feet showering him with questions.

"Sir, what kind of trouble?"

"Who caused it, sir?"

"What can we do to help, Major?"

"Well, it's complicated. A drug lord by the name of Tambu controls part of the drug cartel around Da Nang. He's also into prostitution. He's a sadistic little Arab prick from the poppy fields of Afghanistan. This asshole delights in molesting little boys, and murdering anybody that gets in his way. Three nights ago some of his men attacked Gargoyle outside a bar down the street from the Garden. Looks like they intended to kill him. Several of his friends pulled the men off Henri, then beat the living shit out of them. The next day a note was thrown through the window at the Garden. Tambu is demanding fifty percent of her profits every Friday. I've spoken with the old General in Saigon who gives her political protection. He only has limited control over the drug situation up here. Half the police are on the take anyway. That I can handle. But I need your help to get this monkey off Madame's back. And I must warn you, these people are serious badasses."

"Badasses we eat for breakfast. What do you want us to do, Major?"

Red had spoken for the group. Johnson and the others sat around the table waiting for a response from Major Abraham. First Squad felt a special loyalty for Madame and her girls because of Patrick Abernathy. They also felt a kinship with the Legionnaire whom they respected as one of their own.

"I want you to help me kill them. Otherwise, they will eventually murder Henri and Madame. That's how Tambu operates. Then he moves in and takes over."

Pasamenus raised his hand. "I have a suggestion, Major. We'll reconnoiter the block and the surrounding neighborhood. There's also a place on the roof where we can station a man. You get the information, sir. We'll be there waiting for them when they make their move."

"That's good strategy, Sergeant. This time I'll be with you fellas. I want Tony inside with Madame and Gargoyle in case they get past our perimeter."

Everyone was in agreement. The Major went out into the kitchen to retrieve Dixie. She had prepared cold cuts for them, ice-cold German beer, and mulligatawny broth for the Major.

Two days later a boy appeared at the front door of the Garden with a note from Tambu demanding $2,000 in cash the following Friday. Major Abraham had instructed Madame what to do. Gargoyle was standing behind the door with his pistol in his hand. Madame told the young Vietnamese there would be no payments, Friday or ever. The young man left. Then she telephoned the Major.

Well after midnight, the Major, Tony, and First Squad quietly arrived. They were met at the rear exit by Madame and Gargoyle, Henri with his 9mm German P-38 and Madame holding Gunny's 9mm German Luger. First Squad carried an assortment of explosives and automatic weapons. Cassidy was lugging a heavy roll of barb wire wrapped in a burlap sack. Red had Vera Lynn, his .45 caliber Thompson submachine gun.

"All the girls were sent away as you requested. We have plenty of food and beverages. You'll find beds on both floors. Make yourselves comfortable, gentlemen."

Madame served them sandwiches and tea. Then turned out the lights. Gargoyle positioned himself behind the living room curtains for first watch. The Major seated himself at the kitchen table beside the rear window overlooking the alleyway. The rest went to bed. Streetlights provided enough illumination to spot anyone approaching the building.

Next morning, First Squad surveyed the area. All were dressed in civilian attire so as not to attract attention. Catfish came in from his recon patrol at 1013 hours.

"Sir, there's an alleyway halfway down the block between here and the bar, connecting with the next street over. It has this big open garage. If I was planning an assault on this place, that would be my command center. I can rig a couple of claymores just in case, and wait on the roof. Good visibility up there."

"Sounds good, Cassidy. Henry, you go with Cassidy. Driggins, you stay here with me. You feeling okay, son?"

"Yes, sir. My back healed up just fine, sir."

Calhoun was coming down the stairs from inspecting the roof.

"What's it look like up there?"

"Good fields of fire, front and back, but I can't see nothin' once they reach the building. I'll need some grenades to secure the walls."

"Take as many as you need, plenty of ammunition too. Red, what did you find out?"

"There's a lock on a door about a hundred feet down the alley behind here. Some kind of warehouse, I think. I'll bust the lock and me and Bubba can wait inside."

"Johnson?"

"This place has a ventilation gizmo in the basement wall about twelve inches wide, but I can see out. If Catfish can rig that thing, I can set it off when I see their feet."

"Remember to keep your head down. That is one nasty weapon. The police have been taken care of so we don't have to worry about the authorities getting their asses in a sling. For the record, this is a turf war between drug gangs. The cops have trucks on standby to haul away the evidence. All we have to do is wait."

Red and Bubba took up residence in the warehouse behind the Garden. It was filled with restaurant supplies, tables and chairs, and cases of vodka and rice wine. They carried a shortwave radio connecting them with Calhoun on the roof, the Major inside the Garden, Johnson in the basement, and Catfish down the street.

"You think much about home?"

"Yeah, why?"

"I been thinking about my mom and dad lately."

"What brought this on, cuz?"

"I been thinking about the things they did for me in school. We ain't got much, but my daddy did the best he could on a painter's salary. Mama don't make much herself as a hairdresser, but they always bought me new clothes, things like that. I've learned to appreciate my mother and father, being over here an' all. If I don't make it back I want you to do something for me."

"What's that, jarhead?"

"Tell 'em I always loved 'em, even when I didn't act like it."

"Look here, now. You and me are going home together. I mean it, ole buddy. Don't go gettin' that stuff in your head that you ain't gonna make it or I'll have to kick your butt for ya."

"I could a used some butt kickin' back when I found out I wasn't getting me no football scholarship. I was so pissed off I called my old man a 'loser.' I remember the hurt in his eyes. I ain't never gonna forgot sayin' that."

"Have you written them about it?"

"Yeah, I did. But it ain't the same as bein' there, huggin' 'em. Sayin' you're sorry."

"I promise if you get your ass shot off I'll hug 'em for ya."

Red smiled, then punched Bubba on the shoulder. The two of them understood they would have people to comfort back in The World if either one of them didn't make it.

"I reckon I'll have to marry Suzie if you get your shit blown away."

Bubba laughed. "You know something, Red. You'd make Suzie a damn good husband if I end up in a plastic bag. I'll tell you something else. You and me have changed a lot since comin' over here. We grew up. And we have the best friends on this whole crazy planet. We would never have met Gunny or the Major or Pasamenus or Madame. They don't come no better. Johnson, tha' whole bunch."

"We ain't done too bad for ourselves, have we? I sure wish John was still alive."

"They don't make 'em like John no more. They don't make 'em like our parents no more, neither. Sam and Miss Martha."

"What's the news on Samantha?"

"Suzie wrote me about her cancer. Sam's dying. Said Sam is lookin' forward to bein' with John again. That's somethin', ain't it?"

"I believe we'll all be with John someday. What a reunion that will be. Angels an' singin'. Maybe we'll get to meet Jesus."

"Yeah, I think about that too. I'm worried about Johnson, though. He don't think he's goin' home. That's pretty spooky."

"Them's usually the ones that make it."

"If we keep our shit together we'll get outta here all right."

"I sure hope so. Let's get some shut-eye. If anything happens, they'll call in on the radio."

0315 hours: Calhoun spotted two vans moving up the street with their lights out. "Dog in the Manger! Dog in the Manger!"

"That's our dance number, ladies."

As Catfish predicted, the vans turned into the alley past the bar, but they didn't pull into the designated parking area. Instead, they sat in the alleyway with their lights out and their motors running.

A few minutes later a vintage Lincoln came rolling down the street from the opposite end of the block. Tambu had arrived to supervise his troops.

Fifteen men emerged from the alley to converge on the Garden of Eden. Three more stepped out of Tambu's Lincoln. Then Calhoun spotted another van at the far end of the alley, behind his position on the rooftop.

"Eighteen rats and closing. A third van is in the alley behind Red and Bubba."

"Hold your fire, men. Wait until they're in the alley. Johnson, can you see them yet?"

"No, sir. Not yet."

Seconds ticked by and nothing. Then Johnson began seeing shoes in the dim light. Counting ten pairs, he touched a wire to an electric terminal. A terrific blast rocked the neighborhood, dishes clattered to the kitchen floor, dust and plaster fell.

Cassidy had planted nine pounds of C4 inside his roll of barb wire. When Johnson set it off, thousands of metal shards shot scything out in every direction. Twelve men lay dead on the asphalt pavement, cut to ribbons by the horrible device. Another man was so damaged he lay helpless in a spreading pool of blood. The others ran.

Mistaking the blast for one of their own, the van at the end of the alleyway came roaring down the narrow corridor with seven more apprentices for Buddha's Promised Land. Red and Bubba listened as the vehicle sped past their exit, skidding to a halt before the bloody carnage at the end of the alley. Bubba opened the metal door and stepped out.

"Hey, you! Gook cock suckers! I got ya hangin'!"

Tambu's men jerked around to confront this menace. Bubba and Red opened fire. The driver's brains splattered across the windshield. The others piled out and ran for cover. One made it around the corner of the building with two .45 slugs in his back. The remaining five lay on the asphalt pavement like melting blocks of ice, their lives leaking out in crimson pools in front of their Chevy van.

Realizing he was in a trap, Tambu burned rubber. Calhoun emptied his M-14 into the silver Lincoln, destroying the engine block. Oil and steam hissed from the stricken vehicle. Tambu kicked the door open, running for the protection of his men in the second alleyway. No sooner had they gotten their van underway, than Cassidy blew the claymores inside the garage. Steel pellets shredded the tires, riddling the driver's side of the automobile. Tambu was the only passenger to emerge unhurt. The others were tangled together inside, dead or heading in that general direction.

Down on the pavement, thinking he might still escape, a shadow fell across Tambu from the street lights behind him. He looked up to see Gargoyle and the Major gazing down at him.

"Two thousand dollars, was it, *Monsieur*? I have it right here, Mister Tambu."

The Legionnaire stood over him holding a hundred franc note, and his P-38 automatic. Tony stood behind the Major, holding a dagger in his hand he had taken off the dead Vietcong who attempted to kill him and Red.

Tambu's reputation as a rapist and a killer were well known throughout central Vietnam. Locals called him the Tent Spider because of the spider's white abdomen. Tambu had become unhinged following the failure of his dream to become a famous thespian. Now he resembled a stage actor from a bad Broadway production with his eye shadow, rouge, white facial powder, and purple lipstick. He delighted in torturing his victims before killing them. Tambu had a special chair made up with leather restraints for his guests of honor in a soundproof room. Sometimes he kept them alive for days. The neighbors never heard the screaming, but they sometimes observed large bundles being removed from the fortified compound late at night.

Little boys were his favorite pastime, his sexual pleasure. His men scoured the countryside for the best ones, slender and attractive, ages seven to eleven which they kidnapped. The more they cried and begged him to stop, the more he did it to them. A few died, but the majority he let go after a few days of his amorous attentions. He believed himself generous in that regard.

Tambu knew they were going to kill him unless he came up with a viable alternative, and pronto. Money! That was his ticket to freedom. It worked every time. He would deal with them later after he got the rest of his men assembled. They would pay for their rude insult against him and his organization.

"I'll give you three hundred thousand dollars to let me go."

The Major was amused. "My, such a generous offer. We could live well the rest of our lives. What do you think, Tony? Want to rub elbows with high society in Naples or Madrid?"

"Not enough. Man bad!"

That little son of a bitch. Inside his head Tambu was seething with rage. I'll deal with him personally, strap him to the chair, cut off his ears, his damn nose, his fingers and toes, rip out his tongue, then slice off his dick and cram it down his throat.

"One million dollars! Let me go, and I'll make you rich men."

"A million bucks. We could open our own nightclub and give Madame a run for her money. What say you, Gargoyle?"

"I say he is the degenerate child rapist who knows his time she is arrive."

Tambu rested on the ground staring up at the butchered face of Henri with his black eye patch. Tambu longed to drive an ice pick into that good eye and twist it around, make the man piss his pants and beg for death.

Most troubling of all, he sensed he was running out of options.

"I'll give it all to you. Over two million dollars in a Swiss bank. You can live like kings. Let me go and the money is yours. One phone call and I'll have it wired to your account."

"Tony?"

"Not enough. Not ever enough. Man bad."

The vicious Afghan pleaded for his life, but to no avail. Major Abraham shot him in the kneecap. He screamed, groveling at the Major's feet. Henri shot him in the other kneecap. Tambu went berserk with pain crawling on the ground like a stricken arthropod, raging at them one minute, screaming for mercy the next. Tony rammed the dagger into the man's stomach, ripping the blade up and out. He wiped it clean on Tambu's silk sport jacket.

They left him there, gutted on the pavement, writhing in agony. A victim of his own depravity and insatiable greed. The threat to Madame and her Garden of Eden died in the fetal position, blubbering like one of the little boys he raped, clutching his intestines in his soft, feminine, manicured fingers.

Chapter Twenty-Nine

The Silver Cross

Suzie had never seen the ocean before. Growing up poor had not afforded her such imagined luxury. After her mother died, she devoted her time to cooking and cleaning for her younger brothers and sisters, mending their clothing, shopping for groceries at Cas Walker's, walking the kids to church on Sundays along A Avenue, packing lunch for her father, and graduating from Young High School. They were always short on money, but Suzie had learned to stretch her father's hard-earned dollars from Candora Marble Company in Vestal.

She marveled at the ship's cabin she shared with Samantha, brass fixtures, mahogany trim, queen-size beds, and a real porthole for a window. And flowers. Red roses in a porcelain vase which attached to a table so the sea swells couldn't knock it off on the floor. And sweets on their pillows!

"I love it here. This is so nice. I wish John …" Then she remembered John was with God. "I'm sorry. I didn't mean to say that."

"Young lady, we're here to have fun. I wish your Robert was here too."

Samantha had lost fourteen pounds but still looked radiant. And lovely. Mister Jackson had chartered a cruise for them from Charleston down through the Bahamas, the Windward Passage, over to Jamaica, Nicaragua, Cancun, Miami, then home again to South Carolina. Miss Martha was in the adjoining cabin.

"Let's get Martha and go outside on the deck."

"Okay. Let me use the bathroom first."

Sam sat down to pee, remembering Atlanta and her honeymoon with John Jackson. It seemed like a hundred years since their stay at the Hyatt Regency downtown. She recalled Joe Tierney's restaurant on Peachtree Road, Joe coming over and asking where they were from. They told him, and he said he had a friend from Knoxville living a few doors down from him at the Nob Hill Apartments on Roswell Road. Sam liked Mister Tierney. He flattered her, telling John he was a lucky man. They told him they were on their honeymoon. Joe said he was engaged and would soon be married himself. Then he brought over a free bottle of champagne for them to celebrate.

"Hey, did you fall in in there?"

Samantha smiled. "I'm coming, worrywart. I'm coming."

The Atlantic Ocean was peaceful and serene that summer evening, pale green with a pleasant sea breeze, and little flying fish jumping and soaring above the waves. The sun was going down, creating burnt orange and purple colors inside the clouds where the sun appeared to be sinking into the sea. It reminded Martha of old photographs Fletcher Magbee mailed home from the Pacific during the war.

Huddled together against the railing, Martha broke their reverie. "Know what? We should go to the bar and get ourselves a drink. I feel like celebrating."

"You naughty thing. Let's go!"

The lounge had a Wurlitzer jukebox, mahogany tables and chairs, and a sizable dance floor. Martha chose a table beside the windows where they could watch the sunset and enjoy the music. Suzie put a quarter in the jukebox and they ordered their drinks. The lounge was almost empty.

As Time Goes By began to play.

"Here's looking at you, kid."

They laughed, clinked their glasses and drank, each lost in personal thoughts gazing out at the broad ocean.

Samantha spoke. "I never said this before, but you're my best friends. I'm so happy we came on this cruise together. I wish Fletcher had lived. And John. At least Suzie has Robert. You two will have beautiful children someday."

Martha smiled at the two younger women. "That song reminds me of us. Our separate journeys in life. The things we're been through together. I'd like to turn the clock back in some ways, and leave it just the way it is in others."

"Did either of you see *Lost Horizon*?"

Suzie had turned her attention away from the sea.

"It was about a place called Shangri-la. People never got sick there and they lived a long time."

"I saw that movie when it first came out. I always liked Ronald Coleman. That was before the war. Sam Jaffe was in it. He played in another movie I liked called *Gunga Din*."

"That was on TV not long ago. Cary Grant was so funny. And that big fellow, Victor McLoughlin. There was another man I can't remember."

"You mean Douglas Fairbanks, Jr. He was in *Morning Glory* with Katharine Hepburn, and *Dawn Patrol*, and *Little Caesar* with Edwin G Robinson. All us girls had a crush on Douglas Fairbanks when I was young."

"We had our Shangri-la, didn't we Martha? Suzie is going to have hers just like in the movie."

The sun had set and the moon had risen, casting its silver magic upon the dark waters.

"I remember the thirties when so many people were out of work. Going to the picture show was the only entertainment a lot of people had back then. It was a quarter for adults and ten cents for us kids. Some people couldn't afford that."

"You've seen a lot of things, haven't you, Martha."

"I remember when *The Grapes of Wrath* came out in 1939. None of us realized how bad it was out West. It was only after the war broke out that people began to understand what really happened. Then the Japanese bombed Pearl Harbor and Fletcher joined the Navy. I like to died when I got word he was killed."

"Then you got Sam."

"Yes. That was a blessing from heaven. I never knew who the mother was. I never wanted to know, really. Samantha is my little girl. That makes up for losing Fletcher."

They talked and sipped their cocktails and listened to the music until after midnight. Miss Martha began to yawn so they called it a night. Next morning was a beautiful summer day. They wore shorts and halter tops, taking the sun from their colorful deckchairs overlooking the bow of the Sea Queen.

"Look! Look! Down there."

"Oh, my goodness. Look at that."

A pod of bottlenose dolphins were in front of the ship. Some were jumping and cavorting about, while others swam only a few feet in front of the steel prow.

Beautiful sea creatures with blue backs, large dorsal fins, and white bellies.

"I read about those at the doctor's office. They're mammals, like us. They breathe air and they have exceptional eyesight and hearing. And they're social animals. They're very friendly to people. Oh, and they have big brains, larger than ours."

"Sam, that's amazing. You're plum smart."

"Plum smart aleck is more like it."

"All right, you two rascals."

"Tell us more about the dolphins. I like them."

"Well, let me see. Oh, here's something I bet you don't know. Orcas are dolphins. They communicate by touching and with whistles, like Flipper on TV. And they have something like sonar that helps them fish and communicate under water. They're smart animals."

"Let's go downstairs and watch them from the front of the boat."

They took the stairs down to the main deck. A small crowd had already gathered, peering over the railing. An old lady in a wheelchair was laughing and clapping her hands gleefully.

"I love them. I just love them," she said.

Her gray-haired husband nodded to Martha, stepping aside so she could see.

"Sam, look. Oh, look at them, Suzie." Martha clasped her hands together, smiling down at the lady in the wheelchair. "My name is Martha Fox. This is my daughter, Samantha, and her friend, Suzie Brown. We're from Knoxville, Tennessee. Where are you from?"

The woman's husband touched Martha's shoulder. "She doesn't hear well but she can read your lips. Speak directly to her face."

Martha reintroduced herself. The woman smiled and took her hand. One of her front teeth was missing. Then Martha noticed the numbers on her forearm.

"You … you were in the camps?"

"Buchenwald. Fourteen months, seventeen days. My name is Elsa Lieberman. This is my wonderful husband, Karl Lieberman. We met in Palestine after the war."

Suzie and Samantha were confused. "What's she talking about?"

"Elsa was in a Nazi concentration camp. It doesn't get any worse than that."

Martha turned back to Karl and Elsa. "Please join us for lunch."

The Liebermans were a delightful couple, warm and friendly. They held hands, addressing one another as *Tatelah* and *Mamelah*. Karl made his fortune smuggling weapons into Palestine when the Jews were fighting for their independence against Great Britain. And later on when the Arabs declared war against Israel.

When asked why she was so slender, Samantha told Elsa the truth about her cancer. The older woman patted her hand, telling her there was a place in God's choir for young beauties. Then the conversation drifted back to the camps.

"I'm forty-nine years old. I only look this way because of what they did to me. But I'm one of the lucky ones. I'm still alive and I have my Karl."

"Buchenwald was one of the bad ones, wasn't it, Elsa?"

"They were all bad, Martha. Some worse than others. I suppose mine was as bad as any. Buchenwald was for political prisoners. Something like 61,000 died there. Millions died in the other camps."

"*Mamelah*, tell them about the Russians."

"Yes, the Nazis were *dybbuks*. They treated the Russian prisoners very badly. They used them for experiments, tortured them, gassed them, hanged them. I saw a guard carrying a shrunken head just before we were liberated. I was there when Edward R. Murrow paid us a visit. It was a horrible, filthy, stinking place. We were starving when the Americans came. The soldiers found lampshades made with human skin. The Germans beat us with whips, wooden clubs, rubber truncheons. They murdered thousands in those final days."

"Tell them about the *kapo* in your barracks."

"Karl, the girls. They shouldn't know."

"Tell them, *Mamelah*. It is good they should know."

"Gustafa Mulluer! A terrible man. He was a French Jew. A criminal who helped the Germans manage the work gangs. He was given extra food for doing that. He was a brute, a savage man. He carried a leather club he beat them with. He killed some of the prisoners. Me, he didn't beat. He forced me to his room at night and made me do things. Vile things. The SS killed him before the Americans came. He went into the ovens like all the others.

"When the Americans weighed us, I weighed seventy-eight pounds. At first the Americans gave us too much to eat, and we vomited the food back up. Our stomachs couldn't take it. Then the Americans gave us smaller portions and we kept it down. I remember I cried when they gave us oranges. An orange was considered a delicacy. That orange was the most delicious thing I ever put into my mouth."

"Tell them, Elsa. Tell them how we met."

"Yes. Those were happy days in spite of all the troubles. A number of us Jews were smuggled into Palestine at night through the British blockade. We landed on the beach in little rubber boats. Karl was there holding a rifle and welcoming us. '*Shalom! Shalom!*' he whispered. I was weak, but still a pretty woman then. He helped me out of my boat. A month later we were married."

"But the wheelchair. What caused that?"

"Many Jews helped Karl with his smuggling activities. We were coming across an open field around midnight when the British opened fire. Nine of our party were killed. I was wounded, but Karl carried me to safety. I've been in this silly contraption ever since."

"She was very brave. We made many journeys across the desert before Elsa was shot. Most of the time we had trucks. She helped give birth to Israel. A Jewish doctor who survived Auschwitz saved Elsa's life. We exchange gifts every Hanukkah with Doctor Rubenstein."

Suzie and Samantha had tears in their eyes. They had no idea of the ordeal the Jews had suffered following the end of the war. And ever since 1948 when Israel declared herself a nation. Martha told the Liebermans about John's death, and how Suzie's sweetheart was still in Vietnam. Elsa unfastened a clasp behind her neck, handing Suzie a little silver cross on a worn silver chain.

"I kept this with me in the camp. I used to clutch it to my heart at night, and pray to Lord Jesus to come save us. If the Germans found it I would have been shot. It's yours now to pray for your Robert. It was blessed by a rabbi in Jerusalem."

That night, Suzie dreamed about Butterfly Lake in South Knoxville.

Suzie went there to feed the ducks, but the ducks were all gone. She sat down on a grassy knoll to toss her breadcrumbs in the water for the bass and little blue gills, but none came. That had never happened before.

"Ahoy there, young lady."

She looked around, but saw no one. Suzie got up and looked down Easton Road, behind the leafy redbuds and green cedar trees.

"Hello, Suzie Brown."

"Show yourself. This isn't funny."

"Down here, in front of you."

Then she saw them, dolphins. Four blue dolphins.

"This is crazy. Dolphins don't talk. Besides, we're hundreds of miles from the ocean. I'm hallucinating or something is seriously weird."

"No, Suzie Brown. We have something wonderful to tell you."

"You're not real. This is crazy."

"Was your encounter with Mr. and Mrs. Lieberman crazy?"

"No."

"What about the silver cross? Do you have it with you?"

"Of course I do. I love it."

"You have been chosen as the bearer of the cross. It was baptized in the blood of innocents, and the tears of the damned. The Buchenwald Cross is sacred, an icon of our Lord Jesus Christ of Nazareth."

"Don't say that. You're scaring me."

"There is need for your prayers, Suzie Brown. For First Squad. And for William Kidwell, the man they call as Red."

"Stop it! You're just an old fish. You don't know anything."

Then the four blue dolphins transformed into four golden warriors. Suzie burst into tears, hiding her face. Their brilliance was so grand it blinded her, stealing her breath away.

"We have come to bless your friend, Samantha Gail Jackson."

At the mention of Samantha's name, Suzie regained her composure. "Can you help Robert? And Red? And those other Marines?"

Something about their leader appeared familiar. The warrior was tall, muscular, and flawlessly handsome. His presence glowed with a mysterious blue light, and all around them the atmosphere sparkled.

"Your actions identify you as a woman of God."

"I was bad once."

"We were all bad before. But that was before."

"Is Bubba safe?"

It was then she recognized Patrick Lucian Abernathy from photographs mailed home from Vietnam.

"Pray upon the cross, Suzie Brown. It contains the love and wisdom of generations. Pray for First Squad. Pray for America. And pray for Vietnam."

"Is First Squad okay?"

The golden warriors were starting to recede.

"Don't leave me. I want to talk to you."

Suzie awakened to find Samantha holding her, rocking her in her arms. Suzie was trembling, tears streaking her cheeks.

"What's wrong, baby?

"Sam, will you pray with me?"

Catfish

Boots' Revenge

"Lieutenant Butler! You're back!"

"Hello, Red. How you been getting along?"

"I damn near kicked the bucket, but the sawbones fixed me up good as new. You look well, sir. How long you been back?"

"I flew in last night."

"Come with me, sir. The men are all down at the slop shoot. They'll be glad to see you. I'll buy you a Pabst Blue Ribbon."

When they walked in, the original members of First Squad all stood and shook hands with Lieutenant Butler. Then Catfish and Calhoun were introduced. The conversation went on for some time about their escape from the valley, about John and Gunny. Then Henry asked about Boots.

"Boots is dead."

"You're shitting me! That cat was fine when we come outta them trees."

"I gave her to Lieutenant Ferguson to keep while I was in the hospital."

"What happened?"

"There's a colonel a few doors down from Ferguson. This colonel person apparently hates cats. Boots roamed around the neighborhood quite a bit. From what I gather she sometimes sat on his automobile."

"You mean he killed our cat for sitting on his damn car?"

"He poisoned her with antifreeze. The stuff is sweet. Animals will drink it. He left some in a bowl sitting on top of the vehicle. Ferguson saw it still sitting there after the cat died. He stuck his finger in the stuff and tasted it. Then he had a doctor cut Boots open to see what was wrong with her. That's when they discovered antifreeze in her stomach. Her kidneys had shut down."

"Were does this asshole live, sir?"

"Over in the compound near the main chow hall."

"That's by-God criminal! What kind of fucked-up automobile is this?"

"He's got an old '55 Chevy. Beautiful car. It's red and white, fender skirts, dual exhausts. He loves that old car."

"Sweet Jesus! I liked that little kitty cat!"

Pasamenus steered the conversation away from Boots, knowing full well what First Squad was thinking. He didn't want the lieutenant to get in trouble in case there was an inquiry. He told Lieutenant Butler it was just an old cat, and let it go at that. Later that night First Squad held a meeting in their upstairs squad bay.

"That son of a bitch killed our pussycat!"

"Goddamn right!"

"Brain, you're the smart one. You got any problems with this?"

"None, but we have to proceed with caution. We could land in the brig over this caper. Catfish, this is your department. Any suggest-ions?"

"Let me think … do it at night. I'll need two lookouts with flashlights. A truck or a jeep. A gallon of fuel oil or kerosene. A delayed-action detonator, and a pound of boom boom."

Next day they drove around the mess hall neighborhood until they spotted the 1955 Bel Air convertible. It was parked next to the colonel's living quarters, about five feet from the house.

"We'll have to roll it out in the street or risk blowing the asshole out of bed.

If it's locked, we can hook a cable to the bumper and pull it away from the building."

"What we need is a bumper winch."

"Good idea. Let's get back to the barracks."

Later that afternoon Red called the Major, explaining that he needed a detonator with a two-minute fuse delay and a pound of TNT. The Major asked what for, so Red told him about their cat. Two hours later a 4 x 4 transport truck arrived with a front bumper winch. A taped cardboard box sat on the front seat.

"Johnson, I want you and Tony. No offense, but you're both dark skinned. I'll use burnt cork on my face and hands. "

"None taken. When do we go?"

"Rain is forecast all day Wednesday. We'll go that night. Less chance of the MPs prowling around."

Thursday morning they set out just after midnight in a light rain. The base was quiet except for the occasional motor vehicle. Most of the military personnel were in bed asleep. As they approached their destination, a jeep with two military police drove by. They continued on two more blocks, then turned around and parked.

"Coast looks clear to me. Now remember, flash you lights two times if you see somebody coming. Once I get the Chevy away from the house, I'll do my thing which takes about ten seconds. When you see me blink my flashlight, you come running."

Tony and Johnson hooked the cable to the rear bumper of the Chevy, then spread out forty yards apart to stand guard. It took less than a minute for the powerful truck winch to pull the vehicle clear of the building. Cassidy broke out the driver's window with a tire tool wrapped in the cardboard, activated the detonator, then placed his device on the front seat of the convertible. By the time he backed the truck around for home, Tony and Johnson were back onboard.

Four blocks later an orange fireball appeared in the side mirrors, followed by a loud "Ka-Boom!" Lights began coming on along the street. They heard a fire engine in the distance. Another jeep loaded with MPs roared past. Twenty minutes later they were back at the barracks, explaining the night's adventure to First Squad.

To their surprise, Lieutenant Butler came strolling in.

"I guessed what you were up to. I thought about it myself, but I didn't have the proper materials. From what the Major tells me you people are hell on wheels. He told me about tonight so I waited. I'm proud to be back with you fellas again. The Major's trust in all of us is something extraordinary."

Johnson pulled out his switchblade and pressed the button. "First Squad has a special brotherhood, sir. We'd like you to join our little group."

Lieutenant Butler nodded his head, smiling. "I consider this a great honor, coming from you gentlemen."

The cuts were made, and Butler massaged his blood into Vera Lynn.

Chapter Thirty-One

The White House

"I don't give a hoot in hell who he is! That bastard had no right to call my containment policy a failure in *The New York Times*! Who the hell does he think he is? I'll have his brass balls busted down to latrine sergeant!"

"Sir, you mustn't talk so loud. This place leaks like a sieve. The press isn't exactly our friend these days."

"Fuck the press! I'm the Commander in Chief!"

"And a great one you are, Lyndon, but we must tread cautiously. All that publicity over McNamara and Tet and General Westmoreland casts dispersions over you and your entire Administration. My job is to serve and protect you, Mister President."

"McNamara's a goddamn Harvard pussy! Him and his goddamn Whiz Kids! And Westmoreland was asleep at the goddamn wheel! Ho Chin Minh could a driven a damn hay wagon loaded down with Foo Fighters straight down Fish Head Boulevard slap in the middle of

Saigon. Hell, they damn near captured the General! I could get a better job done with two knot-heads outta the DC phone book."

"General Westmoreland did seem a bit preoccupied with the Offensive. If it hadn't been for General Weyand, God knows what might have happened."

"Good point, Clark. I should have appointed Fred instead of Bill to lead our parade over yonder in Vietnam. And who gets blamed for all this horseshit? Lyndon by-God Johnson!"

"Lyndon, you've done a wonderful job over the years. When President Roosevelt appointed you to go visit General MacArthur and report back what was needed out there, it was your tireless efforts that upgraded our Pacific Theatre of Operations and helped win the war. You saved lives, Mister President."

"I sure do miss my early politickin' days. Hell, Clark, a man could get things done back in the '40s and '50s. Now it's like pullin' teeth with Congress, the Pentagon, and them half-wit media clowns. *The New York Times* acts like a bunch a goddamn communists.

"Now what can I do about that general that pissed on me in the newspaper?"

"As Majority Leader you got the Civil Rights Act passed. President Eisenhower liked you. Sam Rayburn liked you. You fellows worked together as a team right here in Washington. Then you hitched your star to JFK's wagon."

"Ya know, I never did like that Robert Kennedy. He was another one a them snot-nose Harvard brats. Little squirt would smile to your face, then stick a knife in your back. But the President and I got along fine. John was a gentleman. I respected that in him, but that family of his never did cotton to me or Claudia. His problem was he couldn't keep his pecker in his britches. It was by-God awful the day he got shot. They blew the top of his head off. Then they killed Martin. Now Bobby. I'm sorry about Bobby's death.

"What can we do about that damn Army prick?"

"Mister President, forget about that brass hat. All that will get you is more trouble, and we don't need that right now. Especially since you declared you aren't running for reelection. We need to give Hubert a fair shot at taking over around here.

"Remember the 'Daisy ad,' when you put the skids under Goldwater?"

"That was God-awful, wasn't it? I bet he shit his pants when that A Bomb went off."

"You expanded the Civil Rights Act in 1964, and got your Voting Rights Act passed in '65. Then you rolled out your Great Society. Hell, man, you did more for the poor people of this country in five and a half years than all the presidents before you since Lincoln."

"The thing I regret most is Vietnam. I should a never uh got us in that mess. Ho Chi Minh won't negotiate, talk, nothin'. Tryin' to deal with Hanoi is like havin' your nuts in a blender. They'll spend a week arguing over the shape uh tha goddamn furniture."

"Orientals are a pain in the ass to deal with, sir. We solved that problem twenty-three years ago when we dropped the atomic bomb. That's out of the question today. Too many innocent people would get killed. Protesters all over the world, China would shit a brick, *The New York Times* would piss all over themselves. That could start a revolution in this country."

"I'll tell you something in confidence just between you and me, Mister Secretary. I think we've lost this war. Maybe I did go about it wrong. Maybe I should a gone balls out, but it wasn't lost in the jungles or in the air war over Hanoi and Haiphong. Walter Cronkite and that bunch a limp-dicks down at ABC and NBC lost it in the livin' rooms of America. All I ever wanted was to give the people of Indochina a better life and save their asses from communism. Now half the world hates my guts."

"Mister President, I suggest you place your efforts behind the peace process. You succeeded with Medicare and Medicaid. Most of your Great Society programs got through. You've been blessed in so many ways, my friend. Don't let Vietnam spoil it for you."

"All those dead boys. I dream about 'em when I go to bed at night."

"If you're having trouble sleeping, try Valium. I hear it works wonders."

"Sleepin' ain't the problem. I sleep like a whore in church. I keep seein' their faces. Last time I 's over there proppin' up Westy, I musta been introduced to five hundred of 'em. Nice lookin' boys. Lots a Southern men. Nice lookin' black fellas. Ever night it's the same dream. Lady Bird says its 'cause I drink too much. Hell! Since I can't get it up no more from takin' them damn blood pressure pills, drinkin', an' cigarettes is the only enjoyment I get around here."

"What's your doctor say about your heart?"

"Says if I don't quit tobacco and alcohol it's gonna kill me."

"We just had Bobby's funeral. I don't think the country is ready for yours just yet, Lyndon."

"Maybe not. But what's the use a livin' if all you eat is bland-ass food with no salt? And coffee with no sugar in it? And no pussy!"

"Mister President, you're one of a kind!"

"Maybe so. I'm too old to change."

"Do you believe the bombing halt will make a difference?"

"Hell, with them swingin' dicks ya never know. I wanted to do a Great Society in Vietnam, but them commie bastards got their own notions about doin' things. Did you hear about them public officials and "po-lice" they rounded up in Hue and murdered? Goddamn savages! They did it in Saigon, Da Nang, all over the place. I don't understand how they can be that cruel to fellow human bein's. Buried some of 'em alive in Hue!"

"Lyndon, it's time for us to get out. More people are against us now than used to be for us. The college kids are marching in the streets, Cronkite has turned against the war, *The Washington Post* is a major pain in the ass. The Joint Chiefs have no cohesive plan for winning the war or ending the fighting. We're like two blind men stumbling down a dead end street together."

"I guess when Westmoreland asked to blockade the Trail I should a listened. But I had a roomful a peaceniks at the time, don't bomb, don't invade, don't, don't, don't. And like a dumb-ass I went along with it. Now it's too late. If I'd a sent another 200,000 like Westmoreland asked for, they'd a shot me just like they shot John."

"Peking is unpredictable, you never know if they're going to shake hands or send ten divisions your way. I remember how you and Mack agonized over the possibility of China coming in on the side of North Vietnam."

"I worried about it more than McNamara. Them bastards could lose a million soldiers and keep on a comin'. That's why I kept Westmoreland on a short leash."

"Your Great Society helped an awful lot of people, Mister President. That will be your legacy. That and Medicare and Medicaid. In time, years from now, Vietnam will fade from memory. You'll be remembered as a great president."

"I hate leavin' with the Party in a mess, and Vietnam the way it is. In spite of all that, and all the good I've accomplished, I feel like a damn failure. And that damn Nixon is liable to beat Humphrey. I can't stand that ski-nose bastard. The Democratic Party at its worst, is still better than the Republican Party at its best. I love saying that. It drives them Republicans straight up the wall."

"I don't know as much as I should about Hubert. What can the DNC do to get him that majority vote?"

"Well, he looks like forty rows uh bad corn, but he's loyal and he's got a good heart. I bet you don't know how President Truman beat Dewey, do ya?"

"No Lyndon, I don't."

"Back at the 1948 Democratic National Convention, the party was split over the issue of Civil Rights. Hubert and his people wanted to

add legislation outlawin' lynchin' and school segregation, plus job dis-
crimination against coloreds. Most Northern Democrats saw that as a
way to gain black votes. Remember, they was a boatload uh black folks
working in Detroit and all them big industrial cities back then. Well,
the Southern Democrats didn't like that worth a damn, so they split off
and formed the Dixiecrats. Then they ran their own man for president,
Strom Thurman. They figured by splitting the Democratic vote, Harry
Truman would lose, and that would be all she wrote for Civil Rights.

"It backfired! It gained Truman the black vote, especially in them
big industrial towns up north. Truman pulled an upset and like they
say, the rest is history. But Hubert had as much to do with Harry getting elected as ole Harry did himself."

"That's amazing. So the two of you get along pretty well?"

"Hubert helped a lot with my Civil Rights Act when he was Senate
Whip in '64. He got the Peace Corps passed and the Nuclear Test Ban
Treaty when Kennedy was president. We've had our differences, but I'll
support him any way I can."

"What can we do to help?"

"The best thing I can do is stay outta the picture. I'll make the
phone calls and yank all the usual chains, but it might hurt Hubert if
the public sees him with me."

"You have a point there, Mister President. None of us are very
popular these days. I wish this war would end. That would be the best
thing that could happen for America."

"It won't end, not unless we pull out. It's like humpin' a woman.
Pull out too soon, an' you piss her off. Leave it in, an' she gets pregnant.
You lose both ways."

"You have the damnest way of expressing yourself of any man I
know, sir, but you certainly get your point across."

President Johnson relates the French tragedy. "At the battle of Dien Bien Phu in '54, the Viet Minh hauled their guns and ammo from a little town five hundred miles north on the Chinese border. France wanted to blockade the communist supply lines into Laos, a French ally, and draw the Vietminh into a set piece battle. Commie engineers worked on them roads the whole way. They built bridges under water so they couldn't be seen from the air, tied tree tops together to hide their activities on the ground, went through swamps, around mountains, you name it. The last fifty miles was all mountains and no roads, so they built a damn road. In some places, they drug them artillery pieces through the jungle with their bare hands.

"They did all that in three months usin' 800 trucks, 20,000 laborers, and God only knows how many bicycles. A French artillery colonel by the name of Charles Piroth said it couldn't be done. He boasted even if they did it, no Vietminh gun would fire more than three rounds before his artillery boys knocked it out. That Frog bastard was fulla shit!

"General Giap is a lousy general, but he did this one right. He knew his men weren't experienced gunners so he had 'em dig caves and hide their guns on the forward slopes uh the mountains, surrounding General Navarre and his Foreign Legion. That way Giap's boys could see where their shells landed, then make corrections. Sometime after that Piroth committed suicide.

"It was a bloodbath on both sides. The Legion was outnumbered four to one. They damn near won, but after fifty-six days uh gettin' their ass pounded they ran outta bullets and medical supplies. Thousands uh communists got killed, but they kept on attackin' night after night. Fifteen hundred Legionnaires died, 10,000 were taken prisoner. They marched them prisoners two hundred and fifty miles back through the jungle to them prisoner uh war camps. Exhaustion and disease done 'em in worse than all tha fighting. Only 3,900 were still alive when they got released four months later.

"That's what we're up against, Clark. I never knew none uh this when I gave our boys the green light at Da Nang. La Drang taught us what kinda fighters they are, An Lao, Tet. Brave little fuckers ain't afraid to die. That's what you call real live mother-fuckers!"

"We got another problem, Mister President. There's going to be a white backlash in the South and Midwestern states over the Negro riots in the North, and those antiwar protesters all over the country. Nixon will play that up big in the press."

"That self-righteous sumbitch keeps runnin' his mouth 'bout me not usin' our military effectively or our diplomatic people no better. He's got Strom Thurman and John Tower advisin' him now. I'd like to stick that Checkers dog uh his up his skinny Republican ass!"

Clark Clifford spoke: "Eugene McCarthy continues calling for a withdrawal. George McGovern has the same antiwar template every week. Must be something in the water out there in those Western states. Senator Church has become a problem. And now they've got Ted Kennedy in their camp."

"Ted Kennedy, my ass! He can't keep his pants on long enough to be a decent representative. Old Joe was a lousy father figure for all them boys uh his. I don't know who's dumber, Teddy or George Wallace."

There was a knock on the door of the oval office. An aide entered, handing President Johnson a piece of paper from the new telecopier machine. The president read it then placed it carefully on his desk, the color draining from his face

"Mister Secretary, we lost over five hundred men last week."

Chapter Thirty-Two

Colonel Sarkis

Colonel Sarkis

A light rain was falling as a noonday sun shown down on Delta X Ray. Where the raindrops struck the surface of the Se Bang Fui River below the airfield, they made little sparkles like millions of tiny diamonds dancing on the water's surface from the refraction of the sun's rays. The jungle along the waterway was thick and jade green. Blue and white heron waded in the shallows catching sun perch and shark-minnow. Monkeys and parrots gossiped among themselves high up in the giant mimosas, betel, tonle sap, and mangrove trees. Overhead, sea gulls circled and dove on the river's surface, catching dragonflies and snakehead minnows.

"Duke of Earl, I been thinkin'."

"About what?"

"What if I get my balls shot off?"

"Then you really can be Little Miss Buckingham!"

"No! I'm serious."

"What the hell brought this on?"

"That last firefight we had, I found a bullet hole in my pants right below my pecker."

"They missed, didn't they?"

"Yeah, but what if they don't next time?"

"Then you can sing in the boy's choir."

"Damn it, Calhoun. I'm serious."

"Good grief, man. You sound like a six-foot pussy."

"Well, fuck! I want to have kids some day."

"Tell you what, Cassidy. You get married, I'll come over and hump your old lady, then you can have all the curtain climbers you want. And I won't charge you a dime for services rendered."

"Gee, Duke, you're a pal. No, seriously, I'm worried about getting my 'nads shot off."

"Okay, then. Let's go see the Major about getting you a steel jock. We'll call you Iron Box. How's that sound?"

"Sounds like you got a couple a screws loose someplace."

"Hey! Them blondes were great, weren't they?"

"Oh, man! I'd forgotten about that. We gotta go back for seconds first chance we get. Madame said the girls are free from now on."

"Poontang City! Savin' the Garden was the best damn thing we done in this crazy war. That baby doll Tony was with was gorgeous. And that split-tail from Thailand? I'd marry that heifer!"

"I would, my damn self."

"You come, please. Major want see you now."

When Calhoun and Cassidy walked into the Operations Tent the rest of First Squad were already seated. Tony sat up front between Lieutenant Butler and Major Abraham. A map of the region north of the Hien Luong Bridge was pinned up against the blackboard.

Major Abraham spoke. "I pulled a few strings at the Pentagon so from now on you people are stationed here with me. That colonel whose car you blew up was getting inquisitive about the owners of the cat he killed. He has no jurisdiction over here. Anyway, from now on you have special security clearance. You're accountable only to me, and the big brass across the river."

"Sir, can you tell us now if you're with the CIA?"

"Yes, I am. So are you, in a manner of speaking. You can help out around here maintaining the airfield, helping the mechanics, loading ordnance, and helping the Mongs strengthen our defenses. We need more logs and sandbags around those gun emplacements.

"Once in a while I'll have a mission for you, but remember these missions are strictly volunteer stuff. Everyone agrees to go or none of you go. That last detail that damn near got you killed was a foul-up on my part. I would never have sent you out there had we known what you were getting into. That said, you did a hell of a job."

"Sir, what about that map up there?"

"We got a fighter pilot down twenty-four miles north of the Ben Hai River. He's in one of their makeshift prisoner of war camps. This man is one of our aces. He served in World War Two and Korea. The camp is small. Intelligence thinks he's still there because of his transponder. He went down beside the compound two days ago.

"You men feel up for another trip into Charlie Country?"

Pasamenus stood up, asking his Marines if anyone objected to the assignment? Nobody voiced a complaint. Then he asked for a show of hands in favor of the mission. The hand count was unanimous

Red took the floor. "How many guards they got, Major?"

"We don't know for sure. These makeshift jobs usually have five or six guards, sometimes a dozen. There may be other prisoners too. I knew Colonel Sarkis in Korea when he flew Saber jets against the Russian MiGs. This man is a real patriot. He'll be sent to the Hanoi Hilton if we don't get him out of there."

The map on the blackboard indicated a wooden bridge two and a half kilometers north of the POW compound. East were marshlands all the way to the South China Sea. West lay miles and miles of tropical jungle.

Catfish spoke. "Sir, I have a suggestion. Chopper me and Calhoun in near the bridge. I'll rig the thing to blow, then we'll head south. Send in the rest of the squad out a ways from the compound. We can rendezvous using our radios."

"Good thinking, Cassidy. Charlie will be watching the south road. I'll 'copter you and Calhoun in above the bridge. Lieutenant Butler and his crew I can drop a mile or two east. Tony will go with them to watch for mines and tripwires."

Chapter Thirty-Three

The Bridge

"How's she look?

"Like five assholes on a 40mm Bofars gun. Those were great guns back in World War Two, but they're too slow today."

"All it takes is one hit. We're losing ten to fifteen aircraft a week."

"You got a point there. How the heck we gonna get down there without me gettin' my 'nads shot off?"

"I got me a choir book in case that happens."

"You asshole."

"How 'bout us floatin' down the river? They ain't gonna be looking for two assholes jumpin' outta Frogville on their behinds."

"Ya know, Duke, a fellow could get hurt doin' this shit."

"Come on. Bring your 'nads with ya."

Calhoun and Cassidy left their explosives in the underbrush, making their way upstream parallel with the river. A hundred yards above the gun emplacement they located a suitable log, then pushed off to float with the current.

"Sure is pretty country. Birds an' monkeys an' flowers an' all."

"This is one hell of a way to make a living."

They kept in close to the bank to conceal themselves. Frightened by their sudden appearance, a white heron squawked loudly flapping away above the muddy surface of the river. When they floated under the bridge, they let go their log and lay in the cattails, listening.

"Oh, shit! It's on my leg."

"Hold still!"

"Get it off me. I hate snakes."

"Be still, goddamn it."

Calhoun reached down with his trench knife and flipped it out into the river.

The serpent was attracted by the warmth of Cassidy's leg and swam back.

"Awww, Jesus!"

"Be still or that fucker is gonna bite your ass."

Cassidy closed his eyes and remained silent. The snake crawled up his back, curling up between his shoulder blades. Calhoun watched the snake, waiting his opportunity. It raised its head, staring at Calhoun, flicking out its tongue, judging if Calhoun posed a threat.

Noise from above caught the snake's attention. It turned its head. One of the gun crew was taking a leak down their vine-covered embankment.

Calhoun whispered, "Don't move."

Urine rained down on both men. When the Vietcong turned to go, Calhoun grabbed the snake around the neck and sliced off its head.

"That fucker pissed on us."

"Awww, man, I hate snakes."

"Well, it's dead now."

"What do you think it was?"

"Nothing much, just a black-and-white krait."

"What's that?"

"One bite, and you're a dead duck."

Getting up the steep slope without making noise was no easy task. Calhoun slipped and nearly fell. Cassidy grabbed him by his cartridge belt. Five minutes later they were at the crest of the embankment peering through the vines at the North Vietnamese Army personnel.

"Six shots in this thing and five of them. If I miss, you'll have to use your rifle. That's thirty paces."

"How 'bout this? Wait until they're looking the other way. Then we move in closer and you open up. I'll shoot if I have to, but they'll hear us down at the camp."

"Sounds like a plan."

"Shoot slow and deliberate. You'll still have a few seconds after they spot us."

The men lay in the greenery and waited. Minutes passed.

"Let's go!"

Calhoun closed the distance to ten paces before the first Charlie saw them.

He dropped to one knee, aimed, and fired. The silencer went "Pomp!" A second man turned around and he fired again. "Pomp!" He and Cassidy rushed the gunners. Calhoun shot two more. The fifth NVA raised his rifle.

Cassidy leapt across the sandbags, burying his trench knife in the man's chest. The other four gunners were dead. The man with the chest wound lay on his back, wheezing and gurgling for breath. Calhoun shot him in the head to end his suffering.

"Red Dog Two. Come in, Red Dog Two."

"This is Red Dog Two. Is that you Duke of Earl?"

"Yeah, I got Little Miss Buckingham with me. Mission accomplished."

"Good job! Rendezvous in forty minutes. Northwest corner. Check back in thirty minutes. Northwest corner. Time Check."

"0947 hours."

"Check back at 1015 hours, 1015 hours. Got that?"

"1015 hours. Roger that."

Cassidy and Calhoun had walked about halfway to the POW camp when they heard a truck engine start up over in the trees.

"Look at that. Charlie's been takin' hisself a breakfast fiesta."

"Come on. We can use that truck."

The two went dodging through the greenery until they were in a position where the driver would have to pull out onto the roadway. The truck labored and swayed as the driver geared up a grassy embankment.

"Look. It's an old Ford!"

"Wait until he's right in front of us."

As the truck came abreast of their hiding place, Calhoun sprang up onto the running board. "Pomp! Pomp!" He held on to the steering wheel as the dead driver slumped over against his deceased companion riding shotgun. The Ford rolled to a halt. They dragged the bodies out of the cab and back into the trees.

"Let's see what we got in here."

Calhoun backed the vehicle up a few paces so it couldn't be seen from the air. Then they went around back and pulled open the flap.

"Holy Cow!"

Staring back at them was a beaten and bloody American.

"Careful untying him. He might be hurt."

"Boy, am I glad to see you guys. Got any water?"

The NVA had worked him over methodically, black eyes, busted lip, broken nose. Other than that, Lieutenant Kirby was good to go.

"How'd you get shot down?

"It looked like a damn telephone pole. Must have been one of those new surface-to-air jobs. I couldn't shake the bastard."

"We saw some a them things a month ago."

"What are you Marines doing up here above the Zone?"

"We thought we'd mosey up and save some Air Force ass."

The men laughed.

"Hey, we better call in and tell 'em about our truck."

Twenty minutes later First Squad and Lieutenant Kirby were assembled behind a sharp curve a hundred meters above the internment camp. Lieutenant Butler and Sergeant Pasamenus had just concluded discussing tactics. Cassidy had given his M-14 to Lieutenant Kirby. He cradled an AK-47 in his arms.

"Tony drives straight in with six men in back and Kirby in the cab. Tony stops at the north end of camp. We nail 'em when they come out to greet Tony. Then we proceed through the camp. You three right. You three left. Two men will proceed through the boonies on both outer flanks. You two right. Pasamenus and I left. Kirby will cover the open ground from the truck. We need to get this done in sixty seconds, people."

Red and Bubba were on the right flank proceeding behind the rear of the huts when they spotted two guards standing over an American sitting on the ground. His hands were bound behind his back and his face was bloody.

Gunfire!

"That's our cue, bro."

They dashed out before the two guards could react, shot them both dead, grabbed the prisoner under his arms, and dragged him back into the trees.

"Fucking Marines! I can't believe this. I could kiss you bastards."

"Are you Colonel Sarkis?"

"How'd you know?"

"Major Abraham sent us."

"That old son of a bitch! I love it! Listen, there's another pilot two hoochs down. He's in rough shape. Got some busted ribs and a broken leg. Let's get him."

"Can you walk, sir?"

"Hell, yes! Let's go."

"Lead the way, Colonel."

They'd gone only a few paces when a guard came running around the hut in front of them. When he saw the Marines, he threw down his weapon.

"Here's his rifle, sir. Keep an eye on this rice bag. Me an' Bubba will get your pilot for ya."

Gunfire erupted from the other side of the compound. Red peeked around the corner of the hut. Straight across the clearing four guards behind an iron watering trough were exchanging fire with First Squad.

"Gimme your grenades."

Red pulled the pins, bowling the hand grenades one by one across the open area into the NVA position. Four blasts and the gunfire ceased. Pasamenus and Butler emerged from the trees on the far side of the compound. The others came down the sides of the clearing in front of the hoochs. Two additional guards lay dead in front of the truck.

The second pilot was dead. He'd expired from his injuries and the beatings he'd received at the hands of his communist captors.

"Bring that Zipper Head out here!" Butler was royally pissed.

Colonel Sarkis frog-marched the bound prisoner front and center before Lieutenant Butler.

"Tony, ask him who did this."

"Give gun make no noise."

"Calhoun?"

Calhoun handed Tony the .38 Special with the silencer attachment. Tony fired a round between the man's feet. A second round. "Pomp!"

A third round. "Pomp!" Pressing the weapon against the prisoner's crotch, Tony addressed him in Vietnamese.

The young communist was terrified of Tony, his facial scars, and the blue steel revolver pressed against his winkee. A few minutes later Tony knew the location of every enemy camp within a twenty-mile radius, including the location of an ammunition dump two kilometers west in the boondocks.

Henry had a bullet lodged in his forearm. They loaded him and the dead pilot in the back of the truck, then the rest piled in. Lieutenant Butler, Tony, Cassidy, and Calhoun took off in the direction of the ammunition dump.

The rest of the First Squad, Colonel Sarkis, Lieutenant Kirby, and Sergeant Pasamenus proceeded down the south road in the truck. Apache helicopters hit the north end of the bridge two minutes before they arrived. Driving across the structure, they encountered only dead men.

An hour later a loud "BOOOOM" rolled through the jungle behind them. Little Miss Buckingham & Company had blown the ammunition dump. A Huey helicopter was en route to pick them up, escorted by two F-105s.

A smaller explosion was heard a short while later in the distance. Charlie had stumbled across Catfish's calling card at the wooden bridge. First Squad had burned the POW camp to the ground.

That weekend Hanoi Hannah broadcast their names, and the name and location of Delta X Ray over Radio Hanoi.

Chapter Thirty-Four

The Valley

"Men, we got trouble headed this way."

Major Abraham was using a pointer to explain a section of map he'd pinned up on the blackboard. The map showed arrows he'd drawn with chalk to emphasize the enemy advance.

"Intelligence estimates about 2,500 NVA. That's a complete regiment so we must be doing something right or they wouldn't be that interested in us. You people have definitely become a thorn in their side. I could call in the big bombers, but I don't want to do that. We're liable to blow our cover if the media comes in here nosing around over a B-52 strike.

"There are two camps nearby with B-26 medium bombers. We can borrow those if we have to. That would use up everyone's stockpile of bombs. Of course we have our Skyraiders, but that may not be enough. I'm wondering if we can rig some kind of trap where they'll be coming through this valley northwest of here. Otherwise, it would take them a week to go around the mountains and come down from the north.

"Cassidy, can you think of anything?"

"Sir, if you can get me a 1,000 pounds of TNT and 50 barrels of diesel fuel, I got something we cooked up in demolition school that should work."

"Fifty barrels would be roughly 2,700 gallons. That's a lot of oil, Cassidy."

"Yes, sir. The object is to place the barrels in low places overlooking the valley. If we position one barrel every hundred feet, that's a mile. Ten pounds of TNT for each barrel will blast the oil out quite a ways. Det cord connecting the whole 5,000 feet would make one hell of a hotfoot for Charlie."

"That's only 500 pounds of TNT."

"Yes sir. I'll position our last 500 pounds in a special location to bring down the mountain and blockade the trail."

"By God, that should work! And I know just the place. There's a ridge running parallel to the valley for five, maybe six miles. It has an igneous outcrop below the ridge no more than a hundred feet above the valley floor. And the canyon narrows coming through there."

"Sir, you get me the stuff, and we'll have ourselves one hell of barbecue."

For the next two days Major Abraham had his helicopters ferrying 350-pound barrels of diesel fuel to positions a hundred feet apart along the outcrop. It was tricky flying at times due to the valley winds, and in some places the trees got in the way, but finally the barrels were situated to Catfish's satisfaction. Then First Squad set about placing the charges and stringing the detonation cord between the barrels, with Cassidy running back and forth supervising their efforts.

"This shit better work or we'll end up barbecued our damn selves. Or splattered all over the mountain."

"It'll work. You'll be up on top."

"I think I'll bring that new .50 caliber sniper rifle. We may need it.

That's 1,200 yards from top to bottom. M-14s don't pack enough punch at that range."

"Good idea, Duke."

Enemy troops had closed to within two miles. First Squad was dug in on top of the mountain, waiting. Cassidy was three-quarters of the way down the side of the steep elevation with a plunger box and two hundred feet of electrical cord leading down to his detonator caps inserted in ten bricks of explosives.

At two in the afternoon they spotted the scouts approaching. They were thorough, scanning the elevations with their binoculars, and stopping every ten to twenty meters to search for signs of disturbances in the trees and underbrush along the canyon walls.

It took the scouts nearly thirty minutes to reach the area below Cassidy and his fifty fuel drums. The main column was right behind them, winding back two and a half kilometers. Catfish let about five hundred NVA pass him by, then he raised the handle on the plunger box and rammed it home.

Nothing!

He pulled it up again, pushing down hard with both hands.

Nothing!

"It's always something!"

Down the side of the mountain he went, checking the electrical wire as he descended the steep slope. At the very bottom he found it. A connection had separated. He twisted the wires back together and taped them. Back up the mountain he went, staying as low as possible to avoid detection.

He was twenty meters from his plunger box when the first shots were fired. He felt a bullet whiz past his ear. Determined to engage the enemy regiment, he scrambled on his hands and knees to reach his electrical box.

More shots rang out. Rounds impacted all around him. Then the roar of the .50 caliber on top of the mountain answered the bark of the AK-47s down below. An NVA officer standing out in the open was slammed to the earth with his head blown off. The firing stopped as the enemy soldiers ran for cover. Catfish reached for the handle … the lights went out.

Moments later he came to with blood running in his eyes. Again he heard the roar of the .50 caliber sniper rifle. Calhoun was firing the weapon as fast as he could locate targets through his telescopic sights.

The blood tasted salty. Cassidy was thinking dreamily about his father's experiences in the South Pacific during the war. He wondered how his mother would react if he went home in a metal casket. He missed his mama. There was no pain. He reached up a hand, feeling a groove in the top of his head where his helmet should have been.

The .50 caliber roared again. Duke of Earl! Dudley Calhoun was his blood brother, his comrade of war. If anyone could save him it was his buddy, the fabulous Duke of Earl.

Darkness was gathering, closing in around his peripheral vision. He thought about Henry and Driggins and the rest of First Squad. Everything was moving in slow motion.

Miss Head and Heels came to mind. He wondered if she'd care if he died there on the mountain. She might be on the way to becoming a politician by now. It still bothered him sometimes, thinking about her, but that was a long time ago. Another lifetime. Another world when he was still naïve and just a boy.

He gazed up toward the top of the ridge. Red and Pasamenus were running down the mountainside toward him, their rifles held high to avoid falling down. They appeared to be floating above the rocks and brambles.

Red was yelling. "Blow it! Blow it!"

The .50 caliber spoke again with a terrible finality, echoing back and forth between the canyon walls. It sounded far away.

Catfish reached out a blurry arm, slowly pulling up the plunger handle … night descended … escorting him down a dark empty tomb into the arms of Morpheus.

Chapter Thirty-Five

Silver and Gold

"I dreamed about the cross. And … and the dolphins that talked. And the sergeant. And I think you were in it. Oh, Sam, it frightened me."

"Talking dolphins? The sergeant?"

"Yes. And I'm supposed to pray for them. With my silver cross. Because it's special. Or something. I can't remember. And … and the soldiers from God. And …and … you think I'm crazy, don't you?"

"As a bedbug! Suzie, you've always been crazy. That's why I love you so much."

"Sam, you can't die! Nobody in the world understands me like you do."

"John and I will be looking down on you and Robert, laughing our hinnies off. You are just too precious, Suzie Brown."

"That's what the soldiers called me, 'Suzie Brown.' "

"I'm sure they were nice soldiers or they wouldn't have been in your dream. Now put your robe on and let's go outside."

A full moon shown silver and gold high above the Sea Queen from a dark and distant void. The ocean was dead calm. No clouds. A million stars speckled the Caribbean night. Out a ways from the side of the ship two dolphins were playing together, maintaining pace with the ocean liner. The dolphins resembled sea gods with their silver reflections from the distant moon.

Suzie asked again. "Sam, will you pray with me?"

Samantha slid her arm around Suzie's waist. They stood together at the railing, holding the Buchenwald Cross and gazing out across the silver waters. Suzie asked God to watch over First Squad, to protect them from harm and to bring them home safely, and to help the people of Vietnam. Then she remembered Red.

"Please, God, watch over Billy Kidwell. He's a swell guy and we want him back home with us in Knoxville. I have a swell girlfriend for him to meet. And take care of my Robert. I love him and miss him very much. One more thing, God. Samantha Jackson, my best friend, is coming to see you soon. Please find her and John a nice place to live in Heaven. Thank You, Lord. Amen."

Sam hugged Suzie. "That's the nicest prayer I ever heard."

Suzie held Sam in her arms, eyes closed, head on her shoulder, savoring the glow of their friendship. Suzie would remember the Caribbean night and the dolphins and her friend Samantha the rest of her life.

Next morning they got up bright and early, dressed, and had themselves a glass of orange juice and a cup of coffee. Then they knocked on Miss Martha's door.

"Land sakes, you girls are up early. It's only eight o'clock."

"Time to rise and shine, Miss Martha. Let's go get some breakfast."

Downstairs in the dining hall they spotted Elsa and Karl sitting over by the windows. Elsa held out her arms to Martha and the girls as they approached the table.

"Good morning. Come. Sit with us."

After breakfast and the dishes were cleared away, Elsa turned the subject matter to a more serious venue of conversation. Karl sat beside her resting his elbow on the armrest of her wheelchair, smoking his Marlboros.

"That Nassar! First it was the British. Then the Arabs. Then all kinds of mischief and nonsense. Then the Tiran Straits and that Six Day War. Now he's demanding Israel give back the lands they captured. That silly man's a fool. He's liable to start another war, as if Vietnam isn't bad enough already. The world is run by crazy people. Thank the good Lord for Golda Meir and Moshe Dayan."

Karl spoke. "Yes, it's true. Stupid politicians live in every country. The Jews are alone in the world. No matter what they do, it's always wrong in the eyes of many with the United Nations. Israel must rely on herself and no one else. Not even our United States."

"But I thought we had a treaty in case Israel is attacked."

"We do, indeed. But do you honestly believe the United States would bomb Moscow if the Russian-backed Arab armies overran Israel? And wiped her out? The politicians would make great speeches, and say how terrible it was, and do their protests at the U.N. And that would be the end of it. No. Israel stands alone in the world."

"My goodness. I never imagined such dreadful things."

"My friends, I will tell you something else. Israel is a loyal friend to the United States. Great Britain is a loyal friend too. But Israel more so than any other country stands with America. I tell you this today. As it goes with Israel, so it goes with all of us."

"I'm not sure I follow what you mean."

"If the Muslims overrun Israel, and even if they don't, sooner or later they will turn their hatred of Judaism and Christianity against the West. Many conquests have been attempted over the past fifteen hundred years. With all that's happening in the Middle East today, it's only a matter of time before it starts again."

"Let's go outside and get some fresh air. All this talk of war depresses me."

"A fine suggestion. I apologize for climbing up on my kosher soapbox. See what happens, Elsa, when you talk of such things. I become the crazy one, already."

Suzie spoke. "I'm glad you told us. I'm not educated like you or my friends. I find your conversations very interesting. Where else could I learn this stuff?"

Elsa opined. "Your Robert is a very lucky fellow to have such a *sheynkeyt* like you. Yes, indeed."

"What does that mean?"

"It means, young lady, you are the great beauty. And a smart one too."

"Oh Mister Lieberman, you're making me blush."

They took the elevator down to the main deck to see if the dolphins were still there. The pod had grown. Fifty or more were frolicking in front of the Sea Queen. A smaller pod was off the starboard bow.

"I just love them." Elsa clung to the railing, smiling. "They're such beautiful creatures. I dreamed about them again last night."

Suzie and Samantha looked at Elsa in surprise.

"I did too! I dreamed about the dolphins, and they talked to me."

Elsa sought Karl's hand. "You see, my Karl. It's true the things I tell you."

"What's true?" asked Samantha.

"The cross, my dear. I always believed it had powers. Not the hocus-pocus kind, but powers from above."

Suzie took Elsa's hand and stood beside her wheelchair, gazing out to sea. "They spoke to me last night about God and the Marines. And about Samantha."

Karl interrupted. "Elsa used to tell me she had dreams and visions about the cross. Mostly, it was in the camp. I wanted to believe, but I had my doubts. I thought it was her lack of food or the horrors of her living conditions. Then when she was shot, she told me she had dreamed about being in the hospital weeks before. I brushed it off, to her being hurt so badly. Forgive me, my Elsa, for doubting you."

Elsa smiled, playing the coquette. "It's going to cost you."

"And what might that be, *Mamelah*?" asked Karl.

"A little kiss."

Karl leaned down and kissed Elsa. Martha and Samantha clapped their hands, laughing. Suzie whistled and hugged Karl.

Chapter Thirty-Six

Crispy Critters

Pasamenus lost his footing and tumbled headfirst into the foxhole where Catfish had his plunger box set up, landing on top of both the plunger and Cassidy. Red was right behind him, churning up dust in the loose soil and gravel.

"Is he dead?"

"No. He's out cold, but he looks okay."

A bullet whizzed past. More rounds began striking the rocks around them.

"Let's get this show on the road or we're dead!"

"Red, you do the honors."

"My pleasure, Sergeant Brain, sir."

Red adjusted the plunger box upright, pulled the handle up to its full height, then rammed the handle home.

A half ton of TNT went off in a single earthquaking blast. Boiling fire shot out above the valley floor for a full mile. In their final moments, the terrified soldiers below looked up to see the red death above them. The burning diesel fuel rained down on everything. The valley floor and the canyon walls became a raging inferno. Trees, bushes, men burst into flames. Ammunition and grenades went off. Mortar rounds exploded. The wooden stocks on their weapons, boots, uniforms, everything combustible burned. The horrific screaming resembled the pitiful cries of the damned wailing from the bowels of hell's furnace. Flames roared up two hundred feet into the air. Eighteen hundred men perished, burned to charred corpses in seconds, the flesh cooked from their blazing bodies down to their blackened bones.

Farther up the valley, Catfish had lowered the second 500 pounds of TNT into a crevice where the canyon floor narrowed to two hundred feet across. The blast sent tons of rock crashing down on the forward NVA. A hundred and eighty men disappeared beneath an avalanche of boulders, trees, and earth. The forward section of the valley was sealed off. It would take considerable effort to climb over the debris piled up there.

Four hundred men were still alive at the end of the NVA column. Not knowing if they were next, they panicked and ran like the devil himself was chasing them. Many threw their weapons away, whatever they were carrying, and fled into the jungle. They did not return.

Pasamenus and Red were soon joined by the rest of First Squad. Henry examined the head wound, then applied a Red Cross bandage. They rigged a stretcher with tree limbs, and their fatigue shirts stretched in between. They slid the limbs inside the buttoned shirts, up through the arms, and placed Catfish in the middle.

"Let's get him up top."

It took more than twenty minutes to get Catfish to the top of the mountain. The men kept sliding in the loose dirt and gravel. Below them lay the hideous remains of a once proud North Vietnamese Army regiment. The charred smell resembled burned bacon. Metal stocks and bipods had sagged from the intense heat. All the flesh was burned away from hundreds of skulls, giving them the macabre appearance of laughter.

Driggins commented that the place reminded him of Dante's Inferno.

Tony called it, "Big mother fucker."

"Guys, what the …"

"Fellas, he's awake."

"How ya feelin', Cassidy?"

"My head hurts. Did we get 'em?"

"Son, you blew their asses to Kingdom Come! The ones ain't dead run like scared rabbits. Them oil barrels uh yours were un-by-God-believable. It scared the shit outta us and we were up here on top. There's a army uh crispy critters down below. It ain't no purty sight to look at."

"Am I hurt bad?"

"Not bad. You probably got a concussion, but that's about it. You'll need four or five stitches, though.

Back at Delta X Ray, Major Abraham was throwing a victory celebration. The Hmong tribesmen had gathered out front of the operations tent with Larry Cassidy, Tony, and the rest of First Squad. Lieutenant Butler and Major Abraham were serving cocktails.

The Major held up his hand for quiet. "To the best goddamn outfit in Vietnam! You, Mongs! And you, First Squad! I'm proud of every mother's son of you."

The tribesmen began cheering and toasting First Squad. "Number One! Marines Number One!"

First Squad were yelling and laughing, toasting the tribesmen as good as they got.

"Number One! Mongs Number One!"

"How's your head, Miss Buckingham."

"I'm good. Doc says I'll be ready for duty in a week."

Calhoun turned serious. "You scared me. I thought they got you."

"They probably would have if you hadn't brought that cannon along. Half knocked out, I could still hear that thing every time you pulled the trigger."

"When the stuff blew, the whole sky lit up like the Fourth of July. Red set it off. Him and Sarge got down to you within about a minute of your getting hit. They ran down the side of that steep-ass mountain like two billy goats! You owe your life to those jokers."

"I reckon I do. You too, Duke. Without you and that .50 caliber I'd be toast. We done good, didn't we?"

"Damn sure did. The Major says we've hurt them bad. All three missions."

"I wish this war would turn around so we could go home. Our luck's gonna run out one of these days."

"You remember what it's like back there. Political assholes and all them shit-ass war protesters. Maybe we could ship over for Japan or Australia."

"Hey, I never thought about that."

"Men, come over here a minute. I want you to meet somebody.

"Ly Foung, this is Larry Cassidy. He's the one who built the bomb. This is his sidekick, Dudley Calhoun. Dudley was the man on the .50 caliber. Men, this is Ly Foung. His scouts alerted us the NVA were coming across the river. It didn't take long to figure out they were headed our way. You three are responsible for Delta X Ray still being in business. The others certainly helped, but you three men saved the camp. And for that, I thank you!"

"Larry, Dudley, is honor meeting you. I have story to tell. My tribe, the mountain people, are singing songs honoring you. I think soon you become big heroes in Laos."

"Songs? Honoring us? Hot damn! I'll get me one a them fiddles like those bands use in Austin and Nashville. We'll get the Duke of Earl up on stage with his store-bought harmonica. Johnson pickin' on a steel guitar. Henry strummin' a washboard round his neck. Tony bangin' tha drums. Bubba tootin' a jug and shakin' his tambourine. Red on the eighty-eights. Driggins blowin' a saxophone. First Squad will get so big Jefferson Airplane will get bodacious jealous. Tour the Orient, Japan, Australia, Katmandu. Women'll be throwin' their panties up on stage. Hot Damn, I reckon!"

Calhoun and the older men laughed.

"Don't get too big for your britches. There's always a downside. Hanoi Hannah just upped the ante on our heads to $50,000 apiece. That's the equivalent of a million bucks in dong currency."

"And money to burn! What more could a jarhead ask for?"

Calhoun just shook his head. "That crack on the noggin was worse than we figured. He's gonna need some more stitches to keep out the Big Head!"

"Seriously, men. Don't wander off by yourselves. $50,000 is a fortune here in Indochina."

"We won't, sir. Major, may we have another bottle of that Wild Turkey?"

"Drink all you want, lads. You've by-God earned it!"

Chapter Thirty-Seven

Westmoreland

"'Article II Section 2: The President shall be Commander in Chief of the Army and Navy of the United States.' So states the Constitution regarding civilian control over our Armed Forces. That belief in civilian authority has its limitations. Truman gave away the farm in Korea because his Administration was afraid of the Chinese Communists. General MacArthur wanted to bomb China, but he was sacked by President Truman.

"You mentioned Roosevelt. After declaring war on the Axis powers, he left the fighting to his generals. Eisenhower made a good president. He figured out early on that Congress is full of shit so he turned the CIA loose, then went out and played golf. My favorite twentieth-century leader was Winston Churchill. The man drank too much, he was often rude, and he made mistakes, but the old son of a bitch held Great Britain together when some in Parliament wanted to sue for peace.

"Ambassador Kennedy was recalled by President Roosevelt because he was in league with that crowd of losers. Churchill saved England, and possibly the world. The Germans took a beating at the Battle of Britain. By the time we set up shop in England, the Luftwaffe was stretched pretty thin between our Eighth Air Force and the Eastern Front."

"*The New York Times* reported Tet caught you off guard, General. Would you care to comment on that?"

"*The New York Times* is a biased news organization. They don't report on the big picture, just whatever makes the military look bad. The Tet Offensive was a devastating defeat for Hanoi. Their forces were wiped out. It was sheer desperation on the part of the communist leadership. Tet was a Hail Mary, similar to the Battle of the Bulge."

"But *The Washington Post* said you were preoccupied with Khe Sanh, sir. That's how Tet got started, how our Saigon embassy got overrun."

"Tet was in the planning stages for some time, probably a year or longer. You don't plan something that big on the spur of the moment. It takes months to prepare weapons, supplies and ammunition, troop deployment. The communists were losing every battle they fought. Hanoi needed something spectacular for propaganda purposes."

"But weren't you more concerned over Khe Sanh, sir?"

"I still believe Giap's objective was a second Dien Bien Phu. Otherwise, why did he split his forces before Tet? General Giap could have used his Khe Sanh troops much more effectively around Hue and Saigon. But the Marines didn't see it that way. Neither did our news media or the politicians back home. The antiwar crowd needed a scapegoat. I suppose I'm as good as any. It's a shame the way things turned out. The communists are bleeding troops left and right, but Washington has lost the will to take advantage of the situation. Hanoi will lose a million men, and we'll end up tucking our tail between our legs."

"General, how did General Weyand know the attack was coming?"

"You heard about that, did you?"

"Yes, sir, I read about the General's exploits leading up to Tet."

"Then you know he was an Intelligence officer. General Weyand served in the Burma-India-China Theatre. In Korea he commanded the 1st Battalion, 7th Infantry Regiment. He also taught guerrilla warfare at our Army Infantry School. Fred sensed Tet was coming from the increased radio traffic, and heavy fighting along the Cambodian border, which made no sense from the standpoint of the Vietcong. He convinced me to move a portion of our troops away from the border, back to Saigon and Da Nang. Fred was right about the Tet Offensive. He orchestrated a counterattack at Tan Son Nhut, which broke their back at the airbase.

"One of his role models he often referred to was Russell Volckmann. Volckmann was a West Point graduate, a member of the OSS, and a lieutenant colonel in the Philippines when the Japanese bombed Pearl Harbor. The British warned General MacArthur that the Japs were headed his way, but MacArthur, not being overly fond of the Royal Navy, failed to prepare properly and lost his entire air fleet on the ground.

"The Army fought valiantly, but they were ill-equipped and outgunned by the Japanese. General King finally surrendered the Bataan peninsula to halt the bloodshed. His remaining 75,000 Filipino and American troops were rounded up and herded into makeshift prisoner of war camps. The night before the Bataan Death March, Volckmann and several others slipped out under a fence and disappeared into the jungle.

"Colonel Volckmann and a handful of Army and Navy personnel raised a guerrilla force of some 20,000 soldiers. They fought the Japanese with hit-and-run tactics for three years on the island of Luzon, eventually killing more than 50,000 of the enemy. One of his civilian liaisons was Ferdinand Marcos, who later became president of the

Philippines. Volckmann survived the war, becoming the cofounder of our Army Special Forces. *Back to Bataan* is a Hollywood movie about his exploits."

"Was your belief in large military maneuvers supported by General Weyand?"

"We didn't always see eye to eye on tactics in Vietnam, but he was a loyal officer. I believe in maximum firepower, wearing down the enemy by attrition. That worked in the European Theatre during World War Two, and it worked in Korea. The problem we face today is one of national resolve."

"Sir, do you have any regrets about Tet?"

"A good officer always questions himself. Did I do this right? Could I have done that more efficiently? Might I have saved more lives? The Missing in Action never goes away, not completely. You wonder if the enemy has them. The Vietcong and the NVA are a ruthless bunch of characters.

"One of the things I always fear are the civilian casualties. They usually get the worst of it in a firefight in a populated area. Thousands were injured and killed during Tet. The majority of the Vietnamese are dirt poor. If a breadwinner gets hurt or killed, that leaves the mother and children to fend for themselves. The South Vietnamese Government doesn't help much. They don't look after their people the way we do here in the States. It's more of a country with a military but no real government. Certainly not like our country or South Korea.

"Friendly fire, that's another nightmare. There are no front lines in Vietnam so it's difficult not to make mistakes. We certainly made our share in the jungles.

"The thing I regret the most is the Ho Chi Minh Trail. If I had gotten permission from the Pentagon to position two or three divisions across the Trail, the Vietcong and North Vietnamese Army would have run out of guns and supplies in three or four weeks. You hear the argument, they would just move the Trail farther West into Laos.

They could do that, but how long would it take to cut another trail for all those trucks and bicycles through hundreds of miles of jungle? No, they would run out of rice and ammunition long before then and sue for peace. It wouldn't last, but maybe by then we'd have a more resilient group of politicians on Capitol Hill."

The Stars and Stripes reporter had saved his best question for last. It was an impertinent question by military standards, but Albert Gore wanted to make a name for himself once he left the service and entered his father's political arena of power and privilege.

"General Westmoreland, how do you rate the performance of President Johnson as your Commander in Chief?"

Westmoreland gazed across his desk at the young man, recalling his own brashness when he graduated First Captain from West Point in 1936. Wondering too how far this aggressive individual might ascend in the jaded atmosphere of Washington politics?

"President Johnson was a fair-minded commander. He did the best he could with what he had to work with in Washington. As you know, a president has many advisors he relies on for making decisions. His job is no different from a commander in the field who has his captains and lieutenants to assist him.

"The president and I disagreed on certain issues, but that's normal under the best of circumstances. He appointed me his Army Chief of Staff and for that I'm grateful."

"But, sir, you said Washington is losing the war. Doesn't that mean President Johnson?"

"President Johnson had his hands full with the Great Society, Vietnam, and all those obnoxious war protestors, not to mention his own rebellious political party. The next president will inherit all of that and then some. I rate his performance as satisfactory."

Gore sat staring at his notepad. It wasn't much of an interview, certainly not what he had hoped for. No smoking gun. No Walter Cronkite. At least he had been granted the interview. That was more than anyone else had gotten since the General returned home from Vietnam.

Albert smiled, remembering how he had manipulated the university system, then used his father's political influence to get himself assigned to *The Stars and Stripes*, after he volunteered for Vietnam. Gore soon discovered he hated Vietnam, so Pop got him reassigned back stateside to Washington. What a hoot, he thought. The babes on Capitol Hill were coming out of the woodwork.

General Westmoreland didn't like the reporter, but had been told the bright young man had political connections so he acquiesced for the interview. What an arrogant ass, he thought to himself. Too many of the offspring of political families were a species unto themselves in the make-believe world of Washington politics.

"Thank you for your time, General. I appreciate the interview."

"Any time, young man. Good luck to you."

Westmoreland sat staring at the office door after the reporter closed it on his way out. Wouldn't he like to know the truth? he thought in silence. That would blow the lid off the White House, the Pentagon, Congress, and all those corrupt Saigon generals skimming the dong off their soldiers' pay.

LBJ is losing the war because he's afraid of China. Harry Truman did the same damn thing in Korea. We should expand the war into North Vietnam, bomb Hanoi and Haiphong, and blockade the Trail. McNamara damn near shit his pants over my proposals. Now they've kicked me upstairs as Army Chief of Staff.

General Abrams is stuck with it now. He'll find out soon enough that these politicians have no stomach for fighting wars. It's all bluster and bullshit, like that Henry Kissinger blowhard. They all want the quick fix. That new Secretary of Defense, Clark Clifford, is worse than McNamara. Another political windbag, like Eugene McCarthy and George McGovern. None of those civilians are qualified for military command.

The telephone rang. Katherine informed Westy they were invited to a dinner party at a prominent politician's home at seven-thirty sharp. It was nearly six o'clock. He would have to hurry. He showered and changed uniforms, then a Secret Service agent drove him to pick up Kitsy. It was exactly seven-and-a-half bells when they arrived at the Washington address. William Westmoreland adjusted his tie, then pressed the doorbell. Soft music was heard coming from inside. The door opened and there stood Richard Milhouse Nixon.

Chapter Thirty-Eight

Mister Ca Dung

"I shit you not. It's called *Hair*, and they dance around naked."

"Where'd you hear that shit?"

"Shorty told me. His girlfriend lives in New York. She went to see it."

"That's crazy. It's got to be against the law." Red was perplexed. "Brain, what do you think?"

"Apparently, that sort of thing has been going on for some time now. Hollywood too from what I've been reading. They get around the censors by claiming their work is 'artistic.' I believe the porno industry claims the same type exemption."

First Squad was through for the day, sitting around two picnic tables beside the airfield overlooking the river. The sun was going down, painting the western sky with flaming hues of crimson, lavender, and purple. Down below, the treetops glowed pale blue with St Elmo's Fire from an electrical charge in the atmosphere. The river was calm and misty green, and for once the monkeys and birds had fallen silent. "'Red sky at night. Sailor's delight.'"

"Naked on Broadway, huh? I don't know 'bout that shit. Next thing you know, they'll be doin' the nasty on stage."

"Red, I hate to inform you …"

"Don't tell me! They do it under them stage lights like crazed weasels?"

"Yes, they do. New York, Chicago, San Francisco"

"Shit, Miss Agnes! Them assholes is gettin' paid for gettin' poon-tang while we're out here bustin' our chops savin' the world. I need me a transfer to Broadway."

"Red, you wouldn't like it there. Half the men are queer."

"What are the women like?"

"Hot, juicy, and willing."

"I'll take my chances!"

The men were still laughing when Major Abraham approached to address them. There was no saluting at Delta X Ray. Enemy eyes might be watching. VC snipers had killed a number of American officers throughout South Vietnam.

"Men, I'm going to send scout planes out in the morning to recon the area between here and the river. Make sure we got no more of Red's commie rat bastards hanging around. You can go with them if you'd like. I'll have them fly over the Trail so you can get some perspective from the air of what we're dealing with."

Red and the others readily agreed. It would be an adventure seeing Delta X Ray from the air, as well as part of the Ho Chi Minh Trail. Everyone liked to fly except Johnson. Airplane interiors made him claustrophobic, but he wasn't about to get left behind. The others would rag his ass till the cows came home.

They turned in early that night and were up at first light. It was Saturday, not a cloud in the sky. The monkeys and parrots were busy discussing last night's adventures. Major Abraham walked them out to the end of the field where two Pilatus PC-6s were warming up. Known as the Porter, they were rugged eight-seat civilian aircraft noted for short takeoffs and landings.

First Squad carried their M-14 assault rifles. Tony had his German sniper rifle plus two satchels of grenades. Henry was in charge of the First Aid supplies. Johnson carried two bags of extra magazines.

The pilots flew in formation forty meters apart. As they approached the valley where Cassidy had set up his fuel oil ambush, Bubba asked Shorty a question. He was referring to an unusual sight up ahead.

"What's all them birds up there?"

"Mostly buzzards and crows. But you got a little bit of everything mixed in."

"What are they doing?"

"When you guys wasted all those NVA, you left enough chow behind to feed the locals for a month."

"You mean they're feeding?"

"Commie steak tartare. The crows tell me it's delicious."

"Holy shit!"

"I'll fly over so you can see."

Down below they spotted a tiger, two black bears, several smaller animals, and thousands of birds of every variety and color. Eagles, vultures, ravens, the ground appeared to move with their fluttering about. What looked like white sticks were human bones.

"I didn't think bears and tigers got along."

"They don't. But with all that breakfast, lunch, and dinner down there they get along fine. When it runs out they'll turn badass again. Can you smell it?"

"Yeah. Smells like somebody went and burned it."

"I'll fly to the end of the valley, then take a northwest heading. There's something out there I want you to see."

They flew on another forty kilometers, passing over thick jungle, streams and trails leading down to the river. It was all jade green and very beautiful. Some of the trees rose up more than two hundred feet beneath them. The jungle held a special fascination for Johnson who played among Alabama's coastal oaks and yellow pines as a boy.

Shorty pointed his finger. "There it is."

"Oh, wow!"

Down below an ancient temple rose up, surrounded by dense forest. There was a walled courtyard with several outbuildings. The temple itself looked to be six or seven stories high. The floor of the courtyard was covered with rectangular slabs of rock. Here and there saplings had sprouted up between the sections and grown into trees. The temple stone was pale gray, covered with moss and vines from centuries past.

The pilots circled once, then flew east.

"Down there. What's that?"

"Farmers. Villagers. Charlie carries rifles."

They flew on another ten minutes when a sampan appeared.

"They eke out a living trading fish for rice, salt, and vegetables. Those people live a very simple life. I met some of them when I went down in here a year ago. They fed me, gave me a warm blanket. The major found me next day. He gave them $150. You should have seen their faces. I never seen people so happy my whole life. That $150 must have been two years wages for that village."

"What made you crash?"

"Engine quit. Gunk in the fuel line."

"You didn't get hurt?"

"Big knot on my head. They put some kind a herbs on me.

It healed up in a couple uh days."

"That's something. I bet they live happier lives than most people around this screwed-up world."

"Maybe so. The Trail starts up there. See that mountain poking up through the clouds? There's a river down below. That's just part of the Trail. It's ten or twelve miles across in places."

They flew out over the Ho Chi Minh Trail, then turned south.

"Down there! I see a truck."

"You'll see all kinda stuff today. Little guys like us don't spook 'em none. It's the jet fighters and fighter bombers that get their attention. Then they start shooting with everything but the kitchen sink. Most of the time you don't see anything but trees."

"You think there's many of 'em down there?"

"Major says it's like Grand Central Station. Ever' day they got thousands uh laborers and engineers working on the roads to keep things moving along. And thousands more lugging food, medical supplies, ammunition, everything Charlie needs to make a war."

"Don't we bomb the Trail a lot?"

"All the time. The Major says about a third of their stuff gets through.

The Trail is one big-ass graveyard. Thousands of people are buried down there."

They flew on another five kilometers when they came across a truck stuck in the middle of a wooden bridge over a broad creek. Coolies were prying at the wheels with bamboo poles. One of the wheels had broken through the planking.

"That sumbitch is loaded with somethin' heavy or he wouldn't be stuck that way. Wanna fly low and see if we can bust a few tires?"

Shorty laughed. "You fuckers never quit, do you? I'll make one pass if one of you can slide the door open. I'll come in from the east so they'll be looking up in the sun."

Shorty swung around past the end of the bridge, making his run at full throttle. Johnson slid the door back, with Bubba holding onto Red's web belt with both hands.

Red's magazine held fifteen rounds, five of which were tracer bullets. One of the tracers struck a 122mm artillery shell, and the whole load of ammunition exploded like a miniature A Bomb. The Porter was hurled sideways, with Johnson and Bubba hanging onto Red for dear life, who was two-thirds out the door. Calhoun got hold of his boots and the three of them hauled him back inside.

"Men, we got ourselves a problem! Get strapped in. We caught some of it when that thing blew. Look outside and see if you can find the damage."

"There's a hole in the wing about the size of a football."

"That wouldn't cause this yawing. Keep looking."

"I see it. Part of the tail section is gone."

"That hole in the wing? Is anything leaking out?"

"Yeah, looks like gasoline."

"How bad?"

"Like a garden hose. Do we have enough to get back?"

"Not likely. The Major's gonna kill me for this!" Shorty engaged his headset. "Mayday! Mayday! Mayday! Kansas City, this is Ruptured Duck. We've taken shrapnel and are losing fuel. Will not … repeat … will not rendezvous home base. Request pickup."

The second aircraft chimed in.

"This is your upstairs neighbor, Backwater Billy. What's your fuel situation?"

"Forty percent and leaking like gran'pappy's lip. I estimate about twenty minutes."

"Head for the river. They got plenty of sandbars there. Shallow water is pale green. Pale green, Duck Man."

"Ruptured Duck, this is Kansas City. What the hell is going on out there?" Major Abraham was not happy.

"My fault, Kansas City. We're going down."

"Anybody hurt?"

"No, sir. Twenty minutes flying time remaining. I'm heading for the river."

"Good luck. We're on the way."

"When we start down, pull your seatbelts up as tight as you can, and hold your feet up off the floor when we land. Secure those sacks of ammo and your weapons. The minute we're down, release your belts and get out."

They flew on another ten minutes until they saw the river. From 2,000 feet it looked like a long green snake coiling through the jungle. The pilots turned north along the channel in the direction of Delta X Ray. Hank flew alongside. Tony was looking across at them, giving them a thumbs-up. Henry and Driggins just stared through the window glass with concerned expressions on their faces. Pasamenus waved goodbye as they descended below five hundred feet. Bubba sat wondering if this really was goodbye.

"Look for a sandbar, any level place to land."

The engine began backfiring.

"Tighten your seat belts, tight as you can."

The motor labored and quit. Shorty put them into a shallow dive toward the surface of the river.

"Up ahead. That looks like a spot. Hold on tight! The plane may flip when we touch down. Remember to release your belts when we stop moving."

Johnson's life was flashing before his eyes. The Gulf of Mexico appeared that time the undertow got him, and his mother swam out with an inner tube and pulled him back in. Then the hay wagon pulled out in front of him on the old highway, and he ran through Mister Green's tobacco patch with his mother's Buick. And his sophomore year when that big fullback from Fairhope landed on top of him and broke his index finger. Old memories flooded his mind until Firebase Hansel appeared, with all the gunfire and screaming, and stacking dead men like cordwood. Marcus was reliving the mountain and the B-52 bombing attack when Shorty sang out again.

"Here it comes! Hold on!"

The Porter struck the edge of the sandbar at seventy miles an hour, bounced high in the air, coming down hard on the far side, shearing off the wheels and throwing up a huge spray as they plowed into the river.

"Get out! Get to the bank. They got crocs in these waters."

Johnson didn't need any encouraging. Flying always made him nervous. That plane ride was the icing on his by-God cake. Catfish had a bloody nose. Shorty had sustained another bump on his noggin. All in all, they were lucky nobody was seriously injured.

Once onshore, Red took over. "Check your weapons, men. Sling your bandoliers. No talking. We don't know what's out there. Lock and load."

Shorty was amazed at how disciplined they became for Red.

Onboard the PC-6 they were all grab-ass and laughter. Now they struck him as machinelike, something the Vietcong should fear.

"Come on, Shorty. We'll wait back in the trees. Hank's up there circling. The Major will find us."

They had just gotten themselves settled when two villagers came walking down the bank of the river. It was obvious from their excited gestures that they had seen the plane go down. Then half a dozen more appeared behind them. An old villager with long white hair was leading the way, carrying a walking staff taller than he was.

Before Red could stop him, Shorty ran out from their hiding place, yelling. "Ca Dung! It's me, Shorty!"

"Shorty! You crazy man. You wreck again?"

"I can't fly worth a damn. I need you to teach me."

"I teach. I teach you stay on ground where safe."

They embraced, laughing.

"I happy see you. Long time. Much bad happen."

"What's bad, my friend?"

"Bad men come. Take young boys. Make fight in war. Boys here we hide. Bad men come two moons."

"How do you know that?"

"Bad men upriver. Two moons they come."

Red interrupted. "How many bad men?"

The old man held up both hands with his fingers extended. "Ten bad. Take four boys."

"Ten! What kind of weapons do they have?"

"Long guns, like you."

"Ten commie rat bastards with AK-47s. Sounds like a full squad."

Shorty introduced the Marines to Ca Dung and his jungle companions. They were teenagers. The youngsters wore loincloths and carried bamboo spears for catching fish. Each carried a pouch over his shoulder constructed from tree bark and tiny grape vines.

Calhoun motioned Red away from the group. "Why don't we hang around a few days and waste them dirt bags?"

"Sounds good to me. Let's see what the Major has to allow."

Major Abraham gave Shorty a Class A chewing out, calling him an irresponsible bush pilot wannabe, plus a dozen other descriptive nouns. Finally he slapped Shorty on the shoulder, telling him he was the best damn pilot he had, and didn't want him getting his dumb ass killed.

Then he chewed on the Marines a spell before smiling and asking, "Who blew up the goddamn truck?"

Red confessed, then informed the Major about the Vietcong upriver. "Sir, the old chief and his people got a problem." Red outlined Calhoun's suggestion for the Major.

"Mister Ca Dung, do you remember when I came to pick up Shorty?"

"I remember. You good man, help village."

"We can solve your problem, but others will come looking for their commie pals. What about your womenfolk? What will you do then?"

The old man consulted with his tribesmen. A spirited discussion ensued. The younger men kept pointing toward the Major. Finally the old chief came over and stood before Abraham.

"We come live with you."

The Major stepped away, consulting with Red and his Marines for several moments, finally nodding his head.

"All right, it's settled. I'm going upriver with these jarheads. AJ, Lefty, disengage your M-60s and come with us. Paul, you take these youngsters back to base. Shorty, you go with Paul. I want you, Paul, and Carl to fly three choppers back when we're ready. Wait for my call on the radio. We'll be upriver about two clicks. Calhoun, Cassidy, get those extra ammo boxes off the chopper. Mister Ca Dung, you lead the way."

The journey upriver was almost magical had it not been of such a serious nature. Mangrove trees, evergreens, tall teakwood trees, giant strangler figs, and pink and white flowers adorned the riverbank. Fronds, plumeria, hanging vines, orchids, and butterflies, thousands of pretty butterflies. Lizards, snakes, turtles, and rock rats made the jungle setting complete. And always the jabbering monkeys.

A mile and a half upstream they arrived at the village. Major Abraham performed a headcount. Seven young village girls, two grannies, one old grandfather, two children, and two more adult males. Ca Dung and his companion made a total of sixteen. The Major instructed Calhoun and Cassidy to continue upriver another mile and wait there. They were to report back the minute they spotted any enemy activity. First Squad settled in, digging foxholes and cleaning their weapons. The villagers fed them, sentries were posted, then those men not assigned guard duty bedded down for the night.

The first twenty-four hours were nothing to write home about. The villagers went about their daily routines, tending their gardens, fishing, looking after the youngsters, and preparing meals. The second night started off well enough.

0330 hours: "Sir, they're about half a mile behind us."

"How many?"

"Ten. I counted 'em twice."

"Weapons?"

"AK-47s."

The villagers were quietly rounded up and sent downriver out of harm's way. First Squad built up the fire, then spread out to prearranged positions. Major Abraham sat down before the fire with his back facing north, wearing a coolie hat with a blanket pulled round his shoulders. AJ and Lefty waited on the east side of the compound with their machine guns.

The VC leader walked into the clearing accompanied by his nine Vietcong guerrillas. They trampled through the manicured gardens in front of the northernmost huts. Red was inside the first hut with Vera Lynn. Bubba was in the second hooch on the same side of the compound. Johnson, Calhoun, and Cassidy were just below them in foxholes, beside AJ and Lefty.

"Old man! Wake up!"

Major Abraham raised an arm in the air and waved, dismissively.

"You get up now, old man! We come for boys! GET UP!"

Again Major Abraham waved him off.

The leader became furious, not accustomed to a common villager showing such disrespect.

"Get up, old man. Get up now or YOU DIE!"

Major Abraham rose to his feet, slowly turning around, and shot the leader in the face with his .45 automatic. Two M-60 machine guns, four M-14 assault rifles, and a Thompson submachine gun hurled copper-jacketed whupass at the scrambling intruders. Only one made it back to the edge of the clearing. He died there, shot through and through with armor-piercing rounds. The others lay in a bloody pile behind their wounded spokesman. The man watched in disbelief as the Major dropped the blanket from his shoulders.

"Not exactly what you expected, eh, Rice Ball?"

The man tried to speak, to plead for his life, but his lower jaw was shattered from the .45 caliber slug. All Comrade Badass managed to get out was a bloody gurgle. As is often the case when one faces death, his life passed before his eyes. He remembered the villagers he had killed. Some of them wept and begged. Others cursed him before he shot them.

His mental tapes as a young communist guerrilla were still running when the major shot him through the heart.

"Drag this trash to the river. Crocodiles got to eat, too. Throw their weapons out where it's deep. Lefty, you and Cassidy go round up the villagers. Red, you and the others search the bodies before you throw them in. Look for maps, anything that looks official."

AJ spoke up. "I never shot nobody up close before."

Johnson laughed. "You shoulda been with us last month. We killed a trainload uh these suckers."

"Say, where you from?"

"Alabama."

"I thought I recognized that cornpone twang. My gran'maw lives in Mobile."

"No shit! My mama lives in Magnolia Springs."

"Well, shut my mouth!"

Johnson and AJ heehawed. Calhoun stopped work to listen, smiling at his fellow Southerners.

Red spoke up. "Get with the program, you goldbricks. Ever commie rat bastard for five miles heard our guns. Check their pockets, then get 'em in the river. We gotta clear outta here soon as Ca Dung and his people get their shit together."

Cassidy and Lefty returned with the villagers in tow.

Major Abraham addressed them. "Mister Ca Dung, gather up everything you intend to keep. Nothing heavy, no furniture, just your personal belongings. Be ready to move out in fifteen minutes."

"Major, we much happy. You good man."

"Thank you, ole timer. Now get a move on."

Red approached the Major with a handful of papers. "Maps, sir. I don't know what else."

"You may have something there, Red. Where's the radio?"

"We left it in the second hooch. Want me to call the choppers?"

"Yes. Tell them to meet us in forty-five minutes. No, wait. We got old folks. We'll have to help them carry their stuff. Tell Floyd one hour at the crash site. Ask for a Skyraider in case we attract trouble."

The scenery back to the downed Porter was the same tropical wonder as their journey upriver two days earlier. A herd of spotted deer watched as they made their way through a stand of rubber trees. Out in the river a herd of elephants were bathing their little ones. Excited monkeys in the overhead branches gave away a king cobra. Grandfather shooed it away with his walking stick. They were almost to the crash site when Red and Bubba came running down the trail.

"Major, something strange is going on. We saw troop movement all over the top of the ridge."

"Get on the horn and tell Floyd to arm all the Skyraiders. Ask him to call Charlie Tango and request their B-26 Marauders. We been hunting those jokers for weeks now. Looks like you just found Uncle Ho's lost Battalion, the 77th Infantry."

Minutes later Shorty arrived overhead with two Huey escorts. Shorty was flying the HU-1 with a 20mm antiaircraft gun, vintage

World War Two, mounted in the starboard doorway. The metal decking had been reinforced to accommodate the extra weight and vibration from the weapon.

"Major, you got the whole enchilada coming your way about a mile upriver. You better get out of there, pronto. Skyraiders will be here in fifteen minutes. Bombers in half an hour."

"You done good, Shorty. Come on down."

Ten minutes on the ground, and the villagers plus First Squad were loaded and airborne. The Major sent the sixteen Vietnamese accompanied by his two door gunners back to Delta X Ray. He stayed with Shorty and his Marines to coordinate the incoming flights.

"Dragon Lady, this is Love Potion Number Nine. We have liquid refreshments for your party guests. The main entrée is right behind us. Are you clear of the target area?"

"Angels 3,000, two clicks east of the village. Cap the bastards!"

Five Skyraiders appeared from the west, peeling off one by one against the ant-size targets on the ground. The Number One fighter-bomber released his twin canisters into a group of North Vietnamese Army regulars running along the riverbank. The napalm exploded with a flash, covering the length of a football field. They fled into the river, on fire. Number Two aircraft made his bombing run on the village where more NVA were spotted hiding among the thatch huts. A dozen more unfortunates suffered the lethal embrace of the jellied gasoline. Three and Four made their napalm attacks up the trail amid a barrage of small arms fire erupting from the jungle floor. Number Five was starting his run when a missile came streaking out of the trees and blasted a five-foot section off his starboard wing.

"Get outta there! They got Strelas!"

Trailing a plume of black smoke, the pilot headed out over the jungle toward base. Shorty and the men watched in grim silence as he fought to gain altitude. The aircraft rose skyward for several moments, shuddered, rolled off to his left, and started down. With flames bellowing from a ruptured fuel tank and out of control, the pilot bailed out. He was too close to the ground.

"Goddamnit! That tears it! Shorty, hold position at 3,000 meters from the spot that missile came up. Fuck those gook sons a bitches. Strelas don't have the range!"

"Aye, aye, sir."

A missile came streaking out of the trees toward the Huey helicopter. It ran short, spiraling down into the jungle. A second missile was fired. It came within five hundred meters, fishtailing down into the green canopy below.

"Who's your best shot, Red."

"Calhoun, sir. He's better than me or Bubba."

"Son, think you can waste that patch a trees down there?"

"Sir, I'll have to dope it first."

Calhoun pulled the trigger to get a feel for the weapon. It roared automatic fire, belching smoke and flame.

"Man, I like this thing!"

"See if you can manage some payback for Roberto."

His first burst was high, passing well above the intended target. Calhoun adjusted the gun sights, then fired again. Still high. Another adjustment. His third burst went directly into the foliage.

"Send 'em to hell, Marine!"

With Johnson and Cassidy feeding a 20mm ammunition train, Calhoun held the trigger down. Shell casings clattered around the floor, rolling out both doors. A steady stream of tracer fire impacted all through the dark patch of trees. The foliage began disintegrating, white smoke billowed up, flames broke out on the ground, followed by secondary explosions. Calhoun fired another long burst, then swept the area with the remainder of his ammunition belt. Another explosion. An orange fireball came boiling up through the smoking canopy.

"That cooked their goose. Shorty, let's go find Roberto."

Down on the deck they located their pilot, dangling from a tree limb in his parachute harness, out cold but still alive. His left leg was broken, plus he had numerous cuts and scratches, but the tree branches and a tangle of grape vines had broken his plunge to earth. Henry was sticking Roberto with morphine when Roberto opened his one good eye, the left one was swollen shut, exclaiming that Major Abraham was the most beautiful Redskin sumbitch he had ever laid eyes on.

Major Abraham laughed, calling him "a Wop spaghetti snapper from Hoboken."

"I hate they're dropping bombs on the animals. They don't deserve that shit." Red turned away from the planes, remembering their poisoned pussycat, Boots, and the burning fuel drums in the valley. In his mind he could still smell the bodies cooking. Bile rose in his throat, the way it had that day at the mountain when he shot the young NVA in the back. Tremors in his hands had become worse, and for the second time, ever since John and Gunny were killed, he thought that coming to Vietnam had been a mistake.

Four miles away, they could feel the ground quaking from the bomb blasts raining down on the 77th Infantry Battalion from Charlie Tango's B-26 squadron. They watched as the 500 pounders sent columns of black smoke rising high in a clear aquamarine sky. It had been a successful day in the Laotian air war against communism in Southeast Asia.

Only one elephant was killed, a baby female burned to death by the jellied gasoline.

Chapter Thirty-Nine

Buchenwald

"Do you miss Israel?"

"I sometimes miss it. The struggles we went through. Our many friends who died there. We worked wonders, didn't we, Karl?"

"Yes, Elsa. I miss the old days. We were so young and full of ourselves then. We did things people can't imagine today."

"You were my hero, Karl."

"You were the brave one, *Mamelah*, carrying the radio and our medical kit. And that British revolver you favored. When they shot you I thought I would die too. I still have my nightmares, that British machine gun, you bleeding, me pulling you through the sand."

"I don't recall much of that."

"Zack was shot when we were crossing through the wire. I carried you in my arms that last hundred yards. He knew where the gun emplacements were. Without him we would have died out there. Zack saved us both."

"I remember coming to and each of you were beside me. There were a million stars in the sky that night, and I could smell the bell-flowers. After that I remember nothing until I woke up in the hospital room. You were there, my *Tatelah.* "

"I wish I could have been more gentle with you. I fell down several times bringing you out. I blame myself for the wheelchair."

"Nonsense! You saved me. That was enough. We have a good life together, Karl."

"Yes, Elsa, better than I deserve. The men I killed, I dream about them too."

"You're a good man, Karl. A good husband. I read about your dreams in my psychology books. It's normal to dream about tragic events. Suzie said something about that. She said her Marines are troubled with nightmares."

"Suzie is a wonderful girl. She makes me laugh. They're all rather grand, aren't they?"

"Suzie and Samantha are almost like our daughters. They're good girls. And Miss Martha is a sweet lady."

"Do you suppose we should do something for them?"

"When the time comes, yes. You make me proud, *Tatelah.*"

"I love you very much."

"Take me to bed, Karl. Make love to Elsa."

Next morning Elsa and Karl met Miss Martha and the girls for breakfast. A squall was brewing up from the south, causing the ocean swells to crest with whitecaps. They watched as the storm approached, finally lashing against the window panes. Lightning danced about the Sea Queen, surrounding them with rolling claps of thunder.

"Goodness gracious! This reminds me of a storm we had in the camp. The wind was blowing so hard it took the roof off the barracks next to mine."

"Tell us about the camp, Elsa. I never knew such a place existed."

"Are you sure you want to hear such dreadful things?"

"Well, sort of. I think it's something we should know about."

"Tell them, Elsa. The Nazis weren't that different in the 1940s than some of the Arab states today."

"Very well, I will share with you some of those events I can remember. The words *Jedem das Seive* were hung on the front gates. That translates, 'To Each His Own.' What it meant, literally, we deserved our fate. Buchenwald sat on the side of a hill surrounded by miles of barb wire fencing near the town of Weimar, Germany. The fence was charged with electricity. Some prisoners chose electrocution rather than suffer any longer. They threw themselves into the wire fence.

The countryside outside the compound was quite lovely. Tall pines and oak trees. And beautiful green meadows. The camp itself smelled like nothing I can describe in words. It was disease and death and human waste and burning bodies. It's strange the way a person looks after they've starved to death. The skin stretches tightly over nothing but bones, and they have a yellow or brownish waxlike appearance. And we were all covered with lice, making life all the more miserable.

"The Germans fed us once a day, usually a watery cabbage soup with cabbage worms floating on top. And a piece of brown bread cooked with sawdust. And sometimes scraps from the kitchen that nobody wanted. Hunger is a cruel companion. A starving prisoner would do anything for half a loaf of bread. The *kapo* in charge of my barracks used to torment me with slices of cheese and bratwurst. Finally, I did anything he asked me."

Karl held Elsa's hand while she told her story.

"There were two large ovens with three doors attached to each oven. A basement underneath the crematorium was used as a killing room. Then the bodies were raised on a hand lift for the ovens. Toward the very end they were burning two and three hundred bodies a day. With the Americans getting closer, the Germans resorted to clubs and shooting the prisoners. Many starved. Thousands more were marched away to a sub-camp deeper in Germany. I escaped by hiding under my barracks.

"There was one young woman who refused the advances of an SS officer. She was quite attractive with pretty blonde hair. The Nazis dragged her away to the ovens and threw her inside, alive. My *kapo* delighted in telling me how she screamed and clawed at the over door while she burned. I heard they did the same thing to some of the Russian prisoners.

"This was the camp where Elsa Koch, the Bitch of Buchenwald, became notorious for having lampshades made from human skin. She was a horribly vain woman who flaunted her sexuality all over the compound. Her husband was the commandant who was later executed by the Nazis.

"I remember the night my friend Gertrude died. We worked in one of the armaments plants together. She was a cabaret singer and very beautiful. They came for her around midnight. They were all drunk. Later, when they brought her back, she told me she had lost count after eleven of them raped her. Gertrude was a fragile young woman. I held her in my arms while she died from shock and I don't know what else. I took her confession. We did things like that for each other. There was no one else to look after us or give a prisoner the last rites. I could tell you more, but that's enough for today. It troubles me to talk about these things too often."

Samantha and Suzie sat in silence. Even Martha was at a loss for words.

Karl spoke to break the somber atmosphere. "That was an age some twenty-five years ago that cost the lives of 60,000,000 people. The Old World was swept away. The United Nations came into being. Israel was born. Our United States became the light at the end of the tunnel. Now we have the Cold War and Vietnam. I'm truly sorry about your husband, Samantha. "

Suzie responded. "It makes me feel small, knowing all that happened right before I was born."

Martha noticed Sam holding her side. "What's wrong, baby?"

"Mama, it hurts."

Mister Lieberman strode quickly to the telephone on the wall. "Get me the ship's doctor. This is an emergency!"

Chapter Forty

Star of David

Israel

"By the spring of 1967, Nasser's waning popularity, escalating Syrian-Israeli tensions, and the emergence of Levi Eshkol as prime minister of Israel set the stage for the third Arab-Israeli war.

"On April 6, 1967, Israeli jets shot down six Syrian planes over the Golan Heights, which led to a further escalation of Israeli-Syrian tensions. The Soviet Union, wanting to involve Egypt as a deterrent to an Israeli initiative against Syria, misinformed Nasser on May 13 that the Israelis were planning to attack Syria on May 17 and that they had already concentrated eleven to thirteen brigades on the Syrian border for this purpose.

"In response Nasser put his forces in a state of maximum alert, sent combat troops to the Sinai, and announced the closing of the Strait of Tiran.

"In Israel, Eshkol's diplomatic waiting game and Nasser's threatening rhetoric created a somber mood. To reassure the public, Moshe

Dayan, the hero of the 1956 Sinai Campaign, was appointed minister of defense, and a National Unity Government was formed.

"The actual fighting was almost over before it began; the Israeli Air Corps on June 5 destroyed nearly the entire Egyptian Air Force on the ground. King Hussein of Jordan, misinformed by Nasser about Egyptian losses, authorized Jordanian artillery fire on Jerusalem. Subsequently, both the Jordanians in the east and the Syrians in the north were quickly defeated."

"The June 1967 War was a watershed event in the history of Israel and the Middle East. After only six days of fighting, Israel had radically altered the political map of the region. By June 13, Israeli forces had captured the Golan Heights from Syria, Sinai and the Gaza Strip from Egypt, and all of Jerusalem and the West Bank from Jordan. The new territories more than doubled the size of pre-1967 Israel, placing under Israel's control more than one million Palestinian Arabs." (U.S. Library of Congress)

January-February 1968: The Tet Offensive sweeps South Vietnam. Uncle Sam and his allies are caught with their pants down. The US begins shifting most of her air attacks from North Vietnam into Laos. North Korea seizes the USS Peublo with 83 crewmen onboard. LBJ orders 14,787 Army Reservists to active duty. Rumania walks out of the International Communist Congress in protest against Soviet tactics. The world media reports the Tet Offensive as a massive victory for the Communists. US sends 10,500 more combat troops. Israelis deploy fighter jets in a daylong battle with the Jordanians. Republican Senator Jacob Javits calls a military victory in Vietnam "illusionary." The United Nations condemns Israel for her raids on Jordan.

Ever since the Holocaust when those Jews who survived Hitler's gas chambers and his ovens were given a piece of desert in Palestine by the United Nations, war against Israel had become a permanent fixture on the Arab agenda. The Jews transformed their sandy strip of wasteland into a Garden of Eden, and they were hated for doing so. They produced a thriving economy and they were despised for that accomplishment. Most importantly, they established themselves as the preeminent military power in the region in order to survive the repeated Arab attacks, yet they are condemned like no other country or race, before or since, simply because they are Jewish.

Chapter Forty-One

Lost Highway

The doctor gave Samantha a shot and put her to bed in Martha's room. Sam was asleep in minutes. He gave Miss Martha a box of morphine tablets for Samantha, instructing her not more than one every four hours. Suzie was upset so he gave her a pill to calm her down. Elsa and Karl had seen all manner of suffering in Europe and the Middle East so they stayed with the women to talk and make things easier for Suzie and Miss Martha. It was a vigil none of them had expected so soon.

"I never dreamed this might happen. Children are supposed to outlive their parents." Martha was grieving, but had resigned herself weeks earlier to Sam's fate.

Suzie began to cry. "Oh, Martha, what are we going to do?"

"There, there, now. We all knew this was coming someday."

Elsa took Suzie's and Martha's hands. "The woman we love is preparing to be with God. I'll venture to say it's a darn sight better place than down here with us. Samantha is a brave girl. She's going to be with her John soon, and that's as it should be."

Suzie wiped away her tears and blew her nose. "I'd forgotten about that. I guess it's selfish of me crying like this."

Martha patted Elsa's hand. "I'm glad you're here, Elsa."

Karl spoke. "We'll stay as long as you need us. I suggest we take turns sitting with Samantha. That way at least you can lie down and rest."

"I believe some hot tea is in order, Karl. Ask the attendant to bring us a pot of herb or spiced tea. Hot, please, with fresh milk and honey."

Elsa was in her element, reminiscent of running guns in the desert long ago. The attendant brought the tea and left. Elsa poured. Karl declined, smoking his Marlboros instead. Samantha moaned in her sleep which started Suzie crying again.

"Young lady, stop that. It's time for you to be strong. You have to do it for your girlfriend, for Martha, and for yourself. You're no good to anyone falling apart in a crisis. Samantha needs your prayers now. And Martha needs her surrogate daughter to help her get through this. That's you, Miss Suzie Brown."

Miss Martha smiled in appreciation. "You and Karl must have been something out there in the desert. Suzie is a good girl. She's just an emotional sort, aren't you, sweetie?"

"I never called you 'mother' before. May I call you that now?"

"Of course, baby. You're going to be just fine."

Suzie knelt down beside Miss Martha's chair, placing her head in Martha's lap.

The older woman stroked her pretty brown hair, a pair of tears rolling down Martha Fox's rouged cheeks.

Karl stubbed out his cigarette and lit another one. "The doctor said she might be better when she wakes up. Let's hope so. I'll have a bottle of brandy brought up. That may help a little. I'll take the midnight shift. Who wants to come sit when I get sleepy?"

The women talked it over and Suzie was chosen. Martha and Suzie retired to the cabin next door, preparing for bed. Elsa drove her wheelchair down the hallway to her and Karl's room. Karl sat at Sam's bedside, smoking his Marlboros, remembering the scene in the hospital when Elsa almost died. Karl bowed his head and prayed.

"Father, please forgive this old sinner his shortcomings. Thank You for my blessings. And thank You for Elsa. There's a young lady down here tonight that needs Your love and grace, Lord. If this is her time, let it be quick and painless. If You choose to let her stay a little longer, please take away her suffering. May it therefore by Thy will, O Lord, our God and God of our fathers, to forgive her all her sins, to pardon all her iniquities, and to grant her atonement for her transgressions in life. Amen, blessed Father."

Karl often thought about the desert, and the night Elsa was shot. That and the men he killed visited his memory daily.

It had been springtime, and the desert was in bloom. They were coming across an open field in the moonlight, about fifty of them, carrying weapons, ammunition, and medical supplies, when the British opened fire with a Vickers .303 machine gun. Geysers of sand sprouted like mushrooms among the men and women laden with their precious cargo.

Tracers filled the night, shouting, cursing, the hammering of the machine gun. Then one of his men threw a German stick bomb. The grenade exploded, killing the gun crew. Rifle fire. Then another British machine gun opened up.

Zachary was yelling in his ear. "Run for it! We have to make a run for it!"

Elsa grabbed a Sten gun lying in the sand, firing at the British as they ran. Then the tracers came in their direction, chewing up the desert around them. Elsa screamed, knocked to the ground unconscious.

Tracers everywhere, explosions, yelling, dozens of guns firing at once. Zachary grabbed one arm and Karl the other, dragging Elsa along behind them.

Barb wire up ahead. Zachary led the way. Then he was hit, shot through the side, and fell. Zachary crawled on his belly through the wire, Karl inching along behind him pulling Elsa over the sand through Zachary's trail of blood. Nearing the end, they stopped to rest and catch their breath.

Elsa came to and hugged Karl. "I'm done for. Leave me. Save yourself, my love."

Karl never forgot those words. He gathered Elsa up in his arms, following the bleeding Zachary through a quiet zone where there were no British soldiers. Time and again he stumbled and fell, exhausted, but he never let go. They made it out. Zack survived. Most of their party were captured or killed.

Karl exacted his revenge a month later, blowing up a British barracks outside Jerusalem with phosphorous grenades. They came running out on fire. Time passed, a truce was signed, and the fighting came to an end between the Jews and Great Britain.

Samantha stirred in her sleep, mumbled incoherently, bringing Karl back from his vision of the desert. She mumbled again, "John … oh, John," then she lay quiet. Her pajamas had fallen open, revealing her breasts and protruding ribcage.

He buttoned her pajamas back, tucking her blanket in securely around the bed. Her protruding ribcage brought back sad memories of the concentration camps.

Karl sat pondering the plight of the unfortunates around the world. Germany and Japan had created Armageddon for whole nations, 25,000,000 being the last estimate he read regarding casualties on the Russian Front. Now Vietnam was the sausage grinder.

"Mister Lieberman, you're here."

His reverie faded. "Yes, my dear. How are you feeling?"

"I feel much better, thank you. Most of my pain is gone."

"Do you want me to wake your mother?"

"Let her sleep. This has been hard on her."

"You gave us quite a scare, young lady."

"It did me too. I'm close, aren't I?"

"It's hard to say. You have some time left."

"I'm glad everyone is here. I wish John's parents were too."

"Tell me about John."

"That's easy. He was wonderful."

They both laughed.

"I met Johnny at a nightclub. He was pretty full of himself in those days. We dated, broke up, got back together, got married. Then he left for basic training. When he came home we had eight days to ourselves. We lived a lifetime in those eight days. Of course we had dated for nearly a year, but we were together only that one week as man and wife. Then he left with his friends for Vietnam." Samantha began to cry softly.

Karl moved to her side of the bed, placing an arm around her shoulders. "I have lost many friends in my lifetime, Samantha, but I was fortunate with Elsa. I can only guess how I might feel if my Elsa died. It must have been very hard for you."

"Yes … it still is. But I'll be with him soon."

"People of faith are amazing. We endure hardships much better than most people who have no religion. The majority of my people believe Jesus was a prophet. I believe Jesus Christ was the Son of God. So does Elsa."

"Do you think we'll see God when we get to heaven?"

"Samantha, in your case I believe God will come to see you."

"You and your wife are so kind. Was it hard for her getting used to her wheelchair?"

"Not like you might think. She was depressed at first, but I encouraged her. After a while her spirits returned, and I got my old Elsa back.

She's an amazing woman, wheelchair and all. She worries about the way she looks, but refuses to replace that front tooth. Says it reminds her every day that God spared her from the Nazis. To me she will always be the beautiful young lady I met on the beach."

The bedroom door opened and Suzie walked in.

"Sam, you're awake! You're not … you're …"

Suzie ran over and plopped on the bed, hugging Karl and Samantha.

Sam looked at Karl and smiled.

"See why I love this girl so much?"

"Young lady, you are quite the fortunate one to have this Suzie for a friend."

"I know. Now I have two more friends. You and Elsa."

At lunch the next day Samantha pulled out a folded piece of notebook paper she had saved. She found it in a cigar box with her letters to John.

"Mister Lieberman, since you and your wife know about war, I want you to see this. It's something one of John's buddies wrote. I think the censors missed it when they sent his things home."

Lost Highway

God is dead,
That's what The New York Times *tells us.*
We're here to see the Elephant
On the Lost Highway.

Politicians call it Containment,
In Country we call it War.
Roger lost his legs last week
On the Lost Highway.

400,000 was never enough.
Congress says, 'Yes, Mister President,'
Speeding more soldiers up the line
On the Lost Highway.

Semper Fi and a big Moon Pie,
Lonely days and starry nights.
The dead walk among us
On the Lost Highway.

1617280

"What do you make of it, Mister Lieberman?"

"Whoever wrote this had an exceptional grasp of the military situation. The public doesn't know what goes on in Vietnam. I still have a few connections who keep me informed. The President has placed our forces in a no-win situation."

"But why?"

"Johnson and McNamara wanted to stop the spread of communism, but they were afraid Communist China might step in with reinforcements. They didn't want another Korea on their hands. What they've managed, inadvertently, is to create a situation similar to Korea, minus the Chinese Army."

Suzie piped in. "Sounds nuts to me."

"It was, indeed. Johnson doesn't have the political fortitude to attack North Vietnam in a full-scale war. He doesn't want China, or the world for that matter, thinking America is bullying little North Vietnam. So Johnson and McNamara instigated the Gulf of Tonkin incident, luring North Vietnam into attacking one of our destroyers. It was all a political setup designed to fool Congress into giving President Johnson carte blanche with our Armed Forces.

"My sources told me the Chinese Air Force may have been involved from the island of Hainan. None of that has ever been confirmed. I was further informed that the carrier Ticonderoga steamed away from the Gulf of Tonkin to avoid setting off a major sea battle, and possibly World War Three.

"Johnson got his Gulf of Tonkin Resolution passed through Congress, then sent our boys to South Vietnam to act as policemen against the North. What McNamara and Johnson have never understood is that Vietnam and China have been at one another's throats for centuries. The Vietnamese hate China as much as they hate the French. Now it may be too late from a political standpoint to save Vietnam from the communist regime in Hanoi. That aside, we probably should never have gone there in the first place. President Eisenhower made that miscalculation."

"Then why don't we pack up and come home?"

"Politics is the driving factor, theirs and ours. Ego. Saving face. Our Vietnamese friends would be rounded up and slaughtered if we leave. America has a tiger by the tail."

"Does this mean John died for nothing?"

"No, Samantha. John died serving his country. Stupid politicians can never take that away from you. I believe in spite of all our mistakes we have contributed against the spread of communism in Southeast Asia."

"How can you tell?"

"The Cultural Revolution in China, the Soviet invasion of Czechoslovakia, Brezhnev in Russia, Castro in Cuba, North Korea. Communism has been exposed as a dictatorial evil. It has no legitimate legs to stand on. But, sadly, America has damaged her own reputation with Vietnam. Well, enough of this. We must get to bed now or we'll be sleepyheads in the morning."

Over breakfast next morning, Elsa conjured up a suggestion. "Suzie, would you object to Samantha wearing your silver cross?"

"No, not at all. I think that's a swell idea. Let's do it now."

Suzie slipped off her necklace, draped the little cross around Sam's neck, and fastened it.

"Samantha, I want you to wear it the rest of the cruise."

"Sure, is there some reason why?"

"No. I would just feel better knowing it's around your pretty neck. Call it an old woman's intuition. Now let's go downstairs and see if those dolphins are still with us."

That night Samantha said her prayers and went to bed early. A velvet dream from the past came drifting into her bedchamber.

John called, asking to meet with her, telling Sam it was important. She said okay, advising him to come to her place around six o'clock after she got off work. When she opened her front door Sam was shocked by John's appearance. He had lost weight, twenty pounds or more. There were dark circles under his eyes. He looked like he hadn't slept in weeks.

Their five-and-a-half-week breakup had taken its toll on both of them. Sam had lost weight herself and slept fitfully, often experiencing bad dreams.

John apologized for getting drunk at the Carnival Club and hitting the bouncer. He apologized for his drinking, his rude behavior, his arrogance, and the dismal fact he was a spoiled brat. John explained that his mother and father had lived through the Great Depression and World War Two, and had given him all the things they never had as children. They loved him, and were doing what they thought was best for their only son.

Samantha wasn't convinced, believing John just wanted what he couldn't have anymore. Sex had always seemed more important to John than her feelings. She had cried herself to sleep more than once over his selfish behavior. Sam was determined to break off their relationship if that didn't change.

John did his young Perry Mason routine, but Sam remained

unconvinced. The slick talker from South Knoxville had promised to change before.

Then John dropped a bombshell. He had joined the Marine Corps with Bubba and Red.

They would be leaving soon for Parris Island. He wanted to get his head on straight, and become the man Samantha deserved. He loved her and wanted to make her happy.

Fear drifted into her thoughts. Vietnam was a place she had heard about, but never paid much attention to before. What if they got sent over there?

He admitted to Sam that she was a better person than he was, that he respected her for going to church, and that he wanted to become more like her. He would go to church with her, stop drinking, whatever it took to become someone she respected.

The church thing impressed Sam.

John got down on his knees beside the sofa, and took Sam's hand. "I love you, Samantha. I've always loved you. Will you marry me?"

Her heart melted, tears came to her eyes. Sam bit her lip to keep from crying. The things he just told her were those things she had always wanted John to say. She still loved him, just as much as before. John possessed a great deal of potential, more so than any man she had ever known. Sam was sure now. Yes, she wanted this man in her life. She wanted John in her bed. Samantha Gail Fox wanted John Henry Jackson as her lawfully wedded husband.

"Yes," she said. "Yes, John, I will marry you."

She woke up. It was 6:34 in the morning. Sam lay in bed, smiling, until Suzie knocked on the bedroom door for breakfast.

Sam never revealed her dream. At the breakfast table that morning Elsa noticed her cheerful expression. Elsa smiled, remembering the concentration camp and those nights she prayed for God or the Americans or anybody to come rescue her. She recalled the beach and the star-studded night she met Karl Lieberman. Elsa wondered how long Samantha had left on earth before she departed on her celestial journey to rendezvous with her husband and the Lord.

Chapter Forty-Two

100 Proof Women

Samantha, Miss Martha, Suzie, Elsa, and Karl were having cocktails on the stern of the Sea Queen, watching the phosphorous churned up in the water by the propellers. The silver streaks appeared magical, with little flying fish leaping from wave to wave. Except for Sam's physical ailment, it had been a grand voyage. They were two days out from port.

Elsa was in a somber mood, cogitating over the fact she was going to miss her newly acquired friends from Tennessee. She and Karl had discussed the matter at some length the night before.

Elsa sat beside the railing gazing out to sea. "This reminds me of the Mediterranean that night I met Karl on the beach. It was a night much like this one. I fell in love the first time I saw Karl. This dark eyed man holding a rifle, the wind in his hair. I was wet and scared, what more could a girl ask for?"

Everyone laughed. Then Karl spoke. "That night on the beach, I was afraid a patrol boat might spot us. Then this blonde goddess stood up in her dingy and I forgot about everything except her. The Italians have a name for it, 'getting struck by the thunderbolt.' My goose was cooked, flambéed, burned to a crisp!"

Laughter.

Samantha broke her reverie. "That's the way I felt when I met John. At first I wasn't sure if it was going to work between us, but after a while he changed from being a spoiled college boy and we were very happy together."

"We've all come a long ways over the years."

Miss Martha smiled. "Now we're gathered here together on this big cruise ship, almost like it was written in a book someplace."

"Perhaps it is."

Elsa's eyes twinkled. "It isn't often that one meets people they feel at home with and care about right off the bat. That's how Karl and I feel about each one of you."

Suzie hugged Elsa. "I hope my Bubba gets to meet y'all someday."

"He must be rather special to be engaged to you, Suzie."

"Oh, yes, Mister Lieberman. I pray every night for Robert and the rest of First Squad. He and John were best friends, you know."

"Samantha and I talked about John. I wish I could have know him. When is Robert's tour of duty over?"

"Thirty-two more days and he'll be coming home. We plan on getting married at Graystone Presbyterian Church. His buddy Red will be coming with him."

"You haven't told us about Red. What's he like?"

"Billy Kidwell is like me. We grew up poor in South Knoxville. His mama and daddy are nice, they just never had much money. Red went to South High School. The rest of us went to Young. Red and Bubba played football. All of us hung out together at the Southern Circle. That's a drive-in restaurant close to Young High School. All the school kids went there. Babe Maloy's is another drive-in back toward town a ways. We hung out at both places.

"You'll like Red. He's short with red hair and he's funny as can be. He dated a cheerleader at South, but she broke his heart. After that all three of them joined the Marines. I have a girlfriend I want Red to meet when he comes home. She's at the university now in Knoxville."

Elsa spoke up. "It's funny about friends. When you're young you can't imagine ever losing them. Except for Zack and Doctor Rubenstein, we've lost all our closest friends in Israel. Where we live now we know a lot of people, but none of them are what you'd call best friends.

"Karl and I have been talking. How would you feel if we purchased a home in Knoxville? It's not like we'd be underfoot, but it would be nice if we could visit each other now and then."

Miss Martha clasped her hands over her heart, a big smile on her face. "That's one the nicest things anybody ever said to me. I would be delighted if you and Karl moved to Knoxville."

"Yes! Please do. We'd love it."

"Oh, Karl, it would be like the old days again."

"Yes, *Mamelah*, two beautiful daughters, and a very attractive sister."

"That's doggone nice too."

Sam and Suzie chuckled.

"This calls for a second round of drinks."

The cocktails arrived and Karl, teasing Samantha, lit one of his Marlboros. "I've heard some nice things about Tennessee. People there love football, coon hunting, hound dogs, and running around barefoot. Is that about right, Samantha?"

"You left out the part about white lightning and shotgun weddings, Karl."

"I'm looking forward to some of your mountain whiskey, Martha."

"And I know just the place to get it. There's a bootlegger up on Redbud Drive. I'll get us a big Mason jar full for your house warming when you move to Knoxville. I'll cook up some fried chicken with mashed potatoes and gravy and all the trimmings. The boys will be home from Vietnam by then."

"Lord, Martha, you're making my mouth water."

"There's a country club we go to, Deane Hill. They have parties and dancing and bingo and a big pool. We'll have a marvelous time together."

"Do they accept Jews?"

"It's not like that at Deane Hill. If they give you any trouble, we'll have Bubba and Red beat 'em up."

Cocktails came and they clinked glasses to the new adventure.

The next morning dawned with a beautiful sunrise, signaling their last day at sea. They ate breakfast then went outside to sun themselves and watch the dolphins. Samantha asked for a pain pill. A few minutes later she was fine. Nevertheless, Suzie, Elsa, and Martha formed a protective circle around Sam, as if their presence might shield her from the inevitable.

Sam was telling Karl about Knoxville real estate. "I learned about this working for Alcoa Aluminum. There's a place called Bearden Hill west of Knoxville. There's not much out there now, mostly farms and cow pastures. But the planners at Alcoa believe Knoxville will grow in that direction. It's probably a good investment."

"You say this is west of Knoxville?"

"Deane Hill Country Club is just beyond Bearden Hill, right off Kingston Pike."

"Sounds interesting. I'll come take a look."

"Why not come home with us tomorrow? We'll show you around. The Tennessee River runs through the middle of town. We have TVA, Oak Ridge, UT, all kinds of places to go visit. And you can meet John's parents. Mister Jackson made his living in the tire business. Now he deals in real estate. Maybe he can help you find a house."

"Elsa, why don't we do that?"

"I like it. The sooner we get our business settled the better. I'll call our old broker and have her put our house on the market. I want us to be there for Samantha."

"Y'all are so nice. This is like a fairy tale come true."

"Well, it is for us too. We thought about moving years ago, but we didn't know where to go. We have no family left. They all died in the war. Knoxville sounds like a delightful place to live."

"There's a restaurant out east of Knoxville called Helma's. It's fine Southern cooking. We'll take you there when we get back. And downtown is the S&W Cafeteria. You'll like it too. The Southern Circle has Chicken in the Rough. It's great with honey and homemade bread."

"Lord, I'll squash my wheelchair. Karl, you better get us some of those diet pills or I'm liable to roll out in the street and get run over."

"This is so exciting. It feels like Christmas and New Years all rolled together. I'm so thankful we came on this trip. Otherwise, we'd be like ships passing in the night."

"We're going to be great friends and have lots of fun."

"Red said something once, before he left, about me and Samantha. He called us 100 proof women. It sounds awful, but he meant it as a compliment. You know something? We four ladies are 100 proof women. That's about as good as it gets. And Karl, bless his heart, is the glass that holds us all together. Don't you think so, Sam?"

"Suzie, you're 'bout half smart!"

Chapter Forty-Three

The Warehouse

Delta X Ray was running low on food and medical supplies. Their physician, Scott Brown, had used up all of his malaria vaccine inoculating Ca Dung and his newly arrived tribesmen, plus most of his filariasis tablets were gone. And all the toothbrushes and toothpaste had been handed out. Major Abraham needed chow supplies for the mess boys, so he loaded up Tony, Driggins, Calhoun, and Catfish, and lit out in his old C-47 for division headquarters in Da Nang.

Halfway there the port engine began belching puffs of black smoke. When they landed they were told the fuel pump and carburetor were shot. It would take a few days to locate replacements. Major Abraham drove them into town across the Han River Bridge where he rented a cottage on China Beach.

"Oh, wow! Look at all them surfboards. And women!"

"You'll find swimming trunks inside. Be careful and don't go out too far."

"Come on, Tony. Let's go."

"Number One! Number One!"

The men spent the afternoon surfing, flirting with the pretty nurses, and getting a suntan. Next morning Tony was out early walking the beach searching for sea shells when a gorgeous young lady approached. She introduced herself as Su Ling, telling Tony she worked at the base, asking if she could walk with him.

"You pretty lady. Okey-dokey we walk together."

"Thank you, Tony. You're a very handsome man."

"You tease. Tony got boo koo scars from war."

"I think scars are very manly."

"No tease, please. Tell Tony truth."

"Oh, yes, Tony. You're very handsome."

Major Abraham was resting on the front porch, almost asleep, enjoying the ocean view and a gentle breeze when he noticed Tony and the pretty female. He smiled to himself, remembering his younger days. I hope he gets lucky he thought to himself, then drifted away in dreams about the American West and his great-grandfather who was an Indian scout for the Texas Brigade during the Civil War.

By 1400 hours Major Abraham knew something was wrong. Tony would have checked in, female or no female. Guessing correctly that it concerned him and First Squad, he made two quick telephone calls. Ninety minutes later he walked in the backdoor of the Hoi An Hotel where he found the rest of First Squad and Gargoyle waiting for him. Seated with Henri were four tough-looking *hombres*. Gargoyle adjusted his black eye patch, introducing his four companions merely as "my drinking companions." They rose respectfully, extending their hands in friendship. They were veterans of the French Foreign Legion's 1954 battle at Dien Bien Phu.

Henry, Red, Bubba, Pasamenus, and Johnson had two duffle bags stuffed with weapons and hand grenades. German machine pistols were the choice of the Legionnaires. Henri had his 9mm P-38. The Major carried his .45 automatic in a shoulder holster.

"Looks like they've snatched Tony to lure us out into the open. We've put some serious hurt on Hanoi these past few months. They can't afford for that to continue, not after Tet. They want us dead. Tony is the bait. My guess is they'll keep him alive long enough to tell us where he's being held. Remember, Tony is like my son so please be careful. Our job is to locate Tony without them knowing it. That's where you come in, Henri."

"*Oui*, we have out the seventy men searching this very minute, discreetly of course. Adrian and Peter operate the black markets in Hue and Da Nang. They have the many business connections. Fred and Johnny manage the politicians, the military, greasing the palms as you Americans like to say. We have out the $2,000 reward for Tony. That is the large sum for any Vietnamese."

"Thank you, Henri. I appreciate everyone's help. They probably have somebody watching so I left the rest of my people behind to keep our friends company. I slipped out the back door when a very attractive redhead I telephoned came strolling down the beach wearing a polka-dot bikini. It worked, nobody followed me."

"Women will be the downfall of us all!"

The men chuckled.

"In the meantime, we must remain here. The runners know where to find us." Gargoyle ordered a magnum of champagne, and they settled in for a fretful afternoon of wine and cheese.

Two hours had elapsed when a slender young man walked in wearing blue jeans and a sporty blue shirt. He handed Gargoyle a crumpled slip of paper. Henri read the note, nodding his head in approval. He passed the young man a brown manila envelope.

"They're seven miles up the coast in an abandoned warehouse. I know this place. There's a cannery building out back, behind the warehouse. Plantation owners used the cannery during the occupation. There is a low hill behind the cannery, overlooking the buildings. That is where I would station my snipers."

"How can we get at them without giving ourselves away?"

All four Frenchmen pulled out .38 caliber service revolvers with silencers attached.

"We expected the necessary quiet so we brought these."

Red and Bubba smiled at each other. They liked the Legionnaires.

"You guys could make good Marines someday."

The Frenchmen grinned. "You could make the good Legionnaires, yes?"

"We'll need a diversion to distract the men on the hill, if they had the brains to put anybody up there."

"I think we must assume those snipers are there."

"I agree. That's what I would do."

"Perhaps if I start the fire? There are the vacant buildings beside the highway. While they're admiring my potatoes crisping, you come up from behind."

"That should do it. Let's get this show on the road."

They followed Highway 1 along the coast until they were a thousand yards from the warehouse. There they parked their vehicles back among the palms and pine trees and continued on foot around behind the cannery. Henri stayed behind, closing to within one hundred and fifty yards of the warehouse where he struck a match to a pile of dry brush beside a dilapidated frame structure. In minutes the flames were leaping twenty feet into the air.

The Frenchmen fanned out around the left side of the hill, while Abraham and his Marines positioned themselves at the rear and began crawling up the weed-covered bank toward the summit. Up above they heard talking. Nearing the top, they heard the telltale "thump, thump, thump" of the silencers. Then quiet.

"You badass Marines may come up now." Freddie stood at the crest, smiling down at them.

"Great job, you Frog bastard." Abraham threw an arm around the Legionnaire's shoulders.

"Come. Look what I have for you."

Two Uk vz. 59 Czech machine guns sat in the grass sighted in on the roadway below. Four Hanoi secret police lay sprawled in the grass beside the machine guns.

"By God, these jokers mean business! Bubba, you and Red drag these assholes back out of the way. Pasamenus, you stay here with them in case we get in trouble. Watch for Gargoyle. He'll be along in a minute. Henry, you and Johnson come with me."

Seven men proceeded down the left flank of the hill, advancing toward the cannery through a drainage ditch. The stagnant water stank of sewage. Swarms of mosquitoes rose up from the slender reeds and cattails.

"Smells sweet, like the valley of the gods, no?"

"Reminds me of your sister's pussy."

"Pipe down, you pranksters, else we get the asses shot off, yes?"

"I have the mosquitoes up me arse now. Shoot me. Shoot me."

"Don't tempt me, you crazy *merde*."

"Over there, see that?"

"*Oui*, what is it?"

"Some kind of armored car."

"Perhaps we should pay them the visit, no?"

"Perhaps we should pay them the visit, yes."

Fred and the Major crawled through the high weeds until they were only yards from the olive drab machine. It was a bastardized version of a French scout car. They lay silent, studying what to do next. Country music was coming from inside the vehicle.

"Get that revolver ready."

Another secret policeman came around the corner of the building carrying two soda pops. The driver's door opened. He stepped out.

"Thump! Thump!"

Johnson dragged the bodies to the drainage ditch and rolled them in. Then all seven men piled inside the armored vehicle. The motor was still running. They discovered a cooler filled with fruit and sand-wiches.

"We are moving up in the world, yes? Soon now we join the union."

"Hey, this stuff tastes great."

Johnson had a mouthful of *banh mi*.

"Pull up to the corner. We can see the back of the warehouse from there."

The warehouse was large, ninety meters long with five barred win-dows in back. A concrete block structure, with four metal doors evenly spaced across the rear wall which measured eight meters high.

"Henri said the warehouse was empty."

"What do you suggest, Major?"

"Let me think. We've accounted for six of theirs. Probably they got twice that many inside. This thing has an I-beam for a bumper, and gun ports. How do you feel about driving through the back wall?"

"Major, you should have been our commander at Dien Bien Phu. General Navarre was the fucking idiot. Paris was the political whore-house full of lapdogs, yapping and barking at themselves, but no one to help my Legionnaires. You could have won the war all by yourself."

"I read reports on the battle. He underestimated the enemy. Colonel Piroth was just as bad with those field pieces of his. Navarre should never have garrisoned you in that valley without proper air support. Your politicians are like ours, gasbags and idiots. They could have organized a relief column, but they did nothing."

"It was the bloody fucking nightmare from hell. France, she is become the political whore dog. Much the same way your President Johnson is conducting this stinking war. He's making the same stupid mistakes de Gaulle made. But another time, my friend. Adrian, escort our American guests through that cinderblock pisspot to glory!"

"Be careful you don't run over Tony."

They blasted through the rear wall at thirty miles an hour, blocks flying, timbers falling, skidding sideways on a concrete floor. The interior was open, save for three vehicles parked in the center of the building. Tony was hanging by his wrists from an overhead beam, his feet barely six inches off the concrete deck.

Pandemonium erupted, secret police scrambling in every direction for their weapons. Adrian swung the machine around, gunning it toward three men seeking safety against the front wall of the building. Adrian sideswiped them, grinding their bodies into the concrete blocks.

Gunfire!

The windows chipped and cracked, but no bullets penetrated the bulletproof glass. Adrian spun the vehicle around, tires squealling, rubber burning, mangling a fourth victim beneath his wheels. Then he chased a fifth man down and ran over him. Adrian jammed the brake pedal, skidding sideways, wheeling around Tony, crashing into the side of a Pontiac loaded with men trying to get away.

Adrian jerked the gearbox into low, floorboarding the scout car until he had the Pontiac skidding sideways, gathering speed. He drove them into the side wall where their gas tank ruptured, exploding in bellowing orange flames. The men inside were trapped. Their doors were crushed shut. They died beating against the jammed window glass.

Adrian backed up slowly, wheeling around to face the three men standing in the center of the room. Freddie, Peter, and Johnny stepped out of their bullet-scarred vehicle, their Schmeisser submachine guns pointed at the men. The secret police held their hands high in the air in surrender. The Legionnaires opened fire.

Henry was a devout Catholic, but he didn't say a word. He had been informed about the atrocities committed by the secret police in North Vietnam. Some of their specialties included electric drills, chain saws, and blowtorches.

An old Buick rumbled to life, screeching rubber out the open door. It was Su Ling.

"Henry, cut Tony down. We'll get the girl."

Adrian gunned the scout car for the exit. Driving headlong out the open door, a heavy caliber machine gun riddled them front to back from a stand of bamboo across the highway. Armor-piercing rounds shot out their tires and the motor block. The scout car careened off the highway into a ditch. Adrian, Johnson, and Abraham bailed out.

Friendly fire began raking the stand of bamboo from the top of the hill. Stalks were falling about. Johnson lobbed a hand grenade. Adrian emptied his machine pistol. The gun fell silent. Adrian and the Major waited for what seemed like an eternity, then crept out to investigate. The machine gun opened fire again. Adrian fell. Abraham went down with his face split open from his cheekbone to his ear lobe. Johnson threw two more hand grenades. Both machine guns on top of the hill fired until the bamboo was shot to splinters.

Minutes passed as the smoke cleared. The Major walked across the highway, dripping a trail of blood. One gunner was blown to pieces. The other was badly wounded. Abraham stood over them, looking down at the secret police. The policeman cursed him in broken English. He wondered where they recruited such hate-filled assassins. Probably their military or civilian prisons. Maybe they came out of the womb that way, with FU, for "Fucked Up," on their foreheads, which faded after forty-eight hours.

He watched while the dying man fumbled, trying to extract his service revolver. He almost had it out when the Major shot him between the eyes.

Freddie was kneeling beside Adrian when the Major walked back across the roadway. Adrian looked up at them, clasping their hands, blood running from his nose and mouth.

"Do not grieve for me, my brothers. I'll be with God soon. And mama and papa. I enjoyed our adventure, *monsieur*. It was like the old times in Algiers. I hope we made it in time for your Tony. *Au revoir,* Freddie, my dear and good friend. Watch over my little girls, please. Teach them … about honor … and … being the good Suzette. Hug my sweet Lucille … tell her … I love her. I shall be waiting … for you …"

Adrian faded to unconsciousness. And died. Peter came running out of the warehouse. Adrian was Peter's older brother. The tough-looking Frenchman with his big hands and broken nose sat down on the pavement, gathered his brother in his arms, rocking him back and forth like a baby, and cried. Freddie wrapped a Red Cross bandage around the Major's head, tying it in place with strips from a greasy oil rag. Johnson knelt down beside Peter, placing an arm around his shoulders, tears streaking his own dark cheeks.

Back inside, Henry and Johnny had gotten an unconscious Tony loose from the overhead beam and placed him on a cloth on the warehouse floor. Tony had been stripped to his boxer shorts and whipped until his back and shoulders were raw and bloody. Henry shot him full of morphine, then set about cleaning the wounds. Tony began coming around.

"Water, please." Tony drank until the canteen was empty and asked for more.

"Who did this?"

"Woman offer money me join them. I say no. Woman offer self and money me join them. I say no. Woman mad, beat me with whip. I say no boo koo times. Men watch and make fun."

"You're going to be all right. We'll get you some penicillin. You'll become a danged goldbrick. Not worth a plug nickel."

"I no think I live. When wall fall down I know Major come. I happy now."

"I think we lost somebody outside."

"Not Major?"

"No, I heard him talking. Take it easy. He'll be here in a minute."

"Henry?"

"Yes, Tony."

"Thank you."

The Major appeared in the doorway with blood on his shirt and trousers, down to the tops of his leather boots. Johnson and Freddie followed behind him, carrying Adrian between them. Peter had the dazed look of a man in shock.

Abraham knelt down and took Tony's hand. "Looks like that gal got the best of you, son."

"Yes, boss, not happy ending."

"That's what you get for hanging around with loose women."

Tony rose up on his elbows, placing an arm around Abraham's neck. "Thank you, boss. Thank you for come and get me."

At that moment Major Abraham made a decision. He loved the young Vietnamese and planned to make Tony his son. He would adopt him and retire from the CIA and the Marine Corps. Maybe become a consultant. There were a hundred different outfits he could work for and make ten times the money. Tony could go to college, find himself a girl, and they could live a happy life back in The World. Vietnam had been a cluster fuck ever since that first week the Marines went ashore at Da Nang. A lot of good people had died or been hurt for a herd of gutless politicians back in Washington, DC.

To everyone's surprise, Henri came driving up with a woman bound and gagged on the front seat. It was Su Ling.

"How the hell did you get hold of her?"

"Well, sir, when I go to the top of the hill Pasamenus tells me you are down here about to perform the mischief. There was nothing for me to do up there so I started down the highway to get the automobile in case one was required here. I hear the gunfire, turn around, then this crazy lady comes flying out of the building. She turns in my direction, and I shoot her engine with Bubba's rifle."

"Well done, Henri!"

Abraham pulled the gag from Su Ling's mouth. "Who sent you?"

"Fuck you, stupid American pig!"

Abraham slapped her so hard she wet her pants.

"It is no use with this one," Henri said. "She is the hard-core communist."

"The big boys sent this scum. My guess is Ho or the General."

Freddie kept looking at Su Ling. Finally he spoke. "I think we have here the big fish."

"What big fish?"

"That looks like Su Ling. One of the politburo's propaganda whores."

Tony spoke up. "She say her name Su Ling."

"You filthy little traitor." Abraham slapped her again. Blood ran from her nose, dripping off her pretty chin. "One more word, bitch. I will hang your sadistic ass from that steel beam and leave you for the goddamn rats!"

"The French government, they have the reward against this woman for war crimes, 500,000 francs."

"Henri caught her. It's his money."

"No. That would be wrong. Give the money to Adrian's widow."

"This is the kind thing you do, Henri. We will not forget you."

"The Major and his Marines, they saved my life. They saved Madame and our girls. Poor Adrian has given his life saving our comrade, Tony. Is it not our duty to care for his family? Are we not such men of honor? Am I not the fortunate one to have served with such men as you before?"

"Well said, *mon ami. Honneur et Fidelite.* We are the Legion and they the Marines. We fight, we win battles, we die. But the politicians, they are the *linguine spines,* the soft bellies who betray the honor."

"*C'est tres vrai,* my brothers. We fight for our countries. They lose the fucking wars."

Chapter Forty-Four

Lieutenant Butler

Revenge

Major Abraham had assembled the Legionnaires and his Marines back at the bungalow on China Beach. The Frenchmen were in a somber mood over the death of Adrian. Freddie and Gargoyle had prepared Peter a stiff drink to try and relieve some of his stress over the loss of his brother. Adrian was inside the cottage wrapped in a blanket on one of the beds. Su Ling was trussed up like a bad habit on the bed next to his, ready for delivery to the French Consulate. Tony had been sent to the hospital for bandaging and a shot of penicillin. The Major's facial stitches were on hold.

"Men, I want to thank you for your help getting Tony back, and for silencing the plot to terminate my group. Adrian's loss was a tragedy. He spoke of his family and the Legion before he died. Adrian was a decent man and a fine Legionnaire. Henri has graciously volunteered to donate his reward money to Adrian's wife and children. Henri is another example of the heart and soul of the French Foreign Legion.

"Peter, if there's anything we can do for you or Adrian's family, please let us know. I owe you Legionnaires for the lives of my men. Anything you need, contact Henri or myself.

"Sergeant, ask the men to bring a bucket of ice and some glasses out on the front porch. We'll have ourselves a drink before they go. You'll find the Jack Daniels in the kitchen cupboard."

The Marines were gathered around the Legionnaires when the Major came out wearing his Marine Corps flight jacket. Pasamenus poured the drinks, while Bubba and Red busied themselves handing everyone their cocktails. Then Bubba gave the Major his glass of Jack Daniels. Major Abraham walked out in the yard to address the group.

"I'd like to propose a toast in honor of our departed comrade, Adrian Devereux. A man I came to know and respect in a short period of time. Men of war are a different breed. We defend those rights and freedoms the majority take for granted. Here's to Adrian Dev. . ."

The drink fell from the Major's hand as the side of his head burst open, blood gushing from a mortal wound, followed by a report from a sniper's rifle. Saul Abraham was dead before he hit the deck, facedown in the grass.

Back in nineteenth-century France, they were known as vendettas. In the days of King Cotton and mint juleps, these were called blood feuds. Hanoi had never considered any bad repercussions following their assassination of Major Abraham. During the Vietnam War, it was simply called "payback."

Delta X Ray had taken the assassination of their fallen leader personally. So had a handful of patriotic officers in Saigon, Bangkok, and Da Nang. No one else knew except a couple of generals at the Pentagon, and a few former OSS men with the CIA. The Legionnaires had assigned their black market activities to trusted aides, placing themselves in the mix with Lieutenant Butler and his Marines. Gargoyle had gone back to the Garden, informing Madame he was going on a secret mission and the reason why. Madame gave Henri a roll of hundred-dollar bills to help finance the expedition. She felt as strongly as everyone else about the Major's death. Tony was out of the hospital and back at camp, mourning Saul's death. Air America was on standby. Mobilization was afoot.

Lieutenant Butler was briefing his group at the airfield in Laos.

"Our general friend in Saigon says it appears to be the work of a special sniper unit. Those guys live in a small compound with a bunch of technicians. Chinese, they think. And get this, it's a missile complex. They do their thing, arming those weapons against our flyboys. The assembly plant is underground in the side of a mountain. The general said the Air Force couldn't knock it out even if they had permission. That is our target."

"*Oui*, but getting in and out is the bitch. The compound is ringed with the hills, like our little valley of death at Dien Bien Phu. All those guns will shoot down your planes like the shooting ducks in the country fair."

"Right, we haven't figured that one out yet. Bear in mind this is one of Washington's No Fly Zones, so it's not likely they'll be on any kind of special alert."

"All fine and dandy, but it only takes one or two minutes to man those radar guns. There must be the other way. Else we all go home in the ladies' shoe box."

"What about roads in and out of that place?"

"One road. It has multiple checkpoints and multiple guards. Once alerted, we'd never get past all those guards."

"That little river on the map. How deep is she?"

"Not deep enough. It's more swamp than river. The actual waterway is downstream about three and a half miles. Parachutes are out. They'd hear the airplane engines and know something was up."

"Well, shit!" Red was agitated. "Brain, think of something!"

"I was wondering about that rail line going through the mountains. What about the railroad, Lieutenant?"

"Intelligence researched that one thoroughly, Sergeant. There's a checkpoint where they go through the pass. The trains stop there for inspections. Then another one down the mountain where they go inside the compound."

"What if we dressed as North Vietnamese soldiers?"

"Well, if we get caught they'll shoot us as spies."

"They'll shoot us anyway once they know who we are."

Freddie stood up. "It is the good idea. Johnny speaks the language."

Tony spoke. "I speak the commie rat bastard."

Gargoyle rose to opine. "From ten yards away, they won't recognize us."

Butler nodded his head. "All right then, we go as NVA."

Red turned to Bubba. "You lose. Gimme the five bucks."

The Hmong tribesmen supplied the NVA uniforms from a stockpile of weapons and materiels they had accumulated from previous battles with the Vietcong and North Vietnamese Army. The majority would carry AK-47s to blend in with the enemy. Red had Vera Lynn, and Bubba kept his M-14. Calhoun would bring the .50 caliber sniper rifle.

"It's about a hundred miles above the DMZ. We can slip in at night, but we'll need somebody to draw their attention away from our point of entry. Any suggestions?"

Shorty stood up. "Air America can hit the compound. A few bombs. A little napalm. Hanoi will shit a brick, but fuck those assholes. Meanwhile, me and Floyd hug the deck going in, then unload you suckers out a ways on the tracks. A little luck and you'll catch the guards off balance by the time you reach the pass."

"You better get in and get out quick. Those Skyraiders have a distinct exhaust signature at night."

"I got that one covered, Lieutenant. I have a gung ho buddy in Hue I can ask to be upstairs with a squadron of 105s. MiGs don't like tangling with our boys. Last time out they lost two MiG 21s. I'll ask the 105s to buzz the place with afterburners. That'll screw up their hearing down on the deck."

"Okay, Shorty, I'll check with the weather gang to see what they got on the burner. Work up a timetable and get back to me."

By the next afternoon Shorty had his timetable worked out with the pilots in Hue. The next suitable night would appear in forty-eight hours. Shorty and Lieutenant Butler were going over last-minute details with the men in the mess tent.

"One more time now, listen up. We leave here at twenty-five minutes after midnight. Arrive at our destination at approximately 0115 hours. The Skyraiders will do their bomb run exactly at 0105 hours. Out by 0110. Guns on the ridge will be caught with their pants down.

"At 0113 hours the jet jockeys make their run across the compound on full afterburners. The roar is so loud nobody will be able to hear shit for fifteen or twenty minutes. You jokers will land and be on your way up the mountain. Me and Lloyd will put down about forty miles south where Arty will have a blivet waiting for us, gas up, then head for home and a cold one."

Lieutenant Butler then read from a laundry list to his colorful menagerie.

"Freddie and his three men will carry 48 clips for the AK-47s, four .38s with silencers, four boxes of .38 ammo, twenty-eight grenades, and six flares. Calhoun has his .50 caliber, two claymores, and 50 rounds. Red and Bubba will keep their weapons, plus 40 blocks of C4, and 24 clips. Tony has the detonators and det cord, and 12 extra clips. Henry, medical supplies, and 30 rounds for the .50 caliber. Cat, 55 pounds of explosives. Driggins and Pasamenus, eight claymores, 24 clips, one .38, and one radio. Johnson, 30 blocks of C4, 50 rounds for the .50 caliber, and 16 extra clips. I have our map, seven smoke grenades, two claymores, and 12 additional magazines.

"Remember, men, we hide everything before we reach the pass except our .38s and rifles. There should be five or six guards up there. Our job is to walk in and snuff their asses, go back and collect our gear, then wait for the train.

"Those missiles are bound to have a warhead depot someplace. Find it! Cat will rig the thing to blow. If we can't locate one, look for an ammo locker. The inside of that mountain is going to be pitch black. Remember to bring your flashlights. If they spot us, we'll play it by ear. Any questions?"

"Sir, if I get my 'nads shot off will the government compensate me for that?"

"Lieutenant, sir. Little Miss Buckingham has been getting her 'nads shot off ever since we got back over here."

Gargoyle and the Legionnaires laughed.

"We place the 'nads in the pockets. Later we number them for the dice game."

"Guys, this ain't funny, okay?"

A quarter moon made the runway appear silver beneath a misty overcast. Down on the riverbank a chorus of mossy frogs were serenading their jungle audience. Admission was free. Back up at the airfield, an army of fireflies signaled one another in the drifting fog. There was a crisp, fresh smell in the night air from a rain earlier. Shorty and Floyd blinked their landing lights to signal the door gunners. Time to go. The gunners took one last drag on their cigarettes, climbed onboard, and the Hueys lifted off. Operation Payback was underway.

"Red, you ever hear the story about Ed Freeman?"

"Who's Ed Freeman?"

"Freeman was born in Neely, Mississippi. I met the dude in Saigon right after the Battle of la Drang. La Drang is this big valley over in the Central Highlands where a battalion of Air Calvary got their tails in a crack back in '65. Got ambushed by a whole herd of commie rat bastards, and were getting the hell shot outta themselves. It got so bad the MEDEVAC helicopters stopped going in to bring out the wounded.

"The Army boys were in a major shit storm, running out of ammo and you name it. Wounded and dead men strung out a mile. Freeman and his helicopter unit had just transported those boys in there two days earlier. He was back at base when the call came in that they were in trouble. Freeman flew his Huey back in there fourteen times, taking ammunition and medical supplies, and bringing out the wounded. All the while taking enemy fire. That took balls the size of grapefruits."

"Man, that was something."

"That ain't all. Freeman went in the Navy at the tail end of World War Two when he was only seventeen. Came back home, finished high school, then joined the Army. Ed fought in that big-ass battle on Pork Chop Hill in Korea. Him and thirteen others were all that walked away from his unit of two hundred and fifty-seven men. Hell of an indi-vidual. Everybody calls him 'Too Tall' 'cause he's six-four. One of the nicest men you'll ever meet. I think he went home a year ago."

"I'll tell Johnson. He's from Mississippi. He likes stuff like that. I'm goin' home myself after this is over. I've had a bellyful of Viet-by-God-nam."

"Not a bad idea, Red. With the Major gone, I may go with you."

They flew on in the dark for another fifteen minutes

"See that wrecked bomber down there? That's our first checkpoint."

"If we get our tails in a crack, who will come get us?"

"Red, Lieutenant Butler has all of Laos on standby. You get in trouble, the 105s will be there for ya, B-26s, Skyraiders, me and Floyd.

All those people thought the world of the Major. We feel the same way about you guys."

"I'll be damned. I guess we did something right, after all."

"You have no idea, son. Those pilots would bomb Hanoi in the morning if Washington gave the word, and you men were part of the team. People in Laos know about you Marines. You fuckers are heroes."

"Me, a hero? Get back! Gunny was, but not me. I'm just plain ole Red."

"Have it your way. The girls at the Garden talk about you clowns all the time."

"Now there's something we can agree on. Let's go there when this is over."

"You're on. My lady friend just sent me a Dear John letter. She was a snooty bitch, anyway. Hell, we'll all go, take Freddie and Johnny. Peter has to go back and make the funeral arrangements. They got Adrian in a cooler until this is over. Everyone should go to his funeral."

"We sure will. I like those Frenchies."

"There's our second checkpoint. Navigation boys done good."

"Least we ain't lost."

"You hear about Gun Slinger, the rooster?

"A rooster?"

"We got an assload of 155s down around Pleiku. They fire on the Trail whenever they get word Charlie is bringing his trucks through. This old rooster started hanging around the gun pits cleaning up after the gunners when they ate their C rations.

Whenever a gun crew was getting ready to fire, the lead gunner would always yell, "Hold your ears!" First time they fired a round with Mister Rooster present, he took off runnin' in the boondocks lickety-split. Scared the little fellow half to death.

"But that rooster was a smart old bird. He didn't show up for a couple of days. The gunners thought he was gone. Then the third day there he was again pecking at crumbs left on the ground. They got a

Fire Order next day so they loaded up and the lead gunner hollered again, 'Hold your ears!' Know what that rooster did?"

"What?"

"Ran back in one of the tents and waited there 'til the show was over. The gunners adopted him after that, fed him real good, named him Gun Slinger."

"That is one smart chicken."

They could hear the "Crump … Crump" of the bombs, and see the illumination of the fires burning from five miles away. Shorty and Floyd hugged the deck, knowing the 105s would fly over them in about two minutes. Then they heard it, the scream of four pairs of Pratt and Whitney engines delivering 23,000 pounds of thrust, coming their way. The 105s exploded past overhead. It sounded like an avalanche.

"Holy shit!"

"Noisy bastards, ain't they?

"You were right. People down below won't hear shit for a week."

The chopper pilots spotted the rails glistening in the moonlight. Turning toward the compound, they located an open space and set down beside the tracks.

"*Vaya con Dios*, my friends. Be careful out there. No mama sans with snapping pussies. Seriously Red, you fuckers take care of yourselves!"

The men walked single file between the rails toward the mountain, which was silhouetted by the fires burning behind it in the missile compound.

"The ammunition, she is the heavy bitch."

"Yeah, this damn thing weighs a ton."

"Quit your bitchin', guys. We ain't got much farther to go."

"Looks like the flyboys done set the whole place on fire."

"Good thing we had our doors shut when those jets flew over. I never heard nothin' that loud my whole life."

"Blew Uncle Ho outta bed, I bet'cha."

"I wonder if the Major is watching over us tonight."

"The Major will be with us the rest of our lives."

"Well said, Sergeant."

Lieutenant Butler had come to rely on Pasamenus the same way he had trusted Gunny Abernathy. Pasamenus was wise beyond his years. Butler respected his wisdom and his tactical judgment. The sergeant, in turn, fussed over the welfare of his men, as well as his first lieutenant.

"Hey, look. There she goes."

Up ahead the tracks began a steady climb up the side of the mountain. Trees and vegetation were cut back on both sides to accommodate the boxcars and locomotives. Beyond that it was dense jungle. They labored on another two hundred yards until they could see the outline of the pass in the glow of the fires.

"Time to dump our gear, men."

They were hiding their packs and weapons when Henry stood up, cupping a hand to his ear. "I hear something."

"Be quiet, listen!"

In the distance they heard a train whistle. The engineer was signaling the guards in the pass. Another load of war materiels was on the way to defend the motherland against the hated Americans. Butler and his party gathered their equipment back together and waited beneath the trees. The drifting fog was damp and statically charged, producing an eerie glow in the moonlight.

"The Orange Blossom Special will slow down coming up the grade. That's when we hitch a ride. Any train personnel, use your .38s. Let the engineer stop the train before we deal with him and the guards. Sergeant, do you think you can operate a steam engine?"

"It has levers on the engineer's side for going forward and backing up. I remember something about a foot pedal for braking, but engaging the steam system is complicated. I've never seen that done before."

Pasamenus was Red's intellectual mentor and friend. "You can do it, hoss."

"Get ready, men. He's coming up the tracks."

"Reminds me uh back home an' them hoboes jumpin' trains behind my mama's place."

"*Oui*, we are now the hungry hoboes. I wonder what dish they have in store for us tonight."

"Fried 'nads, maybe?

"Duke, you asshole!"

The train passed them at a slow, steady pace, billowing smoke, puff-puff-puffing up the mountain grade. Climbing onboard was easy. Red and Bubba confronted a security guard in their boxcar. Bubba shot him with his .38 before the man could locate his weapon.

The train consisted of five boxcars, a flatbed with two Russian T-55 medium battle tanks, and one steam engine connected to a wood tender. Three more Vietnamese guards were shot and killed without the engineer or the fireman ever realizing they were under attack. The last car was secured with heavy padlocks. Minutes later the engineer pulled to a stop between the gap in the mountain.

The Marines and Legionnaires lay in wait on top of the wood tender. Down below, six guards congregated beside the locomotive, excitedly discussing the air attack with the engineer and his fireman. They never bothered inspecting the cargo. Five seconds later the guards lay dead on the ground.

Bubba and Pasamenus stood inside the locomotive with a revolver pointed at the fireman and the engineer. Tony climbed up, asking the engineer in Vietnamese how it worked. The engineer refused to answer, calling Tony a traitor, and spat in his face. Tony asked him again. He refused, cursing Tony, yanking a knife from his coveralls. Tony jumped down to avoid the assault. Bubba shot the engineer in back of the head.

Tony turned his attention to the fireman, offering to let him live if he told them what they wanted to know. The man was terrified, stammering out details of how the steam system operated, going forward, braking the train, and backing up. Tony translated while Pasamenus took notes. Tony then thanked the fireman. They tied him up and left him in the guard shack.

Pasamenus engaged the steam system, gently applying the throttle. The front wheels spun momentarily, caught, and the engine began to roll forward. Red slapped him on the shoulders.

"Brain, you're a fucking genius!"

"Red, my friend, I take that as a Tennessee compliment."

"Bubba, this place looks like a danged bowl, sorta like Pigeon Forge."

"Yeah. Got them mountains up all around us."

Pasamenus applied the brakes gingerly, and down the grade they went. The second checkpoint lay a mile ahead. As they approached the barrier they saw only two guards standing at the entrance to the compound. Everyone else was busy fighting fires and helping the injured. Pasamenus slowed the train as the guards hailed the cab. Both men were shot dead before they could open their mouths. Johnson jumped down, dragging the bodies to the forward boxcar where the Legionnaires pulled them inside.

The revolvers and their silencers had accounted for thirteen men, and gotten them inside the compound. The place was in utter chaos. Nobody paid any attention to the arrival of the supply train. Dead and wounded were being tended to all over camp. Pasamenus eased up to the loading dock while Bubba tossed more logs in the furnace to keep the steam up.

A massive concrete bunker rose before them in the recessed side of a mountain. Dropping a bomb in there would be next to impossible without flying into the top of the ridge. The concrete entrance, draped with black camouflage netting, presented an eerie sight. The flames behind them cast macabre shadows dancing across the hanging material. "Man! This place gives me the heebie-jeebies. That black curtain looks like Frankenstein's asshole."

Movement of the shadows on the camouflage netting brought to mind the chained prisoners in Plato's *Allegory of the Cave*. Pasamenus' mused about the unreality of the shadows projected on the walls of their dungeon by a fire kept burning behind them, the fanciful delusions of the chained prisoners observing the shadows, and the reality discovered in the world outside the cave by the one prisoner who managed to escape.

Vietnam was like that, an allegory between fact and illusion. Washington and the news media had altered the public's perception of the truth. So had the political fantasies propagandized by the politburos in Peking and Moscow.

Pasamenus and Butler had versed First Squad in the gospel according to all the propaganda and lies manufactured by the politicians around the world. The Legionnaires were painfully aware of the catastrophic results from such stupidity and political arrogance from their own corrupt government in Paris. Plato's form and reality had revealed themselves to Pasamenus in an unexpected time and place, engineering an enemy supply train amid the carnage and horrors of war.

Butler's gallows humor broke the spell. "So it does. Let's go inside and see what Frank has on the slab."

"Yeah. Kick Frank's commie bastard ass!"

"Sergeant, lead the way. I'll be tail end Charlie. If Igor pops out of the woodwork, shoot the hunchback cock sucker."

Dismounting the train, they hurried across a broad concrete apron toward the subterranean entrance. Pasamenus noticed a bronze plaque on the central support pillar. The interior was pitch black, silent, smelling of oil and machinery. For several moments they stood motionless, listening for any movement.

Driggins was the first to switch on his flashlight. Then everyone followed suit. A great assembly room appeared before them. Long rocket gurneys on rubber wheels, an overhead monorail system, cranes, forklifts, compressors, generators. A warhead sat on a wooden bench beside a steel gurney housing an SA-2 surface-to-air antiaircraft missile. Five more missiles sat on gurneys beside the first one. On a nearby wall hung a red flag of the Soviet Union.

"Something isn't right about this, Lieutenant."

"I saw it out front, Sergeant. These are Russians."

"Makes sense. SA-2s are made in the Soviet Union."

"Looks like Moscow's in this war up to Brezhnev's eyebrows."

"You can bet the State Department will hear about this. Leave nothing behind that might identify us, else we're up Shit Creek."

"Sir, there's a few of those rocket things over there in the corner."

"Warheads or missiles?"

"Warheads, sir."

"Cassidy?"

"I'm on it, Lieutenant."

"Fan out, look for combustibles. Anything Cassidy can use for demolition."

They found five more SA-2 nose cones, but no more missiles. The warheads were heavy, 434 pounds each, but that wasn't enough to destroy the laboratory of reinforced concrete and solid rock. Nor were the six missiles enough with their rocket propellant. At best, their efforts would put the place out of commission for five, maybe six months. And they didn't have enough C4 to bring down the ceiling.

"Sir, those tanks on the flatcar outside. If they have ammunition in them we could do some serious damage with that."

"Driggins, Henry, check it out."

"Cassidy, place your charges in the most strategic locations. Stuff they can't live without. Don't forget the monorail, and that big-ass generator."

Driggins and Henry were back in five minutes.

"Sir, they got forty-three rounds apiece, and five boxes of ammo for each machine gun. Those turrets are small inside."

"Hold on a minute, Cassidy. Gentlemen, put on your thinking caps. We're a hundred and ten miles inside the DMZ. Once we expose ourselves it could get pretty hairy around here. We're outgunned, but we do have the element of surprise. And they've already been hit once tonight. I have faith we can pull this off, but if any of you want to set the detonators and bug out now, we all go together. No questions asked. Sergeant, talk it over with the men."

Peter was the first to speak. "Lieutenant, Henri and my men believe as you do. We came here to avenge Adrian and your Major. Johnny and I will man one of the tanks."

Red spoke up. "Bubba says stay. Tony and me can operate that other tank if Peter will tell us how it works."

Each man spoke his piece, paying tribute to Adrian Devereux, Major Abraham, Gunny Abernathy, and John Jackson. They all knew the risks. That didn't matter much. They were there on a mission only warriors understood.

Lieutenant Butler addressed them. "I'm not much on speeches, gentlemen, but I want to say this before we start. You men are something special. Damned special! I'm proud to have served with each one of you. Good luck! Now let's kick some Ivan ass."

Calhoun climbed on top of the wood tender with his .50 caliber sniper rifle. Visibility was excellent. The fires had burned away the fog. Henry handed up two sacks of gravel to steady the rifle for accuracy. Cassidy went to work setting his fuses with thirty-minute delays.

Pasamenus remained in the cab with Butler. Tony and Red climbed inside the number one tank. Peter, a former tank commander, and Johnny commandeered the second tank. Being experienced with armor, their job was knocking out targets in the compound. Red and Tony would fire into the right side of the laboratory, safely away from the antiaircraft weapons. The remainder of the men spread out along the tops of the boxcars.

Ten minutes elapsed.

Finally Cassidy rapped on the side of the locomotive. "I'm done."

"Go tell Peter and Tony."

Cat banged on the tank turrets, delivering his message, then climbed on top of the train with the others. The tank engines rumbled to life, bellowing black diesel smoke. The men let them run at quarter throttle a minute and a half, then idled down. Slowly the steel turrets began to move, their long heavy gun barrels turning as though they were alive, waking from a dreadful slumber, seeking human prey.

Peter sighted in on a flak tower on top of the mountain. Red and Tony pointed their 100mm cannon straight toward the black curtain shielding the laboratory. Peter fired, the flak tower exploded. Tony pulled his trigger. The inside of the laboratory belched smoke and debris. Peter fired again, shattering a barracks building in the compound.

Lieutenant Butler sent out their radio message. "Peter Pan. This is Little Abner. Come in, Peter Pan."

… static crackled over the radio …

"Peter Pan. Come in, Peter Pan."

"Peter Pan here. What's on the menu, Little Abner?"

"We're in Neverland."

"Do you require napkins and silverware?"

"That's affirmative."

"Understood, Little Abner. Lost Boys will deliver the picnic basket."

Calhoun spotted an officer marshaling his troops for action. Placing the cross hairs on his chest, he fired. The man buckled backwards, dead before he hit the deck. The delivery of the .50 caliber was almost as frightening as the 100mm tank cannons. The .50 caliber spat death again and again. Yelling. Confusion. Automatic rifle fire.

Peter swept a cluster of soldiers from beside a burning building. They disappeared in an explosion of arms and legs. An armor-piercing shell fired into the lab by Tony gouged out slabs of concrete from a support pillar. He fired again and the paint locker exploded. Peter sent a shell into a Soviet attack helicopter parked in the center of the compound. It blew up and burned. Tony fired another round, shattering the generator and setting the lubricating oil ablaze.

The .50 caliber fired again. A man with a sniper rifle fell from the roof of the infirmary.

"I may have gotten one of our snipers. He had a scope on that rifle."

"Right on, man, you're the Duke of Earl. Now pop ole General Giap for us."

"Where is that limp-dick pecker head?"

The firefight lasted eleven minutes, the tanks firing round after round. Return fire consisted of small arms weaponry. Bullets were cracking and whining all over the engine and the wood tender. Time was winding down for the delayed-action fuses. Pasamenus engaged the lever, and began backing up the train.

An incoming round exploded where the locomotive had been sitting.

"Get this sumbitch moving. Some asshole's got the range."

A second round came whistling in, bursting in the trees beside the tracks.

"Can you see where it's coming from?"

"Not yet. I can't see shit with all this smoke."

"Back it up! Back it up!"

Duke's first timer detonated the rockets. A cloud of flame shot out the front of the bunker, billowing up into the sky. Muffled explosions followed from the C4 charges going off inside. Then the warheads detonated. A tsunami of smoke and fire blew out two hundred feet into the compound. The fog of war shielded them from the antiaircraft batteries on the mountain. Pasamenus hauled down on the lanyard of the train's whistle. It wailed defiantly. Everyone cheered.

Gargoyle came running along the top of the train. "Lieutenant, I shot it open. There is something in the back car."

"What, Henri? What is it?"

"Dynamite!"

"Sweet Jesus! How much?"

"The boxcar, she is full."

"You hear that, Cassidy?"

"Yes sir. That's enough to waste the whole place."

"Got anything left?"

"Two detonators and two C4."

"Pasamenus, you okay with this?"

"Yes, sir. We can go out on foot. I'll stop by those trees up ahead."

"Peter? Freddie?"

"We are with you, Lieutenant."

"Okay, Miss Buckingham. Do your thing!"

Cassidy climbed down inside the boxcar where he found four hundred boxes of dynamite stacked halfway to the ceiling. Setting his fuses for fifteen minutes, he scurried back along the tracks to warn Butler and the others.

"Sir, there must be 20,000 pounds back there. I set the timers for fifteen minutes. We got about thirteen minutes left."

"Tell me, Cassidy. What will ten tons of dynamite do exactly?"

"We're about a half-mile from the bunker. That Ivan complex down there sits right in front of it. When she blows, we better be behind something or we'll join all those soon to be airborne Russians."

"Men, get down behind the railroad grade. Find cover wherever you can. Sergeant, you better get our Orange Blossom Special under way."

Pasamenus released the brakes and the train began to roll forward. He stayed with it to make certain it didn't stop, then jumped off to rejoin the group. The train picked up momentum, reached the bottom of the grade, clanging into a concrete abutment at the end of the tracks beside the bunker. Small arms fire had withered to only a handful of enemy rifles.

"Dang, ain't it never gonna do nothin'? It's been sitting there all night. What if ..."

Horrific detonation!

An orange thundercloud enveloped the train and everything in front of the bunker. Shock waves blasted vehicles, buildings, people into the air. The front wall of the mountain gave way, collapsing down and burying the entrance to the laboratory. Boxcar parts, railroad ties, tree limbs, and debris rained down around the men. A pair of boxcar wheels landed in the forest farther up the tracks. A broad crater appeared where the train had been resting, as a billowing mushroom cloud rose into the sky. The locomotive lay upside down two hundred feet from the blast. The Russian missile compound was gone, save for a few outlying buildings.

"Let's get the fuck outta here!"

They were climbing the grade when incoming fire from an antiaircraft battery began chewing up the landscape. The smoke was clearing and they had been spotted from the ridge. A hail of 37mm rounds were impacting all around them. A heavy caliber field gun opened fire. Explosions shook the earth. Then another flak battery joined the chorus. Trees were blown apart. The sides of the mountain leading to the pass were being raked with high explosives. Shards of rock and shrapnel filled the air.

"Sounds like Phenix City on a Friday night."

"We have to go another way. We'll never get through there."

Butler pulled out the map. "The only way out of here, short of climbing the side of this mountain or that road to perdition down there, is this creek bed here on the map. Looks like there's an abandoned railroad down there beside the swamp. Ground's probably too soft so they built this one. Stay in the trees. They can't see us from the ridge."

It was a mile to the marsh and the railroad tracks, which led south through the mountains. Shorty and his helicopters weren't due for another twenty minutes. They couldn't fly inside the valley or they'd be blasted out of the sky by the radar-controlled guns. They were too slow to evade the flak batteries. So the Marines and the four Legionnaires were slogging out on foot.

"At least it's downhill. You men got much ammo left?"

"I got seven clips, Lieutenant."

"That should be plenty."

"Sir, I just got two."

"Listen up, men. Distribute your magazines evenly among yourselves. Engage your selector switches to semiautomatic."

A moss-covered riverbank appeared, reminded Johnson of a coloring book he had when he was a little boy. There were cattails and orchids, pretty water lilies, daisies, and hollyhocks. Bamboo grew down to the water's edge, tall ferns and pines. The pine trees reminded Marcus of the sawmill in Magnolia Springs where one of his cousins worked stacking lumber and driving a flatbed truck. His cousin used to let him ride in the cab sometimes when he was delivering lumber.

Farther on they maneuvered through a stand of palm trees with curious brown monkeys overhead. A September moon shown down, making patches of quicksilver on the surface of the marsh. A startled heron shrieked in fright, flapping away in noisy protest. In places they sank up to their ankles in the mud, but they were safe there from the flak batteries high on the ridges overlooking their passage.

Lieutenant Butler and Sergeant Pasamenus were at the end of the column. Tony and Red were on point. They were strung out twenty meters and making good progress. Butler and Pasamenus had been quietly discussing the impact of the Russians and the Chinese on the Vietnam War. They fell silent for several minutes, winding their way through the brambles and trees when Pasamenus suddenly stopped, turning to his lieutenant with sweat streaking his serious brow.

"This ancient battleground … this divided land … will define a Pyrrhic disaster for our United States."

Butler was caught off guard by the sergeant's logic. But it made perfect sense. Pasamenus had put into words what had been troubling the lieutenant ever since they encountered the Russian camp. It was clear to him then. Washington knew Moscow and Peking were there. Politics and fear had forfeited the Korean War. Politics and fear were losing the Vietnam War.

America no longer was the resolute military force she had been following World War Two. Neither were the Western Powers. Uncle Sam and the British Lion had become pusillanimous pussyfooters, political imposters, fearful of world opinion.

Pasamenus pushed aside a large frond. The jungle and the hanging vines swallowed them. Another hundred yards and a large expanse of water appeared on their right with a flotilla of ducks milling around.

"Don't scare the ducks. Pass it on."

They were crossing over a dead tree above a tributary when Calhoun got his rifle tangled in the vines and fell in. The .50 caliber landed beside him with a loud splash. A pair of startled ducks took flight. A dozen rose. All flew, flapping their wings and quacking loudly, making enough noise to wake the dead.

Everyone froze.

A twin-mount 37mm opened fire, raking the water with twenty-foot splashes, firing into the pines, the bamboo, blasting the earth with high explosive antiaircraft rounds.

"Pom, Pom, Pom, Pom."

The weapon was accurate and terrifying. Tracers streaked through the night, slamming into the jungle, blasting dirt and debris, cutting trees in half, showering the men with particles of envy and hate.

"Get the hell outta here! Run for the railroad!"

Chapter Forty-Five

The Kalamazoo

They ran through the briars and thickets with two flak batteries tearing up the landscape right behind them. No matter which way they turned there was the "Pom, Pom, Pom, Pom" from the antiaircraft guns, getting closer by the second. Lieutenant Butler dug out a smoke grenade and pulled the pin. Then a second smoke grenade. There was no breeze in the valley so the smoke hung in the air, concealing them momentarily. The flak batteries continued to fire but they were several meters high, impacting against the side of the mountain.

"Them assholes must have night vision. Russian, Chinese, they both got it."

"Keep moving. There's trees up ahead. We'll rest there."

"Have you seen what's behind us?"

In the distance, coming down the tracks, were the glints of rifles in the moonlight. The men on the flak batteries had radioed for help. A company of North Vietnamese Army regulars had arrived in a truck convoy.

"How much farther, Lieutenant?"

"Three miles. Get to the trees. I'll make the call there."

They ran another hundred meters down the railroad tracks with 37mm rounds impacting against the mountain behind them. Finally they reached the trees where they were safe from the guns.

"Peter Pan. Come in Peter Pan."

"Where are you are, Little Abner?"

"Headed for the back door. Old railroad track. South end."

"We got four MiGs upstairs. Calvary is on the way."

"Are you in the air?"

"No. It's too hot. Uncle Sam is due in three minutes. Will rendezvous your back door when he arrives."

"We may need those heavies. We got our hands full here."

"What's wrong?

"Flak batteries, plus a carload of assholes about two miles behind us."

"I'll call Mother Goose."

"Roger that, Peter Pan."

"Shit! They're on top of us and behind us too."

"Take a salt pill and drink your water."

They rested sixty seconds, then moved out. Tracers appeared in the heavens. Then the flash of heat-seeking missiles. An air battle between Russian MiG 21s and American F-105s was being played out 22,000 feet above their heads.

Bright explosion.

One of the jets was hit, spiraling down in flaming debris. The antiaircraft guns remained silent. They didn't want to shoot down one of their own pilots by mistake.

"Wonder if that's one of ours?"

"Can't tell. Shorty will let us know."

"Pick up the pace. We got cold beers waiting."

"Pasamenus, the slave driver. I never …"

Concussion knocked Catfish and Henry off their feet.

"Jesus! That was close."

"Is ever' body okay?"

Another round uprooted a tree on the far side of the tracks.

"Run for it!"

A third shell blasted part of a railroad tie high in the air behind them.

"Run, goddamn it. Run!"

Bubba staggered and fell.

"Johnson! Get him!"

Bubba's cheek was split open from shrapnel. Red could see his teeth.

"Come on, Bubba. I got'cha."

Another explosion erupted between the steel rails in front of them.

"Into the trees, men."

Lieutenant Butler set off two more smoke grenades. "Is he hurt bad?"

"It ain't real bad, sir, but he's bleeding like a stuck pig."

"Little Abner. Little Abner"

"Go ahead, Peter Pan."

"I got four heavies loading, and five little friends on the way."

"Good job. Looks like we're going to need some help."

"Fix me, Dwayne. I can make it."

"Roger that. I'll check back as soon as they're in sight."

Henry ran a clothespin through Bubba's cheek to hold the loose flesh together, placed a Red Cross bandage over it, then wrapped his head with tape.

"You look like The Mummy."

Red was making jest, but there was concern in his eyes for his friend who was covered with blood.

"Come on, ole son."

Johnson helped Bubba to his feet. They journeyed on through the trees, out of sight of the gunners on top of the ridge.

The jungle became too dense for walking so they angled back toward the tracks.

"Hey! What's that gizmo up there?"

"Thank God! It's a Kalamazoo!"

"A what?"

"A pump trolley. A handcar."

They ran for the machine sitting on the railroad tracks

"Climb on. Let's go."

"The handle. She won't move." Freddie jiggled the handles again. The gears were rusted tight.

"Henry! You got any Vaseline in that medical kit?"

"One tube of railroad grease coming up, Lieutenant."

Peter emptied the Vaseline in the gearbox. Johnson and Calhoun shoved at the handles until the rust broke free. They began to roll, the wrong way.

"Flip the lever switch. It's right there."

Bubba spat out a mouthful of blood. "Got 'er made in the shade now, boys."

Tony laughed. "Go home quick now."

They pumped like madmen, rolling down the tracks for two miles. The NVA were still behind them, yelling, cursing, firing their weapons, but they were beyond effective rifle range. The 37mm guns had lost them in the dark. A wooden bridge appeared up ahead. The marsh narrowed there and ran deep.

"Incoming! Hang on!"

A 130mm round came whistling in, detonating beneath the wheels. The Kalamazoo and everyone onboard went flying through the air.

The contraption landed upside down on the railroad tracks, minus its front axel and wheels. Catfish and Freddie had been blown into the river. Peter landed in the cattails beneath the bridge, breaking his ankle. Bubba lay face down on the railroad gravel, out cold. The flesh on the back of Johnson's right hand was peeled back from his knuckles to his wrist. Calhoun had sustained a broken arm. Everyone had damages, but Tony and Red had caught the worst of it.

Red had lost his legs, one above the knee, the other at his right calf. A shell fragment had severed Tony's spinal column just below his shoulder blades. Both men were conscious. Henry was busy tying off Red's bloody stumps while a shaken Lieutenant Butler surveyed the battle damage.

"Little Abner, come in, Little Abner."

"Peter Pan, we got wounded … have the flyboys arrived yet?"

"We got MiGs out the ass. Two heavies are down. Two little friends. Heavy radio traffic out of Hanoi. I've never seen anything like this. Somebody is pissed off big time. My people are scattered all over hell and back, but we're trying."

Explosions began chewing up the top of the ridge opposite the Kalamazoo. Tracers flew in every direction from one of the flak batteries struck by a bomb. One of the bombers had gotten through. More bombs began falling on the railroad tracks above them. Loud explosions. Another B-26 had made it.

"Pom, Pom, Pom, Pom."

Pasamenus compared notes with Butler. It was six hundred yards to the gap in the mountains. The choppers couldn't fly in or they'd be picked up by radar and shot to pieces. The NVA were up the tracks a mile and a half, approaching as fast as they could run. And the MiGs owned the sky. They were caught in a shit storm. Butler and Pasamenus knelt down beside Tony and Red.

Tony spoke. "Red … we stay, maybe?"

Red rolled over and stared at his friend. "You mean here?"

"You cripple. Me cripple. No good no more."

"Stay here … and man this bridge?"

"Yes … stay here. Yes."

"You sure about that?"

"Yes. We hold bridge. Friends go home."

Bubba had regained consciousness and crawled over beside Red. Bubba's backside was peppered with shrapnel. He couldn't walk. The Frenchmen and the rest of First Squad were gathered around their fallen comrades.

Gargoyle held Red's hand. "I will stay with you and Tony."

"This is crazy."

Lieutenant Butler was bleeding from multiple shrapnel wounds. Henry had powder burns on his face and hands. "We'll carry you out."

Two Skyraiders appeared above the treetops to the east, dove on one of the mountain batteries, frying it with napalm, then disappeared over the mountains to the west, the starboard aircraft trailing a white plume of smoke.

A minute later the port craft flew back over the ridge, hammering another battery with his 20mm cannons, then flew away when a MiG came roaring down the valley. Upstairs, seven American pilots were slugging it out with seventeen MiG 21s. The Americans were doing everything possible to keep the 21s off the Skyraiders and B-26s.

Red made his decision. His day of reckoning was perched on the railing of a railroad trestle. He and Tony had become expendable assets. He would bleed to death or die from shock before they got him back to Hue or Da Nang. Tony was paralyzed and didn't want to spend the rest of his days in a stinking veterans home. But Bubba could make it if Johnson and the others carried him. They could all get out if he and Tony could hold the bridge. Otherwise, they were goners.

"No, Henri. Madame needs you. We're staying here."

Pasamenus understood. He hated it. Loathed even thinking about it. It hurt like a dagger driven in his heart. He felt the post-traumatic trauma he carried inside ever since he and Red had fought their rear-guard action coming out of the A Shau Valley.

North Vietnamese soldiers drenched with flaming napalm, the Air Force overhead, bombs falling everywhere, M-14 magazines being passed back from the Marines fleeing through the jungle toward the rescue helicopters. Him and Red dodging in and out behind the trees, emptying one magazine after another. The intense heat from the napalm, and that horrific screaming from the enemy soldiers on fire.

John and Gunny. Gayle and Mimi. Adrian and the Major. Nothing was real anymore. Pasamenus was looking down at his two comrades on a bloody railroad trestle through the eyes of a stranger. His mind rebelled. He hated the Vietnam War, the generals, the politicians. He hated the cowards in Washington, the Marxist professors, the leftwing news organizations. He hated the mosquitoes, the monsoon, and the stifling heat. He hated the communists, the lying socialists, the greedy, fucking capitalists. He hated the whole malignant nine yards of ass-wipe dictators and scumbag politicians!

He wanted to pick up Tony and Red, make them whole again, give them new bodies, become God. He wanted to end the suffering, the useless, senseless, horrible war. It felt for the moment as though he were going insane.

He longed for the ruby slippers, to click his heels so everyone could be back in The World again, safe and sound with their loved ones, having a cold beer, going to a drive -in movie. But there was no other way, no escape from the responsibility, not if he and Lieutenant Butler were going to get the rest of First Squad and the Frenchmen out alive. Too many of them were injured to carry Tony and Red out quickly enough. And Bubba too. The NVA would overtake them before they made it two hundred yards.

Pasamenus placed a hand on the Lieutenant's shoulder. Butler looked up with tears in his eyes. Then Pasamenus touched Henri's shoulder. He too was overcome with emotion. They knew Red and Tony were right. They knew in their hearts that if their roles were reversed they would do the same thing for their comrades. It was a matter of honor and choice and loyalty among men.

Bubba was semiconscious from loss of blood, but he understood what was taking place. He crawled up to Red and put his arms around his cousin. "I wish it was me and not you."

"You hush now. You got Suzie back home waiting on you. I got no future like this. I'll croak anyhow before they get me out. Tell my mama and daddy I love them. Take my dog tags. I love you, Barthalamaeus. I love you, man. Remember this night. And remember me. You marry that girl, you hear. Now get me the Cat."

Gargoyle motioned for Cassidy.

"Set up the claymores on the bridge. Drag that piece-of-shit pump doodle to this end so me and Tony can get behind it. Leave the flares and some grenades.

"Brain, if they get their hands on us you guys could end up in Leavenworth. Tell Shorty to have the 105s waste this end of the bridge. I'll light the flares for an aiming reference."

An explosion was seen high up in the heavens. One of the MiGs had been hit, and was coming down in pieces. There was no parachute. Moments later another MiG 21 plummeted to the valley floor nose first, exploding in an orange fireball.

"Hey, look! One of our flyboys is still with us."

Coming up the valley was the last Skyraider going flat out and belly to the ground no more than twenty feet off the deck. He opened fire with his 20mm cannons just as he passed over their heads. They could hear the roar and thunder of the fighter jets shooting at one another three miles straight up. It sounded like something wild and terrible had broken loose from the Underworld.

"Pom, Pom, Pom, Pom."

The sergeant kneeled, clutching Red's and Tony's hands. He was torn between his responsibilities as a Marine Corps sergeant, and his emotions as a human being. Pasamenus loathed the thought of leaving Tony and Red. Marines don't leave Marines behind.

"Eshkhan, you got no choice. You have to save the men. Me and Tony will take care of the bridge. Remember that song Vera Lynn sang,

'We'll Meet Again'? I believe it, hoss. We'll meet again. Look after Bubba and Peter. Now get your Armenian ass outta here. There's a pretty nurse waiting for you on that boat."

"Lieutenant Butler?"

"Right here, Red. You need another morphine?"

"Sir, I'm right proud to have served with you. You're a good officer. Don't stay in this lousy war. Politicians are as bad as the Cong. Go someplace and find yourself a good woman. Get married and have some kids. When the Cat gets done, get the men outta here. Take the Thompson. Vera Lynn belongs with you and First Squad now. Ask Dwayne to stick us again, then go."

By the time they got the Kalamazoo positioned at the end of the bridge, Gargoyle and the Frenchmen had improvised a litter for carrying Bubba. Driggins helped Pasamenus and Butler situate Tony and Red behind the hand trolley. Then Cassidy handed them the detonators to the claymores. Grenades and flares were piled between the two men.

Cassidy knelt down, said goodbye to his two buddies, lit a cigarette for each one of them, then got up and walked over to help the injured Calhoun.

"So long, fellas. Don't take no wooden nickels."

"Hurry, please. Friends go home now."

Bubba wept as they carried him away. Peter limped along behind Bubba's grim procession, with Johnny and Freddie supporting Peter between them.

Butler and Pasamenus bowed their heads while Henry said a prayer over their two brothers who were about to die. Driggins was on the far end of the bridge monitoring the approach of the North Vietnamese.

"Lord, it's all gone to hell down here."

Red smiled. He had never heard Dwayne use profanity before.

"Two of our guys are coming your way pretty soon. Please welcome Red and Tony, and find a place in Your blessed kingdom for heroes. They did their jobs well, Sir. We got no complaints. Please tell Major Abraham to be on the lookout for these men. They're both like sons to Major Abraham."

Driggins came running across the bridge. "We got about two minutes."

Tony and Red lay side by side watching their friends disappear into the night. Tony was remembering the afternoon the Major crashed through the warehouse wall in a scout car and saved his life. Tony loved Major Abraham. The Major was going to adopt him and take him back to America before the secret police killed him.

He and Red had become fast friends on patrol out in the boondocks. They had learned to think and move as one while traveling through enemy territory. More important, each man had learned to trust the other with his life. Now neither one of them was going home to America. He felt bad about that, but glad too that Red was with him tonight. He wondered if he was being selfish about his buddy being there. Whatever was right they had one last mission to perform, hold the bridge long enough for their friends to make good their escape.

Red was thinking about the cheerleader he dated his junior and senior year at South High School. Carolyn had been the love of his life. Then she left him for a member of the South High Band. That hurt, but after his experiences in Vietnam he remembered the South Knoxville beauty with a sweet melancholy.

His thoughts drifted back to the man lying beside him on the railroad trestle. They had been through some wild-ass adventures together. Tony was his pal, a brave little man he had know only a few months. The Major had picked a winner in Tony. Now their saga was coming to an end. Red wished he could have taken Tony back with him to Knoxville. He would have loved the Southern Circle and all the pretty girls there.

Across the bridge they heard the scrunch of NVA boots on the railroad gravel.

"How you doin', Tony?"

"Not hurt. Pain gone now."

"You're a good man, Tony. We made a good team, didn't we?"

With eternity staring them in the face, Tony reached over and held Red's hand. He wished he could save his American friend. Red had become like a brother.

"Yes, Red. Good best friends."

"Sounds like we got company."

They could hear boots on the wooden railroad trestle.

"When I say 'now,' you set yours off. I'll save mine for the second round."

"Okey-dokey."

Seconds ticked by. Walking sounds approached the front of the hand trolley.

"Now!"

The ground quaked as thousands of steel pellets blasted into the forward ranks of the NVA. Screaming, gunfire, howls of pain. A barrage of bullets slammed into the trolley, churning up the earth on both sides of the wooden barrier.

"That fixed their commie-ass wagon!"

"Yes, fix damn good!"

Tony stuck his AK-47 around the trolley and emptied a thirty-round magazine. He was running a second clip through the weapon when an enemy bullet struck him in the forehead.

Loss of blood was taking its toll. Red was starting to drift in and out of consciousness. He heard footsteps and lobbed a grenade. Yelling. Gunfire. Red lobbed a second grenade. A third grenade.

A strange blue glow engulfed the atmosphere behind the hand trolley. "Hi ya, Dogface."

"Gunny! I thought you was dead."

"Not likely. We just changed zip codes."

"Get with the program, Red."

"John!"

"You're coming with us."

"I get it now. Is Tony with you?"

"I'm here, my friend."

"You guys look great."

"You look like something the cats dragged in."

"Don't say that!"

"Well, you do."

"Major!"

"You've done an excellent job, William. You're almost through."

"Guys, wait for me. I'm coming with you."

He looked again and saw Tony, wearing his Tiger Scout uniform, standing beside the Major. The Major had his arm around Tony's shoulders. John and Gunny were smiling back at Red. Captain America, the young ARVN soldier, was with them.

Footsteps.

He set off the last of the claymores.

Red popped a flare and threw it off to his left. Then another one to his right. Two more, and he lay in the middle of the burning magnesium. Overhead he heard the whine of an incoming jet aircraft. Abruptly the sound changed. The F-105 thundered skyward to escape the guns.

"Pom, Pom, Pom, Pom!"

The antiaircraft batteries were firing at the lone Thunderchief.

Red imagined himself back at the Southern Circle Drive-In Restaurant in South Knoxville, sharing a Jack Daniels and Coca-Cola with Carolyn Harris, the pretty cheerleader from South High School. It was autumn and the leaves were changing colors. She was smiling at Red. Red was holding her hand. Carolyn leaned over and kissed him.

The Kalamazoo disappeared in a cloud of flame and thunder as a pair of thousand-pound bombs obliterated the bridge and everyone there.

Chapter Forty-Six

Going Home

First Squad was upstairs in the old barracks outside Da Nang, sitting in a circle on the hardwood floor drinking Pabst Blue Ribbon. It was midnight. Henry had just lit an assortment of scented candles. Larry Cassidy had brought incense from the PX. The candlelight and the pungent odors soothed the men somewhat, but they were still in a state of mourning over their losses. Lieutenant Butler sat on the floor with them.

"Brain, what exactly did we accomplish over here?"

"I'm not sure, Duke. We came here with the best of intentions, but the politicians and the media, not to mention our gutless generals, upset the applecart."

"Right on. I don't recall a single one of them ever questioning Johnson."

"Fuck those spineless weasels! They cost us six of our best buddies."

"We're goin' home to a land fulla college pukes and political whores, that's all I know. I can hardly fucking wait! Oh, happy days. The sheer joy of having served my ungrateful country."

"Men, this may not be the time, but you're all a credit to the Corps. I wish I could do something to make things different. I wish I could bring them back."

"You did all you could, Lieutenant. If it weren't for you and Pasamenus we'd all be dead. That bastard Johnson could have won this crummy war if it wasn't for his dumb-ass containment bullshit."

"Things don't seem right without the Major."

"Fuckin' A! They sure as hell don't. Nothin' seems right no more with him and Gunny gone."

"What're you gonna say to Red's mama and daddy?"

Bubba thought for a minute. The bandage on his face had come loose. Driggins took his empty beer can, handing Bubba a fresh cold one. Henry placed two more pieces of adhesive tape across the bandage. Henry had a bandage on his forehead and one on his left hand.

"I'll tell 'em Red died saving his men. And me. I'll say he was a natural-born leader. I'll tell them he was a lot like our gunny sergeant who ever' body liked and respected. I'll say he was a lot more to me than just my cousin. Red was my friend. I'll tell 'em Red asked me to hug them for him if he didn't make it back, and say he always loved them even when he didn't act like it."

"That's good, Bubba. That's a swell epitaph. I sure miss that laugh of his. And that radio he carried around all the time."

"Red was one of those people who could have fun in a paper bag. He loved Elvis Presley and Nat King Cole. Did you know Red was a good dancer?"

"Yeah, I saw him dancing once at the Garden."

"They broke the mold when they made him and Tony. I'll never forget what they did for us at that bridge. They saved our lives."

"You damn sure got that right."

"The Major didn't have no family. I guess we're covered on that account."

"I checked. He left his insurance money to Pensri at the Garden. He did it so she could go to America."

"Him and Gunny were two of a kind. I don't reckon we'll ever meet anybody like them again."

"I got an idea. After we go home and visit our families, why don't we rendezvous in Knoxville and visit Red's parents? Let 'em know we care. It might help a little bit."

"That would be a nice gesture. What do you think, Lieutenant?"

"I think I'm in the company of Marine Corps gentlemen. It's an excellent suggestion. If I can arrange leave, I'll go with you."

"You and Pasamenus have a way with words, sir. That would be Number One."

"What about Tony? I don't think he had any family, did he?"

"He didn't. He told me his mother and father and his sister were killed in a bombing raid."

"What about his stuff?"

"I never thought about that."

"Why don't we put it in a locker box and take it with us? Somebody back home will have a war museum. That way Tony will be remembered."

"That would make Tony real proud. We need to honor him some way. Maybe get his story in a newspaper someplace."

"The Major said we made a difference. We kicked some ass. Too bad Westmoreland and his boys didn't have Major Abraham runnin' the show. With all that firepower we could a wiped out Charlie in a week."

"Fuckin' A! If we'd had them B-52s we'd a blown Haiphong in the ocean, and Hanoi with it! "

"Hell, all they needed was Catfish. Westmoreland didn't need no bombers. The Cat could squirt oil on 'em and set their asses on fire."

"He oughta squirt some on Johnson and that bunch a freaks in Washington."

The men laughed and the tension was broken. Johnson popped another codeine tablet to ease the throbbing in his hand, then handed Bubba his switchblade to slide up under his bandage and scratch his stitches.

"Sergeant, where are you and Gayle going to live?"

"I left it up to her. Australia, maybe, but she's still thinking it over. New Zealand, Hong Kong, whatever she wants."

"Me and Calhoun like Australia. Get ourselves a little spread out a ways from town. Find a couple of Outback cutie pies and settle down. Raise us some kids. And them fuzzy things that live in trees."

"Koala bears, Catfish. They're called koala bears."

"Sounds swell. What about you, Johnson? Madame's leaving for Paris. Henri's going with her. What're you gonna do about Su Su?"

"I called mama and told her the whole story. Know what mama said? Said 'bring that girl to Magnolia Springs, boy.' I damn near fainted!"

"I'd like to come visit, when I get done up Knoxville way."

"Me too."

"Count me in, bro."

"Marcus, if I can get leave I'll swing by after visiting Red's parents on my way back here. Think you can handle all us jarheads?"

"Y'all come, sir. Me and mama will cook up a batch uh gumbo, collard greens, cornbread, red beans an' rice. Ain't none uh y'all tasted food like my mama cooks."

"I'll look forward to that. If I can't get leave, I'll come visit when my tour of duty is over. I'd enjoy meeting Su Su and your mother."

The burning candles cast dancing shadows on the walls, some of them ghostlike, taking Pasamenus back to the train and the Russian missile compound, Red and Tony at the railroad trestle, Shorty waiting for them in the mountain pass, and Plato's Cave.

The chirping of tiny parakeets and chattering of the gray-and-brown monkeys came drifting back in nightmarish fashion, and for a moment Pasamenus was seized with a fear bordering on hysteria. His hands trembled and he wanted to cry, run, anything to get away from the invisible demon in his head. Johnson noticed because he had one too, inside his head. Johnson understood, because in his dreams he was afraid.

Specters, men blown to pieces, burned beyond recognition, guts hanging out, brains drooling down, wandering the corridors of his subconscious. Lost souls searching for a friend, forgiveness, a drink of muddy water, some morphine to ease the pain, refuge from the Iron Storm.

Having one's mind invaded by the phantoms of war is that cross to bear for every combat veteran. They seldom talk about their experiences because it forces them to look back, and remember, and relive their blood-splattered past.

Johnson reached over and nudged Pasamenus. The 1,000-yard stare left him, and he was sane again, back in squad bay with his men. Only Lieutenant Butler knew the severity they suffered from post-traumatic stress syndrome. They asked him not to tell. Gargoyle had warned Johnson, it would stay with them forever. But it would diminish, given time, and they would learn to live with their inner wreckage.

"Sergeant, what do you think we actually accomplished, given the circumstances here?"

"Well … it's hard to say. Johnson is a disaster as Commander in Chief. And the war is probably lost because the politicians in Congress no longer have the backbone to fight like we did during World War Two. That involved whole cities destroyed, thousands of civilians killed. Today they're afraid of world opinion. Truth be known, they're political cowards. That leaves Uncle Sam out on a limb, fighting a relentless enemy who is willing to sacrifice a hundred of his soldiers to kill five or ten of ours.

"Maybe we did halt communism, at least for the time being. India and Pakistan appear sound in spite of their political differences. The Philippines are good. Thailand. Indonesia. Time will tell, especially regarding our next presidential election in November. If Nixon wins, Vietnam has a chance. If McGovern or Humphrey gets in, the ballgame is over."

Lieutenant Butler was impressed. "That's the best political analogy I've heard. Some colonel was giving us a pep talk a while back in the mess hall, but he didn't have the first clue about winning the war in Vietnam. Kept talking about upping the body count, and more search-and-destroy missions. That's typical for most brass coming out of the Pentagon these days."

"Lieutenant, do you think it was worth Red and Tony's lives? Or John and Gunny's?"

Lieutenant Butler stared at the candles, lost in thought. The seven men seated to the right and left of him were closer than sweethearts and wives ever could be. Each man had fought and bled beside every man in the room, Daniel Butler included. They were an elite fighting unit, as good as any in the Southeast Asia Theatre of Operations.

Finally he raised his head and spoke. His voice reverential as the shadows danced about the walls, the candlelight reflecting liquid fire in his eyes.

> *"From this day to the ending of the world,*
> *But we in it shall be remembered –*
> *We few, we happy few, we band of brothers;*
> *For he to-day that sheds his blood with me*
> *Shall be my brother; be he ne'er so vile,*
> *This day shall gentle his condition;*
> *And gentlemen in England now-a-bed*
> *Shall think themselves accurs'd they were not*
> *here,*

And hold their manhoods cheap whiles any speaks
That fought with us upon Saint Crispin's day.'"

"That was written by William Shakespeare in 1599 in tribute to the Battle of Agincourt, back in 1415 between France and England. Henry V and his men were heavily outnumbered by the French Army, sickly, low on morale and supplies. But King Henry rallied his troops and England carried the day. That describes how I feel about being a member of First Squad and the men we lost.

"I wouldn't take anything for the experience, but I sure as hell wouldn't want to do it over again. No, gentlemen, I don't think the American experience in Vietnam was worth all the bloodshed and tragedy. Certainly not the lives of our friends. We never fought to win. We were sent here to bleed and die in a lousy political crap game."

Pasamenus was the first to rise. The others followed suit, helping Bubba to his feet. They stood there, facing Lieutenant Butler in silence. Pasamenus spoke for all of them.

"You and I are brothers, sir, blood brothers. Just as surely as King Henry and his men were brothers. I wouldn't take anything for the experience myself, nor would any man in this room. Wherever life leads us, no matter the distance, no matter our stations in life, we will always be brothers to one another just as surely as the spirits of our departed brothers are with us this night and always.

"I hope you get leave, sir, to come with us to Knoxville. Red was special. While we're there we can look up John's parents. His wife is dying with cancer. Maybe we'll get there in time to say goodbye to Samantha. Tony's stuff we can take with us. That way Tony's memory will live on.

"I don't know how to say this exactly, but I feel like an era is passing. Something great is dying in America. You hear it on the news. The politicians, some of them, talk like traitors. They would have been tried for treason and jailed or hanged back in the '40s. Now it's every day.

We're the bad guys. Poor Charlie is misunderstood. Anyone who believes that chicken shit, In Country or back in The World, is no longer an American, not in my book."

Calhoun stepped to the center of the circle, standing between the candles on the floor, his arm in an elastic hospital sling.

"I lost my best friend last tour. The gooks tortured Billy, then gutted him. Today I have a new blood brother, Larry Cassidy. We're going to Australia to live and raise our families. I don't want to live in a country that doesn't honor their military or their war dead. I'm afraid of what I might do if one of those war protesters got in my face again. Pasamenus is right. The America we knew is dying. It's no longer a country of God and patriotism. It's deadbeats and victims and Big Brother. I wish all of you good luck and God speed. Come visit Larry and me when you get the chance. We'll get shit-faced and tell each other lies about this 'tropical paradise.' "

Driggins and Henry supported Bubba as he shuffled into the circle. "Getting hit in the face wasn't so bad, but this ass business hurts like hell."

They all laughed.

"Ya know, John an' Red an' me were lost balls in high weeds when we joined up. Over here, we changed. We became men. Red and John are upstairs in Glory now with Tony an' Gunny an' Major Abraham. I got me a good woman back home. A real fine lady, but I ain't gonna mind it one little bit when my time comes. I'll be goin' home to be with my brothers. I never knew much about God or politics 'til I came here. But boy, did I learn. I'm gonna miss Pasamenus and his history lessons. And Henry and his Bible. I'm gonna miss all you jarheads. A fellow couldn't ask for no better friends than you fellows. Y'all take good care uh yourselves now, ya hear."

Lieutenant Butler reminded them of something important. "Men, listen up. Never reveal our missions above the Demilitarized Zone or over in Laos. If the wrong people got wind of it back in Washington or in the news media, we could all land in Leavenworth. None of what we accomplished was ever authorized. We'd get nailed for war crimes or some shit by some ambulance chasing prick making a name for himself at our expense. So keep our adventures under your hat."

Driggins took the floor. "The thing I've missed most about Yaupon Beach are my loggerhead turtles. I'm going home to attend Wake Forest, live on campus, chase women, and hopefully forget about this place. But I know I won't. Vietnam has been a fucking horror show. But it was also the best experience I'll ever have. What does one say to men who held your life in their hands? Thank you? Have a nice day? It goes much deeper than that. We evolved into something here resembling magic. Out there in the boonies we moved and thought as one man. It's what kept us alive. Our buddies who died weren't doing anything wrong. It was just the luck of the draw that day. I'm still alive because of you people. And them. God, I'm going to miss you bastards."

Driggins had tears in his eyes. Butler and Pasamenus stepped into the circle and hugged him. Everyone rose and hugged Fred or patted him on the shoulders. Then they sat back down, except Johnson.

"Before I joined the Marines I had some pretty bad notions about white folks. We got the Klan down where I live. They're bad people. But you fellas changed all that. Gunny talked to me one night on fence patrol. He told me you were good people. I wasn't sure at first, even though I loved Gunny Abernathy. He was the daddy I never had. Later on I came to see they ain't much difference between none of us 'cept maybe our skin color. And like Driggins said, I'd probably be dead now if it weren't for you guys. We made a good team, didn't we? So I got this to say. Y'all might be white, but you're all right!"

Catfish clapped his hands. Calhoun whistled. They all cheered and clapped their hands for Marcus Johnson.

Cat got to his feet and stood in the cigarette smoke and candlclight looking down at the men on the wooden floor. Finally he spoke.

"This isn't easy, is it? Saying goodbye after what we've been through. I called my parents and they're cool with Australia. Dad said our country's gone to hell anyway, people burning flags, riots an such. Said Australia might be just the right place to be. Mom wants me to come home for a while so Calhoun and I are going back for a few weeks. We'll rendezvous with you guys in Knoxville.

"I don't hate President Johnson. I think his heart was in the right place with his Great Society. He wanted to help the poor people. But the way my father put it, Washington could fuck up a wet dream.

"Over here he made mistakes. I don't think President Johnson understands war, and I don't think he understands much about China. Pasamenus explained it best, the President is not a man who instills fear in his enemies. To do that he should have leveled their seaport, and closed the Trail.

You guys are my blood brothers. I don't regret coming back for a second tour, but we paid a terrible price with Gunny and the others. Politicians are a bunch of fuckups who couldn't locate their backsides in the dark with both hands. My father has a way with words.

"I wish Shorty was here, Madame and Gargoyle. They're our brothers too, just as much as John and Major Abraham. We should throw a party at the Garden in honor of our missing friends before we go back. Invite everyone who survived that nightmare in the valley. Without those planes and choppers we'd still be out there with Red and Tony. Leaving them was the hardest thing I ever did, but I believe it was the right decision. Not because we're still alive, but because it's the way of the brotherhood. Any man here would give his life to save the rest, that's just the way it is.

"Y'all come and see me and Duke down in Kangaroo Land."

"Sir, I got me a dilemma." Henry stood in the circle. "I study the Holy Bible and I'm just plain confused. First off, I don't believe in Satan, but I do believe in Good versus Evil. Evil is begat by ignorance and poverty. Good is the essence of Jesus Christ in man. The USMC fights the forces of Evil. So here's my question. Do we come into this world as humans, and our souls get attached later on? Or are we immortal souls to begin with, evolving as human beings until we get it right?"

Lieutenant Butler smiled and shook his head. "Dwayne, to paraphrase Major Abraham, you can ask some of the damnest questions! I don't know the answer to your question. But with brains like yours and men like First Squad in the battle for Good, I got a hunch the Marine Corps will be around fighting Evil for another hundred and ninety-three years. Maybe longer.

Semper Fidelis

I can give you nothing
that has not already
its origins within yourself,

I can throw open no
picture gallery
but your own,

I can help make
your own world visible—
that is all

Herman Hesse

Contact the Author

To Contact the Author, visit his website at:
McAnallyFlatsPress.com

Or write to him via the publisher at:
McAnally Flats Press
4809 Riversedge Road
Louisville, TN 37777